# THE CASTAWAYS

LUCY CLARKE lives with her husband and two young children and she writes from a beach hut, using the inspiration from the wild south coast to craft her stories. She has a first-class degree in English Literature and her debut novel, *The Sea Sisters*, was a Richard and Judy Book Club choice. *The Castaways* is Lucy's sixth novel.

Keep in touch with Lucy –

www.lucy-clarke.com
@lucyclarke_author
/lucyclarkeauthor

Also by Lucy Clarke

*The Sea Sisters*
*A Single Breath*
*No Escape* (previously published as *The Blue*)
*Last Seen*
*You Let Me In*

Also by Lucy Clarke

*The Sea Sisters*
*A Single Breath*
*No Escape* (previously published as *The Blue*)
*Last Seen*
*You Let Me In*

# THE
# CASTAWAYS

## LUCY CLARKE

HarperCollins*Publishers*

HarperCollins*Publishers* Ltd
1 London Bridge Street,
London SE1 9GF

www.harpercollins.co.uk

HarperCollins*Publishers*
1st Floor, Watermarque Building, Ringsend Road
Dublin 4, Ireland

First published by HarperCollins*Publishers* 2021
1

A catalogue record for this book is available from the British Library

ISBN: 978-0-00-833412-3 (HB)
ISBN: 978-0-00-845367-1 (TPB)

This novel is entirely a work of fiction.
The names, characters and incidents portrayed in it are
the work of the author's imagination. Any resemblance to
actual persons, living or dead, events or localities is
entirely coincidental.

Set in Sabon LT Std by Palimpsest Book Production Ltd, Falkirk, Stirlingshire

Printed and bound in the UK by CPI Group (UK) Ltd, Croydon CR0 4YY

**MIX**
Paper from
responsible sources
FSC™ C007454

This book is produced from independently certified FSC™ paper
to ensure responsible forest management.

For more information visit: www.harpercollins.co.uk/green

For James, Tommy, and Darcy

# 1

# THEN | LORI

Lori wheeled her suitcase along the humid airport walkway. Loose strands of hair were pasted to the back of her neck. Seeing her gate number ahead, she paused, then glanced back over her shoulder.

Still no sign of her sister.

She slipped her mobile from her pocket, the screen eyeing her blankly. No messages. No missed calls. Her heart kicked hard between her ribs: it was only minutes until they were due to board.

A snatch of their argument arrowed into her thoughts. *I don't recognise you any more . . .*

Lori worked her teeth over the insides of her cheek, finding the smooth flesh, pressing down until she tasted blood.

She tried to picture herself leaving without Erin – taking this inter-island flight to the remote southeastern reaches of the Fijian archipelago. She reminded herself that she'd already done the hardest leg of the journey yesterday – the long-haul flight from London to Fiji. No diazepam needed. But she'd had Erin beside her then, who'd come armed with snacks, music, books, and was so busy colluding about what drinks they'd order once airborne, that Lori had barely noticed the take-off. On arrival last night, they'd checked into a beach-side hotel, planning to grab dinner and some sleep before this morning's short flight to their resort.

Only now here she was, without Erin.

She dragged her suitcase into the toilets. Leaning over the sinks, she eyed herself in the mirror. Her fingertips explored her puffy eyelids, circling to the deep shadows beneath them.

She'd waited up last night, half hoping to hear shambling footsteps along the hotel corridor, a knock at the door, her sister's voice, whisper-shouting to let her in. She'd imagined Erin, gin-drunk, a slur of apologies tumbling out. Maybe she would've let her in, shuffled over in the wide hotel bed to make space. Told Erin to breathe the other way and warned her not to snore. Maybe she would've done that. Or maybe she would only have opened the door a crack, just enough to tell her to leave.

But Lori didn't know how she'd have felt, because Erin hadn't returned.

She took out her make-up bag to give her hands something to do. Her skin had a winter pallor that spoke of too many hours indoors. It had been months since she'd felt the kiss of sunshine. God, blue skies. Swimming in a warm sea. Fresh air. A good book. She deserved this holiday. Needed it.

But what if the whole thing was a mistake? She'd booked it on a moment's impulse. Three in the morning. Her sheets twisted from another wakeful night. She'd taken out her laptop to watch a film – something to lock her thoughts to – and then the advert had popped up. Ten nights on a remote, bare-foot island in Fiji, the dates spanning her twenty-eighth birthday. She'd opened a new tab and checked the joint bank account and seen there was still two thousand pounds left. *Fuck you, Pete*, she'd thought as she'd pressed *Confirm booking*.

At first light, she'd crept into Erin's bedroom, proffering a mug of steaming tea as she'd slipped her legs beneath the duvet.

'I'm asleep,' Erin murmured.

'I've got news,' Lori announced. 'Light coming on.' She'd reached across and flicked on the bedside lamp. 'I've booked us a trip. To Fiji. The second week in January. You said you had annual leave to use up. It's my treat.'

Erin had lifted her head a fraction, opening one eye.

Lori could guess what her sister would be thinking – *But Lori's terrified of flying. She never travels. A holiday is just a plaster across a much deeper wound* – so without giving her the chance to speak, Lori continued, her voice low, certain, 'I need to get away. And the only person I want to do that with is you.' Then a loaded pause. 'Together.'

*Together.* The history and weight of that word pulsed between them.

There was a beat of a pause, no more than a breath of hesitation. 'Okay, then.'

Yet now it was just Lori waiting in an airport. Alone.

She zipped up her make-up bag, grabbed her case and left the toilets.

The walkway was still deserted. She reached again for her mobile, turning it through her hands, deciding. It should be Erin who made the call . . . and yet, she just needed to hear her voice, check she was okay.

She dialled.

Listening to it ring, she watched as a pilot in a crisp white uniform advanced along the walkway. He wore a navy peaked cap, beneath which his eyes were heavily pouched and blood-shot. *The pilot of my plane?* He crouched down, searching for something within his carry-on case, his expression clouded with confusion. He dragged a hand down over his face, pulling the loose skin towards his jowls. After a few moments, he gave up on whatever he was looking for. He took a deep breath, then moved on, eyes lowered.

The sudden click of voicemail snapped her gaze away. 'It's Erin. Keep it short,' then the tone so quickly afterwards it was like you'd been tripped up.

Lori hesitated, a pregnant pause stretching out, her silence recorded.

Her thoughts swam back two decades. Lying beneath a star-flecked duvet, breath warm in the cotton-dark, their mother only dead a week. Lori had squeezed her sister's hand, whispering, *You don't need to be scared, Erin. I'm your big sister. I'll look after you now.*

But what about when Lori needed her? Like right now. What then?

'I'm at the airport,' Lori hissed, lips close to the phone. 'Where the hell are you?'

# 2

# NOW | ERIN

The landing outside my flat is pitch black. The bulb blew last month and I haven't got around to replacing it.

I slide my hand up the door, feeling for the lock. I can smell the leather of my jacket, damp with rain. Behind me there's the man I brought back from the bar. Faded aftershave, the yeasty tang of beer on his breath. *Mark? Matt?*

'I've got a torch on my phone,' he says, just as I manage to press the key into the lock, pushing the door open with a smack.

I pick my way over the day's post, then sling down the keys and kick off my boots.

He follows me into the lounge, his gaze sliding over the flat. I see it afresh, through his eyes: mismatched underwear dried stiff on the radiator; the smell of overcooked food lingering in the carpets; the burnt-out stubs of candles in pools of hardened wax; the coffee mug and cereal bowl left on the windowsill where I sit each morning, the window cracked open, neck strained to try and glimpse a patch of sky beyond the buildings.

I peel off my jacket. Sling it over the back of a chair piled with books.

The alcohol buzz is fading too quickly. I should have put the lamp on, not the glaring downlights that are bathing us in a harsh white blaze. Christ, I wonder if he's regretting this as much as I am. There was a gallery launch and they needed a journo to attend, and I got the nudge. There wasn't time to eat. There was a free bar. We jostled from the gallery to another bar, and then another. I lost my colleagues several hours ago, but found myself in a dark corner of a club with this guy. Somehow he's now in my flat, staring at me with a wolfish twist to his mouth. I realise that we're no longer buffeted by a crowd of smiling twenty-somethings. The door to my flat is shut. We're alone.

I hear my sister's voice. *Erin, you've got to think.*

I close my eyes for a moment, sink deeper into the timbre of her voice.

*If you don't want him here, just ask him to leave.*

'Want a drink?' I say, running my hand through the short hair at the nape of my neck, feeling the brush of it against my thumb. He follows me into the galley kitchen. A cereal box and trail of cornflakes dust the side, leading to an open pack of painkillers and bottle of vodka. Hansel and Gretel for grown-ups.

I open a cupboard, and gesture to the wine, spirts, and half-drunk mixers. 'Take your pick.'

He chooses rum and pours it neat into two tumblers he grabs from the draining board. 'Got any Coke? Lime?'

'Neither.'

'Hostess with the mostest.'

I shrug.

He passes me my glass, we clink them together, knock them back.

He pours us another and we carry these through to the lounge, bringing the bottle with us. I move aside a blanket and sit on the sofa. He stands. 'So, you own this place?'

'Rented.'

'Any flatmates?'

'Not at the moment,' I answer, my gaze finding the painting hanging above my sofa. It's the only thing that adorns the otherwise bare walls. It's an acrylic of the river that ran along the bottom of our childhood garden in Bath. Lori painted it for me using her touchstone palette of rich blues and vivid, earthy greens. She loved to paint in thick swathes of colour. It was a gift to me when I took my first job in London. On the back of the canvas she has written, *So you can have a place to come home to in the city.*

I follow the raised whorls of the acrylic paint, the thick layers she cut through with a palette knife to give texture to the trees on the riverbank. I can see Lori, blonde hair tied back, an oversized shirt of Pete's splattered with paint, music crooning. She never fitted the bohemian image of an artist. She was neat jeans and brushed hair; she was organisation and efficiency; she was painted nails and shaped eyebrows. She wasn't tormented by her creativity – she bathed in its light.

I turn my attention back to the man. He's older than I thought, with facial hair that looks as if it requires a lot of management, too-neat lines and blunt sideburns, the skin beneath his jaw disconcertingly smooth, as if it's never seen air. I'm not even attracted to him. I shouldn't have let him in.

*Why did you, Erin?* my sister's voice pipes up again.

*Because it's a Wednesday night. Because I've been drinking. Because I hate walking into this flat alone, okay?*

He moves around the lounge scanning the bookcase, pausing at the fireplace. It's one of those typical London ones – Edwardian with a blocked chimney breast, so now it houses a glass vase filled with fairy lights. Lori's touch.

'Your birthday?'

The question throws me. I follow his gaze to the mantelpiece where there is a single birthday card propped between two slumping candles. The number thirty glitters on the front.

'Yes,' I say eventually. Easier to lie than to explain.

'Wouldn't have had you down as thirty.'

*No,* because *I'm twenty-fucking-seven,* I think, but can't say.

I finish my rum, heat sliding through my chest, then open Spotify on my phone. I select a chill-hop playlist then, remembering the mother who lives in the flat below, turn it down. I helped haul her pram up the two flights of stairs yesterday – the lift is broken again – and the baby watched me warily, a mushed rice cake disintegrating in his grip. When the mother thanked me, her voice sounded on the edge of tears. I wondered if I should invite them in, check she was okay, but I didn't have it in me.

The man is looking at me, brows dipped, like he's trying to work something out. 'So, talk me through your hair.'

'My hair?' I raise an eyebrow. *Seriously?* 'It's an undercut,' I say, pointing to the shaved arc above my right ear. It confuses people, the lack of symmetry. My hair is black, short. 'Pixie cut' is the term, with a flash of an undercut on one side. It wasn't an edgy fashion choice. I was at the hairdresser's on a student training night. The apprentice, a teenager with a freshly inked tattoo on his wrist, skin still pink and raised, suggested it. I shrugged and said, 'Why not?'

Feels like my response to most things.

*Shall I come back to your flat?*

*Why not?*

I should probably be ringing my eyes with kohl, doing something dramatic with my eyebrows, but I can't quite muster the enthusiasm.

'I like it,' he declares. Then he moves off. For a moment I think he's going to join me on the sofa and I tense. Instead, he crosses the lounge, saying, 'Just going to pay a visit.'

*Pay a visit*. It's like I've invited someone's dad back.

It takes me a moment before I realise he's headed towards the wrong door. I'm on my feet, rushing forwards as his fingers reach for the handle.

'No—' I begin, but the door to the spare room opens, the light switch is flicked.

He freezes.

His back is to me, but I know what he's seeing. His eyes will be stretched wide, gaze pinned to the walls.

I've not been inside that room in weeks – but I know exactly what is in there.

His voice is a notch higher. 'What the hell?'

A pause between songs drops us into silence. The moment draws out, long, contorted, his question stabbing the air.

'The bathroom is the next room,' I say eventually.

'What is all this stuff?'

The walls of the spare room are covered with newspaper cuttings, maps, photos – all connected by pieces of coloured string, and peppered with Post-it notes and handwritten questions. Dead-eyed faces stare back at us, and headlines scream: 'Vanished!' 'No trace of plane.'

I know how it makes me look.

*I know, okay?*

At the centre is a newspaper clipping of a small white plane with a red stripe cutting through its middle. Below are the photos of the two crew and seven passengers.

When I don't answer, he turns and looks at me. 'It's that flight, isn't it? The one that went missing.'

Reluctantly, I nod.

'Is it . . . is this . . . for work?' I catch the note of hope.

'Yes,' I lie.

Relief softens his brows. 'Journalist, you said, didn't you? I remember reading about the flight. Going to Fiji, wasn't it? Plane just disappeared. Went off the radar. No trace. No sighting. No transmissions. No wreck found. Seriously weird, if you ask me.'

My mouth refuses to work.

'It was a while back now, wasn't it? Last year?'

'Two years ago.' *Two years and six days.*

'There were all those theories. You know, that maybe there was a terrorist on board, or the pilot was on a suicide mission. Is that what you're looking into?'

'Mm,' I say noncommittally.

Now he's looking at me warily. 'You often bring your work home? Is this your office or something?'

Another long pause. 'Something.'

His expression shifts, as if he is beginning to realise that something isn't quite right. He looks at the wall, the photos, the cuttings, some of them browned at the edges, Sellotape yellowing – then back to me. I can see he's trying desperately to work it out, to connect to the sense of unease he's feeling.

Maybe it's the alcohol, or maybe he's just a quitter, but he gives up with little fight, saying, 'Bathroom.' He ducks inside and I hear the lock slide.

I stand in the hallway, looking through the open doorway into the spare room. Lori's old room. It's been months since

I've seen these walls. No one in London can afford an empty spare room, me included, but I can't take this stuff down because it'd mean it's over. I'm giving up. I'm letting her go.

But I know I need to.

I take a breath. This weekend. It's got to come down. All of it. Enough.

Or maybe I could just put some of it away, do it in phases. I could start with clearing Lori's bed, which is hidden beneath a spread of books, articles, open files. I should've sublet this room months ago – God knows, my bank account would be grateful – but the idea of a flatmate makes me shudder, someone to hear me pacing at four a.m., or to notice the weird times of day that I eat, or the social life I don't have.

I hear the toilet flush, the cistern refilling. I listen for the sound of the taps turning on, water sluicing into the sink – but instead, the door opens, and there he is once again. Unwashed hands shoved into pockets, eyes sliding away. 'I've got an early start. So . . .'

'Sure.'

He grabs his coat, not even pausing to put it on. 'Cheers, then,' he says from the doorway.

I follow, holding open the door as he steps into the hallway. If I shut the door now, it'll close out the light, leaving him in complete darkness. I should at least wait till he's made it down the stairs, reached the exit.

But fuck it.

I shut the door. Bolt it.

I grab the bottle of rum from the lounge, silver rings clinking against the bottle neck. I traipse into Lori's room, push aside a book about the history of plane crashes, and sink onto the edge of the bed. The air smells musty, untouched, cooler than the rest of the flat.

'Happy thirtieth,' I say, raising the bottle of rum towards my sister's image on the wall.

*Use a glass*, I hear Lori say. I picture her rolling her eyes, feigned exasperation.

I swig straight from the bottle. Grin.

As the rum slides hotly down my throat, I study the photo of Lori slotted amongst the other passengers of flight FJ209. *Passenger Three*, the press branded her. They pulled the photo from her Instagram account, the last picture that was taken before she climbed aboard that fated plane. Her hair had been recently highlighted with warm tones of honey and caramel, and she's smiling, her lips glossy, but it doesn't reach her eyes.

I was sitting right next to her when the photo was taken. They cropped me out, of course. All you can see now are my fingers around her waist. It was shot the night before the flight – before all the mistakes I'd yet to make – but it's as if it's all there in that photo. Lori with a blank-eyed stare, alone – and me reaching out. Trying to hold on.

# 3

# NOW | ERIN

It's gone two in the morning and I'm still sitting in the spare room. I've got to be up for work in a few hours. I should be drinking a big glass of water, setting out two aspirin by my bed and getting some sleep.

I take another swig of rum, teeth knocking against the bottle, as I study the image of the plane. Two years ago that plane was due to travel from Nadi airport in Fiji, to Limaji, a tiny island at the southeastern edge of the archipelago. Only the plane – and the nine people on board – never arrived.

*Disappeared without trace.* That's what the press said.

I look at the list of facts bullet-pointed on index cards on the wall. Captain Mike Brass last communicated with air-traffic control twenty-two minutes after take-off. The transmission reported that everything was fine. Yet, eight minutes later, the aircraft disappeared from radar screens – and never arrived at its destination. A huge, multi-agency search was launched covering a 300-square-mile radius. It turned up nothing. No plane wreck. Not a shred of debris. No bodies. Nothing.

I narrow my eyes, squinting to find something different amid the gaps in the information.

When the plane disappeared, I wanted to gather every shred of evidence. I hounded the police, the British consul, CAAF – the Civil Aviation Authority of Fiji. I demanded to know the search areas they'd covered, ticking them off on my own chart of the Fijian archipelago that is tacked to the wall behind me. I located some of the relatives of the passengers, rallying them to keep pressure on the authorities. I read every book I could find on plane crashes, or survival stories against the odds. I wrote press releases to keep the plane's disappearance on the media's radar.

'It's becoming an obsession,' one of my oldest friends, Sarah, told me during a Skype call from Berlin.

'You've got to forgive yourself,' Ben had chimed in from the background, while pouring white wine into large glasses on a gleaming counter. The sight of the two of them together was still like a fist in my stomach. At school, Ben once said the three of us were like the sides of an equilateral triangle: every side linked, equal, our matching angles making perfect symmetry. Huh. Funny how that shape got flattened when they announced they'd fallen in love and were moving to Berlin together.

There's nothing new to discover sitting in Lori's old room, drunk. But still, I can't help looking. I stretch across the bed, sliding a file towards me. It contains all the correspondence I made in the weeks and months following the plane's disappearance. I started the file because I needed to *do* something. Waiting was dangerous territory. Too much space for my mind to screech and holler, point and blame.

I open the file at random and scan the page, reading an email from a member of CAAF, confirming that although they were no longer actively searching, the incident would remain open indefinitely.

*Open indefinitely.* How do you live with that?

I know the story doesn't have a happy ending. A plane doesn't just disappear because it's landed at the wrong resort and all the passengers are merrily sipping cocktails and swinging their hips in hula skirts. A plane disappears because there is a big fucking problem. I need to know what that problem was. I need to know what went on after that last transmission from the pilot. I need to know what happened to my sister. I need to know who the hell I can blame because, right now, the only person I've got is the one who didn't turn up at the airport like she was supposed to; who didn't get on that plane; who is still here, sitting in the fucking spare room where her sister should be!

I grab the file and fling it across the room. It slams into the wall, the ring binder wrenching open, sending pages and photos fluttering to the floor like broken wings.

Another good reason for not subletting: *propensity to outbursts of aggression.*

In the spill of articles, my gaze lands on one of the passengers: Felix Tyler, age 27 at the time of the flight. In the photo he's wearing a beanie pulled low to his brows, dark hair spilling towards his chin. Peat-brown eyes staring out from beneath heavy lashes. Attractive in a wrong-side-of-the-tracks kind of way. I read everything I could about him – and all the passengers – because I wanted to know exactly who each person was on that flight; why they were flying; what they would have been like in a crisis; who my sister would have been with in that moment of descent.

But Felix, he's the one who made me wonder. He bought

his ticket to Fiji forty-eight hours before flying. I spoke to the resort owner on the island where the plane was bound, who told me Felix was due to head up their water-sports operation for a few weeks to cover for their normal guy. I managed to get hold of a copy of his CV and PADI certificate, but when I looked into it, his references didn't check out and his diving qualification was forged. Felix Tyler was a free-climber, not a diver. A climber who, eighteen months before the flight, had fallen fifty foot onto granite, without a harness or helmet, breaking fourteen bones in his body. He hadn't climbed since.

Something like that must change a person.

I tried contacting his family, but his father died three months after the plane disappearance, and his stepmother refused to talk. Felix's climbing core were impossible to track – a cluster of off-grid types chasing remote peaks and ridges. I emailed everything I'd found out to the British consul and the police – but apparently a forged PADI certificate and fake references don't add much to an investigation into a plane disappearance.

But what I was thinking – what still circles my mind in the middle of the night when I can't sleep – is, *Why? Why did he lie? What else did he lie about?*

# 4

# THEN | LORI

In the boarding lounge, Lori stood at the window rotating the bangle on her wrist. Still no sign of Erin.

The plane waited on the sun-struck tarmac, a red line slicing through the belly of it, as if it had been marked for an incision. Small planes were the worst, she thought, her pulse audible in her ears. Too insubstantial. Every bump or jolt of turbulence, every buffeting of wind and weather – she'd feel it all. She counted the windows on the near side. Eight. Pictured herself climbing the steps, the clang of metal, the sun on the back of her neck. It was just an hour-long flight. She could manage that.

Out on the runway, a man in blue overalls approached the plane, peering at something beneath it. The engine? The fuel store? She'd no idea what went where. He angled his head, looking more closely. A second man approached, dressed in a high-vis orange jacket. They seemed to be debating something, arms gesturing towards the plane, then back towards the airport hangar. After a few more moments, the man in the high-vis jacket strode off, leaving the other man crouched down, brow still furrowed. Eventually, he, too, got to his feet, shrugged, and walked away.

*What's with the shrug? What've you seen? Is there something wrong with the plane?* God, being a nervous flier was exhausting.

She made herself turn from the window. Further along stood a man dressed in chinos and a polo shirt, an expensive leather holdall at his feet. Business traveller, she decided. He glanced towards the gate entrance, a mobile pressed to his ear. 'It's Daniel. I wanted to make sure we've got everything . . . straight,' he said, his voice low, moneyed. There was a pause. He shifted his weight from foot to foot. 'I know,' he said, nodding vigorously. 'I owe you.' He jangled the change in his pockets. 'Second thoughts?' His hand slid free of his pocket, moving to the back of his neck, gaze searching out the plane. There was a sheen of sweat on his brow. 'Maybe.'

Her book. She should read. That would quieten her mind. She made herself take a seat and went through the motions of getting out her book, opening it, setting her gaze on the page. She re-read the same sentence three times, failing to take in the story. Her legs felt restless, twitchy.

She glanced up to see a dark-haired man crossing the boarding lounge. He shrugged a large backpack to the ground, then slumped into a plastic chair at the end of a row. He clamped headphones over his ears, lowered his chin to his chest, folded his arms and closed his eyes. She watched as his shoulders visibly relaxed, fingertips drumming to the secret beat in his ears.

Her gaze travelled to his face. A mess of dark hair hung forwards, meeting the thick stubble that cloaked his jaw. His clothes – slim grey jeans and a T-shirt – looked tired, slept in, matching the shadows beneath his eyes.

She wondered what sort of customer the resort would draw. *Ecologically minded, yet with details of luxury*, it had said on the website.

The man's eyes snapped open and he suddenly drew his phone from his pocket, reading something on screen. His whole body tightened. The edges of his nostrils flared. He sat rigidly still, not moving, not blinking. A glassy sheen swam across his eyes. He pressed his forefinger and thumb hard against his eye sockets. The skin across his right knuckles was flayed, raw cuts yet to fully knit.

*Focus on your book*, she told herself, gaze returning fleetingly to the page – before darting back to this man.

He'd begun typing something into his phone, stabbing at the screen. He paused, reading whatever he'd just typed. He tapped the screen once. Lori watched, surprised when he snapped off the phone case and yanked open the back, digging a fingernail beneath the SIM card to release it. He took a coin from his pocket and scraped it roughly against the matt metal surface.

When it was done, he strode across the room, and tossed both the SIM and his phone into the bin.

As the man turned, his gaze met Lori's. He stopped. Stared right at her.

Heat rose in her cheeks as if he'd caught her spying.

His glare was fierce, defensive. A challenge in it.

She shifted in her seat.

His gaze bore into her, like a wolf's, hackles raised.

Lori wondered if she had time to go to the toilet again. Could you leave the boarding lounge when you'd already shown your ticket? She pressed discreetly against her bladder. Maybe she could hold it. Just nerves.

An American couple were pulling matching wheeled luggage behind them. 'We're celebrating our fortieth wedding anniversary,' the man was telling a young amber-haired woman beside them.

The young woman nodded in a distracted way, something wary or worn in her expression. Her hand was cupped around her front, where a newborn was nestled in a sling against her chest. Lori glimpsed the baby's round head, a pale spray of fine hair. She hadn't expected there to be children flying to the resort. In fact, the remoteness of it, the lack of family-friendly facilities, was part of the appeal.

A baby boy, she saw now, as the mother turned. He must only be a few months old, a similar age to Pete's daughter. Bessy, he'd called the little girl. She'd wanted to hate the name but didn't.

Pete.

Always Pete.

What was it Erin had said last night? That Lori had always put him on a pedestal. 'He let you down, Lori. He cheated, he left.'

*He left.*

She didn't need reminding. She'd lived it.

She pressed her lips together, looked up at the panelled ceiling.

Not now. No tears. If she was going to get herself on that plane, she needed to hold it together.

'Miss? Excuse me, Miss? We're calling all passengers now for boarding.'

She looked up, startled. The airline steward was gesturing towards the walkway, where other passengers were beginning to move down a long corridor. Her gaze searched for Erin, looking for the short, quick strides, the shock of dark hair, the backpack as large as her.

Lori would forgive her. She would. If Erin came now, apologised.

A flush of hot–cold panic washed through her. 'My sister,' she began. 'She's meant to be on this flight. I'm waiting for her. She'll be on her way.' She was aware that her voice sounded thin, near breaking.

'I'm so sorry,' the air stewardess said gently, 'but the gate is closed now. I'm afraid she's too late.'

# 5

# NOW | ERIN

I feed my hands into the pockets of my too-thin coat, lifting my shoulders towards my ears. The jostle of commuters tightens, everyone eager to get home. I plant my feet wide, hold my ground.

My hangover – earlier a flaming heat in my head – has dulled to a baseline note at the back of my skull. I give an involuntary shudder thinking about that guy I brought back last night, his bewildered expression as he stared at the newspaper clippings in the spare room. At least I didn't sleep with him. I'll take that as a win.

The air underground is stale, the faint tang of urine and cooked food drawing through on the body-warmed breeze. I wish I'd ridden my bike to work. I knew I'd regret it, but this morning I slept through my alarm, then woke late in one of my weird-inward-hangover moods, and couldn't muster the enthusiasm for rain-slicked tarmac or the clammy pinch of waterproofs.

The tunnel seems to inhale with the approach of a Tube, the crowd being sucked towards the platform edge. Nothing more enticing than a ready-meal lasagne and a bottle of wine swings in the plastic bag hooked over my wrist, but still I'm eager to get home, stand under a hot shower, wash the day from my skin. I've spent the afternoon traipsing across London interviewing three karaoke singers who've formed a band that's had a Top Forty hit.

*You would've probably loved them, Lori.* I smile into my scarf, thinking about the car-radio wars we used to have as teenagers, me leaning across the backseat trying to eject her pop mix-tape, complaining that my ears were bleeding; Lori ramming the passenger seat as far back as it would go to stop me; Dad threatening to put on Radio 4 if we didn't pipe down.

When the Tube draws in, it is already full. I squeeze my way inside and stand for seven stops, grateful to be in trainers rather than the black patent heels worn by the woman next to me, who is kneading her knuckles into her lower back. Eventually the crowd thins and, by Kennington, I finally get a seat. I pull off my woollen hat and stuff it in my pocket, then roughly scratch my head.

Rotating the black stud in the cartilage of my ear, I glance absently across the carriage. A woman opposite reads an evening paper, her forehead shiny and pink, puffy pouches settled beneath her eyes. Is she going to be opening a front door onto the smell of home-cooked food? Or will she be feeding an electricity meter, hearing the ping of the microwave, sitting under a duvet scrolling the Netflix menu, too?

The woman turns the paper and, as she does so, the front page is exposed.

My skin tightens. My breath halts.

*It's him!*

I stare at a photo of a middle-aged man wearing a white pilot's uniform, with a three-barred gold logo on his left shoulder. His hair is cut short, grey peppering the steel-dark. It's the same photo that's pinned to the wall of my spare room.

Mike Brass, the captain of flight FJ209.

Two years ago, this photo was in the press day after day as speculation slammed into the nation. As days turned into weeks and no new details emerged, the story gradually slid from page one to the middle section of the newspapers, until it was just a footnote, a fading memory in the public's attention. But his face has stayed in my thoughts, burning bright. I've studied this photo, looking for clues in the crinkle of those icy blue eyes, the lips that turn into a slow smile. Now, here he is once again, on the front page.

*Why now?* I'm wondering, pulse flickering in my throat. It's not the anniversary of the plane's disappearance. There's been no new information for months. The story is dead in the water.

I must see the headline. I'm out of my seat, stepping across the carriage. 'I need to . . .' I say as my fingers reach out.

The woman gasps, drawing the paper towards her chest and – in that moment – I see it, the full stretch of the headline, stamped in black capitals.

*'DEAD' PILOT SPOTTED ALIVE IN FIJI*

The carriage retracts. My vision narrows.

My whole body begins to tremble: fingers, legs, teeth.

The Tube lurches to a stop and I stumble into the woman clasping the paper. She cries out and everyone turns to look. She gets to her feet, dusting herself off as I mumble an apology. She tosses the paper into her vacated seat and makes for the doors, head shaking.

I snatch up the paper. I'm aware of the rush of blood in

my ears, the inky smell of damp print. The Tube doors close and we rattle on, wheezing underground.

The paper feels sticky in my sweating palms. I'm blinking too quickly, breathing too hard. I begin to read.

*Captain Mike Brass, pilot of flight FJ209, which disappeared somewhere in the South Pacific two years ago, has been found alive. In the early hours of this morning, he was admitted to a Fijian hospital by his employer, after he collapsed. He was recognised by a member of the nursing team, who contacted the local police.*

*It is believed that he has been living on Fiji's main island, Viti Levu, under a false identity since the disappearance of flight FJ209. He has been using the alias Charlie Floyd, while working as a handyman at a resort in the interior of the island.*

*His wife, Anne Brass, who lives in Perth, has been interviewed by the police and claims she had no idea that her husband was alive. 'He hasn't tried to contact me.' Anne and Mike Brass have a son, Nathan Brass, who also lives in Perth.*

My thoughts are screaming.

The pilot survived.

Breathe. Breathe.

I scan the rest of the article, which reframes the original details of the plane disappearance. It ends with a final paragraph, reading: *A spokesperson from the Fijian government commented, 'Captain Mike Brass is currently in the care of a team of doctors. We are hoping his condition will stabilise so he can help us with our investigation into the disappearance of flight FJ209.'*

The pilot has been alive this whole time.

I look up, catching myself in the reflection of the darkened Tube window. My face is leached of colour, brows knitted, lips pulled tight. Saliva pools in the back of my throat, the tang of bile chasing it.

It's impossible, isn't it?

I've imagined it, hypothesised about it, dreamt about it. I've been desperate to believe that there could be some explanation, some reason that defied logic to mean the passengers could walk out of the wreckage alive.

Everyone told me to let it go.

Let my sister go.

There was so little information to go on – no black box recording, no plane wreck, no sightings – that it was as if the plane simply disappeared into thin air. All manner of theories were raised in the media and conspiracy forums: hijackers; thermostatic conditions causing spontaneous combustion; an act of God; pilot suicide.

No word. No clue. Not for two years. Nothing. Not even a trace.

Until now.

Now there is a pilot.

# 6

# NOW | ERIN

With my mobile wedged between my shoulder and ear, I let myself into the flat, heart knocking hard against my chest. Piano music trills as I continue to hold for the British Embassy.

I hurry through to the kitchen, removing the wine from the carrier bag. There are no clean glasses, so I slosh it into a mug, hands shaking, heart drilling. I push two painkillers from a foil sleeve and wash them down with the wine.

Someone from the embassy comes onto the line, telling me that Captain Mike Brass has been interviewed by the police, and a transcript will be emailed shortly.

Taking my wine, I head for the spare room, swipe the desk clear of books and articles, and fire up my laptop.

I click on my emails.

Nothing.

My fingers drum the desk. After a moment, I open a host

of national and international news sites, including News24, Fiji Times, CNN, *The Guardian*, as well as Twitter. In less than a minute I have a dozen different sites loaded and I begin scrolling. I'm surprised I didn't find out about the news at work. I might write for a weekly, but we still cover news from a human-interest angle.

I inhale sentences, headlines, lead-in paragraphs, quotes, opinion pieces. I'm looking for any new facts I can gather, but there is little except for the bare bones of what I already know.

It's an hour before I shrug off my coat. Two, before I remember to kick off my trainers. I forget about the micro-wave lasagne sweating on the kitchen side and eat cereal straight from the box, dry granola showering my chest as I push handfuls into my mouth, eyes on the screen, washed down with gulps of wine.

I've hit refresh on my emails so many times that my fingertip pulses with heat.

Glancing at the wall of articles above me, I study the faded handwriting, the curling edges of the photos. I'd shut the door on this room. On Lori. Even my obsession began to wane. Now words and images swim before my eyes, jostling for attention. All those questions, those leads, eventually coming to dead ends. The wrench of guilt tightens and suddenly I'm on my feet, reaching for today's newspaper, tearing the front page clean off. I pin it firmly in the centre, over the top of Captain Mike Brass's photo.

*'DEAD' PILOT SPOTTED ALIVE IN FIJI*

I read the article afresh, my gaze hovering over the line, *It's believed he's been living on Fiji's mainland under a false identity.*

He stepped off that plane, alive. He *chose* to hide.

Why?

Staring at this face, the cold blue eyes, I'm wondering what happened on that flight that the pilot didn't want the world to know about. I already know a part of his story that no one else does. But it's not enough. Not nearly enough.

I place my hands flat against the desk, palms to the wood, and concentrate on breathing deeply, right into my diaphragm. I draw in another breath, closing my eyes. My head hangs forward. There's a deep pressure in my sinuses, and a knot of tension running along the back of my neck.

The pilot is *alive*.

Think.

Where is the plane now? Where are the other passengers? *Please, Lori. What happened when you boarded that plane? Tell me. Tell me what happened?*

I wait to hear her voice, to feel it inside me. Tears leak hotly from the corners of my eyes, but there's no voice this time. No gut instinct.

Just silence.

My mobile rings, startling me. 'Yeah?'

'It's Pete.'

My fingertips reach for my temple. I haven't spoken to Lori's ex-husband in over a year. 'Oh,' I say, nothing else coming to me.

'I've just switched on the news. Heard about the pilot's reappearance. I can't believe it, Erin. Is it true? He's alive?'

'Yes. He's been interviewed at the hospital. I'm waiting for the transcript to be emailed.'

I lean forward, click *refresh* on my inbox.

Nothing.

'Right. Jesus. All this time he's been alive. Didn't come forward. I can't believe it.'

I don't say anything.

'What do you make of it?'

I don't answer his question. Instead I ask my own, a

sharp little bite, that I'm surprised I've got the energy for. 'How's Zoe?'

I briefly find myself hoping that it's over. That Zoe has suffered some terrible, tragic demise. A fatal injury with a kettlebell, or perhaps a deadly trip over her yoga mat. But then I think about their baby – a particularly cute and chubby-faced little girl with Pete's wide smile – and I'm forced to adjust the direction of my ambitions, hoping instead for a vaguely amicable split.

'Zoe's fine. What about you though, Erin? How are you doing?'

The last time Pete asked me that was at Lori's memorial. What a God-awful day that was. I fiercely opposed the memorial, furious at the concept of letting Lori go. Nothing in my body wanted to let go – it wanted to hold on by the teeth.

I'm saved from answering by a ping as an email lands in my inbox. 'The transcript's arrived . . .' I lean close to the screen, brows knitted.

'What does it say?'

I ignore Pete. Read.

The transcript is preceded by an email from Dr Alba of the Central Hospital of Fiji, explaining that a CT scan has revealed that Captain Mike Brass has a brain tumour, which they believe is the cause of his collapse. I glance over the details about issues with memory recall and verbal reasoning and click straight on the attached transcript.

It's short, barely two pages. My gaze burns through sentence after sentence as I inhale the pilot's responses. In moments, I've reached the end. 'No . . . no . . . that can't be all.'

A note at the end advises that the interview had to be terminated by request of the doctor as the patient was too unwell to continue.

Pete is asking, 'Are you there?'

'Yeah . . .' My legs are trembling beneath the desk. I jam my heels into the cold floorboards, forcing them to still.

'What does the transcript say?'

'Barely anything . . .' I read it aloud to Pete.

*Officer Enrol: Can you confirm that you are Mike Brass, captain of flight FJ209?*

*Mike Brass: Yes.*

*Officer Enrol: Twenty-two minutes into the flight, you contacted air-traffic control and reported everything was fine. Eight minutes later, the plane disappeared from radar and hasn't been seen since. Can you explain what happened after the final transmission?*

*Mike Brass: A . . . problem . . . (Pauses. Coughs extensively. A nurse fetches him a beaker of water, directing the straw into his mouth.)*

*Officer Enrol: Can you elaborate? What sort of problem? A technical problem?*

*Mike Brass: (No response.)*

*Officer Enrol: We are assuming that the plane got into difficulties. Weather data has shown that there was a band of heavy weather which was stronger than forecast. Did you have to perform an emergency landing?*

*Mike Brass: Tried to . . . (Silence.)*

*Officer Enrol: You tried to perform an emergency landing?*

*Mike Brass: Couldn't control it . . . (Silence.)*

*Officer Enrol: Can you tell us where the plane is now?*

*Mike Brass: (No response.)*

*Officer Enrol: I'll repeat the question. Can you tell us where the plane is now?*

*Mike Brass: (A long pause.) I don't know.*

*Officer Enrol: What do you mean by 'I don't know'? Did the plane crash on land or into the sea?*

*Mike Brass: (No response. Mike Brass shuts his eyes.)*

*Officer Enrol: Were there any other survivors from flight FJ209?*

*Mike Brass: (No response.)*

*Officer Enrol: I'm going to repeat the question. It's important that you answer. The relatives of the passengers on flight FJ209 will all be receiving a transcript of this interview. They have the right to know what happened to their loved ones. Please, can you confirm, were there any other survivors from flight FJ209?*

*Mike Brass: None.*

*Officer Enrol: To confirm, you were the only survivor?*

*Mike Brass: Yes.*

*Officer Enrol: As the only survivor of the plane crash, can you elaborate on how you survived? Did you deploy the life raft?*

*Mike Brass: (No response.)*

*Officer: We understand it was the anniversary of your daughter's death the day before the flight. Were you in the right frame of mind when you captained that plane?*

*Mike Brass: (Pause.) Yes.*

*Officer Enrol: You have been living on the mainland, working as a handyman for the past twenty months, under the alias, Charlie Floyd. Why did you not come forward to the police and inform us of your safety?*

*Mike Brass: (Coughs extensively for half a minute, clutching chest. The nurse and doctor discuss his condition. Pain relief is administered. Mike Brass closes his eyes.)*

*Officer Enrol: Were you in contact with your wife or son during this time?*

*Mike Brass: (No response.)*
*The interview is terminated on the request of Doctor Alba, who confirms that the patient is too unwell to continue.*

My stomach feels hot, liquid. 'That's it. That's all there is.'

'A crash,' Pete says slowly. Then, almost whispered, 'No other survivors.'

It's what we all assumed. What alternative was there? But to read it right here, after all this time, knocks the breath from my lungs.

'I can't believe it,' Pete says. I hear him swallow. 'So, Lori . . . her body . . . Is it still there? In the plane?'

The question is too awful to think about, her strapped to a seat alone all this time.

'I don't . . . I can't . . .'

We're both silent for a long while. My eyes don't leave the transcript.

When Pete speaks, his voice has softened. 'I'm sorry that you're having to go through all of this. I know what you and Lori meant to each other.'

There. That last sentence. It hits me right between the ribs. I hold the phone away as I suck air into my lungs, tears spiking the corners of my eyes.

Lori and I only had each other. Our mother died when I was eight, Lori ten. Bowel cancer. Our father a decade later with a ruptured brain aneurysm. There. The facts. Easier like that. Better than remembering how our small, fragile world was slammed up against a cold brick wall of loss. After Dad died, we rattled around in the family home for months, playing at being grown-up. Except at night. At night I'd climb into Lori's bed, like I'd done as a child, and we'd curl up together, falling asleep with our heads on the same pillow.

Over time, Lori learned to harness her grief, using it like a bitter wind to sail forward, building a career, a home with Pete, a marriage. My grief felt different; it buffeted me in one direction and then the next, leaving me unsure, directionless. The one safe harbour in any of it? My sister.

Now there's no harbour. Just endless ocean.

So no, Pete doesn't know what we meant to each other. Pete has family – parents, two sisters, aunties and uncles, grandparents – and now he has Zoe and their baby. Losing Lori was like . . . like someone had just reached up and plucked the sun right out of the sky. There was no wall to be slammed against. Really, there was just no wall. No nothing. My world fell out of orbit, lost its rhythm. It's two years on and I still barely sleep. When I'm awake, it feels like I'm sleepwalking, disorientated, as if everything I do, or say, is one big performance. I'm pretending to feel alive.

You don't admit things like that to people like Pete, with their big sunny families and bundles of optimism. It makes them uncomfortable. 'I've got to go.'

'Wait, Erin. Please. Are you okay? Have you got someone with you? Who's looking after you?'

'I don't need looking after,' I say, before hanging up.

I let the mobile slip through my fingers. I leave the spare room and cross the darkened lounge, moving towards the window. I push aside an empty mug and perch on the windowsill, knees drawn to my chest, watching the rain bleeding down the dark pane.

In the apartment block opposite, a man drains a steaming colander in the sink, his head stretched away to stop his glasses steaming up. There's something comforting about the rhythms and movement of all the separate lives being lived in parallel – just metres from me. I often sit here, watching these tableaus of domesticity framed in rectangles of light: the woman who practises the flute for twenty minutes each night while her husband reads; a little boy who sits on the back of a sofa as he's babysat by the glare of a television screen; a red-haired man who spends an hour of each evening on the phone.

*I don't need looking after*, I told Pete. But I know he was thinking: *Yeah, you do*, because that was always Lori's role. When we finally sold our family home, I moved in with Lori and Pete, taking one of their spare rooms that should've been a nursery. In the years I lived with them, we never once fell out. Maybe it was that the house was bigger, we weren't circling each other like we did in the flat. Or perhaps Pete's presence balanced us. Somehow, it just worked.

So I thought it would work when I invited Lori to stay in London after their marriage ended. But the moment she arrived, dragging her wheeled case into the spare room, lamenting – *but you don't even have a wardrobe* – it just felt different.

We tried though. We ate dinner together, usually something wholesome that she'd cooked – a thick soup with fresh soda bread and salted butter, or a bolognaise simmered with porcini mushrooms and red wine. She'd be up before me, the heating firing, fresh coffee brewing on my crappy two-ringed hob. She brought a new rug to cover the dark stain in the lounge left by the previous tenants, and a duck-egg-blue throw for the sofa that she'd straighten each evening before bed, plumping the cushions so that the space looked fresh, clear for the morning. When I lived with her and Pete, I'd always loved being cooked for, looked after, mothered – but somehow, in my own flat, her gentle chiding felt like criticism. *You live like a student*, she accused me one night.

No. Not one night.

*That* night. Our last night.

I yank open the sash window and stick my head into the drizzling January night. I inhale deeply, the air sharp against my teeth. Rain mists my face. I lean further forward, head hanging down, feeling fine droplets of rain gathering on the back of my neck.

I stare towards the concrete courtyard several storeys below. My fingers grip the window frame as I lean a little further forward, the balance of weight shifting.

Four storeys. It would be a broken neck. Worse.

*Get back from the edge!* I hear Lori's voice in my head.

I lean further still, breathing into the night, seeing the exhalation mist white.

My thoughts turn through the transcript, revisiting the pilot's answers, and the many, many gaps they left. It's hard to picture that flight, to really put my sister inside that plane, airborne.

*Did you stow your carry-on bag – the one you'd checked against a tape measure, making sure it met the airline's guidelines – or did you keep it at your feet? How did you feel when the seat-belt light flicked on? Were you calm, or did you sense the danger that was coming? Did you turn to the seat beside yours?*

*My seat.*

*Empty.*

*Together, that was always our promise.*

*Only, I never showed up.*

Guilty heat draws up through my belly, sticky and cloying. I make myself imagine how she felt as the plane began to descend, fear taking root, its piercing grip stealing her breath.

*Did you see the earth come rushing towards you? Did you scream? What were you thinking in those final moments?*

Below me, the dark, frostbitten concrete spins and slides.

I whisper it to the night, to Lori.

*I wish I'd been on that plane, too.*

# 7

# THEN | LORI

Lori felt her stomach contract as the plane door was closed, sealing them inside. Suddenly the plane seemed exceedingly small, a minibus with wings.

She strapped the belt over her lap, tightening it until she could feel the nylon cutting into the tops of her thighs. She leant back in the seat, the headrest pushing her neck forward at an awkward angle. Who designed these seats? She didn't know what to do with her hands. She held them above her thighs for a moment, watching the way they trembled, fingertips twitching – then pressed them down onto her lap, feeling the sticky heat of her palms.

She glanced about the plane, taking in the faded upholstery, torn in places, wondering how old the plane was and trying to avoid fear-exacerbating hypotheses like, *older plane = increased likelihood of death*.

The window. Look out of the window. She focused on the

stretch of tarmac, the green mountains beyond, tipped with blue sky.

When you're afraid of flying, most people think you have a fear of the motion of flying, the take-off and landing, or the fear of crashing. But it wasn't *only* that. If Lori had to pinpoint the precise quality of her fear, it was a single thought that looped: *What if I want to get off?*

Because the thing is: you can't. Once the plane is moving, that is it. You have no choice in the matter. You are handing over control to the pilot. There are no exceptions. You are stuck, trapped on a plane with its tiny secured windows and processed, pumped air. You are sealed into a vacuum and there is no way of accessing the world beyond until you reach your destination.

She glanced at the empty seat beside her.

Erin's seat.

She still couldn't believe that Erin wasn't here.

Nothing would be the same between them after this.

Would Erin really go back to London without her? *When you get home, your shit will be packed.*

Would it be? It would be crazy – and yet didn't this, right now, feel crazy? She swallowed. Her mouth was paper-dry. She took a small bottle of water from the bag and sipped it.

In the seats adjacent, the retired couple were taking out crossword puzzles and bags of chocolate-coated raisins. Perhaps she'd strike up conversation with them. Lori loved to talk. Loved learning about other people. She turned towards them, but saw the husband snapping off a pen lid, reading aloud the first clue to his wife.

She glanced about the plane. It was less than half full. Most people had two seats to themselves. She did a head count: seven passengers.

Seven strangers.

The smartly dressed man, whose call she'd overheard, had one ankle crossed over his leg, his leather brogue tapping anxiously. Daniel. That was his name. A hint of pale skin was exposed between sock and trouser hem.

Daniel kept glancing across the aisle. She followed his gaze to where the dark-haired man, who'd binned his mobile, was sitting. He was holding a near-empty plastic water bottle, his fingers clenching and unclenching around it, the plastic shrinking and expanding in his grip.

Daniel glared, a muscle in his jaw working hard.

The dark-haired man continued to massage the crackling plastic.

'Can you stop that?' Daniel snapped.

The dark-haired man stopped. His gaze met Daniel's. There was a charge of tension, a challenge in his expression. Then, with a shrug, he stuffed the plastic bottle into the seat pocket.

The air stewardess, a Fijian lady with black hair oiled into a perfectly round bun, was moving down the aisle towards the front of the plane. Reaching the cockpit, she knocked once and then pushed open the door.

Lori caught a glimpse of a strange tableau: the pilot was hunched over, head hanging down. His fingers were cradling the back of his head, tufts of grey hair sprouting between his fingers. It was the pilot she'd seen earlier. She noticed the slack, loosening skin at his jaw, a hint of greying stubble. *Is he unwell?*

A moment later, he raised his head, readjusted his pilot cap, and turned to face the air stewardess, lips dragging upwards into a smile. She couldn't hear what the air stewardess was saying to him, but he nodded rapidly, giving a cheery thumbs up.

*No, I'm just being twitchy*, she told herself.

But, as the air stewardess slipped from the cockpit, Lori caught the light furrow in her brow. A moment later, her bright smile returned. 'Right then, let's get on with the safety briefing.'

Lori listened closely, memorising how to open the emergency exit, how to fit an oxygen mask, where the life jackets were stowed. Ever the conscientious student.

In front, the young mother was trying to settle her baby, tiny mewing cries escaping from its gummy pink mouth. The mother held the baby against her chest, her lips pressed to the crown of his head. She could imagine the sweet, biscuit scent of his skin, the soft brush of his hair. She felt the familiar yearning to reach out, to hold that tiny little being. Babies always elicited such a complicated response in her. Some days she wanted to be near them, to study their tiny, wrinkle-less hands, the perfect nub of their noses, and others it was easier to pretend they didn't exist.

'Please could I get some hot water for his bottle,' the mother asked once the safety briefing was over.

'Course,' the air stewardess replied, resting a hand on the seat back. 'How old is your little one?'

'Sonny. He's four months.'

'He's beautiful. You must be besotted.'

Sonny's mother glanced down at him, a smile on her lips. 'Besotted – and exhausted. I'm hoping sleep deprivation will be easier in the sun.'

'Where are you from?'

'Chicago. The winters are tough.'

'I'll bet. No one can prepare you for the lack of sleep, can they? I remember it so well with my daughter. She's seventeen – and now the problem is getting her out of bed! You got family around to help?'

She shook her head. 'No one. I'm doing it solo. But I do

enough adoring for everyone, don't I?' She pressed another kiss against her son's head.

The plane began to turn on the runway, wheels rolling across the tarmac, the sun streaming in as they turned east. Lori peered through the window, noticing a band of dark cloud ahead. It loomed like smoke on the horizon, thick and dense.

As they began to taxi on the runway, the sun slipped behind the layer of cloud, the cabin darkening. In the distance, the palm trees at the edge of the airfield began to bow and quiver.

She felt the empty space of Erin's seat beside her. *God, I wish you were here.* Erin would've gripped her hand, reminding her of what waited at their island destination: cocktails, and warm, white sand, and the cool slip of the sea.

The baby was still crying as they taxied along the runway – a low wailing sound, broken by hiccupping gasps. His mother jigged him lightly against her chest; he was red-faced, tiny fists curled. Lori sensed the mother wanting to be on her feet, walking him up and down the aisle.

The air stewardess approached, saying, 'I'm so sorry, but you're going to have to put your little boy in the bassinet now. We're about to take off.'

'But he'll scream even more,' the mother said, voice thin.

'I'm really sorry. It's protocol. The moment the seat-belt light is turned off you can get him out.'

The mother unpeeled the baby from her and placed him into the bassinet. His screams became piercing as he writhed, his mother desperately whispering to him as she circled a hand over his tummy.

The tarmac was sliding beneath the plane wheels, the airport disappearing behind them. At the front of the plane, Lori saw the smartly dressed man, Daniel, signalling to the air stewardess.

He said something that Lori missed beneath the baby's cries, but whatever it was caused the air stewardess's eyes to widen. She shook her head. 'You can't! We're about to take off.'

He signalled to the window, said something else. Lori caught the end of it '. . . off the plane. Now.'

There was no panic in his voice, just a clear, firm request. An instruction.

What was going on? Had he been watching the bad weather approaching? She remembered overhearing him on the phone earlier, something about second thoughts. Her skin prickled. Nothing felt right about this flight. She shouldn't have got on the plane without Erin. It was a mistake. This wasn't where she was supposed to be – buckled into a plane that was about to buffet its way through the skies above the South Pacific, alone, without her sister.

Her hand moved to her seat belt. She needed to get off the plane. Panic felt hot and flush in her throat. She snapped open the buckle.

Daniel's voice was raised. 'We haven't left the ground yet!'

'We're moments away from take-off,' the air stewardess said firmly.

Lori felt the acceleration of the plane. Her stomach knotted, heart lifting into her mouth. G-force pinned her to the seat. The engines roared as the plane powered forward. Her fingers scrabbled for the seat belt. Ahead of her, the baby screamed.

At the window, the throbbing clouds had closed in, rain smattering against the panes.

*It's wrong*, she thought as they gathered speed. *Everything feels wrong.*

Across the aisle, the retired couple had bowed their heads in prayer. 'Our Father who art in Heaven . . .'

As she clicked her seat belt back into place, she felt the wheels lift. That's it. They were airborne. There was no turning back for any of them.

# 8

# NOW | ERIN

The plane falls from the sky, a flaming arrow. Smoke pours from the tail. It lilts and shudders, plummeting downwards.

'Lori!' I scream, over and over, from where I'm standing on the ground, eyes skyward.

The plane is so near now, I can see the white terror of my sister's face pressed to the window. I scream her name again, but she doesn't see me. Doesn't know I'm there.

I lift my arms as if I can catch her.

But I can't.

She's alone as the plane hits the earth in an explosion of flames.

I wake, like I always do, gasping, skin coated in sweat.

I'm out of the flat early, pedalling hard through London's dawn-grey streets. I fly past construction workers drilling into hard tarmac, concrete dust and fumes at the back of my throat. My thoughts race with me, spinning through the gaping spaces in the pilot's transcript.

I pedal harder, lactic acid biting into my calves. I'm so consumed that I don't see the lorry backing out of a side road, the reversing beeps swallowed by the noise of my own thoughts. Then metal pushes back against me, clipping my front wheel, and I'm flying forward, arms windmilling through air, my mouth stretched with surprise.

Airborne, everything rises and distorts, the windshields of vehicles slanting at the wrong angle, the streetlights seeming too bright as I look up into them. Everything is flipped, curved. It feels as if I am flying endlessly, further and further from my bike, the road, the ground.

I think of Lori. It feels as though I have forever to do so. I wonder at her last view as the plane plummeted. Food trays slipping, air pressure dropping out, the earth roaring towards her.

There is a thud, a crack of my helmet. My body connects with pavement, air pushed from my chest.

I lie still. My brain feels as if it's been rattled within my skull.

A vehicle door opens. Heavy boots pounding towards me. 'Jesus! Y'all right, love?'

It takes me a few seconds to draw enough air to answer, 'Yes . . .'

The pavement is frost-cold. More feet close in – leather shoes, dirty-white trainers and jogging bottoms, black tights and heels.

The lorry driver is shaking his head, talking fast, voice high with panic. 'You didn't look! You didn't fuckin' look! Didn't you hear the reversing beeps?'

Emotion is welling in my throat. 'Sorry.'

Another man is stepping forward, crouching down. Narrow-jawed, earnest. 'I'm a first-aider. Do you need help?'

I've no idea how badly I'm injured. All I know is that I'm close to tears. That there are too many people near me. That I need to get away.

I push myself to my feet, staggering a little, as if my body is uncertain about the direction it should return to. I search for my bike. Somehow it's behind me, a long way behind me, and my brain is trying to work out how I have landed so far away, the distance I must have flown through the air, but I can't hold onto this thought, because tears are pricking hotly at the corners of my eyes.

'Let me help you,' the first-aider is saying.

'Sorry,' I say again, the only word at my disposal. I am limping towards my bike, picking it up from the ground – hoping, hoping that it will ride, that the wheel isn't buckled – and then I am straddling it, reaching for the pedals.

I'm aware of the burning sensation in my elbow, a damp warmth on my knee. I hear the lorry driver calling after me, asking if I'm okay.

'Wait!' someone shouts.

But I don't.

I pedal harder, away. Away.

At the office, I go straight to the toilets and tidy myself up as best I can, cleaning the grit from the cut on my chin. My favourite black jeans are torn across the knee. When I roll up my left sleeve, I find my elbow bleeding. I press a wad of tissue against it, then pull my sleeve down, hoping it'll hold it in place. There'll be a first-aid kit somewhere in the office, but locating it will involve hunting down the person with the key to the supply cupboard and getting into a conversation about the perils of cycling in London. I'll take a coffee over a plaster, I decide, leaving the cubicle.

The office kitchen is busy with colleagues ahead of our

nine o'clock meeting. No one notices me come in, picking up a chipped Keep Calm and Carry On mug from the draining board. As I wait for the kettle to boil, I study its coffee-ringed interior, wondering whether it would be possible to age the mugs in the office, as one ages a tree by counting the rings on its trunk.

'It's like that case, do you remember?' Thalia is saying to a small group with their backs to me. 'The couple who disappeared in Panama for the life insurance. Pretended to their own kids they were dead. All for a hundred grand.'

'You can't believe people can be so selfish,' someone else chips in.

'Maybe the pilot wanted to get the life insurance for his wife?'

Someone turns then and sees me. The others look around and the room falls silent.

Everyone knows that my sister was on that plane. It's something that people just *know*. I don't talk about it. I began as a PA to the editor three years ago, then a writing role came up covering someone's maternity leave, but the woman never returned, so I am, somehow, still here. Still racing after stories, still wondering whether this is where I'm meant to be. Every month, keen, fresh interns arrive in the office and I *smell* their hunger to be in this industry, to have a permanent job in this building. It makes me feel fraudulent, as though I've slipped into a role that was never meant for me.

Darren, my one friend in the office, stares at me. 'What happened to your chin?'

I raise a hand to my chin and feel the hot graze there. 'Came off my bike.'

'Looks nasty. You all right?'

'Course.' I say it so crisply that Darren lifts a hand to his forehead, saluting.

46

'Come on,' he says, taking the mug from my hands, 'let me at least make you a coffee. The meeting is about to start.'

We sit around a large table, notebooks out. I take a sip of my coffee. Darren added twice the amount of milk I'd have used. 'Thanks for the latte.'

He grins, then opens his notebook, which is filled with cartoon doodles bursting with little speech bubbles. After a moment, he turns towards me. I can feel him looking at me. He leans closer and asks, 'Really, are you okay, Erin?'

Thankfully, I'm saved from answering when Rebecca, our editor, strides into the room. She is tall, bone-thin, and has a hint of an East End accent embedded in her vowels.

Every Friday we have a meeting to pitch ideas for the following week's magazine, to show our hand as to what we've got. There's an etiquette to it. You come prepared. You don't share your ideas outside of the meeting room, in case they get snagged by someone else. Some people race through sharing every whim or thought. Others say nothing, then dazzle.

Rebecca's pale blue gaze assesses the room, then fixes squarely on me. 'Erin.'

Everyone turns to me. Heat creeps into my cheeks.

'The pilot,' she says. Two words. Nothing more. Darren says she's spent so long as an editor that she speaks in headlines.

She knows my relationship to the story – because that's what it is to her: a story.

I open my notebook. It is blank. Darren will see my gaze moving along the empty lines.

I'm silent as I look down at the wordless page. My hands are still trembling after coming off my bike. I'm aware that everyone is watching me, that my cheeks are on fire.

I take a breath. Begin. 'The relatives of the passengers of flight FJ209 were emailed a transcript of an interview with the pilot – but he's not talking. Not really. All we know is that the plane crashed and he was the only survivor. He's not given any indication of what happened on the flight, or where the plane is now, or how he is still alive.' I look up, my gaze meeting Rebecca's. 'I want to find out what the pilot is hiding.'

I know it's true as soon as the words spill out of me. It's not enough to read a few stilted, broken responses in a transcript. I want to look the pilot in the eye, hear the tone of his voice, watch his expression as he speaks. I want to know what happened the moment that plane came crashing down. I want to know how he crawled out of the wreckage alive – when my sister didn't.

He was the man who was in charge of the safety of each of those seven passengers, yet they are dead and he isn't. I want to know why he didn't get in touch with his family. His friends. The police. I want to know what makes a man *choose* to leave his life behind.

That's when I decide. 'I want to go to Fiji and interview the pilot.'

# 9

# THEN | LORI

Lori pressed her nose to the plane window. She could see nothing through the layers of thick cloud, just wisps of it rushing by like smoke.

She checked her watch. They'd been flying for forty-five minutes. They must be almost there. She rubbed at her forearms, wondering why the air conditioning was always set to freezing on planes. As she was about to reach for her cardigan from the overhead locker, there was a sudden drop, as if the plane had hit a speed bump. The water in her bottle sloshed.

*Just turbulence,* she reminded herself, heart flaring. The seat-belt sign pinged, illuminating red. She tightened her belt, shoved her drink into the seat pocket, and set the tray in the upright position.

The air stewardess appeared in the aisle. 'There's a band of heavy weather on our course, which the pilot has been skirting. We may just brush the edges of it, so we'll keep the seat-belt sign on for now.'

Turbulence is perfectly normal, she reminded herself. Not a sign of a problem. Absolutely not. She'd Googled an explanation of turbulence last week. Knew it was simply disturbed patches of air caused by different forces, like mountains, jet streams and storms. But research had also told her that weather forecasts and pilot reports are often relatively blunt tools for predicting turbulence. All anyone could do was buckle in and ride it out.

She gasped as there was another bump, as if the plane had hit something solid. Her gaze shot to the window, her heart hammering, but the view was still swallowed by a thick layer of cloud.

The baby, woken by the bang, began to yell, its cries urgent and sharp. Lori watched the mother reaching into the bassinet, but the air stewardess called across the aisle, 'Please, leave him there until we're through the turbulence.'

The plane gave another lurch.

Lori's head snapped back against the seat.

'Jesus!' a man cried out near the front.

She gripped the armrests, knuckles white. What was going on? Was this normal? It felt more than turbulence. Her gaze was pinned to the window.

Cloud. Rushing cloud. Nothing else.

She wanted to land. Feel earth beneath her feet. Get out of this fucking tin can!

The plane stalled to the left, the wing tipping downwards as a grinding metallic noise filled the cabin. *No! This isn't right!*

At the front of the plane, Daniel swivelled in his seat, face pinched and white. 'What's going on?' he yelled above the strain of the engine.

'Everything's fine!' the air stewardess called back, who was holding onto a seat back. 'Just keep your seat belts fastened.' She pasted on a smile as she navigated unsteadily towards the cockpit.

Every pair of eyes was trained on her as she opened the door.

Lori caught a snatch of hurried words shouted by the pilot: 'Left engine behaving erratically . . . switch to auxiliary tank . . .' Then the door slammed shut behind the air stewardess.

'It's the engine!' the American woman cried, hands clasping her husband's.

Sweat was pooling beneath Lori's arms, a band of tightness squeezing at her chest. The noise was astounding, loud and rasping.

The young mother had circled her arms around the bassinet, speaking only to her child.

The American couple began to pray again.

Lori could smell something metallic, burning.

The air stewardess stumbled out of the cockpit. Her face was white. 'There's an issue with the fuel,' she shouted above the roar of noise. 'We need to make an emergency landing. Everyone must be strapped—'

Without warning, the plane dropped. A rush of air tore through the cabin as if the windows had blown out. The air stewardess was flung upwards, her back smacking the ceiling, feet pedalling against nothing but air.

Someone screamed.

Shots of pain burst in Lori's ears and behind her eyes. Her hair danced above her head. Everything around her was rising, lifting. A book took flight. A phone cracked against the ceiling. A shoe was pinned to the overhead lockers. Everything being sucked upwards with unstoppable force.

All around her people screamed. The mother had hunched forward over the bassinet, her body a shell.

A deep pressure was constricting Lori's chest. She tried to reach for an oxygen mask, but her hand couldn't rise against the force of the pressure drop.

Then a juddering lilt. A shift. Spinning, as if the axis of the earth had swung.

The door to the cockpit flew open, and she caught sight of the pilot, his profile terror-bleached, eyes wide as he strained to keep control of the plane, teeth bared.

Through the plane windscreen she glimpsed a flash of land through the cloud, spinning dangerously close. Then sea and sky.

Her eyes felt as if they were being sucked from her head. A pressure expanding inside her, splitting her open.

They were going down.

*This is it*, a voice inside her said.

Lori didn't think of her sister, or even Pete. Her life didn't flash before her eyes. What she thought of was the life she hadn't yet lived, the mother she'd never had a chance to be. It was like a film about to be paused halfway.

And then there was the earth, green and dazzling, rushing towards them, so close . . . too close.

# 10

# NOW | ERIN

*I'm in Fiji*, I repeat to myself as I exit the terminal, squinting into the searing light. Yesterday I was at the office in London – and now, somehow, I'm here.

I hire a car, which I stall three times on the way out of the airport, causing the rental guy to wince. I'm jet-lagged as hell – eyes gritted, bone-weary, mouth furred.

I don't have a car in London, so I'm rusty, I'll admit that – but I still drive how I've always done – fast and sharp on the brakes. I motor along curving main roads, passing dilapidated shops and bars and litter-strewn verges. The sun radiates through the tinted windscreen against my chest and I lean forward, fiddling with the air conditioning, until I'm finally rewarded with a blast of cool air.

It's only when I've put some miles between me and the airport that the landscape begins to resemble the Fiji I remember – the red-hued earth beneath glistening vegetation, the fruit stands on the side of the road selling fresh coconut and huge bunches of small green bananas, the turquoise glitter of sea glimpsed around a bend.

I pass an art gallery framed with a wide, well-lit window and slow the car. I glance at it a second time, realising we must have come this route before, because I remember Lori turning to look at the beautiful oil seascapes in the windows – and leaning forward, hands on the dash, saying, 'I need to see that painting.'

I'd pulled over, two wheels bouncing up onto the pavement edge, and Lori had slipped out, crossing the road, hair loose against her shoulders. Disappointingly, the gallery had been closed, but she'd stood in front of the window studying the oil seascape. In the glass reflection, I caught the way her expression transformed into something contemplative, almost serene. As I watched, hands on the wheel, indicator ticking, I thought how much I wanted that. A passion. Something that makes you pull over, just to *look* at something. To *feel* it.

'We'll stop again on our return,' I'd promised Lori as she'd climbed back into the rental car.

But there was no return. Not for Lori.

The sat nav confirms that I'm approaching my destination. I turn left into a wide entrance, framed by stone pillars and an elaborate sign announcing the Hotel Pacific. I pull up outside a vast white hotel, the pristine lawn decorated with sprinklers. I sit for a moment, looking at the bloom of brightly coloured flowers and carefully sculpted trees.

I made the booking on my phone at the airport, but now that I'm here, I wonder why I did it. Why I chose the exact same hotel.

The last place I saw my sister.

\* \* \*

It's been two years since Lori and I climbed these marble steps into the luxuriant, high-ceilinged lobby. Memories shimmer as I recall the swish of Lori's dress as she'd turned a circle, head tipped back, staring up at the domed wooden ceiling carved with ornate flowers. 'It's beautiful,' she'd marvelled.

We were due to stay for just one night – a stopover on the mainland before flying on to the tiny island of Limaji where the real holiday was supposed to begin – but in one evening, everything changed.

Instead, the following day, I found myself returning to the hotel, hungover, unslept, and suffused with guilt that I'd abandoned Lori and our holiday. I was already telling myself that I'd book another flight, find a way to make it up to her, when the hotel manager stopped me in reception to tell me that British consul Steven Wills was waiting to see me.

*Me? But, why?*

I'd crossed the lobby – this lobby – thinking they'd made a mistake. I went to say as much, but Steven Wills, a slight man with a lion's handshake, began speaking. 'Are you Erin Holme? Is your sister Lori Holme? Was she travelling on flight FJ209 to Limaji? Were you meant to be travelling with her?'

*Yes. Yes. Yes. Yes.*

Then came the blade, so unexpected, so swift, I didn't even see it drawn. 'The plane your sister was on never arrived at its destination. The Civil Aviation Authority of Fiji are trying to make contact and a full-scale search has been launched . . .'

And so it began.

I spent the next three weeks in this hotel, stalking the corridors in search of the best place to get a Wi-Fi signal, hounding the local police for news, being visited by the consul with his insufficient updates, fielding calls from Lori's concerned friends.

Now I wait at the reception desk as a slim young man

checks in the couple in front with smiling efficiency. When he turns to me – perhaps it's my weary expression – he leans closer, and with a sincerity that reaches his eyes, tells me, 'I'm so happy to have you staying. I'm here to help in any way you need. I'm Tyia. You can always ask for me.'

There is something familiar about him. It's his smile, the way his whole mouth opens, showing both his upper and lower teeth. I wonder if we've met before – whether he was working here two years earlier. He looks too young. In fact, he looks as if he should be in school.

I thank Tyia, declining the help of a porter, or the glide of the lift, and instead I make for the stairs, backpack slung over one shoulder.

As I follow the corridor towards my room, I pass a drift-wood-framed mirror and catch a glimpse of myself: a dark-haired girl with a backpack on her shoulders. Something stirs deep inside that I can't quite put words to. This girl I see, she has flown halfway around the world chasing shadows. Her skin is wan; bruised eyes give away that she doesn't sleep, not properly, and there's something about the hunch of her shoulders, as if she is curling in on herself.

Yet, I also see the padded straps of her backpack – a backpack that should speak of adventures and paths to tread – and I feel a deep yearning, something core and essential that I don't know how to answer. Staring at my reflection, it's like I can see myself – but also a different me, just glimpsed, the breath of someone I'd rather be. But I don't know how to reach her.

I pace on, feeling a little spacy, too intense.

*You? Intense? Never.*

I catch it, the smile in Lori's voice, and I find myself smiling, too.

Inside my hotel room, the air is ice-cool. My eyes are

gritted and dry from the flight. I fiddle with a couple of switches on the air-conditioning unit and turn it off, then go straight to the balcony doors and throw them open. I step out into the thick heat. The day is closing, buttery rose clouds dusting the sky.

A thrum in the air alerts me to a plane travelling overhead. The reverberation tingles across my shoulders, through the tips of my fingers, in the lightest of vibrations beneath my bare soles. I've become attentive to planes – it's like an extra sense I've developed. In London they're part of the fabric of my day. I'll hear them before breakfast, as I cycle, through the tall windows of the office, in bed at night as I try to sleep.

In the early months following Lori's disappearance, the sound of a plane would root me to the spot, cause me to crane my neck, shoulders tensed, breath held. I'd be waiting to see whether the plane would continue smoothly on its path – or whether it would stutter, begin to lose height, spiral to the earth. I'd stand frozen, watching, until the plane had safely left my vision, just a vapour trail in an empty sky.

Over time, I've worked hard to give less energy to planes. But out here – seeing this small plane flying right above me, perhaps headed to one of the outer islands – the tightness in my chest returns, like thick hands squeezing at my ribcage. Everyone on that plane will safely reach their destination, I know that. I've learned the stats. The odds of being in a plane crash are one in eleven million.

One in eleven-fucking-million.

*So, why you, Lori?*

By comparison, the odds of being killed in a car crash are one in five thousand. When you set foot on a plane, you are effectively relinquishing all control – handing over your safety to the pilot. The doors are locked, the plane is moving, there is no getting off. All you can hope is that your pilot, on that day, in that moment, is thinking straight. Is making the right decisions. You might hope they're in good health, that they've slept well, that their mental faculties are sharp.

I picture Captain Mike Brass as the press have presented him: a 53-year-old Australian with an unblemished flight record, his press photo capturing a man with silver-dark hair and pouches beneath his eyes. A husband. A father.

But that's not the full picture.

Tomorrow I'm going to be face to face with him. I don't have an appointment, a strategy, a brilliant plan. I will simply turn up at the hospital and do whatever it takes. I only need a few minutes. Enough time to look him in the eye, ask: *What really happened?*

The transcript provided the bare bones of the pilot's story – but what about the flesh, the ligaments, the blood, the emotion?

I've had two years to think about the disappearance of flight FJ209; two years to examine the questions that twist hot and insidiously through my thoughts at night. I've played out every scenario, followed those possibilities down winding rivers of imagination to see where they stream.

My thoughts turn through the transcript now, revisiting the pilot's answers, and the many, many gaps they left. They pause on one question.

*Officer: We understand it was the anniversary of your daughter's death the day before the flight. Were you in the right frame of mind when you captained that plane?*

*Mike Brass: Yes.*

His answer is a lie.

Captain Mike Brass is lying about what happened the night before the flight. I know that for a fact, because I've been lying, too.

# 11

# NOW | ERIN

The next morning, I'm wired, jittery, as I swing the rental car into the hospital car park. My feet slip within my flip-flops as I try and park, causing me to stall. I reach for the key to restart the engine, but it's one of those bloody keyless ignitions. I fumble around and accidentally lean on the horn, which sounds a loud honk.

*Nice, subtle entrance, Erin. Great job*, Lori pipes up.

I step out into the full heat of the morning, skin flushed, the backs of my knees licked with sweat. It was a mistake to drink coffee on an empty stomach, I realise, feeling the rapid pound of my heart, but I couldn't face eating. Now I'm over-caffeinated, jet-lagged, twitchy. My mind is racing through an assault of questions for Mike Brass.

I rang the hospital earlier to check his ward number, claiming to be a member of the local police. I'm not sure whether impersonating a police officer is a criminal offence in Fiji, but I withheld my phone number, so I'll take my chances. I learned three facts during that phone call: one, the pilot is still alive. Two, he has been moved into a hospice situated at the rear of the hospital grounds. Three, his condition has deteriorated.

I locate the hospice, a single-storey beige building, with a decorative water fountain fronting it. An elderly Fijian man sits alone in a wheelchair watching two bright-plumed birds bathing, wings sending a spray of water arching. He wishes me good morning as I pass and, as I return the greeting – my mouth tight, my voice knotted – I remind myself to lose the scowl. Lori once teased me, 'You know what your resting face says? *Pissed Off, So Don't Even Bother.*'

Inside the air smells of bleach and food – the combination turning my stomach. At the reception desk, two staff members talk with their heads bent together. I snap past them, eyes ahead.

All the rooms appear to be privately occupied. I slow my pace as I approach each doorway. A Fijian woman in a vivid green dress is curled on the side of her partner's hospital bed, eyes closed, her palm laid against his chest. In another room, a teenager in a rugby shirt lies alone watching a television screen.

The next open doorway I look through is his.

Mike Brass. Captain of flight FJ209.

My fingers are curled at my sides, my breathing is ragged. I stare at the man who crashed my sister's plane. Who survived when everyone else died. Who made it back to the mainland, but hid from his family, the police, the press. The one man who can give me the answers I need.

He lies on his back, lips slightly ajar, eyes closed. His hair has been shaved close on one side and, if I were in a lighter mood, I'd think of something funny about our matching undercuts. But I'm not. An IV line runs into his left hand, a bag of clear fluid hanging on a stand beside his bed. Beyond him, a machine with a black and green screen beeps lightly in the background.

I take a deep breath, step fully into the room, pulling the door behind me. I move to his bedside, perching on a plastic chair. 'Mike?'

No response.

I try again, saying his name more loudly the second time.

But there's still nothing. The room is too hot, my top sticking to my back.

I don't know how long I have. My hand hovers above his arm. His wrist is circled by a hospital band, thick white hairs sprouting around it. I squeeze. 'Mike?'

His eyes flicker beneath crepe-like eyelids. The rhythm of his breath alters.

'Mike?' I say again, squeezing harder.

This time, his eyes open. He blinks several times, murmurs. His fingers splay. He seems to be grasping for something.

On the table beside him, I find a paper cup of water with a straw in, and hold it near his mouth, directing the straw towards his lips. He takes a sip, without even acknowledging me. Then I remove the cup and his gaze lifts to my face, focuses.

For a long time, he says nothing. Then I see the moment recognition arrives, his brow dipping, the slow blink of eyes.

I'm waiting for it.

When he speaks, his voice is thick. 'It's you.'

Mike Brass studies me for a long moment. He remembers.

I think of the bar at night, the cool clink of ice in glasses. 'Yes.'

There is silence. We stare at one another, both remembering different fragments of the same evening.

'You didn't tell anyone,' he says.

The silence stretches. A stream of emotion runs through me, a thousand tiny electrical currents pulsing beneath the surface. 'Not yet.'

He tries to sit, pushing himself up with the heels of his hands; a puff of stale air escapes his mouth. The movement seems impossible and he collapses back into the pillow.

My voice is steel. 'My sister, Lori Holme, was on your flight.'

A shadow of something passes over his face. His eyes leave mine.

'I want to know everything that happened.'

'There's . . . a transcript.'

'It's bullshit.' My teeth clench. 'I want the truth.'

He glances to the doorway as if there may be someone to help him. The door is shut; we're alone.

'You should never have flown that plane. We both know it.' But I'm not interested in excuses or apologies. I want facts. 'Where did you crash?'

'An island . . . somewhere . . .'

'Where?'

He shakes he head. 'We were off course. There are . . . hundreds of them.'

I've learned enough from interviewing people to recognise when they're wary, skittering away from the truth. Typically, I would work the questions to bring someone into an easy rhythm of answers, so they'd lower their guard. But there isn't time. 'After the crash – then what?'

He swallows, the sound dry, rasping. 'I managed to survive.'

'Congratulations.' Acerbic I can do. 'What about the others?'

He blinks. 'Me. Just me. They would have told you that.'

'I need to hear you say it. Not read it from a transcript.' I reframe the question, so it is solid, black and white. 'Is my sister alive?'

There. I've asked. The question I've been quietly nursing ever since the plane disappeared. Because there was no body, it left space for hope. However small. Is that the right word, *hope*? Hope is a positive word, optimistic – yet it flies dangerously close to desperation. Hope is all that remains when concrete, tangible facts have scattered. It's no firmer than the wind, and yet it is there, all around me. Hoping, hoping, hoping.

Mike looks at me with a strange, bewildered expression – as if he's surprised that I'm even asking this question. He should know that anything is possible when you walk out of the shadows after two years. If he's alive, why not Lori?

Slowly, his head shakes. 'She is dead.'

The words are blunt, hard blows to my gut.

I don't have to believe him. I can choose *not* to believe him. But there's something small and curled within me that knows.

I hear myself asking, 'Where's her body?'

'I'm sorry . . .'

No. That is not enough. I am not accepting an apology of an answer. Fuck him. I lean forward, right over Mike Brass. 'Where's her body? Where is Lori's body? I need to know where my sister's body is! You have to give me that. Is it still on the plane? Did you leave her there? Please, please tell me you didn't.' *She was terrified of flying . . . to have crashed and then be left there . . .*

'No . . .' the word is little more than a whisper.

'No, you didn't leave her there?'

His brow furrows, as if a deep pain is pushing at him. He reaches for the cord at the side of his bed, controlling his pain relief. He misses. I could pass it to him, but don't.

'What did you do with my sister's body? With all of the bodies?'

I wait. My fingers are curled into my palms. The bite of

nails against skin. I'm fizzing with energy, it needs to be directed somewhere, but his stillness, his weakness absorbs none of it. It's as if all my anger is reverberating around this hospice room.

'I didn't want to . . . honestly . . .'

I wait.

And wait.

'What didn't you want to do?'

Nothing.

'Mike?' I'm leaning closer, my nose almost touching his. 'What didn't you want to do?'

His eyes glaze. He has retreated somewhere within himself that I can't reach.

Beyond the door, I hear voices. I look up and see a nurse with her back to the door. She's talking to a young man with a heavy brow line. I recognise him from his photo: it's the pilot's son, Nathan Brass. He's standing beside an older woman with grey hair pinned low against her neck, who must be the pilot's wife. Their gazes are on the nurse and haven't found me yet.

We have moments before they'll be upon us.

I squeeze Mike's arm, hard. He jolts awake. 'Tell me! Where are their bodies?'

Eventually he speaks. Just one syllable, so I think I've missed it.

'See.'

I wait, thinking there's more. 'See? What am I supposed to see?'

He says nothing further. And then I realise: *sea*.

'The sea? You put them in the sea?'

'Couldn't bury them . . . no spade, nothing to dig with.' He reaches again for the button and this time his fingers grasp it. He squeezes. A dose of pain relief floods his system. His body slackens. 'The heat . . . horrific to leave them. We had no choice.'

I blink.

I can feel each beat of my heart. Strong, clear. '*We?*'

He looks at me. His eyes widen just a fraction, or perhaps it is simply the light.

'You said, *We had no choice.*'

His breath is laboured. 'No. A mistake . . .' His eyelids are beginning to flicker, to slowly close.

I can hear the hinge of metal as the door handle is being depressed.

'Mike? What did you mean, *we?*'

His eyes close, breath slowing. He's being dragged away on the current of drugs.

'Did someone else survive the crash?' I'm squeezing his arm, fingernails pressing into paper-thin skin. 'Tell me!'

A rush of noise spills into the room as the door is opened wide. I glance up to see the pilot's son staring at me, as I grip his father's arm. 'What the hell?'

My face is close to Mike Brass's as I hiss, 'Other people survived that crash, didn't they?'

His head moves an infinitesimal amount and I wonder if it is a nod, or the movement of him swallowing. I can't tell.

'Who else survived?' I demand, hands moving to his shoulders, pinning him. 'Was it my sister?'

But Mike Brass lies completely still now. There's no answer, nothing more, just the rush of Nathan Brass's footsteps, the feel of his large hands on my shoulders, pulling me off.

I'm wrestled from the room, eyes swivelling towards Mike, as I beg, 'Tell me! Who else walked off that plane?'

But the question is left hanging there, unanswered in my wake.

## 12

# THEN | LORI

Nothingness for long, undefined moments. Emptiness deepening and shallowing, dark and hot. Not thoughts but sensation: a thrumming ringing; burning air; crushing weight.

Then a slow awareness dimpling the surface.

Her cheek. Pressed against something hard, angular.

Lori blinked. Only one eye peeled open. Images swung. A flash of distortion. A moaning wail, low and throaty.

*Where? What?*

She swallowed. Tasted blood in her mouth.

She tried to raise her head. Pain crashed through the front of her skull. There was a whirring sound, like a long, slowing exhale.

Her fingers, searching, crawling, met something solid, stable. She blinked again, raising her head through the blinding wince of pain. Oxygen masks hung limp from the ceiling. Overhead lockers gaped open. Luggage was strewn everywhere. A trail of smoke was rising somewhere behind her.

*Plane. I'm in an aeroplane . . .*

Her gaze skittered and slid to the aircraft window. Branches were butted up against it, thick leaves crowding in. She blinked rapidly, taking in a dark thatch of trees, limb-like branches reaching. Everything felt distant, removed.

*We crashed . . .*

The deep wailing continued, desperate and broken, twisting through her.

*Me*, she realised slowly. *The cry is coming from me . . .*

She dragged in a breath, chest heaving. She turned her head a fraction.

Adjacent, the American couple were fastened to their seats, unmoving. The man's head hung forward, chin resting on his solid, still chest. Blood was already drying on the side of his face, his glasses hanging from one ear.

*No . . . this isn't happening . . .*

His wife was slumped against his side, her neck at an awkward angle, exposing a gold chain cutting into the flesh. Her mouth was open, eyes rolled back in her head. The sickening understanding settled: *Dead. They're both dead.*

A wave of nausea swam up, her throat turning liquid. She wanted to screw her eyes shut. Sink down into the folds of darkness. Disappear. But a primal part of her told her she needed to move. Now.

Smoke.

She tried to stand, but the belt held her fastened to the seat. She fumbled with the metal clip, thick-fingered and clumsy. The belt finally released and she pushed into the armrest, making to stand, but felt the lock of her legs. The seat in front had been forced back, pinning her legs. She tried again, ramming her hands against the seat, pushing.

Smoke was thickening in the cabin, billowing from the rear of the plane. Panic sparked in her chest. 'Help!'

She shoved the heels of her hands hard against the seat in front, pushing with all her force. Pain ripped through her shoulders and neck. There was a fraction of release – and she used that moment to draw up her knees, dragging them from the crush of seats, shin bones screaming, as she wrenched herself free.

Her head spun, the ground tilting and flexing. Clinging onto the seat back to steady herself, she panted unevenly, staring down at her torn and bloodied legs. Through the wash of pain, she dragged herself along the aisle.

Slumped on the floor at her feet, the air stewardess lay on her back, unnervingly still. Her eyes were open, blood pooling beneath her head in a gruesome slick of red. A gurgling sound was bubbling from her mouth, as if she were breathing in liquid.

'It's okay . . .' Lori said, her voice strange and thin.

Pain shot down her legs as she knelt. She could taste blood in her mouth, pressed her tongue into a hole in her cheek. She wanted to gag but made herself take another breath.

'I'm going to help you,' Lori told her.

The air stewardess's lips moved as if she were trying to speak. A liquid, bubbling sound came from her lungs. The words that followed were so weak, Lori wasn't sure she'd caught them . . .

'Stopped him . . .'

'It's okay. I'm going to help you,' she repeated. The plume of smoke was thickening in the cabin. She needed to get her out. Fast. She glanced over her shoulder towards the exit. The door was open, daylight spilling into the plane.

An intensity pierced the air stewardess's expression as her gaze locked with Lori's. Her fingers reached up, grasping at Lori's wrist. 'I . . . should've stopped him.'

Whatever energy had pushed the air stewardess to speak, suddenly dissolved. Her grip withered, her gaze slipping away.

'Hey! Stay with me!'

The air stewardess's eyes were completely still and unfocused.

She grabbed the collar of her shirt. 'Hello? Can you hear me?'

Nothing.

She squeezed her shoulders hard, pressing her nails into her blouse. 'Hello? I'm going to help you! You've got to stay with me!'

No response.

Lori lowered her head closer to the woman's face, listened: the gurgling had stopped. Her chest wasn't moving.

*Oh God, oh God . . .*

She made herself take a steadying breath, then placed her fingers against her neck, feeling for a pulse. Her own heart was rocketing so hard, she couldn't feel, couldn't think, couldn't even fucking count – but she knew. She knew. This woman was dead.

But still, her hands went to the air stewardess's sternum and she pumped hard, fingers locked, the heels of her palms compressing her chest. *Thirty beats. Was that right?* She pinched the woman's nose and covered her mouth with her own. Breathed, breathed.

Then thirty more pumps. Her shoulder burned, her head splitting with pain.

Two breaths.

More compressions, hard and rhythmic.

A breath. A breath.

Over and over . . .

She could taste the other woman's lipstick in her mouth, faintly sweet, against the metallic tang of blood.

*Smoke,* Lori thought distantly, that lurching warning in her thoughts. *I need to get out.*

There was movement as someone else was staggering to their feet. Lori looked up to see the long-haired man from the boarding lounge unfolding himself. A trail of blood was inching from a gash at the bridge of his nose, disappearing into the stubble on his jaw. His eyes were wide, blinking rapidly. He lurched into the aisle, his gaze meeting hers, then falling to the air stewardess.

There was a clunk as the door to the cockpit swung open and the pilot stumbled out. Blood trailed from a gash at the side of his head, thin rivers of it like cracks in a skull. His face was whitewashed as he lurched forward. The uneven tilt of the plane caused him to stagger. He grabbed onto a seat for support, gaze darting around the plane.

A yell yanked Lori's attention away. The long-haired man had moved and was now holding a bassinet in his blood-stained hands. 'Here! Take the baby!'

*Baby? Oh . . . the baby . . .* She lurched forward, gripping the bassinet. *Please . . . please be okay.*

The baby was lying still on its back. Navy eyes open, unmoving.

Then he blinked, his gaze refocusing on Lori.

A burst of relief. 'He's alive!'

'Get the baby out!' the pilot instructed, as he shook himself into action, unhooking a fire extinguisher from its wall mount. His face was grim, determined, as he pushed towards the thickening smoke at the rear of the plane.

Lori rushed towards the exit, legs biting with pain. In the open doorway, she hesitated as a wash of heat and the scent of earth roared towards her. Disorientated, she stared into the shadowy knot of trees. A wall of green. Waxy, dark leaves. Shadows and light, shafts of sunlight spilling through a dense canopy.

*Where are we?*

She set down the bassinet, using both hands to lower herself onto the crackling, earthy ground. Teeth gritted against the pain, she grabbed the bassinet and stumbled from the smoking plane, bare feet on leaf-strewn earth.

The air around her whispered and shimmered with heat. Her legs gave way and she collapsed on the ground beside the bassinet.

She was aware of the rapid chatter of her teeth. Her brain was offering up strange, minute details of her surroundings. A bright-winged bird perched on a branch, the black bead of its eye watching. The incongruity of the metal-white plane slammed into trees. The whirl of a turbine slowing. Looming trees dripping with vines.

'Where are we?' a voice called from behind her.

She turned. Daniel was bent over, hands just above his knees, a trail of saliva hanging from the corner of his lip. He wore a pale pink polo shirt, which was torn at the sleeve and smeared with dirt. He wiped his mouth, then straightened.

'I don't know . . .' she said, looking around, a shudder of pain travelling down her neck.

They were surrounded by trees, a thick canopy above them shaded out most of the sunlight. There were deep gouges in the earth where the plane must have careered through the jungle, flattening bushes and shrubs. She stared at the plane, the nose butted between two hunkering trees, crisp green-white hearts of snapped branches exposed. Part of the left plane wing had crumpled, wire entrails snaking skyward. She blinked several times, as if adjusting her vision might help smooth the scene into something less surreal.

The mewing cry of the baby pulled her attention back to

the bassinet. Instinctively, she reached for the child, lifting the tiny weight of him into her arms. She stared at his milky-smooth skin, his tiny nose, the fine mist of pale hair.

'Where's his mother? Someone needs to help his mother . . .'

From within the plane, the pilot hollered. 'Hey! Help!' His cap was askew, face smeared with black. 'You!' he said, pointing at Daniel. 'We need you!'

Daniel moved on command, disappearing into the smoking plane.

Lori looked down at the child. 'I'm going to check you over, okay?' Her voice sounded strange, distended, as she narrated what she was doing, running her trembling fingertips around the baby's scalp, looking for any cuts or bumps, then moving downwards over his neck, the tiny curve of his shoulders. She could feel the rapid beat of his heart as she unbuttoned his white cotton vest and moved her fingertips across his chest and torso, carefully stretching out his tiny arms, then legs.

He watched her curiously, not protesting nor struggling. Nothing seemed to cause him discomfort. The bassinet must have been the safest place for him. A strange fact about car crashes arrived through the fog – that passengers who were asleep during an accident usually fared better as their bodies were relaxed.

*He's okay*, she repeated to herself, trying to feel the relief in that knowledge. Carefully, she returned him to the bassinet – but the moment he left her arms, his mouth screwed up in complaint and he began to cry.

'Oh.'

His face reddened, sharp little mew-like cries flooding from his mouth, until she gathered him again. Something told her that motion was what he needed. She clenched her jaw against the flare of pain as she stood. She cradled him close to her body, his cheek against her shoulder. 'Shush, shush.'

She looked up to see the pilot staggering towards the exit of the plane, holding the baby's mother beneath her armpits. Her head had lolled back, amber hair trailing towards the earth. She saw the whites of her eyes, the dark stain of blood matted to one side of her face.

Daniel emerged white-faced, gripping her ankles, eyes anywhere but on the mother.

'Is she . . . ?' Lori called.

The pilot shook his head. 'She's dead.'

*Oh God, no!*

Lori cradled the baby closer, turning to shield him. Above his low, mournful cry, she began to hum. The rhythm of a forgotten lullaby was dredged from the deepest reaches of her memory. Her voice was shaky, too high, but as she repeated the chorus, she started to move, pacing a few steps forward, then back, matching the rhythm of the lullaby.

Gradually the baby began to soften in her arms. Her throat vibrated as she hummed, head nodding with the tune. She kept on humming, wouldn't stop, and all the while, the men moved in and out of the plane, carrying the dead.

## 13

# THEN | LORI

The plane smouldered in the panting jungle.

The baby was asleep in Lori's arms and, behind them, the four bodies of the dead were laid shoulder to shoulder on the earth.

*Our plane crashed. Crashed.*

Words and phrases kept repeating in her head. It was like her body had been rattled with such force that the stream of her thoughts had separated into droplets, each landing in a random, pelting order.

There was heat, movement within her arms. She looked down, surprised afresh to see a baby asleep in her arms, his breath warm against her neck.

Sonny. That's what his mother had called him. She had the overwhelming sensation that she wanted to hand him to someone. But who?

Thirst clawed up her throat. She needed water. She'd had

a bottle with her on the flight – but she couldn't climb back into the smoking barrel of the plane. She pushed her tongue around the insides of her cheeks, which felt tender and swollen where her teeth had pushed deep into her cheek.

Ahead of her, Daniel held up his mobile, squinting at the screen. 'No fucking signal! Not a bar!' He paced across the jungle floor, eyes on the screen. He was wearing cotton socks, pale blue with fashionable stripes of orange cutting towards the ankle.

*He's outside in his socks.* The thought locked there, disconnected. She watched dead leaves snag against the cotton, dirt collecting on the heel print as he moved.

'Hey!' he called to Lori. 'You tried your phone?'

Phone. Where was her phone? It suddenly felt of incredible importance that she had it. Pressed buttons on it. Called someone. *Erin!* she thought. *I need to speak to my sister. I need to let her know what's happened.*

The pilot shambled from the cockpit, arms braced in the plane exit. Below his cap, the wound on the side of his head looked nasty. Blood had dripped onto the white collar of his uniform.

'Are you okay?' Lori called. 'Your head . . .'

He reached his fingers towards the wound. Looked surprised to find his fingers slick with blood. He wiped them across the breast of his uniform, an eerie red-striped logo smearing the badge pinned to his shirt. She squinted, reading it: *Captain Mike Brass.*

'What the fuck happened?' Daniel demanded from the jungle floor.

The pilot – Mike – opened his palms, saying, 'The fuel . . . the fuel line malfunctioned . . . I don't know . . .'

'Where are we?' the long-haired man asked as he emerged beside the pilot, an extinguisher still in his hands.

'I had to make an emergency landing . . . there was nowhere clear, no landing strip, not for miles. This island – that's all there was.'

*An island. We're on an island.*

'Couldn't control it . . .' Mike was saying, head shaking. 'Tried to slow . . . tore through the treeline . . .'

'Did you radio for help?' Daniel cut across him. 'Is a rescue team on the way?'

'The control console has been damaged. Nothing's working.'

'Nothing?' Daniel repeated, voice high. 'But you have a satellite phone?'

'Planes this size aren't equipped with kit like that.'

Daniel gripped the back of his head – the motion seeming to send a fresh shock of pain through him. He dropped his hands, rolled his left shoulder towards his ear. 'There must be some sort of radar or GPS device that gives out our position?'

The words . . . they were all too fast. Lori couldn't hold onto anything. She kept glancing down at the baby in her arms. *What do I do with you?*

Mike was talking, saying something about primary and secondary radar. 'It's line of sight only. The aircraft drops off the radar when it's below the horizon.'

Lori felt her insides turning icy. 'So, what happens now?'

Mike turned and looked at her properly for the first time. His eyes were bloodshot, pupils enlarged. He was blinking rapidly. 'They'll launch a search.'

'A search?' Daniel laughed. 'A fucking search?' He shook his head, his smile shifting into a snarl. 'You crashed our fucking plane and now you're telling us there's no way of radioing for help? No satellite phone?' He opened his palms, turning on the spot so that his gaze pulled in Lori and the long-haired man. 'You hearing this bullshit?'

He pulled his phone in front of him again. Swore at the

screen. 'I'm not waiting around for a search party. There must be a signal somewhere on this island. Or, better still, people. I'm going to see where exactly we are.'

'We came in this way,' the long-haired man said. He pointed in the direction the plane had wheeled across the forest floor, leaving a crush of trees and flattened bushes, wheel marks gouged into earth.

She followed the others towards the edge of the jungle, the baby in her arms. She was barefoot, her sandals lost somewhere within the plane debris. She searched out tree roots and jagged branches, planting her feet carefully on the leafy earth.

The dappled shade ended and they stepped out onto a coral-white beach, blindingly bright. She shielded Sonny's head from the fierce beam of the sun. The deep sand was burning hot against her feet. Without a breath of wind, the sun pulsed above them. Her thirst flared as they trudged forwards, the sand littered with the dried husks of coconuts and long-dead palm fronds.

They came to a standstill on the shoreline. The empty stretch of ocean eyed them indifferently. It was a brilliant azure, crystalline clear and shallow. The strange beauty felt obscene against their bloodied, torn bodies.

Half a kilometre out, the shallow bay was fringed by a curving reef that appeared to circle the island. There, the ocean darkened to a deep navy, ruffled with white water from breaking waves.

Looking left, she could see the beach ended in a cluster of huge elephant-hide boulders that inched out to sea. Looking right, the sand stretched emptily before being cut off by a dense mangrove forest wading into the water.

She turned on the spot, facing the cloak of dense jungle at the island's centre. There was no interruption to the stretch of green – no buildings, no roads, no sign of habitation. It was disturbingly serene, a postcard of paradise with a smoking plane concealed at its centre. Her gaze scanned hungrily for something recognisably manmade – a fishing hut, a boat, the most basic of accommodation – but there was nothing.

'It's fucking deserted,' Daniel whispered.

'How long until they find us?' Lori asked Mike. 'The baby – it needs milk. Needs to be out of this heat.'

He squinted against the glare of the sun. 'I don't know . . .'

Daniel said, 'From our flight path, they'll know where the plane went down. Right?'

A muscle in Mike's jaw was clenching and releasing. 'There was a band of heavy weather. I had to divert to avoid it, so we hooked round wide.' He paused. 'They may not be expecting us to be in this area.'

'What?' Daniel shot. 'They'll have no fucking clue where we are?'

She remembered looking at a map of Fiji back in Erin's flat in London. The southeastern area, where they were headed, was remote and rarely visited. The archipelago was dotted with thousands of islets, and more than three hundred uninhabited islands.

Mike squatted low to the ground, knees clicking. His cap was still at a drunk angle, the cut beneath it beginning to dry in the heat. She watched as he reached a shaking hand into the sand and began to draw.

The shape of the mainland began to form, marked with their take-off point. Sweat pooled in the furrows of his brow as he drew a rough representation of the island chain. 'This was our destination.' He marked a cross. 'This is the flight path we were supposed to take – and I made my last contact with air-traffic control about here.'

Lori noted it was a third of the way into the journey.

'The heavy weather was coming across from the west, so I diverted and tried to reroute.' He thought for a moment. Then he leaned forward. 'I think we went down somewhere around here.'

The rest of them came closer, their shadows falling over the sand map. She could smell the sour tang of vomit, the stench of smoke.

'So when they launch the search,' the long-haired man said, his dark T-shirt soaked with sweat, 'it will be from the point of your last transmission?'

'That's right.'

'So that means . . .' he said, inching forward to see the full expanse of the map. 'That means the search area will cover hundreds of miles.'

Her head swam. She squeezed her eyes shut, holding the baby close. *I can't do this.*

She desperately wanted to hear the churn of helicopter blades, feel the roar of a rescue plane cutting through the sky, see a lifeboat racing across the bay. But when she opened her eyes, all she saw were the bloodied, scared faces of strangers, and beyond them, the blank blue eye of the ocean.

# 14

# NOW | ERIN

I'm wrestled – still yelling – from Captain Mike Brass's hospital room.

I shrug off the pilot's son, who is demanding, 'Who the hell are you?' as I stalk down the corridor.

*We had no choice.*

The words echo in my head, growing louder with each footstep.

*We.*

Other people survived that plane crash. Not just Mike. Who? Who?

The pilot's son is following me, his footsteps heavy and fast. 'Hey! You! Wait!'

But I don't. I break into a run. I need air. I need to get out of this hospital. I take a sharp left, pushing through heavy doors into a stairwell. I jog down them, flip-flops slapping at my heels, and duck around a visitor. Reaching ground level, I slam my palms into the hospital doors, pushing through and out into the rush of sunlight.

I gulp in air, warm, humid – but fresh.

I stand for a moment, catching my breath, hands on hips.

No news for two years. Nothing.

And then the pilot – alive – right there in front of me.

He knows something. He *knows*.

Behind me there's the clunk of boots.

'Hey! You!'

I turn.

The pilot's son, Nathan Brass, is suddenly before me, energy buzzing from him. He's all shoulders, veins in his neck, khaki shorts, work boots. Thick hands open in front of him. 'What the fuck was that? Who are you?' he demands in a hard, Australian accent.

He is glaring at me. I square my shoulders, raise my chin. 'Erin Holme. My sister was on board the flight your dad crashed.'

That knocks him. He blinks. 'Why are you here?'

'I've got questions.'

I look at Nathan. I know things about him. I know that he cried when his older sister moved out. I know that he played rugby to a national standard until a shoulder injury ended it. I know that he didn't speak to his father for eighteen months after his sister died. I know that he married a girl at twenty-three and was divorced by twenty-five. I know that he now lives in Perth, twenty minutes from his mother's house, and works in a boat yard.

'My father's dying,' he says matter-of-factly.

'That's why I need to speak to him. I won't be palmed off with some bullshit transcript that's been scraped together by the authorities. I want the truth.' Adrenalin loosens something and rage pours out of me now, unstoppable, muscular. I square up to him, which is hard, seeing as I'm eye-level with his collarbone. 'I want to know why my sister got on that plane and has not been seen since. I want to know how the hell the pilot – your father – is still alive. I want to know why he didn't hand himself over to the police. I want to know why, when I asked him all these things – where the island was, what happened – he refused to tell me. Why, when he admitted that he put the dead bodies of the passengers in the sea, he said *We had no choice*. Not *I*, but *we*.'

Nathan has taken a slight step back and stares at me, confounded.

'He's lying to us,' I finish.

There's a long silence between us. Then Nathan says, 'I know.'

I was expecting defensiveness – not agreement. 'Why? What's he hiding?'

'Y'think I know? My father let me think he was *dead*.' His lips pull back over his teeth. 'We had a memorial. We mourned him. My mother drank a bottle of wine a night for six months after the plane went down. The press camped outside her door for three of them. She lost her job. She moved in with me. And just when she was beginning to move on, to be happy, we get a call from the police to say my father's alive. Has been alive – and living in Fiji – the whole time. So now we're back here, staying in some hotel with the press glued to the fucking door again.'

'You really didn't know he was alive?'

His jaw juts forward, as if the question is offensive to him. 'Course we fuckin' didn't!'

We stand there for a moment in the beating sun, listening to the shuffle of a patient in slippered feet who passes us, progress slow. Above, a plane cuts through the sky and I glance up into the dazzling blue. 'He should never have flown that plane,' I say, each word a hard stone of truth.

Nathan scrutinises me. 'What does that mean?'

'Nothing,' I say quickly.

He's still looking at me. 'You meant something by it. What?'

My lips are pressed tight.

'He was a brilliant pilot. Had a flawless record. Flew all over the world.' For a brief moment, I can picture Nathan as a boy, sitting in the cockpit, his face expansive with joy, his father demonstrating dials and switches.

'Maybe. But not that day.'

'There must've been a mechanical fault,' Nathan says, but there's no conviction there.

'Then why not come forward? Why hide away in Fiji for two years and not return to your family?' I pause. 'You know the only reason for someone to do that?'

He stares at me, eyes narrowed.

'Guilt.'

The word hangs between us, loaded, poised.

'Nathan?'

We both turn.

The pilot's wife is standing a few feet away. She looks thin, frail. Her hands are clasped together. There's a question in her brow as she looks at her son. 'Nathan, the doctor is waiting to speak to us.'

He nods. 'Right.'

He glances back at me, hesitates a beat, as if there's more he wants to say. Then a moment later, he moves on, the two of them disappearing back inside the hospice.

I stand for a moment, watching the doors swing emptily behind them.

*We had no choice.* The words loop in my head. I picture the pilot scrambling from the plane wreckage, other passengers, too.

The cracks are already appearing in Mike's story. I know he's lying to us. But, why?

# 15

# THEN | LORI

Lori made herself return to the broken carcass of the plane. A fresh wash of terror pushed through her, tightening her throat. Oxygen masks dangled lifelessly from the ceiling and a charred, acrid smell hung in the air. The rear of the plane was blackened with smoke and the damp mess of the fire extinguisher.

Trembling overtook her entire body. Sonny fussed and writhed in her arms, fresh bullets of pain shooting down her neck as she fought to cradle him.

*Milk. He needs milk.*

She'd seen his mother preparing a bottle of formula during the flight. There had to be more.

Forcing herself forward, legs unsteady, her gaze skirted the bloodstained aisle. A single navy court shoe was jammed beneath a seat and, somehow, the sight felt more disturbing than the blood. The stir of nausea was a hot threat whispering in her belly.

Her heel crunched against something hard. She looked down and saw her mobile, the glass screen shattered, a web of cracks spreading across it.

Awkwardly, she reached for it, pressing the Power button. Waited.

Tried a second time.

There was nothing, not even a flickering white logo. She left the phone and moved on.

The overhead lockers gaped open, empty of luggage, the impact of the crash firing bags across the plane. She spotted her tan satchel, which was wedged between two seats, but her gaze passed over it, focused only on milk. She crouched as best she could, looking beneath seats, the skin on her shins burning as it stretched taut.

There! A floral spill-proof bag with numerous pockets. She reached for it one-handed, managing to unzip the main section. She searched through nappies, spare vests, a travel-sized changing mat, a baby sling – but no milk. Just an empty bottle, the dregs of milk clouding the teat.

*Shit!*

Sonny's cries had deepened into an insistent scream.

She hurried towards the exit of the plane. In the walled green of the jungle, Daniel was hauling the main luggage from the hold. His polo shirt had risen, exposing a pale stretch of his back smattered with dark hairs.

'I need the mother's case!' she called. 'Sonny needs milk.'

Daniel pulled a cheap-looking purple case towards him. 'Could be this one?'

With difficulty, Lori climbed from the plane while supporting Sonny. He felt hot and damp in her grip, his skin flushed. 'It's okay, sweetheart,' she said, undoing the poppers on his cotton vest to let some air reach him. A fly buzzed around the cuts on her legs.

Daniel tugged open the zip to reveal folded sets of tiny white vests and baby grows, little sunhats. She pictured the mother folding each of those cotton vests, setting them in neat piles, and felt a ball of emotion roll right through her. Crying was no good, not here. She needed to keep it together.

Daniel pulled out a tin of formula, bottles, too.

'Thank God!' she said, jiggling the baby. 'You need to make up a bottle.'

'Me?'

'Add the powder to some water. Read the instructions – it'll tell you how much.' She'd seen friends of hers preparing bottles, but wasn't the water meant to be sterile, warm?

Daniel ran a hand across his brow as he concentrated on the back of the tin.

'How old is it?' he called, above the baby's screams.

*It*. Lori had heard his mother telling the air stewardess Sonny's age. 'Four months.' He felt rigid in her arms, little fists shoved against his gummy mouth. 'Sorry, sweetheart, it's coming.'

Blood had dried on the side of Daniel's face. His brow furrowed. 'Can't you get him to shut up? I can't think!'

Lori flinched.

Daniel shoved the tin of formula towards the long-haired man, whose name she'd learned, was Felix. He was laying out the supplies from the plane: crisps, bottles of water, cartons of fruit juice, chocolate and nuts. 'You do it!' Daniel said, stalking back to the luggage.

Felix looked at Lori, eyes dark above the bloodied swelling across the bridge of his nose. 'What d'you want me to do?'

She told him to grab one of the bottles of still mineral water and add it to the baby's bottle with some powdered milk. He did as she said, scooping the formula into the bottle, a dusting of it falling to the earth.

'Put the teat back on it,' she said, watching as he fumbled to secure the plastic ring, the black ink of his wrist tattoo flashing.

He handed her the bottle. Sonny's little fists batted out hectically, connecting with the bottle, sending it flying from her grip.

'Shit!' Lori cried, as it rolled between her feet, milk dribbling into the damp earth, the teat flecked with dirt. She tried to reach for it, but the baby bucked, suddenly feeling as slippery and precarious as an eel. She used both hands to steady him against her chest.

She could feel a slick of sweat beneath her arms and behind her knees, Sonny's screams travelling right through her.

Felix picked up the bottle and rinsed the teat clean with the remainder of the water. It wasn't perfect, but it would have to do. He handed it to her a second time.

Sonny thrust his arms towards the milk, back bucking. She was ready this time and lightly caught his arm with one hand, bringing the teat slowly to his mouth, her grip firm. Sonny opened his mouth wide, pink gums latching on. The crying stopped instantly.

'There you go. Slow it down,' she said as he sucked fiercely, eyes wide, gulping in milk. She could hear his noisy, uneven swallows.

After a minute or two, the rhythm slowed, and relief washed through her, softening the tension in her shoulders.

When she looked up, Felix was watching her. 'Have you had anything to drink?'

She shook her head.

He moved to the pile of supplies and reached for a large bottle of water. She didn't have a hand free, so he placed it at her feet. 'Keep hydrated.'

'Thank you.'

He nodded once. 'I'm gonna take a look around the island . . . we'll need more water soon.'

Mike was laying out the charred remains of a life raft. A section of it had been completely scorched and was now a melted mass of orange plastic. He wiped the sweat from his top lip, his face grim.

'It's ruined?' Daniel asked, who was standing with his hands on his hips. A hard-shelled silver case lay open at his feet, freshly ironed shirts incongruous in the jungle surrounds.

'Yeah,' Mike said, 'but the grab bag survived. We've got two flares, a first-aid kit, desalination tablets, a lighter, rope.'

'No satellite phone tucked at the back of there?' Daniel asked.

Mike didn't respond. He pushed himself to his feet. Lori saw the way he staggered, as if one of his knees was giving out. He managed to right himself, but she caught the grimace of pain that twisted his face. Dirt streaked his forearms and she could see the age spots on his sun-damaged skin.

Lori returned her attention to Sonny. His feeding had relaxed and his eyelids began to blink more slowly. She studied his tiny fingers, which were trying to grip the bottle, nails cut neatly, skin fair. He had a soft fuzz of light hair, thinning at the back of his scalp where she imagined it rubbed in his cot. She watched as his eyelids began to close, lips loosening from the bottle.

He'd taken about half the milk. Was that good? She'd no idea how many feeds a baby his age needed. When would he need more? Even in the shade, the heat pulsed thickly, her skin dewy with perspiration. Beyond them, she could hear the ocean, moving, shifting, surrounding them.

She heard a sound, something faint, metallic.

Daniel was kneeling on the ground, a sea of luggage open

around him, as if the cases had been subjected to an autopsy. His expression was intent as he studied the item in his hand.

She could see the silver glint of it, the deadly edge.

From a black sheath, Daniel had drawn a knife.

'Where did you get that?' Mike asked, looking at the blade, several inches long, one edge needle-sharp, the other serrated into jagged teeth.

'One of the bags.' Daniel turned the knife, examining the dual edges of the blade.

Lori felt a prick of unease spike at the base of her neck, trail down her spine. Why would any of the guests be travelling with a knife? They were going to a holiday resort, a tiny island where everything was catered for. Lori had packed sundresses and sandals, books and bikinis.

*A knife?*

'What else have you found?' Mike asked, approaching.

'A pair of binoculars, and this,' he said, pulling out something that looked like a metal spear attached to a harpoon by a black elastic loop. 'Looks like a spear gun. There are fins, too.'

She realised all of the cases had been opened, items spread out across the earth at Daniel's feet. He'd made a stack of their passports, every bag searched. Her gaze went to her case: unzipped, the inner straps unclipped, her belongings rifled through. The pale lace strap of one of her bras had been unsettled, and the wisp of a black thong had been pulled out. She felt the disturbance of Daniel's fingers moving against the fabric of her underwear.

Why had she even packed lace underwear for a holiday with her sister? She'd also treated herself to a manicure, choosing a neon pink that felt like just the right pop of indulgence for a tropical holiday midwinter. Now the glossy varnish felt ludicrous. Obscene. Who was the underwear for? The manicure? The expensive highlights? Not Pete – not any more. Maybe it was just so *she* felt good about herself, as if a coat of nail polish could change a thing.

No, not now. No tears. Not out here. Not about Pete, for God's sake! Her scattered thoughts seemed to warp, sliding back to that day.

May half-term. Lori at home, sorting out the art cupboard. Hardened paints and stiff brushes spread across the kitchen table as she decided what to salvage and what to toss. She'd heard the front door open, then glanced at the kitchen clock: midday. Strange. Pete hadn't said he'd be back for lunch.

The moment he walked into the kitchen, she'd seen his expression – wide-eyed, slack-mouthed, white-faced – and thought: *Cancer.* He's going to tell me he's got cancer.

Instead, his gaze had fallen to the floor, where he pressed the nose of one of his work boots against the loose edge of the skirting board. He was shaking. 'I'm really sorry, Lori. I can't believe I'm about to say this . . .' He swallowed. When he raised his head, looked right at her, she noticed his throat was flushed red. 'I . . . I'm leaving you.'

She wasn't the only woman in the world to hear some permutation of those words, but the impact felt physical, like the words were made of rock or stone, slamming into her chest. 'What?'

It was as if his lips had numbed, slurring his words. 'I'm sorry. I'm leaving,' he repeated.

In the crush of disbelief, her hands reached for the support of the table. 'Why?'

'I've been having an affair.'

'What? Who?'

He'd looked away. Shaken his head.

Gripping the edge of the kitchen table, the skin beneath her fingernails was bloodless. 'I know her, don't I?'

He'd nodded. It felt like a perverse game of Guess Who?

'Not one of my friends. Please,' she said, her head beginning to shake.

'Zoe.'

She'd felt the weight of understanding arrive in one go, hitting her at the back of the knees, so that she slumped into the kitchen chair. Her stomach seemed to rise into her throat.

Zoe was the PE teacher at the school where Lori headed the art department. She'd started last academic year, moving down from Birmingham with a boyfriend, who she'd parted from in the first term. She thought of Zoe's lean little body, taut and firm in her pleated PE skirt; the bruised, sharp shins. Nothing like Lori's body, like the body Pete had always professed to adore. Curvaceous. Full breasts. Something to hold at the hips.

'Get out.' She waited for him to turn, slink from the room.

Only, Pete didn't move. He'd looked at her square in the face, steeling himself. 'There's more.'

She'd blinked. How could there be? What could possibly be worse?

'Zoe is pregnant. Fourteen weeks. It's my baby.'

The world tilted. She'd hinged forward.

'I'm sorry, Lori. I'm so sorry. I know this is the worst thing . . . after everything we've been through. It was an accident—'

Her head snapped up. 'Accident?' The word was growled, teeth bared.

'I didn't mean to say that—'

A furious heat pushed through her body. Her hands slammed against the lip of the table, flipping it with one violent movement. The jar of turpentine shattered against the fridge, raining glass and liquid across the room, paint brushes clattering across the tiled floor.

Pete lurched back, palms raised. 'Lori—'

Her voice was rage, spit, fire. 'Get. Out. Now.'

He blinked, frozen for a long moment. Then he turned and hurried towards the door – and left.

*Left.*

A deep tremble had overtaken her body. She wasn't sure how long she'd stood there, rooted to the spot, but she knew the light had moved across the wall of the kitchen until she was in shade.

Then, finally, she'd reached for her phone.

Dialled.

Two rings. Her sister answered on the third. 'Sis?'

Lori offered a single sentence – *I need you* – and Erin was in her car, on her way, bringing the compass of how they'd navigate through this together.

Now Lori looked up at the dense thatch of jungle, the plane crumpled at its heart. All she wanted was to pick up a phone, ring her sister. Tell her: *I need you.*

# 16

# THEN | LORI

The day was closing, sealed with heat. Lori stood on the shoreline, gaze pinned to the empty horizon. Her skin was sticky with layers of cooled sweat, dried blood, dirt. She hugged her arms around her middle. Pain sparked in her neck. She cupped a hand there, rubbing at the knot of muscles.

Looking out across the inky water, she knew it was coming. Night.

The final disc of sun had already slipped below the line of the horizon, leaving a brief blush of colour. She'd watched, silent, as it bled away to nothing.

She'd give anything to spot the search beam of a rescue boat, ploughing through the thickening dusk. Her gaze travelled to the furthest edge of the bay where a band of deep water met the reef. There, waves crashed, frothing white water sucking and exposing dark reef. A boat would have to navigate through head-high waves breaking onto a boneyard of rock and hull-wrecking coral. In the daylight it would be treacherous. At night, impossible.

The certainty of it settled over her skin: they would be spending the night on this island.

At her feet, Sonny slept in the bassinet. She crouched awkwardly, newly knitted cuts stretching open. A warm trickle of fresh blood slid down her shin bone. For a moment she listened to the gentle draw of his breath, and felt her pulse slow. She'd tucked a cardigan of his mother's into the bassinet, hoping her scent might be locked in the weave of the cotton. For now, he looked peaceful, content. But soon he'd wake and would need feeding again, changing, comforting. All in the dark. No running water. No sterilised bottles. No changing table.

No mother.

The drumbeat of anxiety marched faster: it fell to her. *In loco parentis*. She was way out of her depth. Wanted to hand the responsibility over – but to who? Daniel wouldn't touch the baby. Felix had been gone for hours, and Mike seemed unsteady on his feet, his head injury worrying her.

A drift of wood-smoke blew across the beach. She turned to look over her shoulder and saw the signal fire was blazing now. Mike had used the lighter from the grab bag to get it started, tearing up the dried husks of coconut and thin twigs as kindling. He was crouched in its glow now, feeding a branch into its belly.

A vivid flash of the plane crash burst into her thoughts. It kept happening whenever she was still – a strobe of images, visceral and punctured with horror, screening behind her eyelids. That first drop as the plane plunged, the screams of terror, the dull crack of the air stewardess's body as she was flung upwards, connecting with the ceiling.

She shook her head to free the images, but the movement

sent another spike of pain arrowing between her shoulder blades.

Through the half-light, she became aware of a shadow moving along the shoreline towards her. Gradually she could make out the long, unhurried strides of Felix, hands thrust in pockets, head lowered, dark eyes looking up. At her.

As he neared her, she could see the trails of dried blood snaking from the bridge of his nose. His left eye was beginning to blacken, the bruising unbalancing the symmetry of his face, giving him a haunted expression.

Her thoughts flicked to the knife, the flash of silver as it had been drawn from its sheath, the two sides of the blade equally deadly. It was his, Daniel had discovered, pulled from his backpack, along with the spearfishing gun.

She stood.

He came to a standstill at her side. She could smell something earthy, salted. Him?

Her skin prickled, unsettled by the knowledge he'd brought a weapon to the island.

'How's Sonny?' he asked, voice low.

'Okay, I think. Sleeping – for now. Did you find anything? Water?' The provisions from the plane would last them a couple of days at best.

'There's a stream. I followed it to its source. There's a small pool at the centre of the island. Clean, drinkable. There's not much else, though. No sign of habitation. Not even a fishing hut or shelter. I climbed a ridge at the far end of the island that gives a good vantage point – but there's nothing much to see.'

'Oh.' She didn't know what she'd been expecting, yet the confirmation felt like a blow.

'Plenty of fruit trees, though. Mangoes, banana, coconut, breadfruit.'

'That's good.' And it was. It was good news – yet she didn't feel a kick of optimism. All she wanted was to be told that rescue was on its way. 'Did you check for signal?'

His expression shifted, eyes lowering. 'Didn't have my phone.'

She remembered then: Felix hunched over his mobile in the boarding lounge, destroying the SIM card, then pacing over to the bin – throwing the whole lot in. He'd looked up, caught her watching.

Now, his gaze lifted to meet hers, eyes sunken beneath the contours of the swelling.

The way he was staring at her, was he affronted? Humiliated? It was difficult to tell in the growing darkness.

'Got rid of my phone before flying. It was old, out of contract. I liked the idea of being off grid for a while.'

She said nothing.

He shifted his feet through the sand; she heard a stone or shell being turned with the toe of his foot.

A mosquito buzzed near her ear. She checked the inky horizon for any sign of life, but there was nothing. 'No one's coming, are they?'

He looked at her for a long moment. 'No. They're not.'

She shivered, suddenly wanting to be near the blaze of the fire with the others.

Lori sat in the dark, cooling sand, Sonny beside her. The signal fire blazed, red tongues of heat licking at the night.

God, she wished Erin was with her. It was selfish – to want that. To want your sister to be involved in a plane crash. But she did. That was the truth. She wanted Erin here. Right now. Swearing and fighting her way through the wreckage of what had happened.

Earlier, Mike had dragged several branches from the jungle,

grimacing as he'd manoeuvred them onto the beach to spell out 'S-O-S', large enough to be visible from the sky.

A signal fire and a driftwood message: it wasn't nearly enough. Hidden within the treeline was the shell of the plane, wheels grounded. It would be better if it had landed on shore – something to mark out this island.

Sonny stirred, fingers suddenly splaying as if surprised by his dream. Lori gently rocked the edge of the bassinet, making a low, soothing noise until he settled again.

Mike, who was sitting across from her, pushed himself up onto his feet. She saw the effort it took him to rise, the clench of his teeth as he took the weight through his knees, ankles. He said nothing, just fetched another branch, then fed it to the flames, sending fresh sparks skyward.

'Here,' Daniel said, pulling out a multi-pack of energy bars from a bag. 'Who wants dinner?' He took one and passed on the pack. Mike and Felix took a bar, but Lori declined. Her stomach felt knotted, bunched too tight to feel a stir of hunger. 'I just . . . I can't get my head around any of this,' she said. 'I keep thinking, why us? Why did *we* survive? Why did the others die?'

'There's no reason,' Felix said, voice low. 'It's not luck. It's not fate, or any of that bullshit. It just happened. Things happen and you deal with it because there's no other choice.' He sniffed hard, then swore in pain. He explored the bridge of his nose with his fingertips. Even in the firelight, Lori could see the swelling and guessed his nose was broken.

The fire hissed, an ember spitting onto the sand. She watched it burn itself out, cooling to ash. 'You think our families will have been told?' Lori asked.

'Yes,' Mike answered. 'They'd have been contacted a few hours after the plane failed to arrive. The airline follows a protocol.'

'So what,' Daniel said, 'my wife will get a knock at the door?'

'I'm not sure,' Mike said. 'A phone call, maybe.'

'Will she have someone with her?' Lori asked.

'We live in Epsom. Her mother's nearby. She'll be over like a shot. She'll probably be going through my study looking for the life-insurance documents.'

She tried for a smile. 'Got any kids?'

There was a beat of hesitation. 'I was an arsehole as a kid. Couldn't cope with another me – and I'm certain my wife couldn't.'

'Why were you in Fiji?' Lori asked him.

'Business. Potential property deal.'

Mike looked up. 'Where?'

'On the island we were headed to. Expansion opportunity, you know?'

She thought about Daniel's phone call she'd overheard in the boarding lounge, something about *second thoughts*. She wanted to ask him about it, but Mike was saying, 'Did anyone talk to Sonny's mother? What was her name? Why was she travelling alone?'

'Holly Senton,' Daniel said. 'I checked all the passports.'

'I heard her talking to the air stewardess,' Felix said. 'There was no father in the picture. No family at all.'

Daniel added, 'She was telling the American couple that the trip was a bit of a marker in the sand. Survive the first few months with a newborn and she'd reward herself with a holiday – sunshine, meals prepared for her, that kind of thing.'

Lori couldn't imagine any of her friends wanting to travel alone with a baby that young – and yet she could understand the decision. Holly was a single mother who'd made a decision to be kind to herself.

'What about you?' Daniel asked Felix. 'What brings you to Fiji?'

A shrug. 'I was headed to the resort to look after the water-sports activities. The current instructor is a mate of mine. Fractured his ankle, though, so he's out of action for three months. I was meant to be filling in.'

'Explains the spear gun and fins,' Daniel said.

Felix cocked his head. 'You've been through my stuff?'

'Pooling provisions. We went through all the luggage. You've got a knife, too.'

Felix held his gaze. 'It's a dive knife.'

From the jungle she heard the low, vibrating trill of frogs calling.

A spark drifted into the sky. Lori watched it floating upwards, burning out, like a tiny shooting star. She kept her gaze lifted, staring into the depths of the star-studded sky. It should be beautiful – it *was* beautiful – and yet, it felt too big, looming. Like if she looked at it for too long, it would swallow her. She wanted a ceiling. Walls. A lamp to switch on. She wanted to be in Erin's boxy rented flat. She wanted to be sitting on her cheap sofa together. She wanted her sister to do that annoying thing of shoving her cold, bare feet under Lori's thighs. She wanted a box-set and a takeaway and wine. She wanted to talk shit with Erin about inconsequential things that had nothing to do with rescue, survival, or food supplies. She wanted her sister.

'Lori?'

She blinked, drawn back to the fire. Daniel had asked her something. 'Holiday, was it?' he repeated.

'Holiday, yes. I was meant to be flying out here with my sister.'

'What? Your sister was on board?'

'No, no. We arrived in Fiji yesterday. We were meant to

get the inter-island flight together this morning . . . but . . .' She hesitated, looking down at her lap, a finger sliding to the bangle Erin had given her years ago. 'We were having dinner last night . . . ended up arguing. We both said some things.' She shook her head. 'She didn't turn up at the airport this morning.'

Daniel whistled. 'Must've been some argument.'

Across the fire, she could feel eyes on her. When she looked up, she found Mike staring right at her. 'What's your sister's name?'

'Erin.'

In the shifting light of the flames, a strange, unreadable expression passed over his face.

'Why?' she asked.

He blinked, the expression disappearing. He shook his head. Tried for a smile. 'No reason.'

# 17

# NOW | ERIN

I've spent the afternoon trying to contact the relatives of the passengers on flight FJ209. I've left messages with Felix Tyler's stepmother; Daniel Eldridge's wife; the air stewardess's daughter. I want to speak to someone else who understands what this feels like. Who might even say, *Yes, I think other passengers stepped off that plane alive, too.*

But no one's returned my calls.

I fling my phone onto the bed, pick up the key card, and leave the hotel room.

I've not had a proper meal since arriving in Fiji and my stomach feels hollow. I stride down the stairs, cross the lobby, and head for the hotel restaurant.

At the entrance, I hesitate, pulse quickening. The smell of warmed spices and roasting meat drifts from the room. I shift my weight from foot to foot. I know I need to eat. I need to walk into this restaurant and stop giving a shit.

So that's what I do.

Eyes down, I hurry to a table in the far corner. I angle my chair so that my back is to the terrace. I open a drinks menu, pretending to concentrate on the list of wines. But my gaze is eventually drawn to the terrace overlooking the floodlit gardens. I search out our table – the one where I sat with Lori on our one night in this hotel. It's vacant, a candle unlit in a glass jar.

I blink, and suddenly I am right back there, sitting opposite my sister, ribs pressed against the table edge as I leaned forward, and hissed: 'Enjoy your holiday for one.'

Ice clinked against my teeth as I drained my cocktail, fresh lime cutting through the sweet warmth of the rum. I set the glass down, feeling the familiar loosening of alcohol. 'Another?' I asked Lori.

She didn't check her watch nor deliberate over the half-full drink in front of her. 'Definitely.'

This boded well.

I ordered two more Mai Tais, and we waited, candlelight flickering between us, the warmth of the evening washing away the air-con dryness of our long-haul flight. Lori was wearing a new dress, a trim of shell beading at the neckline. Her hair was loose, trailing down bare shoulders in waves of honey, and I thought, as I often did, how much she looked like our mother.

'You okay?' I asked. There was something vaguely edgy about her, a restlessness I didn't expect to follow her out to Fiji. I told myself it was because this was a stopover destination – both the start of the holiday, yet also not quite.

'I'm fine.' She smiled, her lips tight, eyes roving.

The drinks arrived, held aloft on a bamboo tray scattered with virgin-white frangipanis. The waiter, a young man with a long thin nose, laid the cocktails in front of us with reverence.

Lori thanked him, marvelling at the pineapple spliced on the glass, the sprig of mint perched on crushed ice. 'Would you mind taking our photo?'

Men have always done whatever Lori asked. As a teen, I studied her closely, trying to put my finger on the essence of this. It was nothing as obvious as her full, expressive mouth, or her caramel-smooth skin. I decided it was something to do with the way she held eye contact, just a beat longer than most people, so you were drawn right into her. Once her attention was turned on someone, they didn't want to extract themselves from it. Who wants to step out of the sunshine and into the shade?

The waiter indicated that we should move closer to get us both in the frame. I slid my chair over, catching the apricot scent of Lori's conditioner piqued with the fresh note of recently sprayed perfume. Maybe I should've made more of an effort for dinner; I hadn't changed out of my travelling clothes and my cotton trousers were creased and bunched, my dark vest stale from the flight. I felt guilty for my lack of enthusiasm in the build-up to the trip; even as I was packing, I'd been thinking I'd rather stay in London, have the flat to myself. It was ungrateful and, now I was here, I realised how good it felt to have arrived somewhere, a fresh story waiting to be written.

Beyond the restaurant, the night was warm and fizzing with the scent of the sea. I went to squeeze Lori, to communicate something about the moment, that the two of us were here together, that she'd be okay, but the click of the shutter went and Lori was already pulling away, taking the phone and checking she was happy with the image.

She spent a moment editing it, neck bent, eyes on the

screen. I tried not to mind that she uploaded it straight to Instagram, the moment no longer just for us. Her phone remained on the table, like an uninvited guest. The screen flashed every few minutes with notifications, Lori's attention pulled towards it to see who'd liked the photo, whether they'd left a comment, if Pete had seen it.

I reached across the table and turned the phone face down.

'Wow,' she said, an eyebrow cocked.

'Let's not make tonight about Pete, yeah?'

'Yeah?' she mimicked. Last week, over breakfast, she'd told me that I sounded like the Year 10 class she was covering.

'Delete him,' I said, not for the first time. 'Get him off your social media. Why do you want to see what he's doing? It always upsets you.'

'Maybe I want him to see what *I'm* doing.'

'So that's what the holiday is about? Two fingers up to Pete?'

'Don't be prickly.'

We'd never been sisters who bitched and raged at one another, but that didn't mean we didn't have our resentments. I wondered if that was more dangerous, the heat quietly building like a pan set on low that will eventually boil over. Talk of Pete had consumed everything for the last nine months and I just wanted a break from it, to sit in a restaurant in Fiji, watch the lights twinkle over the sea, sip cocktails with my sister and forget. 'This is my holiday, too.'

A tightening in the lips. 'And who is paying for your holiday?'

I made a show of glancing at my watch. 'In Fiji for four hours and you've already reminded me you're paying.'

'I'm stating a fact.'

'You are – and here's another. I'm not a teacher. I only

have twenty days' annual leave, and I'm using half of them coming to Fiji.'

'What, and you have a better way to use your annual leave?'

The facetious tone, the raised brows, spurred me. 'Now you're asking, Fiji wouldn't be my first choice.' It was the truth. There were plenty of other trips I couldn't afford. I'd never been to Africa. To India. To South America. I hadn't hiked in mountains, or been inside a temple. I'd done little except move from Bath to London.

'Then why come?'

I shrugged. 'Because you needed me.'

'You're here out of sisterly duty?'

'Not duty.' Although it was half true. Lori had a host of friends, but they were mostly married, pregnant or already mothers – none of them available to jet off to the South Pacific on a moment's notice. 'All I meant is that this isn't exactly my type of holiday, is it? Glamorous resorts, lying around in hammocks, sunbathing. When have I ever managed to lie in the sun? My skin has the colour range of a pack of marshmallows: white or pink,' I added, trying to the lighten the tension.

Two vertical lines settled between Lori's brows. 'Did you say *Yes* to me moving into your flat out of duty, too?'

'Course not,' I answered, but I mustn't have sounded convincing as Lori leaned back in her seat, folding her arms across her chest.

That arched brow again. 'You don't even want me in London?'

'I never said that—'

'No, but it's been apparent from the moment I arrived.'

'What?' I said, stung.

'When you lived with me and Pete, I looked after you. I did everything for you. I cooked. I did your washing. I practically found you your job. I set you up on dates with friends of ours . . .'

'Jesus, Lori – you sent me on a date with a fucking accountant. He wore a tie to the pub.'

'He played in a band.'

'He played the fiddle in a folk band.' I hoped my sister might crack a smile at that, but she'd found her stride and wouldn't slow.

'My marriage ended. I had to leave my job because of Zoe. Sell my home.'

I hated it when Lori did that – listed her misfortune.

'Yet even with all that going on, I'm still the one looking after you.'

That caught my attention. 'Sorry? How?'

'I cook your meals, do the food shopping—'

'You *took over* the food shopping. Wanted to set up a grocery delivery.'

'Your cupboards were always bare. You're living like a fucking student, Erin!'

A burst of anger rode hard in my chest. 'Sorry that I don't cook homely meals or have an Ocado delivery plan in place, but we didn't all study at the Lori School of Golden Ease.' I'm not exactly sure what I meant by that last comment – something to do with my frustration that everything always comes so easily for Lori – but my sister sniffs out the message with the speed of a hunting dog.

'Not everything. You might have noticed – since you were living with us at the time – that I went through four rounds of IVF. You might have noticed that the one thing I really wanted, more than anything, was to be a mother. That hasn't come so easily, has it? Maybe you've also noticed that the man I love, who I thought I'd spend my life with, is now having a baby with my friend.'

There. Again with The List. 'You put Pete on a pedestal – like he's still the golden boy at sixth form who took you to prom. But he's not. He let you down, Lori. He cheated, he left. It wasn't Zoe's fault. It was his.'

'If Zoe hadn't fallen pregnant, he wouldn't have left. She trapped him. It was a mistake, a one-off—'

'No! It wasn't!' My palms slammed down on the table.

Lori sat back with surprise.

We stared at each other. I felt her gaze narrow as she studied me. 'What do you mean?' Her tone was crisp, each word enunciated precisely.

*Shit*. I picked up my drink. Swallowed half of it, the ice-cold liquid making my head feel compressed.

I could feel my sister's gaze on me. 'What do you know?' Her voice was low, steely.

'It was just a remark. I didn't mean—'

'Tell me.'

I could feel colour rushing into my cheeks, a throbbing heat spreading towards my earlobes. I couldn't speak. Couldn't look at her.

But she could read me. 'Zoe wasn't the first, was she?'

My lips felt thick, slow. I couldn't organise my thoughts, respond with the speed she demanded.

In my silence, Lori suddenly pitched. 'You?'

'Christ! No!' I said, head snapping up. 'Of course not! Never! Lori, how could you even think that—'

'Who, then?'

She was leaning across the table, so close I could see myself reflected in her dark eyes.

I swallowed.

'Please,' she said, reaching across the table, taking my hand. Her fingers were icy from her cocktail glass, her grip too firm.

There was nowhere for me to go except straight ahead,

delivering the bullet of truth. 'It was a long time ago. Two, three years. I saw him with another woman – just once. Not an affair. He'd been drinking, made a mistake—'

The waiter returned, gaze seeking out Lori, asking if we wanted anything else. We didn't. The axe-sharp tension had him retreating as smoothly as he'd arrived.

Lori hissed, 'Tell me everything.'

Reluctantly, I explained about the hotel in Winchester where I'd bumped into Pete. He'd stepped out of the lift with a woman. Saw me. His mouth opened and closed, ludicrously fish-like. He had tried to say something about being on a work thing, but bullshit to that. I told the woman he'd just screwed to fuck off, and Pete to get in my car. We sat in the car park, sleet settling on the windscreen, Pete rubbing his hands to keep warm. He promised me it was a one-off. Begged me not to tell Lori. They were midway through their third round of IVF and he didn't want to jeopardise that. He loved her. He was sorry.

I wanted to believe him.

I looked straight at my sister. 'I'm so sorry.'

I'd practised those words, said them in my head through all the imaginary conversations I'd held where this truth eventually rose through the surface, lava-hot, but now the apology felt hollow, too little.

'You kept his secret.'

'I didn't want you to get hurt.'

'Or was it more about you?'

'Sorry?'

'You were scared of losing Pete from *your* life.'

The words were a slap. 'What does that mean?' But I knew exactly what it meant. After we lost our dad, it was just Lori and me in the family home. We couldn't afford the mortgage and there was no life insurance, so we eventually sold. Lori and Pete had been talking about moving in together for a while, so they bought a little terraced house on the edge of Bath – and I went with them. Made a home of their spare room. It suited me; I was eighteen by then – and even though I disappeared off to university for months at a time, I liked having somewhere to come home to, to spend the holidays, to return to after I graduated.

Lori shook her head as she said, 'You knew what Pete had done – and yet you lived under our roof, said nothing, let me carry on as if everything was normal. If I'd known back then, Pete and I could at least have tried to work things out. But you said nothing, because it would've rocked your world. You needed that stability – me and Pete.'

Was she right? I'd let Lori teeter closer to the precipice of her marriage's end and didn't even try to haul her back. I told myself I was protecting my sister – but maybe I was protecting myself.

Lori leaned forward, face pinched. 'Remember that promise we made when we lost Dad?'

I nodded, throat dry. We'd been sitting on the riverbank after the funeral, black dresses hitched up, feet pressed onto the long, damp grass. Lori had put an arm around my waist and I leaned in, head on her shoulder. We listened to the river twisting below us, shifting silt and small pebbles. 'It's just us now,' Lori said, her voice strangely adult. 'Whatever happens, I'm always going to be here for you, Erin. Let's promise to tell each other everything.'

I nodded hard. We were safeguarding our relationship, preserving the foundations. Lies and omissions were cracks in the walls, and we thought we were better than that.

'Me and you,' Lori promised. 'Together.'

We wrapped our arms around each other, wet-cheeked. '*Together*,' I echoed.

In the restaurant, Lori had looked at me and said, 'You let us down.' She picked up her cocktail, fresh, coffee-dark, icy. I tensed, expecting to feel the clash of ice against my face. Instead, she drained the drink, then carefully set down the glass. She rose to her feet, the gold bangle I'd given her glinting on her forearm. I knew what word was inscribed on the underside of that bangle because I'd chosen it.

'Go home, Erin. This trip is over.'

There was something about the way she said it, a haughtiness in the tilt of her jaw. Her disdain struck me like a match. I was on my feet, too. 'I never even wanted to be here. You know the real reason I came on this trip? Because I knew you weren't brave enough to do it alone.' I saw the words slice right into my sister. Felt a flash of triumph. 'You surround yourself with other people,' I continued, 'so that you don't have to spend a minute in your own company. Because I don't think you like what you see.'

It made its mark. I watched as Lori's lower lip quivered and her eyes filmed with tears. *Shit.* I'd gone too far. 'Lori—'

'Want to know the real reason I invited *you*, Erin?' she said, cutting me off. She was leaning across the table, nose almost touching mine. 'Because I felt *sorry* for you. At least I've got friends. Who've you got? Since Ben and Sarah moved away, who are you left with? Name one person you actually care about? Or who cares about you?'

*You*, I thought. *You.*

That was all.

She was all I had. But I didn't say that. 'You're right – there's no one,' I spat. 'Enjoy your holiday for one, Lori. When you get home, your shit will be packed.' It wasn't even dignified. Or true. But that's what I said.

That was the last time I saw my sister.

## 18

# THEN | LORI

Sleep was futile. Lori felt the rawness of the night as she shifted in the cool sand, pulling her jacket close to her chin.

She'd underestimated the coolness in the tropics at night. It wasn't that the temperature had plummeted – it was the exposure, the cool sand beneath her, a dampness in the air. It had been a mistake to use the spare blankets from the plane to cover the bodies. But it was done now. There was no chance she would be getting to her feet, creeping into the earth-dark jungle to tug blankets off the dead. No. In the morning she'd go through the luggage again. There must be a spare beach towel to cover herself with. At least Sonny would be comfy enough, tucked into the bassinet beside her.

A drift of smoke from the dying fire wafted over her. She thought of a funeral pyre and covered her mouth with her arm. An image arose of the dead passengers, lying bloated and still in the jungle. There could be animals prowling, or insects beginning to crawl over their skin. She wondered how long it took for a body to begin to decompose. What would they do if they were here for more than a night? Two . . . three . . .

She shuddered.

Beyond the fire, the jungle hummed and vibrated with noises she didn't recognise – unseen insects, the scuffle of something through the leaves. There was a stillness, as if the trees were panting. She tried to set her mind on the sea, follow the sound of the waves, but rather than calming her, it felt oppressive – surrounded by all that water, just the swell of the ocean circling the island.

Darkness was pressing too close, right up to her face, filling her nostrils, the hollow drum of her ears, her throat. It was a weight, desert-black, against her chest. She wanted to reach for a light, for music, for a person – anything to push it back a little. But she had no defence, so she lay on the island floor, fear skittering in her chest.

She could feel her breath coming in short gasps. Her head blared with the thought that she was lying here, on an island with no name, when all she wanted to do was run. Run from this feeling, this situation, this waking fucking nightmare.

But there was nowhere to go. She was living it.

Suddenly she was on her feet, searching out the others. Was anyone else awake? In the dying glow of the fire, she could just make out the shape of Daniel sleeping on his back. His body was stretched out, hands resting together on the dome of his chest. The dead-stillness, the closed eyes, the unflattering play of shadows hollowing his eyes brought to mind a corpse.

Felix was on the other side of the fire, a coat thrown over his body. She couldn't tell if he had his eyes open in the darkness.

Her gaze circled the rest of the beach, scanning for Mike. She paused on the darker patches beyond the glow of embers, then turned and looked towards the shoreline, which was faintly lit by a crescent moon. No sign of him there, either.

She didn't know any of these men. They were strangers. She desperately wished the other passengers were here, too. Holly, or the air stewardess with her sunny chatter, or the American couple.

Erin, that's who she really wanted. She'd be awake, too. God, what must be going through her mind? There's no way Erin would be sitting still, waiting for news. She'd be rallying people, demanding answers, researching flight routes, ringing the British Embassy. She wondered who Erin would call at home. Pete, maybe? She wanted him to know. Wanted him to worry!

A mewling noise, then a cry. Sonny. She peered into the bassinet. She'd fed him a couple of hours ago – but he'd only taken a third of a bottle. He must be hungry again. The spare bottle was in the hold of the plane. Shit, she should've thought ahead.

'Back in a minute,' she whispered to him, then grabbed one of the sticks by the fire, shoving it into the flames, waiting till it caught. She held it out in front of her as a lantern, flames licking the sky, then hurried towards the jungle, legs stiff, sand spreading beneath her toes.

She picked her way through the dark treeline, keeping her gaze lowered, aware of the human-shaped mounds lying beneath blankets at the edge of the clearing. She wondered if she were imagining it, or whether there was the smell of something decaying in the air.

The sound of Sonny's cries had been swallowed by the noises of the jungle. The air was alive. Insects, the hum of trees and branches muffling everything. If she called out now, from this distance, no one would hear her.

The sticky tangle of a spider's web caught against her arm and she brushed it away, shuddering. The air seemed denser within the jungle, as if she could taste peat, the rot of leaves. She halted. Through the dim light, she could just make out the plane wreck, shocking in its incongruity in the deep reaches of the jungle. There was something obscene about the splintered, torn trees, stubs of thick branches severed where the plane had torn right through the jungle.

The horror of the crash rushed at her, stealing her breath. The shear of metal; the dark plume of smoke filling the back of the plane; the white-hot fear alive in her body.

Her stomach contracted and, without warning, she was bent double, retching. Bile dimpled the jungle floor, splattering against her bare feet. The acidic taste was foul in her mouth. She crouched there, breathing hard, tears stinging her eyes. She wanted to give up – right there – just make all of this fucking stop!

But there was Sonny. Crying, hungry, alone.

She wiped her mouth with the back of her hand. Straightened. With the flaming stick raised in front of her, she moved on. Her whole body trembled as she approached the plane. The hold was already open, but the luggage had been pushed right to the back. She stabbed the stick into earth, then used both hands to haul herself inside. Her knees protested as she crawled into the cool metal mouth, a freshly scabbed cut on her shins knocked off, releasing a warm trickle of blood.

The air was cooler in here, stale. Ridges of metal left depressions on her knees and shins and the heels of her hands. She located Holly's carry-on bag and began to pull it towards the exit. Somewhere beyond the hold, she sensed movement: the creaking of a branch, the passing of a shadow. She had a sudden image of the hatch door slamming shut, swallowing her in the pitch black of the hold. She scrambled for the exit, losing her balance and tumbling onto the jungle floor.

She grabbed the flaming stick, scrabbling to her feet. Glancing around, there was nothing but trees . . . and, in the far edge of the clearing, the covered bodies, shoulder to shoulder. Beneath the blankets, she imagined them with eyes open, bodies stiff, a pulse of decay beginning.

She made herself move slowly, calmly, as she picked up Holly's bag and began to walk back to where the others slept. A loud clunking sound startled her. She froze.

Waiting, pulse ticking.

A sliding of something metallic.

Spinning around, she saw a faint light moving within the cockpit.

One of the men?

She edged closer, just enough to see through the cockpit window, where a torchlight from a phone was being shone. She caught the gold bars of the pilot's uniform. Mike. She was about to step forward, announce herself, but as she did, he turned to the side and halted. There was an expression on his face that she hadn't seen before, an intensity, focused and burning. He was concentrating hard, his hands working on something.

She stepped closer still, head angled to one side. He was in the cockpit with his back to her.

He looked around suddenly, as if becoming aware he was being watched.

They stared at each other through the cracked windscreen. Then he disappeared for a moment, before reappearing at the exit to the plane.

'What are you doing?' she asked.

'Painkillers,' he said quickly. 'Thought I had some up here.'

'We pooled all the medical supplies.'

'You're right, we did. Thought there was another pack up here somewhere. Must've dreamt it.'

She nodded.

'How are you? Sonny okay?' he asked, his voice warmer.

'Just getting his bottle.'

'Want some help?'

'I've got what I need, thanks,' she said.

It was only when she was walking back towards the shore that she let herself think about his expression when she'd asked what he was doing – the strange flicker of something she couldn't quite read. She sensed it though: the hot whisper of a lie in his answer.

## 19

# NOW | ERIN

'I don't trust the pilot,' I tell the British consul as we cross the hotel lobby.

His footsteps are soft in smooth leather loafers. My flip-flops thwack as I keep pace. He's given me the promised hour of his time, and now our meeting has come to its end.

I've done my best to keep my voice level, my questions concise. I didn't order the Bloody Mary I desperately wanted in the hotel bar. I made a conscious effort not to fidget, to keep my hands still as I spoke. I've tried so fucking hard, but now he's leaving and I'm no further forward.

I want him to exit this hotel ready to rally, push, probe, make waves on Lori's behalf. Two years ago, when Lori's plane failed to arrive at the resort, it was this man, British consul Steven Wills, who visited me to deliver the official news. He was my main point of contact, communicating on behalf of the local police, CAAF, and the Foreign Office at home. He was kind, sympathetic, and helpful in a limited, procedural way. But now I can tell he's surprised to find me back in Fiji. I'm not a British National who's found myself unwittingly in the centre of a current crisis. I'm someone who has flown here with the sole purpose of digging for information, when I should've waited at home like a good girl, like the other relatives. I'm exactly the sort of difficult person that gives him a headache.

We exit the hotel, pausing atop marble steps that lead into the evening. 'The pilot wasn't the only survivor,' I say again, as if repeating the assertion will solidify it as a fact. 'I told you that, when I saw Mike Brass, he said, "*We* got rid of the bodies." It wasn't a slip-up. The pilot said it because it's true. Other people survived on that plane.'

'Like I said,' the British consul tells me calmly, patiently. 'I will pass this information on to the relevant authorities.'

'Yes, but the police need to be pushing harder for answers. The pilot is lying to everyone. I mean, why hasn't he told anyone the location of the island? He's hiding something . . . covering something up.' I'm aware I'm speaking too quickly, that I'm standing too close.

'I assure you; I'll do everything I can to make sure you get the answers you need.'

It's a pat response, and we both know it. 'What exactly does that mean? I want to know who you're going to call. What questions you'll ask. I want to know that you're going to do absolutely everything—'

'Like I say,' the British consul interrupts, 'finding the wreckage is the priority now. They're putting another search plane out there.'

'It's not the wreckage that's important! It's what the pilot knows! What he's not fucking telling us!'

His mouth tightens. 'I do understand how deeply frustrating this is.'

'You do? Did you have someone you loved on that plane, too?' I know I'm being facetious, but fuck, this guy is a puppet. 'This whole thing is a mess for the airline, for tourism, for business, and so no one is putting the resources into finding out answers. No one is pressing hard enough. Mike Brass is dying! We're running out of time!' My hands are poised mid-air, fingertips splayed. I lower them to my sides and remind myself to breathe.

My attention is caught by two young women who are ascending the lobby steps, legs tanned, bags hooked over shoulders. They fall into the same rhythm of step. I spot it immediately, the similarity in the straight length of their noses, the same tan colouring of their skin, the smooth length of their forearms that are linked through one another's: sisters.

I watch as they pass close to us. They don't look up, their attention is focused solely on each other, heads dipped, mouths working hard, eyes bright as they talk. I turn as they pass, magnetised. I want to reach out – as if their closeness is something physical that can be touched or inhaled. I want to be in their orbit, feel the warmth of the sister bond emanating from them.

I think of Lori and me, right here on these steps, two years ago. We climbed them together, luggage dragging behind us, the sun hot against the backs of our necks. I took that easiness between us for granted. Sometimes I railed against it, butting up against the solid walls of my sister's love because I liked to test it, feel the strength of it. Now I wish I could do everything differently. There would be no argument this time. I would never have left the hotel restaurant, gone on alone. I wouldn't have made all the bad choices that followed.

'Erin?' The consul is saying something that I've failed to catch.

'Sorry?' I shake my head.

'I said, you've got my number if you need anything else.'

'Yes . . .' I've lost my momentum and he seizes the opportunity to leave.

As he descends the steps, his shoulders are already beginning to soften, relieved our meeting is over. I imagine him returning to his air-conditioned home, clocking off for the evening, sitting at a plush, leather-topped desk, the day's newspapers waiting for him, grateful that this meeting is off his to-do list.

I need to keep on pushing forward – no one else is going to do it for me. I saw the pilot yesterday. I know the prognosis. Days. I need to find out as much as I can right now while there is time.

I keep replaying our conversation, examining it for clues. *I couldn't bury them . . . there was no spade, nothing to dig with . . . We had no choice.*

*We. We. We.*

It could so easily have been a mistake, a slip in speech, caused by the tumour or medication. But what if it wasn't?

There was something in the pilot's expression that I couldn't quite reach. I sensed it just beneath the surface, as if my fingers had dug through the earth and touched something hard, concealed. I should have kept my cool, slowly brushed at the edges, carefully loosening the soil to prise it free.

I need to get in front of him again. Dig carefully. Reach right down into the earthy darkness of his secrets and pull out the truth.

# 20

# THEN | LORI

Lori woke to the sensation of something crawling across her cheek. She swatted at her face. A dark-shelled insect slipped from the ledge of her chin onto her chest. Lurching to her feet, she slapped at her body, knocking the insect to the ground. She shuddered, skin studding with goosebumps, as it crawled away, black legs burrowing deep into the sand.

Disorientated, she lifted her gaze, heart racing. Seeing the smouldering remains of the fire where she'd slept, the memory of the plane crash slammed into her afresh. She wrapped her arms around her middle, letting out a small whimper.

'You okay?' Daniel was lying on the other side of the fire, hair rucked up, polo shirt crumpled.

She shook her head – and the movement hurt. Her fingertips explored the knotted, stiff muscles around her neck. She experimented with carefully turning her head from one side to the other, investigating the range of movement.

She glanced around the charcoal remains of the fire. There were two body-shaped depressions in the sand where Mike and Felix had slept, beach towels spooled nearby. She peered into the bassinet, relieved to find Sonny still asleep, his tiny chest rising and falling. After his feed last night, she'd struggled to resettle him. She'd tried rocking him, singing to him, changing him, feeding him – but nothing worked. The humidity, the darkness, the temperature of the milk, the chirruping of insects, Lori's smell rather than his mother's – it was all wrong and Sonny knew. Finally, exhausted from sobbing, he fell asleep in Lori's arms as dawn broke.

The morning was overcast, but thick with heat. 'I'm going to splash some water on my face,' she said, leaving Daniel with the baby, and walking down to the shoreline. Her legs were bruised in a rich palette of pinks, reds and grape-purple, and protested with each step. She waded into the shallows, grimacing as salt water bit into the cuts criss-crossing her shins. A tiny fish darted between her ankles, disappearing into the bay.

Crouching, she cupped a handful of water to her face, splashing it over her cheeks, letting it run down her throat. She wanted to peel off the clothes she'd slept in and wash the filth and blood and wood-smoke from her skin – but Daniel was on the beach. She settled for washing briefly beneath her arms. Even that was reviving.

The view was disturbingly empty, just the wavering line of the horizon disappearing into sky. Looking into the dizzying void of endless space, there was nowhere to focus her gaze except on more nothingness. Her head swam; her legs felt the tow of vertigo. Staring at the looming ocean, her thoughts sparked with anxiety. *Find us! Please, find us! We've got to get off this island! We need to do something! We need to light more signal fires . . . dot the whole bay with them. Or, maybe we should start making a raft, or . . . what else? We need to think of a plan. I need to be doing something. I can't stay here. I can't just wait and wait and wait . . .*

Her sister's voice cut through her panic.

*One step at a time, Lori.*

Erin never needed a plan, never needed to know how everything would work out, or where the next turn in the path would lead. She didn't direct life – she went with it. Right now, Lori needed to do the same. She had no control over what would happen next. All she could do was live minute by minute.

She glanced at the rose-gold bangle on her wrist. Her talisman. With an index finger, she circled the inside of the band, feeling the inscription Erin had chosen: *Together.*

She took a breath.

First, Sonny. She needed to get a fresh bottle of milk prepared for when he woke. She crossed the beach, moving into the treeline. She slowed, noticing that Daniel was on his feet, standing completely still, neck craned as he stared into the bassinet. She wondered if Sonny had stirred. Daniel's expression was curiously blank. After a moment, he edged closer, brow dipping. He reached a hand tentatively into the bassinet, his features pinched.

Then she heard a short, sharp cry from Sonny – and Daniel shot back as if scalded.

Sonny began to wail. Daniel seemed frozen, just standing there, staring. Then, after a few moments, he glanced up and down the beach, before disappearing into the jungle, leaving Sonny helpless in the bassinet, screaming.

Later, after Sonny had finally been calmed and fed, he fell asleep in Lori's arms. They were sitting together on the shoreline when Mike approached.

He was still wearing his bloodstained pilot's uniform, and

beneath the rim of his cap she could see the deep cut on his head. He shrugged a bag from his shoulder, pulling out a bottle of water. 'Filled all the empties at the stream. Want this?'

'Please,' she said, slipping her arm from beneath Sonny and reaching for it.

'Here,' he said, untwisting the cap for her.

She took a long drink, tasting a hint of earth and something salted in the water, but grateful for the cool liquid.

Mike pulled a bunch of small green bananas from his bag. 'Found these, too. Want any?'

'No, thanks.' She still had no appetite, her insides knotted and tight. She'd try and eat something later.

Mike lowered himself into the sand beside her, knees clicking, breath laboured. 'How's the baby?'

'Okay, I think.' She'd draped a sarong across Sonny, shading him from the bursts of sunlight emerging between billowing clouds. She lifted it a fraction, peering at his closed eyelids and the pink bud of his lips. 'Still sleeping.'

'Lucky you're here,' he said. 'He needs you.'

'It's his mother he needs.'

She didn't mean the remark to come out so sharply – but Mike flinched. His head hung down. He kept his gaze on the ground as he said, 'I'm sorry. I'm sorry she's dead. That they're all dead. I'm sorry that you're here. That Sonny will grow up without his mother. I—'

'It was an accident, Mike. No one wanted this.'

After a long silence, he nodded slowly.

'You think they'll find us today?'

He lifted his shoulders. 'I don't know. I took a walk to that ridge top Felix was talking about. It's a good lookout spot – you can see right around the island. I'm gonna station myself up there with the binoculars and flares. Best place to spot boats or planes. Keep watch for rescue.'

'Good idea,' she agreed. It was something.

They both set their gazes on the water, falling into silence once more. Felix was swimming across the bay, the spear gun at his side, dark flippers on his feet. He cut a smooth, sleek line through the clear blue.

'He had any luck?' Mike asked.

'Not sure.' She watched dark shadows of clouds travelling across the sea. 'Is it dangerous out there?

'The ocean? Not for swimming. You get the odd sea snake and you've gotta watch where you put your feet. Fire corals are nasty. But if you keep alert, you'll be fine.'

'And out further?'

'I wouldn't be going out further. Particularly not with a spear gun. You catch something out deep and there's a cloud of fish blood swirling around your bare legs; well, it's a pretty good signal to predators to come and investigate.'

'You mean sharks?'

He nodded. 'Blacktips, grey reef sharks, bull sharks – and the odd tiger shark, too. They're all out there. Most wouldn't give you the time of day – but you add a bloodied fish flapping on the end of a spear and suddenly it's a dinner party.'

Felix swam towards the shoreline and she watched him emerge, hair otter-dark. He sat in the shallows as he pulled off his mask and fins and unloaded his spear gun. On his back, a pink scar ran above the line of his board shorts. He turned then and walked up the beach towards them.

'Anything?' Mike asked.

'Couldn't equalise 'cos of this,' he said, pointing to his broken nose. The skin beneath his eyes had darkened to a painful-looking bluey-purple. 'There's plenty of reef fish in the shallows, but I'm guessing the eaters are out off the ledge.'

A cloud shadow rolled across the beach, a patch of dark hovering over them. Mike looked up at the sky warily. To the west, clouds had gathered, a moody blue. She could feel the humidity pressing against her.

'Rain's on its way,' Mike said.

'I was thinking we should set up shelter near the plane,' Felix said. 'It's rainy season, right?'

Mike nodded. 'We got lucky last night that there weren't any downpours. But tonight we want to be ready.'

*Tonight?* Lori thought.

Lori pushed hard against the fallen trunk, feeling the burn of her muscles as she inched it across the earth. Felix worked the other end, the two of them rolling it into the clearing near the plane.

'There!' he said, letting go. He straightened, hands on his waist, a triangle of sweat darkening his torn T-shirt.

Lori rubbed at the spasming muscles in her neck. They'd rolled four logs into the clearing, positioning them around a ring of stones that marked out a fire pit. Beside it was a pile of deadwood Daniel had collected.

'What d'you think of this?' Mike asked.

They turned to see the remains of the life raft lashed between the trees to provide a basic shelter. They'd all agreed that no one wanted to sleep in the plane. The horror of the crash clung in the bloodstained aisle and crumpled shell, and plus, with the seats bolted to the floor, there was no space for anything but sitting.

'You really think we're all going to fit under there?' Daniel asked, who was sitting in the shade of the plane wing, eating an energy bar. The hems of his chinos were rolled up, exposing pale, slender ankles.

'Lori and the baby get the shelter. The rest of us manage,' Mike said.

'Who made you chief?'

Mike gave no rise.

Felix hauled a log stump across the clearing and set it at the edge of the fire circle. Then he took his dive knife from his pocket and stabbed it into the stump. 'Camp kitchen.'

Her gaze travelled to the other edge of the clearing where the bodies of the dead lay beneath blankets. She didn't know if she could sleep here in the jungle, so close to them. When the rain arrived, it would slide from the trees, snaking over the bodies, making dark rivers beneath them.

Following her gaze, Felix said, 'We'll need to think about what we're gonna do with the bodies if we're here much longer.'

'We won't be,' Daniel said, firmly, pushing to his feet. 'I'm getting the fuck out of here. If we're hiding out in the jungle, no one's going to see us. We need to keep the signal fire burning on the beach. Build more along the bay.'

Felix nodded. 'Then we'll need more wood.'

'Let's get started,' Daniel said.

One by one, the men left the camp.

Without their company, the jungle seemed to crouch closer. Huge trees stretched towards the light, their mammoth trunks dripping with vines. Creepers and tangled branches made a wall of green so dense it stilled any breeze. Her skin glistened with sweat. She felt light-headed and faint – and remembered she hadn't eaten. She fetched one of the bananas Mike had foraged and, as she did, something liquid poured from the undergrowth, sleek and glossy.

She froze, breath held.

Snake.

It moved slowly, a whisper of a trail left behind in the earth. It slid towards the blanket where Sonny lay on his back, stripped down to his nappy. He was gazing contentedly at the canopy above.

The snake hesitated, black eyes on his small shape.

Instinctively, she wanted to grab Sonny, lift him away from danger – but she knew sudden movement would be a mistake. She forced herself to remain still.

*Don't move*, she willed Sonny. *Keep very, very still.*

The air quivered. It smelt of decay and rot and the breath of a thousand plants.

The snake's tongue, forked and red, protruded from its mouth, sampling.

She felt the collective hush of the jungle, everything paused, waiting.

Sonny drew his knees towards his tummy, kicking.

The snake's beady eyes watched. After a few more moments, it lowered its head, slunk away, melting into the undergrowth. She rushed to Sonny, lifting him into her arms. He cooed, eyes brightening to see her.

Behind her, she became aware of Holly's corpse, silent beneath the blanket. Sonny was her little boy. She had birthed him, loved him, died with her arms around his bassinet trying to save him. Now the responsibility had been passed to Lori to keep him safe – and she was failing.

'I'll do better,' she whispered, to Sonny, to Holly, to the watchful eyes of the jungle.

# 21

# NOW | ERIN

After the British consul leaves, I return to the cool of the hotel lobby. I'm heading for the lifts, when I notice the two sisters who passed me earlier. They're waiting at the entrance of the restaurant, talking animatedly.

The taller one picks up her sister's hand and lifts it towards her face, examining something – her sister's nails or jewellery, perhaps – and then she says something that causes her sister to laugh, head tipped, mouth wide.

I want to be near them, breathing the same air, remembering what it feels like to have that easy intimacy. I find myself moving closer, joining the small queue of diners waiting to be seated. I stand as close as is socially acceptable, catching the scent of perfume as the taller sister turns, pointing towards two plates of food being carried to a nearby table.

'I'm ordering whatever that is,' she says, emphatically, her accent British. 'Red snapper maybe? Is that a mango salsa?'

'Look what that guy is eating,' the other sister says, pointing towards a man who hovers a fork above a curry decorated with fresh herbs and petals. 'I'm not sure if I'm in a curry mood, or if want that lobster bisque again.'

'You can't have the same!'

'But it was soooo good.' She makes a throaty, drooling noise.

Lori and I loved food talk. Whenever we ate out, we'd paw over a menu, calling over the waiter to ask questions, seek recommendations. I'd lobby her into agreeing to complicated plate shares, because I could never settle on one thing, and we'd spend the meal reaching across each other's plates, sampling, testing, before usually favouring the same thing and wishing we'd just ordered two of them.

'How's your day going?'

I blink, realising I must have been staring.

Both young women are smiling at me encouragingly. I push my hands in my pockets. 'Good, thanks.' That's all I've got. Lori was my smoother, the one who filled in the gaps, who channelled conversations so they flowed around the more awkward edges of my personality.

The taller sister confides, 'We've been ogling the food. Incredible menu, isn't it?'

'Yes,' I answer, then come to another halt. My mind is literally blank. I've forgotten how to do pleasantries.

'Who are you here with?'

I can't say, *It's just me.* Or, *I'm alone.* I cannot say those words. I don't want them to be true. I don't want to see their faces flicker with pity, or faux cheer as they say: *Good for you*, but are really thinking: *Glad that's not me.* So instead I find myself saying: 'My sister.'

'Snap,' they both say, then look at each other and laugh.

'She's still getting ready,' I add, even though they haven't asked.

'You're British?' the shorter sister asks.

'Yes, from Bath, originally. We live in London now.'

*We.* That feels good.

'You live together? Lucky! We did once, but we're married now.' They both lift their hands, showing me the evidence, rings glittering. 'This is our annual escape. We started it years ago – used to go to London for a weekend every January, you know, see a show, go sales shopping, cheer ourselves up after the Christmas slump – but this year we've upped the stakes.'

'Our husbands are onto us, though.' They both laugh and the sound is so warm and inviting that I join in.

'We're going to have some drinks later. There's a cool little beach bar about ten minutes' walk from here. You and your sister should join us.'

I want to say, *Yes!* I want Lori to be in our hotel room, right now, dusting her cheeks with blusher, then pouting and doing her mirror face. God, I miss getting ready together for nights out. Even though I teased Lori for her long routine – the face mask and bath, followed by the blow dry and styling, then the carefully applied make-up and contouring – I revelled in the ceremony. Just being in her bedroom, music on, cheap wine in glasses on the carpet. Lori leaning into the mirror to apply her lipstick. Me cross-legged on the bed with a hand-held mirror and kohl pencil. Air scented with perfume, body lotion, hair products. Lori turning to ask my opinion: *This dress, or the black top? No bra – or is it too much nipple?* The way she'd stand, side on to the mirror, checking which pair of heels to wear. The floor strewn with make-up, hair straighteners, cast-off outfits, handbag options, eyeliner-streaked cotton buds, tissues blotted with lipstick.

I want every bit of that.

I want to see Lori crossing the lobby right now. I want to meet these sisters at a beach bar. I want to hear my sister's laugh one more time. I want to remember what it feels like to be happy, to feel alive.

My eyes prick hotly. *Don't cry. Don't you fucking dare!*

I bite down hard on the inside of my cheek, but tears still threaten. There's a pressure building in my throat, and my temples feel drum-tight. Tears begin to leak hotly from the corners of my eyes.

One of the sisters is stepping forward, asking, 'Hey, are you okay?'

I cover my face, mortified. Then turn, apologising, as I hurry across the lobby. The thwack of my flip-flops quickens as I make for the lifts, desperate to get to my room, hide.

As I reach the lifts, finger jabbing at the button, I hear someone calling my name.

I hesitate.

The lift doors open and I'm about to step in.

'Erin?' the voice repeats.

The hairs on the back of my neck stand on end. I don't know anyone in Fiji – and no one knows me.

I turn, eyes narrowed, searching for the voice.

Nathan Brass is standing in the lobby, his expression darkening as he stares right at me.

# 22

# THEN | LORI

Lori glanced over her shoulder, checking for any sign of the men, then undid her shorts and squatted over the hole she'd dug with a stick.

Shitting in the woods. Just another way her life had shifted so far from its original shape that she barely recognised it. It was day four on the island. No rescue team had arrived. No search helicopters had been spotted. No boats had passed the shores. Nothing.

Her hair was tangled and sun-dried, scooped on top of her head. Her scalp felt hot and itchy. Her legs were streaked with mud and stubble, the bruising darkening and speckled with scabs.

She rested her elbows on her knees and examined her fingernails. The neon-pink varnish looked faintly grotesque; the edges were already chipped, half-moons of dirt embedded beneath her nails. Her feet were filthy, dirt settling into the dry, cracked skin, the soles of her feet scratched and bloodied from walking barefoot.

It seemed crazy that less than a week ago, she'd been standing in Erin's tiny bathroom, applying a layer of fake tan over her goose-pimpled winter skin. Now what she cared about was making sure Sonny stayed hydrated, fed. She cared about checking the ground for snakes. She cared about the number of fruit trees on the island. She cared about fetching fresh water from the stream.

*Survival.* That was the word that rippled beneath every action and decision.

Hunger growled deep in her stomach. The provisions from the plane had already run out and now they were eating food foraged from the island: bananas and mangoes when they could find them, along with coconut and breadfruit. She'd measured out Sonny's formula, scoop by scoop, and worked out there was enough in the tin to last for four weeks. Rescue *had* to come by then.

She felt in her pocket for the packet of tissues. Just one left. Tomorrow it would be leaves.

When Lori was finished, she kicked dirt over the hole, stamped it down and returned to camp.

*Camp.* That's what they were calling it now. They tried to keep a fire burning throughout the day – in part to keep away the mosquitoes, but also so that they didn't have to struggle to light it each evening if the wood became damp. They only had one lighter on the island and they needed to use it sparingly.

She checked on Sonny. He was sleeping in the bassinet beneath the small shelter Felix had erected from the remains of the life raft. His lips were pursed, neck long, giving him an almost regal look. He rarely settled in the bassinet, prefer-ring to sleep in the sling in the daytime, his body pressed

firmly to hers. At night, she'd abandoned the bassinet alto-
gether, Sonny sleeping on her chest, or in the crook of her
arm – when he slept at all. Mike had reassured her that the
snake she saw two days ago wasn't venomous, which was
some relief when she had to set him down.

She glanced towards the treeline, just able to glimpse the
sea beyond. It had become instinctive, the way her gaze
moved to the horizon, always searching. With the island
ringed by reef and breaking waves, she wasn't even certain
a boat would be able to reach them here. Even from a
distance, the waves looked like huge, towering things, sucking
the reef bare, exposing ribs of rock and coral.

They'd discussed building their own life raft. There was
easily enough wood, and certainly enough vines to lash it
together. If they did manage to make one, launch it, stock it
with enough supplies, it was unlikely they'd even make it out
past the reef without getting slammed against the rocks. Even
if they did, she couldn't take a four-month-old baby out on
a raft, exposed to the blistering sun, or risk him going overboard. Not only that, but without knowing exactly where
they were, they could drift on the currents in any direction
and find themselves lost in the vast South Pacific Ocean. She
knew what the islands of Fiji looked like on a map – a tiny
cluster of them in the middle of the ocean, with no other
land nearby for hundreds of miles. The risk was crazy.

'I don't think it's a good idea.'

She turned. Beyond the plane wreck, the three men were
standing with their backs to her.

'I'm not sure,' Felix said, hands linked behind his neck.

Daniel had hooked the neckline of his polo shirt over his
nose and was breathing into it.

Lori came closer to see what held their attention. The
blankets covering the bodies had been removed. The shock

of human hair and stiffening limbs made her gasp. 'Oh, God!' she said, covering her mouth.

The three men turned.

Mike's skin was flushed with the midday heat, a vein pulsing in his temple. 'The bodies. We need to do something with them.'

She stared at the mottled flesh. There was a mulchy, fishbone scent in the still air. Jack – the American retiree – lay on the earth, his Hawaiian shirt strained against his chest where his body had swollen. His wife lay beside him, her skin stretched taut, mouth gaping open. A fly landed on her lower lip.

'*He*,' Daniel said, pointing at Mike, 'wants to throw them in the sea. Let the fish have them.'

'I don't want that,' Mike countered, teeth gritted. 'I want them to have a proper burial. But instead they're just lying here, rotting.'

*Rotting.*

'Can't we bury them?' Lori asked.

'If we had a spade, sure,' Mike answered. 'But digging graves deep enough for four people will be almost impossible with bare hands.'

'But their families . . .' Lori said.

'We've got to think about ourselves,' Mike said solemnly. 'Leaving them here, like this . . .' He shook his head. 'There's a risk of disease.'

Lori made herself look at each of the bodies in turn to confront what had happened. They had died. People on the same plane as Lori had died! She'd learned each of their names from their passports – Holly Senton, Jack Bantock, Ruth Bantock, Kaali Halle – but repeating their names didn't help humanise the sight before her. Their skin was greyish, limbs bloated, as if waterlogged.

A sob choked from her mouth. 'I can't . . .' she said, staggering away. She rushed through the jungle, slapping aside branches and ferns. She stopped only when she reached the beach, the sand hot and giving beneath her feet. She raised her head to the sky. Breathed.

After a few moments, she sensed footsteps behind her.

'You okay?' Felix asked.

She faced him. 'What do you think we should do?'

The swelling around Felix's nose was beginning to subside, but his left eye was a strange tie-dye of greens and yellows. After a few moments, he said, 'The priority has got to be survival. I think we need to take them to the water.'

'I disagree,' Daniel said, walking out of the jungle, unhooking his shirt from his mouth. 'What if a rescue boat arrives this evening? What do we tell everyone then? *Oh, sorry, we ditched the bodies!*'

'I get that,' Felix said. 'But what if rescue doesn't come for six weeks? For six months?'

Lori's skin prickled with fear. 'Don't!'

'Maybe the real question is,' Mike said as he joined them, face drawn, 'if it were one of us, what would we prefer? To be left on the island, or put in the ocean?'

Lori thought of the stench of the bodies, the flesh already beginning to decompose. Then she shuddered. 'I wouldn't want to be left to rot on this island.'

Holly Senton was the last.

Mike took her ankles, and Felix held her by the wrists. Her head lolled back, amber hair trailing through the sand. Her eyes seemed bulbous, pushing from her skull. Both men were sweating as they staggered under her dead weight.

On the shoreline, Lori clasped Sonny, her stomach knotted. Were they making the right call? She'd wanted the bodies off the island – couldn't sleep with the thought of them slowly decaying, trapped gases expanding, stretching their skin, pushing at their organs – but was this right? The sea? It was too late to change their minds now: Jack, Ruth and Kaali were already drifting out towards the reef.

Daniel was staring at Holly, his face white. He wiped the heel of his hand across his eyes. 'This is fucked!' His gaze swung to Lori. 'Don't you see how fucked this is?'

'I—'

'I'm not sticking around to watch. I want no part in it.' He stalked off, disappearing into the jungle.

She wrapped her arms closer to Sonny, dipped her nose to his head. 'It's going to be okay,' she whispered. She felt the unjustness of it all – that she was standing here, alive, cradling Holly's baby. 'I'm sorry . . .'

Mike and Felix waded up to their waists, then guided Holly's body out to sea. Her dress ballooned and her long hair fanned, mermaid-like. For a moment, it looked as if she were waving, fingers splaying at her sides.

Lori stepped into the shallows, the warm water reaching over her knees, darkening the hem of her shorts. Sonny's little legs kicked excitedly at the feel of water against his toes.

She watched as all four bodies drifted slowly away from the island, floating on unknown currents.

No one spoke. No one prayed. No one held hands.

Yet they stayed there, watching, without agreement. Instinctively it felt as if it was the right thing to do. The passengers' lives – and deaths – needed to be acknowledged.

Lori raised her hand, which contained four frangipanis she'd picked earlier with Sonny. She lowered each in turn to the water. One for Ruth Bantock, and another for her husband Jack. The third for the air stewardess, Kaali Halle. She paused at the fourth flower, looking at the thick white petals, the tender pink centre. She held it out in front of Sonny. 'Here,' she said, as his chubby little fists came towards it, closing around the white petals. 'Will you put this in the water?'

She lowered him closer to the sea, guiding his hand towards the surface, imagining the touch of the water would make him release the flower, wanting to dip his fingers through it. It felt right for this tiny baby to be out here in the hem of the South Pacific, letting go of a flower for his mother. But instead, his wet fingers lifted the flower to his mouth, shoved it right in.

'Oh!' She quickly prised his gums open with a finger, hooking out the crushed petals.

Sonny chuckled. The delicious lightness of the sound broke the tension and Felix and Mike turned to look at him.

Lori lowered the mangled flower into the water, gum marks pressed into the virgin white petals. She smiled because she hoped that Holly, a girl she'd never even spoken to, would somehow like it.

Then they turned back towards the beach, waded in.

'There, that's done,' Felix said gravely.

The pilot nodded, but his face looked colourless. His voice was so quiet, she couldn't tell whether he was speaking to himself or the others. 'We had no choice.'

Lori returned to camp with Sonny. In the clearing, Daniel was snapping thin sticks across his knee. His face was flushed, a sheen of sweat clinging to his brow as he snapped another branch, then tossed it onto a pile of wood at his feet. Without looking up, he said, 'They did it, then? Dumped the bodies?'

'They weren't dumped.'

'He wanted them gone though, didn't he?'

'Who?'

'Mike.' He slapped the back of his neck. 'Fucking mosqui-toes!' He examined his palm, then smeared the dead insect on his shorts. 'You trust him?'

'Mike?'

'Of course Mike! Here's Exhibit-fucking-A,' he said, indi-cating the plane wreck.

'It was an accident. A mechanical fault.'

'So he says. That's all we've got, isn't it? His word.' Daniel turned to look at the plane. His polo shirt was streaked with dirt and charcoal, the collar pushed up to keep the sun off his neck. 'Plane crashes don't just happen nowadays because of a simple fault. There are safety checks. There's radar, air-traffic control, a series of measures—'

'Except they do happen. The Malaysia Airlines flight had over two hundred people on board and it just . . . disappeared.'

'It didn't disappear,' Daniel corrected. 'They found part of the plane debris in the ocean. Think how long that search took. How the media went crazy over the story, desperate for answers. What do you think the reaction will be about our plane? I know it's smaller, but people love anything to do with planes. There's something almost, I don't know, mystical about flying, right? I mean, how many people board a plane under-standing the science of how flight actually works? You?'

She shook her head.

'Me neither. There's a runway, a plane, acceleration. There are equations to do with force, lift, pressure – but how the actual thing works, most people like us don't know. Every time you step on a plane, you are putting your faith in the pilot – that he or she will get you safely to your destination. Except Mike failed us,' he said, his voice gaining momentum. 'The press are going to be after him. They'll crucify him when they find us. He's not going to want the truth coming to light.'

'What truth?'

'Think about it,' Daniel said, coming closer, near enough that she could catch the sour note of his breath. 'If you or I were driving a car – and it crashed because of a mechanical fault, like the steering suddenly went, how would you feel afterwards?' Like most questions posed by Daniel, he didn't require a response. 'I know how I'd feel. I'd be furious. Outraged. I'd want to know exactly what happened. What went wrong. How the hell a manufacturing fault could've caused that crash. I'd go over and over it.' He looked straight at her. 'So why isn't Mike? Why isn't he replaying the details of the crash?'

'Maybe he is. We don't know what he's thinking.'

'The only thing he's thinking about is how he's going to cover up the fact it was pilot error.'

Around them, the jungle hummed with the chirrup of insects, the weight of moisture in the air. Lori remembered coming across Mike in the cockpit on that first night. How he'd swung around, seen her, his expression white-faced as he'd claimed to be looking for painkillers.

Daniel was watching her. 'You've noticed something too, haven't you?'

She glanced down at Sonny. He'd fallen asleep in the sling, his cheek against her chest, mouth slack. She curved her palms around him, holding him close. 'I don't know. I'm not sure.'

'Not sure about what?'

She glanced over her shoulder towards the treeline, checking they were still alone. Then she explained about finding Mike in the cockpit. 'I just got a strange feeling about it. He looked . . . caught out.'

Daniel's features tightened. 'What if there is a radio or transmitter in the cockpit that he's not telling us about? Maybe he doesn't want us to get off this island.'

'Come on, that's crazy.'

'Is it?' His voice was low and urgent as he said, 'If we're right and it was pilot error, he could be trying to cover it up. What if Mike only suggested putting the dead bodies in the water because they're evidence?'

No, she wouldn't entertain that idea. 'We're the evidence. You, me, Felix and Sonny.'

Daniel looked at her for a long moment. 'Only if we're alive when they find us.'

Her eyes widened. 'You're serious?'

'I don't know anything about the man. I don't know what he was thinking when he stepped on that plane. And I sure as hell don't know what he's been thinking since we've crashed.'

'None of us wants to be here – Mike included. He's got a wife, a son. You think he wants to be sleeping on the dirt with us every night?'

Daniel didn't answer. He began moving towards the plane.

'What are you doing?'

'Whatever he's hiding, I'm going to find it.' He hauled himself into the plane, disappearing into the cockpit.

Through the shattered windscreen, she watched Daniel fiddling with various switches and controls. Then he reached into an overhead locker, running a hand along a panel.

She turned away. She didn't want to be around Daniel when he was like this – paranoid, jumpy, quick to rage. Her hands circled beneath Sonny, experimenting with taking a little of his weight in her palms, giving her shoulders a moment's respite. Her spine felt crooked from the constant bending and lifting and carrying – and although she should probably be putting Sonny into his bassinet for naps, she liked the re-assuring warmth and weight of him against her body.

'Lori!' Daniel shouted, from the plane.

She turned.

Daniel was standing in the plane doorway. 'You need to see this!'

She heaved herself into the plane. The trapped heat throbbed and the air smelt faintly metallic and charred. She followed him into the narrow cockpit, taking in the shattered windscreen and smashed control board.

Daniel was pointing to a bundled blanket. 'This was stuffed in the footwell. Look!' His voice was too loud in the cramped, hot space. He was pointing to a collection of miniature bottles of spirits, all empty. 'There was alcohol on board! He kept it! Stashed it up here – drank the fucking lot!'

Lori stared at the empty bottles. There must have been twenty or thirty of them. When they'd pooled the food and drink, Mike had said the plane supplies had been limited to crisps, chocolates and soft drinks.

'Lying bastard!' Daniel said, spittle flying from his mouth. 'He crashes our plane, trapping us here, and all the while he's mixing himself fucking gin and tonics!' He yanked open a small drawer, then turned out an overhead cupboard.

'Listen—'

'What else has that bastard been hiding?'

Mike's flight bag was on the pilot's seat and Daniel ripped open the zip, then emptied it, possessions clattering over the floor. He toed through a couple of items. 'I'm going to fucking kill—' He stopped, reaching down.

He was holding a mobile, his brow furrowing. 'This isn't Mike's phone. I used his after the crash to try and get signal at the edge of the bay. Why would he have a second phone?' He found the power button and switched it on, the welcome tone tolling to life.

'Has it got signal?'

A rectangle of light lit Daniel's face in the dimness of the cockpit. He blinked, brow creasing as he stared at the screen. Confusion spread across his face.

'Daniel?'

His body was rigid. He said nothing, just continued to stare.

'What is it?'

'The screensaver photo,' he said, turning the screen towards her, so she could see the picture clearly. 'It's you.'

## 23

# NOW | ERIN

Nathan Brass, the pilot's son, is standing in the hotel lobby staring at me.

I wipe away the evidence of tears with the back of my hand. I've no idea what he's doing here or how he knew where I was staying.

'I need to speak to you,' he tells me. His face is drawn, eyes dark. He wears the same sun-faded cargo shorts and work boots he wore at the hospital, and looks out of place in the understated elegance of this lobby. We both do. He shifts his weight slowly from foot to foot, giving the impression that he is swaying.

Behind us, there's a loud eruption of laughter and we both turn to see a group of women moving through the lobby. One has a veil pinned to her head and is flanked by three other women in strappy sandals. They're followed by a group of men of mixed ages, who are talking about something that happened in one of their hotel rooms, prompting a further outburst of laughter.

Nathan's gaze flicks to me. 'Wanna talk outside?'

I don't fancy being surrounded by all this glittering cheer, but I'm also unsure what Nathan wants. 'Okay,' I say eventually, 'but I've only got a few minutes.'

Outside, the evening is still and thick with heat. We follow the floodlit path through the grounds, which are tastefully lit with a wash of green and white lights. Curved tree trunks look almost prehistoric, and wide canopies of leaves are toned with light and shadows. We walk in silence, the clomp of Nathan's boots breaking the light tinkle of sprinklers freshening thirsty grass.

As we move through the night, I'm aware of the physical presence of this man – his height, the length of his heavy strides, the hard suck of air in and out of his lungs – and I decide I don't want to go any further. We reach the hotel pool, elaborately styled with rockery and exotic climbing plants, the chlorinated water glowing an eerie pale green – and I pause here among the cushion-less sun loungers and the closed pool bar.

I turn to face him, pushing my hands into the kangaroo pocket of my dungaree dress. 'How did you know where I was staying?'

'Rang around.'

I wonder how many calls it must have taken to track me to this hotel. 'Why?'

'At the hospice you said something. You said my father should never have flown that plane. What did you mean?'

I look at him in the semi-darkness, trying to decide what happens next. 'I just meant,' I begin, 'that I *wished* he hadn't flown it.'

Nathan stares at me, silent. 'No. I don't think that's what you meant.'

Heat is building in my cheeks.

'I know you've got questions. But I have, too. My dad disappeared for two years, and now he turns up, saying shit-all about it. I can't . . . I can't get my head around any of it. I don't know what to think . . . I . . . I'm going out of my mind . . .' The deep strength of his voice dissolves. All I hear now is uncertainty and fear. 'My mum, she's shell-shocked. You said you've been lookin' into things. What do you know? Why did you say that?'

For two years I've kept the secret. I've not told a single person that Mike and I met. If those first words between us hadn't been exchanged – the dim lighting, the warming smell of beer, the wrench of regret desperate to be softened – then everything would be different.

I wouldn't have lost my sister.

# 24

# THEN | LORI

Lori's fingers were white where she gripped the mobile. Why was there a photo of her on this phone's screensaver?

Daniel stared at her, waiting.

She blinked, studying the photo of herself: she was looking away from the camera, laughing with someone out of shot. Lori knew exactly who'd made her smile like that, causing a sunburst of lines to fan from her eyes.

Erin.

The photo had been taken on the lawn of her and Pete's old garden. It was Pete's birthday and April sunshine held the sky blue all afternoon, and the air was scented with the first blossoms from the plum trees. Bonobo was playing from an outdoor speaker and Lori and Erin had polished off a jug of mojitos, dropping alcohol-soaked mint into their mouths. Lori couldn't remember what Erin had been saying to make her laugh as she clicked the shutter – was it something about the birthday cake Lori had baked? The icing had run in the heat and Erin had said it looked like a dog's tit. Was that it? She couldn't remember – but she could recall that feeling of laughing so hard that her chest and shoulders shook.

When Daniel spoke, his voice was hollow. 'Why is there a picture of you on Mike's phone?'

Lori's hand trembled as her gaze travelled over the wooden phone case, examining the scratched and worn edges. In the back corner of the case, she felt the raised edge of a tiny oak leaf sticker. 'This isn't Mike's phone,' she said, blood draining from her face as she understood. 'It's my sister's.'

Daniel blinked. 'What? Why is it in the cockpit?'

'I . . . I've no idea. It doesn't make any sense. I . . . I don't understand. My sister's never met Mike.' Sweat was beading across her forehead. The weight of Sonny in the sling was pulling down on her shoulders. Beyond the plane, the under-growth crawled with hidden life – the clicks and whirls and chirrups of a thousand unseen insects.

'You said your sister came out to Fiji with you.'

She nodded. 'We spent the first night on the mainland, in a hotel near Nadi airport. We had dinner together, but then . . . we had an argument. Erin left, and I went back to our hotel room.'

'Then what?'

Lori squeezed her eyes shut, flooded with shame. 'I don't know. She never came back to our room. Didn't turn up for the flight.' A creeping feeling of dread was travelling through her very centre, turning her stomach to ice.

Lori heard the scuff of leaves underfoot and turned. Mike and Felix were returning to camp, their expressions grave. Their clothes were sodden from wading into the sea to dispose of the dead bodies.

Daniel pushed past her, jumping down from the plane. He stepped directly in front of Mike, forcing him to halt. His chin was raised, eyes narrowed. 'We want to talk to you.'

Mike raised his palms. 'Look, I understand you didn't want the bodies—'

'It's not about that.'

Felix glanced sideways at Lori, the rise of his brow intonating, *What's going on?*

Daniel and Mike were a similar height, but Mike had the heavier build, a solid neck and thick arms. The edges of Daniel's lips quivered as he spoke. 'I've been looking through the cockpit.'

Mike's expression held steady.

Somewhere in the canopy above, a bird shrieked.

'We found your little stash of booze,' Daniel spat. 'Turns out the plane was better stocked than you had us think.'

Colour flooded Mike's face. 'Listen, I'm sorry. I should've told you about the alcohol. But . . . I couldn't sleep at night . . . The crash . . . Kaali lying in that plane aisle . . . lifting Jack out of the plane . . . all their faces . . . I keep seeing them over and over. I needed something to take the edge—'

'You think we're sleeping soundly?' Daniel spat. 'Every time I close my fucking eyes, I've got a horror film playing on loop. Someone's scream at the back of the plane. The smoke. The smack of the earth as we hit. All that fucking blood on Holly's face! You don't think the rest of us might need something to help us sleep?'

'You're right. I'm sorry.'

'Those empty bottles,' Lori said. 'They're not all we found.'

Everyone turned to look at her.

'This phone was in your bag. It belongs to my sister. I want to know,' she said, staring hard into Mike's blinking gaze, 'what the hell you're doing with it.'

# 25

# NOW | ERIN

'I met your dad the night before the flight,' I tell Nathan.

God, everything about that evening was a mess. I'd left Lori in the hotel restaurant and stormed through the grounds out onto the lantern-lit beach. I needed motion. All that crap we'd said to each other, looping around and around. I couldn't make sense of it – how quickly everything escalated. I just kept on walking until the beach ended in a headland, and I had to veer towards town, finding myself on a side street lined with bars.

Maybe everything would've turned out differently if I was the type of person who let things cool off, or who had the grace to return and apologise. But fuck, no.

I tell Nathan, 'My sister and I had had a fight. I needed to take the edge off – so I headed for a bar.' I remember ordering a double rum and Coke, nerves jangling, fingers drumming against the counter as I waited. All the things Lori had said, they were there, locked in my thoughts. I shredded a beer mat, tiny little pieces of cardboard dusting the bar like a colourful snowdrift. Anything, anything.'

I go on. 'On the bar stool next to mine there was this bloke, a glass of whisky propped in front of him. He was just staring at it. There was something about his expression – I don't know . . .' I shrug, not sure how to explain why I felt a kinship with this sad-looking man who would've been about my father's age. 'I slid my drink across the bar, clinked the rim of his glass. Told him to *Drink up*. He looked at me.' Jesus, his eyes. Two pools of desperation right there in the centre of his face. I don't know what he saw when he looked at me. But he nodded slowly, just once, as if a decision was being made. 'He raised his glass – said *Cheers* – and we knocked back our drinks.'

Nathan holds my gaze, doesn't move a muscle.

'I didn't know he was a pilot. Or that my sister and I were meant to be on the plane he was flying the next day.'

His brow creases. 'You were meant to be on that plane, too?'

I nod, eyes down. I'm already giving away too much of myself. I clear my throat, plough on. 'So, me and your dad. We became drinking buddies.' I don't know why I say it like that, flippant.

'Did he tell you?'

'That he's an alcoholic? Yeah, Later.' That was a fucking good moment. Sitting in a bar with a man who's been sober for the past three years and you've just gone and sunk half a dozen rounds together. 'That first whisky – the one he was looking into like there was a map of his life at the bottom – he said he was testing himself. Needed to know.'

Nathan buries his hands deep in his pockets. There's a faint shake of his head that I can't read.

'He told me about your sister. That it would've been her birthday that night.'

He swallows. 'Natasha. She'd have been turning twenty-six.'

The depth of hurt is right there, etched in his voice, like he hasn't said her name, her would-be age, in a long time. Not even to himself. I know all about that. You lose both your parents by eighteen, and you get familiar with the contours of loss.

'What else did he tell you?'

'That it was also the anniversary of her death. That he missed her. That she was a brilliant singer. That she had this voice – like a soul singer, deep and gravelly – and no one knew where it came from. That when she sang, the whole room fell silent. That everyone just listened as this powerful voice belted out from a narrow, blonde-haired girl. That the rest of you don't have a musical bone in your body, he said.'

I catch the edge of a smile at that.

'He also told me that things went bad. Drugs.'

His expression hardens, mouth tightening. He looks at me as he says, 'He tell you he threw her out the house? Changed the locks? Slung all her stuff on the lawn? That she was out there on her knees, begging him to let her stay, but he wouldn't let her back in?'

'Some of it,' I say quietly. Mike told the story as though it had been locked up so tight that when the words were released, found air, an audience, it dragged out something so damaged that he couldn't catch his breath.

'Some of it? Did he tell you that after he chucked her out, she had nowhere to go? No help, nowhere to stay, no friends left. So what does she do? On her twenty-second birthday she buys some cheap fucking shit from a dealer and injects it deep in her veins. All of it. One go. Enough to reach oblivion – and stay there. He tell you that part?'

I nod, slowly.

Nathan is quiet for a moment. He rubs the back of his neck. Exhales hard. 'He never speaks about my sister. Never talks about her with me. With Mum. It's like she didn't exist. She's a fucking ghost. And then he meets *you* in a bar and suddenly you know our life history.' Anger and hurt roll off him in waves.

'We were strangers. It's easier. Plus the drink: there's no filter. We both told each other things. That's how it works. A dingy bar, a stranger's ear.' I think of how I'd sat there, knees agitated beneath the table, flicking my mobile over to check the screen in case Lori called.

'What happened after that?'

'Not much. Got to closing time. We said goodbye. Staggered away in opposite directions.' I shrug. 'That's it.'

Except that wasn't it. But Nathan doesn't need to know the rest. I remember Mike hugging me. The two of us swaying together – both sad, bummed, but maybe also exhilarated and released by the confidences we'd shared, or perhaps I even felt an echo of my own dad, someone there to just listen – but then Mike kissed me. Thirty years older. Married. Face creased with shame and hurt. Dry, wrinkled lips, the sour breath of whisky, arms locked around my shoulders like I was some fucking lifeline. I couldn't breathe, couldn't move. Just knew I wanted it to stop.

I yanked myself free, wiping my face, humiliated, angry – at myself, at him – and then I disappeared. Got straight out of the bar. Ran. I didn't go back to the hotel – couldn't even think of letting myself into the room where Lori would be sleeping, smelling of expensive moisturiser and eye cream and toothpaste – so I stumbled along the beach until I crashed out on a sunbed. Woke hours later in the blinding morning light, mouth dry as cracked clay. If I'd shaken myself into action, if I'd hurried, maybe there would still have been time to make my flight. But instead I'd crawled off into the shade, nursing my misery – leaving Lori to board that plane alone.

Nathan looks out over the pool. I catch the distant sound of music from the hotel, the drift of voices, laughter. When he turns back to face me, his expression has slackened. 'Why did he fly? He could have got to the airfield and said no. He could've called in sick. But he didn't do any of those things.'

'I don't know.' I've tried to picture Mike climbing into the cockpit, alcohol still flooding his system, his head a mess of grief. Why did he risk his passengers' lives?

Nathan says, 'When you heard about the crash, you must have seen a picture of the pilot. Realised who he was.'

I nod.

'You didn't tell anyone about the drinking.'

'No.' I look down at my feet. 'It wouldn't have helped the search, so what was the point?' I pause. 'That's what I told myself. But really, I was ashamed. I felt responsible.' I swallow. I need to get these words out, say them aloud because it's what haunts me. 'If it hadn't been for me, Mike Brass wouldn't have climbed in that plane over the limit – and those passengers would still be alive. My sister would be alive.'

For a long moment, Nathan stares hard at me. His gaze moves to my mouth, then back to my eyes. When he speaks, his voice is quieter than before, but firm. 'You're wrong, Erin. He went into that bar. He ordered the whisky. He would have drunk it. He was so like her. Natasha. That's why he can't talk about it – can't get over it. That's why they found it so hard – there's this thing in them both. They can't fucking stop.' He shakes his head. 'He didn't need someone to tell him to drink up. He'd gone to a bar, ordered a whisky. He'd have drunk it with you there or not.' He looks right at me as he says, 'It's not your fault.'

Tears sting my eyes. Those words – *It's not your fault* – I've needed them.

I find myself stepping forward, into Nathan, my arms wrapping around him, my head against his chest. Tears slide down my cheeks.

Nathan doesn't move, but I can feel his heartbeat, the heat of his skin through his clothes. After a few seconds, he carefully puts his arms around me. I feel the spread of his palm against my back, a slow stroking motion, like someone reassuring an unnerved animal.

A rising heat stirs in my chest, taking me by surprise. My head is jammed too full to think, and all I am aware of is my body, how good it feels to be held, the warm and steady pressure of his hands, the earthy smell of him, grounding me.

A beat later he releases me, stepping back, planting his hands deep in his pockets. 'I should go,' he says, eyes lowered. 'Mum's on her own at the hospital.'

I nod, quickly, wiping my face.

He goes to leave, but I find myself calling after him. 'Nathan?'

He turns, looks at me.

'I need to see him again. Your dad.' I pause. 'He knows things. He's the only one.'

He's silent.

'Please.' A current of something fizzes between us.

Eventually he nods. 'Go see him if you need to, but, Erin – you've already got your answer.'

'What do you mean?'

'You wanted to know why my dad didn't come forward after the crash.' He pauses, gaze resting on my face. 'It's because he couldn't live with the guilt that he'd been boozing before captaining that plane – just like he couldn't live with his guilt about Natasha's overdose. He's never owned up to his mistakes. Didn't have it in him. He'd rather abandon his wife and son – live in the shadows – than admit culpability.' He looks right at me, emotion glassing his eyes. 'There's no great mystery to any of this. My father's a coward.'

# 26

# THEN | LORI

They all listened as Mike talked, eyes lowered to the earth. Dappled sunlight pulsed through the canopy, mottling his expression, shifting it from light to dark.

Lori tried to imagine the scene he described: her sister sitting across from Mike in a Fijian bar. She felt the weight of Erin's mobile in her palm. That's how Mike came to have it – Erin left it in the bar.

'That's how I met your sister,' Mike said eventually, eyes finally lifting to meet Lori's.

At her shoulder, Daniel snorted. 'I don't care about how you met! Or why you have that mobile!' His lips drew back from his teeth. 'What I care about is that you spent the night before our flight in a fucking bar!'

'I had one drink,' Mike said, eyes still lowered.

'You expect us to believe that?' Daniel took a step closer. A streak of charcoal blackened one of his cheeks. 'Then why've you been stashing the plane's bar in the cockpit?'

A sheen of sweat was building on Mike's brow.

'Come on, Captain. How much did you really have the night before you flew? Did you need a couple of extra shots to perk you up in the morning? Get you back on your feet?'

Mike held his gaze, said nothing.

'Answer me!' he shouted.

Sonny let out a startled cry. Lori moved away from the men, whispering a gentle *shushing* sound close to Sonny's ear.

'Easy, mate,' Felix said to Daniel, placing a brotherly hand on his shoulder.

Daniel shrugged him off. 'Answer the fucking question, Mike!'

Mike pulled at the dirt-stained collar of his shirt, as if he needed more air. 'Yeah, I went to a bar the night before the flight – but I had one drink. That was all. Course I didn't drink the morning before flying.'

'No? Then how come we crashed?' Daniel's sun-cracked lips pulled back over his teeth as he said, 'People died because of you. The air stewardess—'

'Kaali Halle. Ruth Bantock. Jack Bantock. Holly Senton. Four people,' Mike said, his words blunt, as if letting them out too quickly would cause a rush of emotion to sweep him away. He kept his chin raised, but Lori could see his hands trembling. 'They all died because of me. And all of you – and the baby – you're here because of me, too. You think I don't know that? You think I wanted that?'

'Then why have you been lying to us, stashing the alcohol?' Daniel said, hands curled into fists, rage shimmering from him.

'It was wrong, all right? I just needed something . . . but it was a bad decision. I'm sorry. I'm sorry for everything! That what you want? Does it make any of this better?'

'Nothing except a fucking rescue boat makes this better.

And after that? When we're back on the mainland, you know what makes it better then?' Daniel said, jabbing a finger against Mike's chest. 'You locked up in a fucking cell.'

Daniel stalked off, crashing through the jungle. Felix went in the opposite direction, towards the sea.

Mike leaned back against a tree, exhaling. He looked deeply tired, his hands still trembling.

'So you met Erin,' Lori said at last. 'Did you know we were sisters?'

'Not at first. But later you used her name – said there'd been a fight. I put it together.'

'You didn't tell me.'

He shook his head but offered no explanation. 'I liked her. Erin. She's smart, wry. I bent her ear off, boring her with an old bloke's woes.'

She wouldn't have been bored. Erin loved other people's stories. At a party, she would be the one sitting on a wall outside, listening to someone else's problems. People opened up to her because she never judged.

'She's a good listener,' Mike said. 'When you've been through loss, well, you understand, don't you?'

Lori looked at him.

'She told me – about losing your parents.'

The words jolted her, as if he'd pulled something private out into the light. 'We got through.'

'Because you had each other. Grief, well, it either cements a relationship, or corrodes it.'

There was something about the way he said it that made Lori wonder about his marriage. 'Did Erin say anything about that night? Our fight?'

He smiled a little. 'Boy, was she steaming. All fired up, you know, in that way people are when they need their side heard.

But then she'd had a couple of drinks, y'know? Took the lid off the pressure cooker.' He looked at Lori. 'You know what she said about you?'

She waited, lips pressed together.

'That you were everything. That's how she said it: *My sister, she's everything.*'

Lori needed air. Space. Everything was too raw, too much.

The sand was hot beneath her feet as she hurried to the water's edge, plunging her feet into the shallows, the soles stinging. Her shoulders fizzed beneath the weight of supporting Sonny in the sling.

At her ankles, the water was so spectacularly clear it seemed to sharpen everything beneath the surface: the cracked pedicure on her toes; the contours of the sea bed, shaped by waves and tide; fragments of sea-smoothed white coral and pink-hued shells.

She felt in her pocket and pulled out Erin's mobile. She thought of her sister's fingers touching this screen, her bitten fingernails always unpainted, a silver ring on her thumb. She switched on the phone and felt the tiniest flicker of optimism seeing the battery symbol read ninety per cent.

No signal, of course. They had checked the whole island and there was not a single bar of reception to be found anywhere.

She studied the picture on Erin's home screen. Her sister had chosen a photo of Lori to be the first image she saw whenever she reached for her phone.

*My sister, she's everything.*

She swiped to the photos, needing to see Erin. God, she wanted to see her face. Opening the camera roll, the last photo was taken at Heathrow – a selfie of the two of them in a bar in the departure lounge, holding up ice-cold beers.

Their skin was winter-pale, jumpers on. She couldn't remember what it was like to feel that cool. To be sitting on
a chair, holding a cold drink. It seemed like another lifetime
– pictures in a storybook she couldn't reach.

She continued to scroll through half a dozen shots from
Christmas Day. Lori and Erin had spent it at a London pub
with a group of Australians Erin knew from her office. It
had been a fun day of drinking – and it hadn't felt like
Christmas at all, which was exactly how they wanted it. She
scrolled through photos of nights out, of blurry images of a
gig, of pictures of the two of them taken in summer. She
went right through the gallery, swallowing once ordinary
sights that were now completely absent from this island.

When she reached the end, she looked up – and all she
saw was the endless, empty stretch of horizon. Her chest
tightened as she sucked in air. All this space – but trapped,
pinned by it.

God, she missed Erin. She desperately wanted her here, to
say something acerbic, to make a snaky little comment. She
missed the way Erin could make a joke of anything or get in
a fury about the smallest details – never quite knowing which
way the pendulum would swing. She wanted to speak to her
spiky little sister so badly it felt like a physical pain in her gut.

On instinct, she scrolled to the camera and hit the video
button. The screen suddenly filled with her image. What she
saw shocked her. Her hair was lank and sun-scorched, and
when she tried to brush it back from her face, it was stiff
with salt. There was a cluster of insect bites at her temple
and a deep scratch from a low branch cutting across her
cheek. Maybe it was the absence of make-up, but her eyes
looked dulled and flat. There was nothing she could do about
any of it, so she pressed *Record*.

'Erin,' she said, and her sister's name on her lips made her stomach fold. 'I can't believe I'm recording this, that I'm even saying these words, but our plane crashed. We're on an island somewhere.' She looked over her shoulder, moving the camera with her. 'No one knows where. We were off course. There's a baby. Sonny,' she said, angling the camera to show him strapped to her chest. 'He survived, but his mother—' she broke off, shaking her head. 'He's amazing, Erin. So tough, so incredibly sweet, but he's just a baby – out here. I'm doing my best . . . but I'm scared for him . . .' She could feel her voice beginning to crack.

She sucked in a deep breath. Refused to cry.

Raising the camera to her face, she continued, 'You met Mike Brass the night before the flight. In a bar. He told me he picked up your phone. That's how I've got it. Are you okay, Erin? I hate that we fought. This is all so messed up. Our fight. You going to that bar. My plane crashing . . . and now this. None of it – none of it – should've happened. It feels like I'm living in a nightmare. I want to wake up and be back in London, in your flat. I wouldn't even care about your shitty electric hob burning my coffee. I would worship it! Or the crap view of the tower block from the lounge window. I would kiss those bricks! I would kiss the spare bed! The walls! The fridge! I would kiss every-fucking-thing in your fridge! I want it back. All of it. I want *you* back.'

There was something about speaking aloud, imagining Erin listening, that pulled loose everything she'd tried to lash down. 'I know you'll be looking for me. I know that. Don't let the rescue teams give up. Keep hounding them. Because I need you, Erin. I need you to get me off this island . . .'

## 27

# NOW | ERIN

I pull into the hospice car park and cut the engine. With the air conditioning off, the morning sun scores through the windscreen. It's only moments before sweat builds beneath my underarms and behind my knees. The steering wheel turns tacky in my grip.

Once I leave this car, I've got to cross the sun-bright tarmac into the hospice, hoping no one stops me and then, when I get to the pilot's room, I've got to hope he is still lucid enough to speak – and that he'll speak to *me*. Tell me the truth.

The heat is becoming overwhelming. I can't stand it a second longer. I push open the car door and step out into the car park.

Immediately I have the sensation that I'm being watched. I can't say why exactly . . . it's just a feeling, a creeping sensation of someone's gaze on my back.

Slowly, I turn. The sun glints off the windscreens of the

parked cars, making it impossible to see inside the vehicles. I glance around, but there is no one about, just the thrum of early morning traffic on the main road. I begin walking towards the entrance, gaze alert as I look around me.

My mobile startles me in my pocket. As I'm pulling it out, I accidentally hit *answer.*

'Erin. What've you got?'

*My editor!* It must be evening in London. Still at the office, of course.

I checked my emails first thing and had a flurry of messages from the magazine. I only glanced at them, but the gist was clear: the magazine wants the story right now, so they can capitalise on the public's interest while the pilot's reappearance is still fresh. Plus, they'll be getting nervous about budgets. Flights to Fiji don't come cheap, and neither do four-star hotels. Everyone in the office knows I wouldn't have been considered for this story had it not been for my relationship to it. In fact, no one would have. Ironic how my sister's disappearance is now turning into the biggest assignment of my career.

Funnily enough, it was Lori who got me the job at the magazine. I was still living with her and Pete, pulling pints at our local, while thirsting for an adventure, for change. Lori came into my room one evening with a printout of the job description.

I read it, cross-legged on my bed, peeling a satsuma. 'You honestly think I'll make a good personal assistant?'

I was wearing an old Nirvana T-shirt I slept in and a pair of leggings that were thinning at the gusset. I thought she was going to make a joke – *Dressed like that you won't.* Instead, she met my eye. 'I think, Erin Holme, you are capable of whatever you set your mind to.'

So I went for the job. I worked hard to make my CV sing.

When I got an interview, I turned up in an outfit of Lori's – a tailored pair of trousers that bunched at the waist and a structured blouse that I failed to fill out. The night before, Lori had made me watch a TED talk about the power of body language, so I disappeared to the toilets and practised some Wonder Woman poses in a cubicle where someone had graffitied: *Three-day weekends should be law* ☺ But whatever. It worked. I got the job. Erin Holme – PA to the editor.

After I'd spent a year of booking Addison Lee cabs and making restaurant reservations, one of the feature writers went on maternity leave. I put myself forward to cover her role and, when she didn't return, I became permanent.

I once thought of journalism as something frontline and essential, that educates, informs, grows awareness. But now I'm not so sure. There's a salacious underbelly to it, because what we're really selling is fear.

I straighten, stilling my hand that's lifting towards my throat. I make sure my voice comes out clearly, level. 'I was just emailing you.' Lie. 'I had my first interview with the pilot yesterday.'

'What did you find out?'

What I want to say is go fuck yourself and this story, but that's not conducive to remaining employed. I manage to squeeze out something vaguely complicit. 'There's a lot more to his reappearance than the public has been told.'

'Oh?' she says, and I can hear the interest in that single syllable, as if the phone has been pressed closer to her mouth.

I know she want facts, not hunches. 'The pilot is hiding something about his reasons for not coming forward to the authorities, not getting in touch with his family. Also, he claims not to know where the island was, but I don't buy it.'

'Have you got any evidence?'

For some reason, I keep the '*We had no choice*' remark

to myself. For now. I've learned that when speaking to my editor, you don't answer a question with the word *no*. 'I'm at the hospital – about to see him. These things can only be done in stages. I'll need more time.'

'How much?'

'There are other people I need to speak to. His family. The flight authorities.'

'You've not spoken to them yet?'

My jaw tightens. I think I might actually hate my boss. I need to give her something, so I decide to say, 'I interviewed his son, Nathan Brass, yesterday.'

'And?'

'They have a troubled relationship. Hadn't spoken in a few years. I'm certain he didn't know Mike Brass was alive.'

'You got enough for a teaser article?'

A teaser article, in my editor's vocabulary, is a rehash of what's already out there in the news, just with an added quote or two – in this case, from Nathan Brass. I think of our talk last night, the chlorinated air by the poolside cut through with jasmine, something vulnerable in the lowering of his gaze. I don't want to take his words, stretch them to fit a headline. 'Releasing something like that at this stage could close doors for me out here. Let's hold back. There's a bigger story here. And I'm close, Rebecca.' Yeah, I hate myself a little.

'How much time do you need?'

'A week.'

'Impossible. I want the story for this Saturday's magazine.'

That gives me four days. There's almost no chance I can get everything I need in time.

'Call me after your interview,' she instructs, then hangs up.

\* \* \*

167

I push my mobile back into my pocket, palms sweaty, heart racing. I hate how edgy I am after dealing with my editor. As I wipe my palms against the sides of my top, a shadow falls over me.

I look up, squinting into sunlight. Nathan Brass is standing in my pathway, feet planted wide. His face is in shadow, but I can make out the hard glare of his gaze.

'You're a *journalist.*' The word is spat, an insult.

Heat flushes to my skin. 'Nathan . . .'

His jaw is set. 'Bitch.'

It's not the first time I've been called a bitch – but when you actually deserve it, the word cuts. 'What you just heard – it's not what you think—'

'What I think is you're a fucking journo,' he seethes, jaw jutting forwards, 'and you're using my family to get a story!'

I think of the dark poolside, the way he'd shifted from foot to foot as he'd talked, eyes on the ground, unsure. That heat that had struck between us as I leaned into him. 'Honestly, that's not how it is . . .'

'*They had a troubled relationship.*' He squeezes his voice an octave higher to mimic mine. 'How dare you!'

'I wasn't going to use that . . . I just . . .' My cheeks are flaming. 'I had to make my editor think . . .' I trail off, unsure how to explain. The sun is right in my eyes, making them water.

'Insider story, is that what you promised?'

I've got no response, because that's exactly what my editor is hoping for.

'You people.' He shakes his head, jaw locked. He turns from me as if he can't bear to be in my presence a moment longer, but then just as suddenly he swings back around. 'When that plane went down, the media stormed my mother. She was hunted down when she went to buy milk, when she stepped into the garden to hang out her washing. She couldn't go anywhere. Couldn't open her curtains without a camera being pointed in her face. Now it's happening all over again. But you – you're the first to play the relative card.'

'I'm not playing anything. Honestly, Nathan. I'm not.' I want to reach out, grab his arms, make him look me in the eye – and see, really see. 'I'm here because I want to find out what happened to my sister.'

'Yeah? Then here's what happened: my dad crashed a fucking plane. Somehow, he made it out alive – then felt so guilty about surviving when everyone else died – that he went to ground. Lived in the fucking hills to stay out of sight. Spent two years fixing up bure huts for some German bloke. He chose that rather than coming back to Australia, to his family.'

My face remains neutral. 'If he felt so guilty, then why isn't he telling us where the plane wreck is? Why can't he remember the location of the island?' I shake my head. 'He's a liar.'

'And so, journalist Erin Holme, are you.' His face looks strained, eyes bloodshot, as if he's been crying.

I deserved that. But I will not back down. I hold his gaze, chin lifted. 'I'm not leaving without answers.'

'Yeah, you are.'

'Nathan, please—'

'Go!' he bellows.

'I just need a few minutes, that's all . . .'

He steps forward, the breadth of his body casting me in shade. He's so tall that his chin could rest on the crown of my head. 'If I have to carry you to your car, I will.'

I could bargain, beg, shout, but there is something determinedly resolute in the set of Nathan's jaw. He has shut down, closed off to me.

My gaze breaks away first. I lower my head, knowing I've messed up, lost my chance.

I turn, begin to walk away.

*You're quitting?* It's Lori's voice. *You're giving up, just like that? That's not you, Erin.*

I hesitate. My whole body is trembling. I want to run. I want to disappear from the face of the fucking earth. And yet my sister's voice, buried right at the core of me, makes me turn back.

Nathan is still standing in the same spot, watching. 'I'm sorry,' I tell him, 'but I'm going to speak to your father whether you like it or not.'

His head shakes. 'No, you aren't.'

'Then you'll have to stop me,' I say, as I sidestep around him and walk slowly, but purposefully towards the entrance.

He doesn't move to stop me, just calls out something, but I'm not listening.

This is it. All I have left.

I will make Mike Brass talk. For Lori. For me.

I stride down an over-lit corridor, passing an empty wheelchair. My fingers curl into fists, swinging at my side as I pace forward.

I ignore the receptionist, who asks who I am here to see, and I hurry directly to the pilot's room. The door is half open and I am already through it before I notice a nurse wheeling a piece of machinery away from the hospital bed.

'Oh,' she says, startled. 'You can't be in here.'

'I have his son's permission,' I lie.

Her brow dips. 'Are you family?'

'I just need a minute to talk to Mike.'

Her gaze flickers towards the hospital bed. 'But I'm afraid . . .'

And then I realise.

There is a white sheet covering Mike Brass. It is pulled over his face.

I blink, understanding.

I'm too late: he is dead.

## 28

# THEN | LORI

Daniel gripped the knife in his fist, dragging it down the gnarled trunk. The jagged slash exposed the green-white flesh of the tree.

He took a step back. His face was raw with sunburn, and he'd tied a tattered shirt of Jack's around his head, keeping the sun off the thinning patches at his scalp. 'Fourteen days,' he announced, counting the tally of slashes.

Then he turned, gaze snapping to Lori, who was kneeling on a blanket, changing Sonny's nappy. 'Two fucking weeks and we're still here!' He stabbed the knife into a log and crashed through the clearing. It was the only thing he'd said all day.

Had it only been two weeks? It felt longer. A lifetime. Time passed differently on the island. Hours merged and blurred, days losing their shape because they were no longer punctuated by breakfast, lunch, and dinner. Instead, they grazed throughout the day, eating fruit when they felt like it and occasionally fish if Felix had been successful spearfishing. Last week it was Lori's birthday – twenty-eight years old – but she'd lost track of the days and the date had passed. It scared her, missing her own birthday like that, the framework of normal life slipping away.

Lori adjusted the tab of Sonny's nappy and clipped the poppers on his vest. She'd begun lining his nappies with rags, which she washed and hung out across branches to dry. It meant she could make each disposable nappy last for twelve hours, sometimes twice that if she changed the rags often enough.

He was grizzling lightly – had been unsettled all day – and she wondered whether she should try another bottle, or if it was a nap he needed. She lowered her face to his, staring into his deep navy eyes. 'What is it, baby?' she whispered. 'What do you need?'

He stared back at her, lower lip protruding, eyes watery. 'Please tell me,' she begged.

Holly would have known. A mother would know what he needed. *You've no idea what you're doing. The baby has sensed it*, hissed her inner critic.

She scooped him into her arms, wondering if a cuddle could help. She pushed to her feet, vision swimming with black dots.

*You've no maternal instinct. The baby knows you're useless.*

This – a baby in her arms – had been her dream once. It had been clear, laid out like a stone stepping path into the future. Marriage. A family. Four children. A warmly chaotic house filled with blaring music, artwork stuck to the fridge, home-cooked meals, laughter spilling from open doorways. Noise and people and love. That was everything she'd wanted. She'd never been driven by the promise of a high-flying career, hankered after a big pay packet, or wanted to march out into the corporate world. She wanted a family. She wanted to be a stay-at-home mum. That wasn't something you admitted these days. Women wanted more than that – to work, to mother, to cook, to be cooked for – and good for them. Lori was wholeheartedly cheering them on. But that wasn't what she wanted. Just a family.

Most people didn't understand infertility. They thought they did – that was the worst thing. Everyone knew about IVF. It was part of the lexicon of the twenty-first century. *I'm going through IVF.* But until you take those injections in the soft, childless flesh of your stomach, or until you lie on a hospital trolley having your eggs extracted by an embryologist, your greatest hopes shrunk right down into the tiny cells, you can't know. Even before Lori began IVF, when they were just 'trying to conceive naturally', it was still brutal. The unrelenting rollercoaster of a single cycle, repeated month after month. Sex, which had always been at the heart of her and Pete's relationship, had eventually – despite their best efforts – become something goal-orientated, predicated on a temperature reading, followed by a notation on an app. Then began the hope-tinged, anxiety-pricked days afterwards when she'd wonder: *Do my breasts feel tender? Am I bloated? Am I more tired than usual? Could I be . . . pregnant? Or is it my period coming?* And then the blood-red disappointment.

Every. Single. Month.

It was easier to close herself off from the world, protect against the insensitive comments from well-meaning friends that pierced right through her previously robust heart. She couldn't face baby showers. She couldn't shop in the M&S food hall as it meant passing the baby clothes section on the way through. She changed her route home from school, so she didn't have to pass the park and see the new mothers with their babies swaddled in snowsuits. All around her, friends, colleagues, strangers, teenagers, forty year olds, were falling pregnant, and she watched the miracle of their bodies changing shape, doing this instinctive, natural act.

But her body had betrayed her. It had failed at this one simple thing it was designed to do. We're always told to follow our gut instinct. She'd read somewhere that 90 per cent of the time our guts are correct. So what if her body knew – on some deep, intrinsic level – that she shouldn't be a mother? That she wasn't good enough. That she would do a terrible job.

That's what she believed on the darker days, when the blood was fresh and the cramps hollowed out her middle. The struggle to conceive robbed her of her sense of purpose because the only purpose she was desperate to fulfil was to be a mother. All those layers and layers of loss felt as if they were stacking up, tiny hairline cracks around her heart.

And then Pete broke the news.

Zoe. Pregnant.

Right there, in their kitchen, where they'd sat together, elbows on the table, gazes on a calculator, working out if they could afford a fourth round of IVF.

The Zoe bomb had cracked her open – and what spooled out was such darkness, such loneliness and sadness, that she was scared to even look at it. Scared to let anyone else see. So she pressed her shattered self together and carried on. She got up in the mornings. She put on make-up, combed her hair. She kept her six-weekly highlighting appointments. She cooked. She ate. But inside she was broken, as if her heart rattled as she walked. She began supply teaching, trying to win over kids and infuse them with the desire to paint – when she hadn't picked up her paintbrushes since Pete left.

Booking the holiday to Fiji was never going to fix anything, but just the act of committing to something positive – seeing it in the diary – had given her a little spark of light. She wanted to find the Lori she had been before she and Pete had started trying for a baby. She liked that Lori. She was light and fun and popular. She loved her body. She loved sex. She loved going out on a Friday night and having too many drinks, and then lounging in bed on Saturday morning, making love, eating croissants and sipping coffee, buttery flakes of pastry flecking the sheets. She missed that Lori, the easy one.

She realised now that that was the Lori who Erin still saw. Erin clung to that version of her sister because she needed her to exist. Lori was her rock, her stability, the platform she reached for in the turbulence of her own life. But she wanted to tell Erin, *That's not who I am any more. I didn't want to show you the darkness in me. I was scared by it. I liked how you saw me, Erin. I liked that me more. The big sister. 'The golden girl', you called me. I wanted that me. So I let you believe that's the me who was still there. But Erin, she left. That Lori has gone. Can you love this one?*

She had never found the words to explain that Pete's betrayal was too large for her to bear so, instead, she'd packaged up her heartbreak and directed it at Zoe. The label of temptress was easier than accepting that Pete had let her down. So when Erin had pulled away the security blanket, revealing Zoe wasn't the only person Pete had slept with, it broke something within her.

Lori had been betrayed by her body. Then by her husband. And finally by her sister, who'd kept his secret. That's why she'd told Erin to leave. That's why she'd got on the flight alone.

And now, she thought, looking at the sheared plane wreck at the edge of their camp, that's why she was here.

She moved to the tally tree, freeing a hand from beneath Sonny and running her fingers down the fourteen white slashes. She could feel the sticky grip of sap oozing from the freshest marking and breathed in the sharp resin scent.

She took another step, circling to the far side of the trunk. There, her fingertips found the letters *R.I.P.* She lowered her hand, exploring the words that had been carved beneath:

*Holly Senton, R.I.P.*

*Ruth Bantock, R.I.P.*

*Jack Bantock, R.I.P.*

*Kaali Halle, R.I.P.*

A list of dead passengers.

When she came to the end, she felt the rough grain of the bark, an empty canvas waiting for more. She shuddered, picturing each of their names being added one by one, until there was no one left.

## 29

# THEN | LORI

High above in the canopy, Lori heard the leathery flap of wings. Large fruit bats took to the wing at sunset each night. Goosebumps shivered across her neck as she peered at the black cloud of them gathering to hunt. Sliding one hand out from beneath Sonny, she tucked her hair beneath the neckline of her top. She must've seen it in a film somewhere – a bat getting trapped in a woman's hair, panicked claws scratching at a scalp. She shuddered.

Lori continued to circle the camp fire, Sonny in her arms. She passed Felix, who was laying out four coconut shells. Earlier he'd caught a trevally, which was now roasting in the flames, speared on a water-soaked branch. She could smell the crisping skin, the warming flesh. Saliva pooled in her mouth. Breadfruit, wrapped in banana leaves, were nestled on the hot embers at the edges of the fire. She didn't love their starchy bland flavour, somewhere between a potato and pumpkin, but they were good enough when sweetened with coconut milk.

'Mike's normally back from the ridge by now,' she said.

Felix glanced towards the dark jungle. 'I know.'

He was often absent, spending his days on the ridge top at the far end of the island. She'd climbed up there only once, a 200-foot rocky stack, which offered a vantage point from which to survey the whole island. Mike spent his days up there on watch, Jack's binoculars looped around his neck, returning in the evenings for food on the good nights, or just the warmth of the fire on the hungry ones.

Felix removed the fish from the flames and began to strip the flesh from it, dividing it equally into four bowls. When he'd finished, he said, 'Yours is ready. Want me to take Sonny so you can eat?'

'No, eat yours while it's hot,' she said.

'Hey, I've got something Sonny might like.' He disappeared into the shadows, returning a moment later holding what looked like an arch of driftwood. He brought it closer to the fire and she could see a series of shells, feathers, and stones, each attached to the wood with vine. 'It's not quite a baby gym, but I thought it'd give him something to look at.'

Lori's face broke into a wide smile for the first time that day. 'It's . . . incredible,' she said, surprised by his thoughtfulness.

'Here,' he said, grabbing a blanket and placing the driftwood arch above it. 'See what he thinks.'

She carefully lowered Sonny onto the blanket.

He lay still for a moment, unsure. His brow creased and Lori feared he was about to cry. Then one of his little hands reached out, batting at a shell. He missed. Tried again. This time he hit a shell, which clinked pleasingly against another. His face lit up, delighted, and she heard a gurgle of pleasure.

Felix grinned, teeth white against the dark weave of his beard. The expression softened him, made him reachable, boyish.

'Thank you,' she said, with meaning, touching his arm.

His gaze lowered to where her hand was resting on his arm. Slowly, he looked back up at her.

Lori felt a stirring of something deep within her. 'I'll let Daniel know it's ready,' she said, ducking away, unnerved.

She left the fire, picking her way carefully over the rooted dark earth. Moonlight barely filtered through the thick canopy above, but she was growing familiar with the short path that led to the beach.

Looking towards the shoreline, she could see the half-dozen signal fires that Daniel kept lit each evening. He spent his days tramping around the island, searching for deadwood. She walked towards him through the cooling sand, watching as he poked a long branch into the flames. His face lit up as sparks shot skyward, watching the mesmeric pattern.

'Daniel?'

He didn't turn, just continued stirring the fire, blinking rapidly.

'Daniel,' she said again. 'The fish is ready.'

He turned, staring into the darkness, face blank, as if he couldn't see her – or didn't recognise her. After a moment, he shivered, as if someone had walked over his grave, then followed her back to camp.

At the fire, Daniel took his bowl of food wordlessly, then sat on the log bench, feet planted wide, as he shovelled in the fish with his hands.

Lori ate too, inhaling the steaming warmth of fish and coconut, eyes closing, saliva glands releasing. She didn't speak.

Didn't think about anything except the warmth of food sliding down her throat. She tried to eat slowly, to savour each bite, but she was ravenous, pushing it into her mouth, chewing and swallowing. Within what felt like moments, the bowl was empty, fingers scraping at the veined coconut shell, searching for more. She lifted the bowl towards her mouth, licking the final fragments of fish from the wood. Then she sucked each of her fingers, one by one, not minding the dirt trapped beneath her fingernails, just desperate for every last tinge of flavour.

When she looked up, Daniel was watching her, his gaze on her mouth. His lips were parted. She could hear his breath drawing in and out of his lungs. His face was pocked with bites, patchy stubble thickening on his jaw. He'd lost weight like they all had, hollowing his cheeks and making his eyes seem set back further. He looked ravaged, as if the island were consuming him day by day.

The chorus of insects fell silent, as though a conductor had paused the baton. Lori heard rustling beyond the dark line of the camp. Turning from the fire, she peered into the darkness. She could see nothing but the looming shadows of trees.

The breeze shifted, sending a drift of smoke washing over her, stinging her eyes. She listened, waiting.

The snap of wood underfoot, the ragged draw of breath. Then Mike came shambling from the trees, shoulders rounded, limping. As the fire cast him in light, she could see a fresh cut on his cheek, like the clean slice of a knife.

'Mike,' she said, going to him. 'Are you okay? What happened?'

'I'm fine,' he said, raising a hand. He moved towards the camp fire, sinking heavily onto a log bench.

Lori fetched him a bottle of water she'd filled at the stream.

181

His hands trembled as he drank thirstily. He wiped his mouth with the back of his hand, breathing hard. 'Left it late leaving the ridge. Got disorientated in the dark.' His voice was throaty and thick; it was clear he hadn't used it in hours. 'Caught my foot on a root – took a fall. No big deal.'

Across the fire, she could see Daniel watching him steadily, his expression rigid.

'Are you hurt? Do you need anything from the first-aid kit? That cut on your face—'

'I'm fine.'

No one spoke for a time. The crickets started up their chorus once more.

'There's food for you,' Felix said, indicating the bowl perched on the makeshift table.

'Thank you,' Mike said, rising unsteadily to his feet. He picked up the bowl, asking, 'What did you catch?'

'Trevally.'

Mike ate standing up, lifting handfuls of food to his mouth. Lori watched, stomach rumbling. More. She always needed more.

'See anything up at the ridge today?' Daniel's tone was sharp, pointed, as he stared at Mike.

'Nope,' Mike replied, eyes down, mouth stuffed with food.

'All day you're up there with those binoculars. Panoramic view of the ocean. Yet, nothing. Not a single boat . . .' He let that statement hang there.

There had been a gradual shift between the group over the past few days. At first it was subtle, as if Mike's stashing of the plane booze had caused a hairline fracture, not necessarily visible, but undermining a previous strength or structure. When they were all together, they manoeuvred around one another carefully, warily, as if they weren't sure where the landmines were placed.

Mike looked up. 'What does that mean?'

'That I hope we can trust you.'

'I want to get off this island just as much as the rest of you.'

There was a pause. 'Do you?' Daniel got to his feet. He crossed camp, passing right by Mike, his elbow catching him, knocking Mike's bowl to the ground.

Daniel stopped, turning to look at the food at his feet. 'Whoops.' And then he was gone, striding off through the trees.

After a moment, Mike lowered himself down to the ground, knees clicking, and began to scoop the dirt-flecked meal back into the bowl and continued to eat.

Later, Lori crossed the moonlit beach, drawn to the water. The mosquitoes were less ferocious away from the hunkering trees. At the shoreline, she sank into the cooling sand, allowing the mellow draw and suck of waves to soften the rhythm of her breathing.

She rolled her shoulders back, straightening her spine. She'd left Sonny sleeping in the bassinet near Felix, but she couldn't settle. Didn't like being apart from him. If he woke, it was her he'd want.

Lori slipped her hand into her pocket and felt the hard press of Erin's mobile. She slid it out, the glass and metal warm from being against her body. When she pressed the Power button, the screen lit up as if it were a magic trick. The battery was now down to forty per cent. She was being cautious with it, switching it off immediately after recording a message for Erin. It didn't matter that her sister wouldn't see the videos – it was the act of talking aloud to Erin, imagining her somewhere, listening, that made Lori feel like, well, Lori.

She slid her finger to the *Record* button and saw her image reflected faintly, face leached of colour by the moonlight, eyes glittering. 'Me. Again. Still here.' She thought of all the things she could tell her – how she was worrying about Sonny's formula running low, or how Daniel's behaviour was growing increasingly erratic – but all she wanted was to disappear from this island, if only for a few moments.

'Do you remember that walk we did in the Purbecks the summer before Dad died? We got up early and drove while it was still dark, you eating toast in the car, the dream catcher swinging, me telling you to keep two hands on the wheel. And then we parked up at Durdle Door, layered up with waterproofs and wellies, and walked out onto that clifftop path. You had borrowed Dad's wax jacket – and we found a condom in the pocket! Ha! Your face! It was like you'd pulled out a dead rat. I didn't tell you – but I put it in there when we were walking.' Lori laughed now, remembering it all. She'd planned to tell Erin later at the pub, but a group of mountain bikers had turned up, asking to share their table, so they'd squeezed on together, enjoying pints and pasties, Erin drinking so much that they had to check in to a B&B and drive home the next morning. Whatever she did with Erin, it was fun. Unexpected. That's how it used to be. Before things had shifted, inch by inch.

'I'm sorry I was so hard to live with,' she said in a rush, her mouth close to the phone. 'You were right – I did criticise your life. It wasn't fair. Out here,' she said, glancing up at the stars, 'it's like I've got all this time to think about things. I feel like . . . like I can see more clearly. I wish we were together. I want to know how *you* are. What's going on with you? Because, Erin; I don't think you're happy, are you?' She thought about the camera roll of photos she'd scrolled through, absent of good friends, of a lover, of memories to cherish. Instead it was peppered with pictures of drunken nights out, or screenshots of other people's Instagram photos, as if she were storing up a life she wanted, but wasn't living.

'I wish I could hear your voice. God, I miss you.' Her throat thickened with emotion. 'Oh dear, here they come. Promised myself I'd get through one message without crying. Massive fail,' she said, her voice choked.

Through the blur of tears, she glanced at the bangle her sister had given her. She raised her wrist, bringing it close to the screen. She didn't need any more words. Erin would know.

# 30

# NOW | ERIN

I sit on the floor of the hotel room, hugging my knees. Closer to the minibar this way. Reaching across to the too-small fridge, I take out a miniature bottle. I've been through the good stuff, ticked off rum, vodka, gin, and now I'm down to whisky and no mixers.

The tiny cap twists off with ease, and I aim it at the bin, hear the clink as it hits the rim and bounces back onto the carpet. I drink the bottle in one, feeling the familiar burn in my throat. Then I tip back my head, stare up at the blank white space of the ceiling.

He's dead. The pilot is dead.

It's all over. I wasn't fast enough. I didn't do enough.

*What now, Lori?*

*Lay off the minibar. Wash your face. Stop feeling sorry for yourself.*

I reach for another miniature bottle of whisky. That's the

good thing about talking to your dead sister – you can pick and choose when you listen.

As I'm lifting the bottle to my lips, my mobile rings. I growl at the interruption. Glancing at my screen, I see it's my editor again. Does the woman never sleep?

*Leave it, Erin. Don't answer. Not right now, it's not the right time.*

'Rebecca!' I say, numbed lips feeling thick and heavy.

'I've just heard the news,' Rebecca says, coolly. 'The pilot is dead.'

'Yes,' I say, toasting my bottle to the air. 'Death at fucking last!'

A pause. 'Sorry?'

There's a long silence, which I fail to fill with anything more than a low burp.

'Why didn't you call it in? Why am I paying for you to be in Fiji, yet I am reading this on the news like everyone else? What's going on out there, Erin?'

'Well, right now,' I say, pushing myself to my feet, staggering a little, 'what's going on is I'm sinking my way through the minibar in my hotel room.'

I catch the edge of a curse. 'I shouldn't have sent you. It was too much. Look, I'll book you on the next flight back.'

I nod. She's right. It was too much. All of this is too much, I think, catching sight of myself in the mirror, mascara smudged beneath my eyes, deepening the hollows there. My hair sticks up, unwashed.

'We can still piece together something. You've at least met the pilot and his family now. We'll get a story.'

'A story?' My head shakes. 'I'm not interested in a *story!*' I hiss. 'I'm not interested in packaging this into something fucking sensational so readers can get their kicks. All I'm interested in is understanding what happened to my sister!' I know this isn't how you speak to your boss. I know I'm drunk. I know I should hang up. Instead, more words spill out. 'I'm done. Done with this job. With the magazine. It's bullshit.'

There's silence.

'Erin, I understand you're emotional right now. Why don't we talk about this when you're back in the office—'

'I'm not coming back to the office. I'm done.' As I say those words, I realise how good they feel. How true they are. 'I quit, Rebecca. I quit.'

She begins to say something, but I hang up, then sling my mobile onto the bed. I stand, swaying in the centre of the hotel room, alcohol souring in my throat.

I need air. I lurch towards the balcony, pushing open the doors. The night is humid, thick against my skin. There's no air. Just darkness. Emptiness.

I just want it all to stop. I want that tightness in my chest to leave. To feel space again. I want to stop the racing circle of thoughts. I want to stop hearing myself saying to Lori, 'I never even wanted to be here. You know the real reason I came on this trip? Because I knew you weren't brave enough to do it alone.'

*But the truth is, Lori, I want to be everywhere you are. That's the only place I want to be. Not here. Not any more. Not without you. It's me who isn't brave. I can't do this any more.*

I clutch the balcony, knees clanking against the wooden slats, ribs pressed against the railing. My head is spinning as I lean forward, looking down at the floodlit grounds three storeys below, the blue-green twinkle of the pool in the distance.

*Two years ago, I was here in this hotel, with you, Lori. I had everything then and didn't know it. What if I'd just got on that plane with you?*

I drag the sun lounger across the balcony, hearing the scape of plastic against tiles. I stagger onto it, reaching for the edge of the balcony, pulling myself up onto the railing, a hand pressed to the wall for balance. I straighten my knees, standing upright, toes curled over the edge of the railing. My legs shake as I peer down into darkness.

*I should have been on that plane with you.*

*Get down, Erin!*

I ignore her. My shoulders pull back. I feel my fingers leaving the wall. I raise my chin.

It's all there beneath me. A choice.

The night surrounds me, whisper-dark. My body feels fluid, boneless, like I could melt into the darkness. I don't want to feel any more. I want it all to disappear. *I* want to disappear.

*Get down. I mean it. Please, Erin . . .*

I stand completely still, but my legs are trembling, my head spins. Everything is so loud inside me.

'Give me one fucking reason!' I yell into the night.

I wait. Feeling tears streaming down my face. 'I need a reason. Give me a reason, I am begging you.'

And then it comes, a whisper of words somewhere in my heart.

*Because I love you, Erin.*

Tears. Stars. Raining down. Pouring from my body, from the sky. Darkness and heat and endless, endless night.

The choice is a footstep in either direction.

There is love. But which side is it waiting on? Forward or back?

I can't breathe with the emptiness.

*This isn't your path, Erin.*

*What is? Please. Tell me, what is?*

Everything spins, nausea rising, a swelling of grief over-whelming me.

I wait. I wait to hear her voice again.

But there's only more emptiness.

*I'm begging you, Lori. Tell me what to do!*

There is no answer.

Nothing.

I wait, legs trembling, body swaying on the edge of the night.

*You know, Erin.*

That's all she gives me. A statement as big as it is small. As rounded as it is pointed.

Everything and nothing.

My hands reach for the wall, solid, hard, trapping the earlier heat of the day. I push against it, stepping down onto the sun lounger, legs giving way, sobbing and gasping as I curl into myself.

# 31

# THEN | LORI

*What are you doing right now, Erin? Talk to me.*

Lori lay awake. The darkness was so complete, so thick, it felt as though she couldn't breathe for the weight of it against her chest. On nights like this, when the cloud layer pushed low and closed out the moon, she could hold a hand in front of her face, but not see it. She searched the night for pinpricks of promise – a blinking tail-light of a plane beyond the tree canopy – but there was only black.

As kids, she and Erin used to camp in their back garden every summer. She thought of the smell of the tent, the pile of books and magazines they'd stack in the tent pockets, along with sweets for their midnight feast. They'd pull the zip shut, certain that the thin layer of polyester would protect them from the night and anything that lurked beyond.

Now she longed for a tent. A zip to pull. Her sister beside her.

\*    \*    \*

Out of the darkness came the cry of Sonny. She pushed herself to her knees, her hip stiff, her right-hand side drilling with pins and needles. Despite her exhaustion, a rush of pleasure washed through her at the feel of his body as she lifted him to her. 'Shush,' she soothed gently, chin ducked to his head. She circled the flat of her palm against his warm little body, 'Shush, baby. Shush,' she whispered.

His crying increased, enraged. He'd been unsettled all afternoon, only taking half his milk at each feed, fussing and agitated.

He arched in her arm, his body strong and lithe, tiny fists drawn up to his mouth. She glanced at her watch, saw it was only midnight. He didn't usually wake for a feed at this time, and his cry seemed furious, unsettled. She felt his nappy: dry.

'What is it, sweetheart?' she said, adjusting him into her other arm, facing him outwards this time so he could see the glow of the flames.

Firelight illuminated the red mottled skin at the edges of his lips. She'd noticed a few marks there earlier in the day. A dribble rash? Scratches? Something worse? Holly had packed a bottle of Calpol and a sleeve of anti-diarrhoea tablets, but there was no other medication if he got sick. She placed the back of her hand against his forehead. He did feel hot – but what did she know? It was just something she'd seen mothers do: hand to forehead.

'Let's get some air to you,' she whispered, opening a few poppers on his vest and freeing his arms. 'Is that better?'

But Sonny's cries were growing, his cheeks wet with tears. In the firelight, she could see the little bubbles of saliva on his lips as he grizzled.

'Oh sweetheart. Perhaps you're thirsty?' He hadn't taken much milk earlier and the risk of dehydration on the island was a constant worry. 'Here you go,' she said, reaching for the bottle she'd prepared before nightfall. She tried to set him in the right position in her lap, but he was writhing, his little body stiff and uncompliant. Each time the bottle came near, he twisted away, fists batting out. Lori could feel tears pricking at her lower lashes.

Her arm was beginning to ache from supporting his weight. She'd seen mothers doing this, feeding colicky babies as they paced rooms, or rocked on the spot, the motion settling something in their newly formed digestive systems. She remembered thinking at the time – just sit down. Rest. But now she understood – the fear of breaking their flow, of them not finishing a bottle when they desperately needed the milk. So she continued to walk the perimeter of the fire.

'Is he okay?' Felix asked, startling her. He pushed aside his blanket and came towards them, rubbing his eyes, hair rucked up. She felt a surge of gratitude that he was up, too, asking after Sonny.

'I don't know. He feels hot and he's not taking his milk. I'm going to give him some Calpol. Will you take him?'

'Sure,' Felix said, reaching for Sonny. 'You havin' a rough time, buddy?'

Lori scrabbled around in the dark, finally locating the Calpol. She returned to the fire, angling the bottle towards the flame to read the dosage. She loaded the syringe. 'Here, this will help,' she soothed, popping it in his open mouth, slowly dispensing the medicine.

His crying stopped instantly, delighted by the sweet taste. Once it was emptied, his gums continued gnashing down on the syringe, searching for more. When she tried to remove it, he screamed once again, so she left the syringe for him to chew on.

She looked across at Felix, who was watching them both.

'What if he gets sick out here? Or what happens when the formula runs out?'

'We're just going to do our best, every single day, until we're off this island.'

The *we*. She needed that.

She glanced down at Sonny, the perfect curve of his head, the tiny button nose. 'What if I'm doing it all wrong?'

'You're doing an amazing job, Lori. Anyone can see that.'

Tears pricked the edges of her eyes as she looked at this little boy, gums still clamped around the plastic syringe. 'Teeth. It's his teeth!' she announced. The near-constant grizzling, being off his milk, the red dribble rash, the temperature. 'You poor little thing – it's your gums that are hurting, isn't it?'

She eased her little finger into his mouth. Carefully she explored the smooth, wet upper gums, sliding her fingertip across them. Then she repeated the same on the lower gums. There! In the middle she felt a sharp spike, the tiniest shard of a tooth just beginning to break through the skin. 'No wonder you've been complaining,' she said, placing a kiss on the crown of his head. 'The Calpol will help,' she promised, rocking back and forth on her heels. She cradled him, humming lightly as she moved. The rhythm began to relax Sonny and she let the rise and fall of notes fill her throat, her humming curving around the song.

Felix crouched beside the fire with an armful of sticks from the woodpile. Using a branch, he stirred the molten-red embers. Then he began to lay the fresh branches across them, smaller ones first, building to larger ones. He knelt close, blowing low against the fire, tiny flames beginning to lick at the new wood.

With the warm weight of Sonny cradled to her chest, she continued humming, tilting her chin towards him. Slowly, his crying began to ease, only the occasional hiccup-sniff drifting into the sky, like the sparks leaving the fire.

By the song's end, Sonny was asleep, his mouth slack. When she looked up, she noticed Felix was staring at her, something intent burning behind his eyes. 'What?' she asked, feeling a blush of self-consciousness.

He shook his head as if letting something leave him. 'That last tune you were humming,' he said quietly. 'What was it?'

'Oh. Um. I'm not sure.' She knew the tune, but couldn't think of its name. She hummed the first few notes to herself, but it wouldn't form.

He smiled, shaking his head. 'Never mind. I think my mother used to sing it to me. Hadn't heard it in years.'

She returned Sonny to the bassinet, gently laying him down and tucking the mosquito net securely around it. Then she straightened, stretched. God, it felt good to move her arms freely. She reached above her head, then bent to one side and then the other, feeling the lengthening of her spine. She rolled her neck slowly, feeling a gentle release.

She was tired, but somehow wasn't ready for sleep, for lying alone with her thoughts. Felix was still sitting on the log bench, so she joined him.

'So, Friday night,' she said.

'Friday,' he repeated.

'What would you be doing right now if you weren't here? Your perfect start to the weekend?'

He thought for a long moment. 'If we're talking perfect, then I'd be filling my pack with climbing gear, piling in the back of a car with my mates and driving west. Setting up camp somewhere. Then waking at dawn and climbing all day. No one around except granite peaks, birds, sky.'

Lori smiled, able to picture Felix in that setting. He didn't strike her as the night-out-in-town sort of guy. Driving off to the mountains, yes. She found something appealing in his voice, warm and wave-swept, a hint of a drawl, like some adventurer who's been to so many countries that his accent has become untraceable. She asked, 'Has climbing always been your thing?'

'Was. I took a fall a year or so ago.'

'A bad one?'

'Bad enough that I haven't climbed since.'

'I'm sorry.'

He shrugged. 'I was free-climbing in Wales. It should've been straightforward. A warm-up climb. Dunno what happened. Lost concentration, maybe. Or was unlucky. Maybe both. Reached for a handhold, thought I saw the right shape, but it was the light, the way the shadow fell, and there was no depth. No grip. I had no purchase. Felt my fingers slide right off. It jolted me enough. Lost my footing. Was holding on by my fingertips.' A pause. 'And then . . . I wasn't. I was just dropping. Fifty feet. Hard earth. Fourteen broken bones. A shattered radius in my wrist. A punctured lung. Eight weeks in hospital. A wheelchair for a while. Months of rehabilitation. That was the end of it.'

'I'm so sorry,' she said, understanding he was giving her the husks, dried little pellets of information. 'It must've been hard adjusting after the accident.'

'Had to move back in with my dad and stepmum. Twenty-seven years old and being brought food on a tray. Needing help to shower. Having your clothes laid out for you. Fuck that. I wanted to be wild camping in the mountains, sleeping in rocky crevices, cooking up food on a stove, climbing looming mountain peaks.' He stopped abruptly. Shook his head. 'Sorry.'

'Don't be,' she said, imagining the snap of wind as he

clung to a rock face, every muscle in his body working together to hold him steady. 'Will you be able to climb again?'

'My wrist is fucked. Some people manage to climb one-handed, but I don't want it. I could still go into the mountains, hike, take the trails, but I don't know, it's not enough. I don't want to be walking in places I once climbed. Every day would feel like a compromise. So, I stopped. Cut it all off.' He shrugged. 'People don't get it. How I can leave it all behind. But it's easier.'

'Is that why you chose Fiji?' she asked. 'Nothing to climb.'

'It could've been anywhere. I just needed to get away.' He kept his gaze on the fire. Didn't say anything more.

She thought of him in the boarding lounge that first day. The fresh cuts on his knuckles. She wanted to ask about it – but something stopped her. 'Spearfishing,' she ventured instead. 'Where does that come in? You were headed out to look after the water sports, you said.'

He nodded. 'Got into breath-hold stuff during rehab. I had to go to the pool every day for physio, which I hated. My physio cut me a deal. When I completed my pool exercises, she'd let me have free use of the pool before her next client. The faster I got through the exercises, the more time there was for breath-holding. I got a set of weights and would sit at the bottom of the pool like some watery Buddha. Then, as I got stronger, I began weight-walking along the bottom of the pool, stretching myself. I liked it. Everything closed out, y'know? Pushing it. Finding an edge.'

Lori tried to imagine it, the feeling of lungs contracting as the air left them, the crushing absence, the burning desire for oxygen. It must have overridden every other pain in his body, every thought and feeling, until it was simplified to a single goal: breathe.

He was so unlike Pete. Unlike anyone she'd met. There

was something unreadable about him that both appealed to her and unsettled her. She made herself hold his gaze. Look at him, properly.

Those tattoos. The shadows beneath his eyes. That way he had of closing down, turning away as if there was only so much he could take. She'd never understood the appeal of those skulking bad boys her friends had liked. Was Felix one of those? The boys at school who'd ring their eyes with liner and smoke rollies, loafing about in their worn-out black boots.

She couldn't see that either – so who was he?

There was a depth to him she wanted to examine more closely. The way he looked at her when she held the baby, as if he was breathing in the two of them. A vulnerability. And yet she sensed that there was a metal edge, too. That in certain contact he could spark.

'What about you, Lori? Why did you book this trip? What were you hoping to find?'

She looked up. Thought of the Lori who'd sat in her sister's flat scrolling the Internet in the hopeless hours of the night; lost, searching, looking for anything that would give her relief. 'Honestly, I don't know what I was hoping for.' She took a breath, said, 'When the plane went down, that moment when I saw the earth right there, rushing towards us, all I could think about was the life I hadn't lived.' She looked up, wondering if he understood.

Slowly he nodded, his gaze on hers, pulling her towards him.

'Why did we survive,' she said, voice low, a whisper, 'and not the others?'

He thought for a long time. 'Honestly, I don't know. But now we're here, it feels like a gift. Not the island, necessarily. But life. This time. It's a gift.' A pause. 'And my life hasn't felt like a gift in a long time.'

She sat there, gaze locked to his, divided by desire and fear.

It felt as though she was trying to swim towards the shore, but could feel the pull of something indistinct, unfightable – a current, the swell of a wave – pulling her back, right out of her depth, towards him.

Then they were moving together. Stubble against her cheek. The taste of salt on her lips. The feel of breath, hot and moist. The skin on his fingertips was rough, yet his touch was gentle against the back of her neck, her shoulders.

The air shifted, retracted. The jungle drew back. The canopy disappeared. It was only them, their mouths, skin, bodies.

Her need, her hunger for Felix – it felt too much. She was aware of the sensation of falling; slipping into something so deep, dark, that she was scared she wouldn't emerge from it – or whether she'd even want to.

Then, just as suddenly, he was lowering his face from hers. Turning away, eyes to the ground. 'I'm sorry.'

# 32

# NOW | ERIN

I stand in the shower, water pouring over my body. The hangover physically hurts. I lean into the pain because it's something I can feel – a thundering head, a rocketing heart rate, an acidic burn low in my gut; those are sensations I understand.

Beyond the bathroom, I know the balcony doors are shut. Curtains drawn.

It was the alcohol, that's what I tell myself.

That's where I'm leaving it.

I snap off the shower and stand for a moment, panting in a cloud of steam. I experiment with rolling my head from side to side; the pounding moves with me.

I can hear my mobile ringing. I step out of the shower, dripping water across the tiled floor as I pad into the bedroom. I reach for my phone. A UK number I don't recognise. 'Yeah?' I say, holding it away from my wet cheek.

'Is that Erin Holme?'

'Yeah.'

'I'm Kiera Tyler. Felix Tyler's stepmother. You've left me some messages.'

Water drips from my body, forming a small puddle at my feet as I say, 'Oh. Right.' When news of the pilot's survival broke last week, I'd tried to re-initiate contact with the relatives of the other passengers. I'd done the same two years before, only managing to get responses from Jack and Ruth Bantock's daughter, Sarah, who was living in Miami at the time. The others weren't interested in making contact, which I understood. So I'm surprised Kiera Tyler is returning my call now.

'The pilot died last night,' she opens with. 'Got the email from the British Consulate.'

The email was sent to all the relatives, informing us of the pilot's death and that 'the search for the plane wreck remains a priority.'

*Like hell.*

'I got it, too,' I say, choosing not to mention my trips to the hospital, my contact with Mike.

'Turned into a media circus again,' Kiera Tyler is saying. 'I wish the pilot had done a better job of staying hidden. I just want to move on with my life.'

Tucking the phone between my shoulder and cheek, I pull on a dungaree dress. I can't have this conversation naked. 'Thanks for getting back to me,' I say, stepping into my pants, still trying to understand why Kiera is returning my message now. 'I left you a voicemail as I'm trying to find out a bit more about who was on the plane with my sister, Lori Holme.'

I hear a glass being moved on a counter. A drink being poured. 'You're out there, aren't you? Fiji.'

I hesitate. 'Why do you say that?'

'When you left me a message, your number showed up with the foreign dial code. Plus, you're a journalist.'

'You've done your research.'

'Just like you're doing.'

I catch it now, the slight slurring of her word endings. I check the time: it's midday here, so it must be eleven p.m. in the UK. No one makes a call at that time of night unless there's something on their mind.

'I take it you tried to speak to him. The pilot.'

I hesitate for a beat. 'Yes.'

'And? What did he tell you?'

'Nothing more than was in the transcript.'

She's silent for a moment, perhaps deciding whether she believes me. 'He was the only survivor?'

'That's what he claimed.' I prefer to be the one asking the questions, so I change tack. 'Were you and Felix close?'

There's a sharp bark of laughter. 'Us? I was the wicked stepmother!'

I move to the bedside table where the file on the plane disappearance rests. I thumb through it until I reach the section on the passengers. I'd done some research into Felix's family: his mother died in a car accident when he was fourteen; his father married Kiera within a year; Felix left home at seventeen, dropping out of college. 'What was Felix like?'

'I'm not the best person to give him a character reference. He was a source of constant conflict between his father and me. He was never easy, even as a boy. He had this intensity about him. If it was put to good use he could be quite spectacular. But if not . . . well . . .' She slurs to a stop.

'There was a climbing accident,' I prompt.

'Taking the risks he did, it was inevitable. These extreme sports people – it's like their brains work differently – always needing to find the edge, seeking out danger. Adrenalin junkies

– that's what people call them, and it's true. Like a drug, always looking for the next fix.' There's a pause, and I hear her lifting a glass to her mouth, swallowing.

Is the alcohol for Dutch courage? What is it she really wants to talk about? 'Why was Felix in Fiji?'

'The resort hired him to look after their water-sports activities. Diving, snorkelling trips, that sort of thing.'

'But his PADI qualification – it wasn't even valid.'

'I wondered if anyone would clock that. That was Felix for you. Thought the rules didn't apply to him. Always pushed things one step too far. Thought he was special.'

'What sort of state of mind was Felix in when he went to Fiji?'

When Kiera speaks again, her voice has changed. It's low, serious. 'He was someone you didn't want to be around. If Felix hadn't left when he did, the police would've been banging down his door.'

'Why?'

'He was a dangerous piece of work – and someone was finally brave enough to call him out on it.'

A drip from my wet hair trails down the back of my neck, like a cold fingertip.

'Anyway, why do you want to know about Felix?' she asks, her tone shifting again, suspicious.

'Like I say, I'm just interested in finding out a bit more about who my sister was on board with.'

'But *why*? What difference does it make? They're all dead.'

I'm silent.

'You think there were other survivors, don't you? That's what your calls have been about. That's why you're in Fiji.' She makes the claim with satisfaction, as if she's proven a hypothesis she's been working on.

'That's what I thought to begin with.'

'And now?' It sounds as if her mouth is pressed close to the receiver, her tone hushed. 'Do you think the rest of them are dead?'

I finally understand: what Kiera is really asking me is, *Do you think Felix is dead?*

'Yes, I do,' I lie.

There's a beat of silence. Then I catch it: the small, low sigh of relief.

# 33

# THEN | LORI

'I'm going to the stream,' Lori called to Daniel, who was lying on his back, arms pillowing his head.

He said nothing.

He'd not moved in hours, gaze turned up to the canopy. A fly buzzed around a swollen bite on his elbow, but he didn't bat it away.

'Want me to fill up your water bottle?' she asked, looking at the crumpled bottle lying in the dirt.

Still nothing.

Daniel's stretches of lethargy were often followed by a burst of feverish energy. Sometimes he'd break into a conversation with no awareness that she was already talking, or pace over when she was trying to soothe Sonny to sleep, saying, *If we lashed some branches together we could make a floating platform . . . we don't need to even sail it, just set it adrift with a message . . .*

She tucked his water bottle into her bag and left camp.

The stream was a ten-minute walk, following a path that Felix had marked by tying strips of palm fronds around tree trunks to indicate the direction. Lori made the trip most days and had become familiar with the path, but there was something about being alone deep in the jungle that she didn't like, as if it were pressing too close, crowding at her shoulder.

The earth was damp underfoot, teeming with insects and rotting leaves. She concentrated on the path ahead, checking for snakes or potential hazards, not wanting to lose her footing with Sonny fastened to her in the sling.

*God, these bloody sandals,* she thought as a twig scratched against the side of her foot. The gold strap was already fraying and the soles were thin and without grip. She'd treated herself to them for the holiday, imagining wearing them to dinner under the stars – but out here they were woefully inadequate for navigating the muddy paths marbled with tree roots.

Lori had always been good at treating herself: a new handbag, a pair of heels, the occasional blow-dry if she needed a pick-me-up. There were worse habits. Erin teased her for it – *You could set up a distillery with all these bottles of perfume* – but she liked taking care of herself. It made her *feel* good. She looked down at her stubble-flecked legs, the skin streaked with dirt and scratches.

*If you could see me now, Erin.*

Thick, ancient trees leaned close, sealing in the heat of the day so that the air throbbed. Only a whisper of a breeze wheedled through palm fronds, waxy leaves gossiping. Bamboo canes marched high and she sensed something malevolent in the shadows, as if the jungle were alive, stalking her. She searched for a patch of sky through the dense canopy, but it seemed dizzyingly far away. She began humming to lighten her unease, but the sunny tune felt disturbingly out of context in the dark heart of the jungle.

Shortly, she caught the sound of running water. She followed the light stream ahead, climbing over a rocky boulder and skirting a huge spider's web that stretched across the path.

A large pool of water, deep enough to swim in, curved before her, before narrowing over a hump of boulders and returning to a stream. Sunlight reached in here, the edge of the pool streaked gold, the air feeling lighter.

She laid her towel in the shade, checking the ground first for snakes or scorpions. Carefully, she unstrapped Sonny, supporting his head as she lowered him down. She studied him for a moment as he slept on, absorbing the fine, mauve-shadowed closed eyelids, flickering lightly as if lost in a sweet dream. The curl of tiny fingers. The creases at his thighs, the sweet fluff of hair that smelled like biscuits. She pressed her lips lightly to his forehead. 'You are perfect,' she whispered, her heart full.

Then she wriggled free of her filthy clothes and untied her hair, which was so stiff with salt and dirt it seemed to stand up on its own. After only a moment's hesitation, she walked into the stream. The temperature was cooler than the sea, refreshing and startling in the humid heat. The cuts across her legs stung briefly, but soon began to feel pleasingly numb. She hadn't washed properly in a few days and her hair felt lank and heavy with wood-smoke. She slipped beneath the surface, feeling the water close above her head, a perfect seal. She opened her eyes, looked up at the blurry shimmer of the surface, feeling the bubbles pop in her ears.

When she had no breath left, she let herself float upwards, breathing in the warm rainforest; earth and heat and something fragrant and verdant.

She swam a little, the stream wide enough to take a few strokes, to feel the delicious sensation of weightlessness. She glanced back to check on Sonny, who was still dozing in the shade. She rolled onto her back and let herself float, the warmth of the sun reaching through the trees, dusting her skin.

She floated there, feeling the pulse of heat in her body.

That kiss.

It turned through her memory, hot and vivid. Followed by that sudden retraction; Felix disappearing into the night, leaving her with no explanation. She'd not seen him this morning. He'd woken early, slipping off with his spear gun at dawn.

There had been no one in the eight months since Pete had left. Erin had told her that she needed to put herself out there. Maybe she'd held back because it validated her position as the wronged party. Or maybe the truth was smaller, harder to digest, in that she simply hadn't wanted anyone else. No one had made her want to take the risk.

Until now.

Lori swam over to the rocks, where she'd laid out her washbag and clothes. She sluiced water over her body, feeling the grime and stickiness loosen, the salt-clung sweat wash away. She ran the bar of soap along the back of her neck, then set it carefully on the rock. It had become a precious commodity – a travel-sized bar, a little luxury in its waxed paper, the scent of vanilla and cinnamon reminding her of home, of comfort. She'd no idea how long this soap would need to last, or how long the small tube of toothpaste would stretch. She thought about the complacency with which she'd slung them in a shopping basket, grabbing a packet of face wipes, some shampoo, a bottle of sun lotion. At the checkout there'd been a bag of chocolates on offer, so she'd bought those too. She'd eaten them in the airport lounge, not even really tasting them, just dropping them into her mouth one after the other.

Satisfied that her body was clean, she set to work washing her clothes. She lathered shampoo into her top, her underwear, twisting and rubbing the fabric together to work deep into the fibres. When she was finished, she wrung the water from them, then lay them on the rock to bake in the sun. Naked in the stream, her skin was covered with goosebumps, a relief to be cool after the heat.

Behind her, she heard the crackle of leaves underfoot. Her heart rate flared as she swung round, searching out Sonny. He was still lying peacefully in the shade.

The noise came again from the edge of the trees. Slow footsteps approaching.

She clamped her arms to her chest. Every hair on the back of her neck stood on end.

Through the shadows, Felix appeared in the clearing. His brow was furrowed, dark gaze lowered. He'd lost weight, his ribs straining against his darkening skin. There was something distant, almost lost, about his expression.

Lori picked up her towel from the rocks, the cotton sunwarm against her wet skin.

Felix's gaze snapped up.

His face changed, eyes lightening. 'Lori . . .'

Her pulse quickened.

'Where's Sonny?'

'Asleep,' she said, pointing. She moved towards Felix, dried earth clinging to her soles, shafts of sun spilling over her bare shoulders. She stopped in front of him.

His gaze moved over her body.

She could smell earth and salt on his skin.

That kiss.

'Last night . . .' she began, but then stopped, unsure what she wanted to say.

He was looking right at her.

Desire was hot and heavy at the centre of her.

Was it this island? Stranded?

Alone. Lonely.

Or was it more? Was it Felix, wherever he was – an island, a city, the edge of a craggy mountain top? Would she want him anywhere?

She could question everything, or she could just let go.

'I don't know what this is,' she said, looking right at him.

He said nothing, just held her gaze, steady, level. The dark irises, pupils dilated.

'Neither do I.' She could feel it in the air, a pulsing energy, as if the air between them vibrated with it.

Her lips parted.

There were no more words. She found herself stepping into him, her hand loosening from the towel, the fabric slipping away. Tanned, damp skin, waiting.

In the sun-dappled forest, they paused, holding each other in their gazes. She felt the surprise that out here – on the edge of the world, the edge of themselves – there was this. Not asked for. Not searched out. But here it was. Longing, yes, but also peppered with hesitancy. If they dived into this, they would have to confront whatever it was, feel the shape of it, the rhythm. On this island, there was nowhere to run.

Lori felt as if the island were a vast mirror, and there was no place to set her gaze, except to level it at herself. Look herself right in the eye – and see.

It was terrifying.

And electrifying.

A glance – once – towards Sonny. Soundly sleeping. Safe. Then, there was no more thought as their bodies were drawing close. She looked at his mouth, sunlight caught in the thick stubble. The single blink of his eyes, which seemed to drink her in.

Desire. Fear.

The threat he posed.

He was like this island, unknown.

Then, the hot salt of his mouth. The clash of cheekbones. Her teeth against his shoulder. Muscle and skin beneath her palms.

The scorch of desire left her throat as a sigh.

Knees, thighs, ankles all entwined. Sweat-flushed skin.

She had the sensation of coming unstuck, like the sea bed shifting beneath her; or being on a train when another passes in a blur of metal and glass and humming air – and no longer knowing whether you are the carriage that is rushing forward or rooted still.

The hard gasps of breath.

Pleasure, molten-hot, winding right through her.

An ocean.

Head tipped back. Light. The sun falling from the sky.

# 34

# NOW | ERIN

'You said that if Felix hadn't left for Fiji, the police would've been banging down his door. Why?'

I'm still on the phone to Kiera. There's the sound of a bottleneck clattering against a glass.

'For what he did to me.'

A storyteller's response: leading, provocative. I make a noise of interest, encouraging her to go on. It's clear she wants to tell this story – and I want to hear it.

'The morning before Felix flew to Fiji, he came to the house. He would've been expecting his father home, not me – but his father was at the garden centre. Felix wanted to pick up some things. He'd moved all his crap back in when he was staying with us after the accident. The spare room was crowded with boxes of records, guitars, climbing gear he was never going to use again, plus *three* suitcases stuffed with his mother's things. Ten years, she'd been dead! A whole decade and he still kept her clothes, her books, her jewellery. It was odd. Probably kept it just to spite me. That's exactly the sort of thing he'd get a kick out of. We'd asked him to collect his stuff so many times. Warned him we'd get rid of it if he didn't. I'd been wanting to turn the spare room into my art room – you can hardly get creative surrounded by suitcases filled with your husband's dead wife's clothes!'

She pauses. I hear her take a drink, set the glass back on a counter or table. 'So anyway,' she continues, 'I broke the news that I'd done it: all this stuff that'd been gathering dust for months had finally been taken to the charity shop. I know it might sound hard – but we'd warned him.'

I listen without comment, catching the note of righteousness.

'The anger,' Kiera says slowly. 'It came down like a red mist. Wasn't the first time I'd seen it happen. All I had to do was mention his mother's name in the wrong tone, and that was that. But I'd never seen anything like this. He lost it. Started shouting, abusive language, the works. I told him I wouldn't listen to it – tried to shut the door – but he shoved me aside. He thundered upstairs, straight to the spare room. Tearing open the wardrobe, looking beneath the bed, knocking down my easel. He went through the rest of the rooms – and when he finally realised it was true, everything had gone – well, he really lost it.'

She describes what happened next and I listen, picturing his fist slamming into the mirror, glass shards raining to the floor . . . A vase hitting a wall in a spray of china . . . A row of framed photos swiped from a windowsill . . . The crunch of glass and china and rage underfoot . . . The yammer of a chair tossed down the stairs . . . The crash of a coffee table being thrown at a television . . . A case of red wine, each bottle hurled at a wall in a series of blood-red explosions.

'He was out of control,' Kiera says, voice shaking. 'It was terrifying. He punched a wooden door, slicing his knuckles, blood everywhere.' She pauses. 'I was just standing there, watching him destroy my home. I asked if he thought his mother would be proud of the man he'd become.'

I can imagine the sting of that comment. When you lose a parent young, it is the very question you whisper to yourself, the measure of all your actions, the root of everything you loathe about yourself.

'The next thing – his hand was around my throat and I was pinned up against a wall. I couldn't breathe. Couldn't move.' The bitterness slides from her tone and I can hear it, the trauma in her voice. 'I thought . . . I thought that was it.' She breaks off, sobbing.

I realise now: Kiera didn't return my call to talk about Felix and his death. Kiera called because she was afraid he was still alive.

## 35

# THEN | LORI

Afterwards, Lori lay spent beside Felix, sweat cooling on her skin. Beyond them, Sonny slept. A yellow-breasted bird dipped low to the stream.

Lori rolled onto her side, looking at Felix. He was staring upwards, eyes distant. 'What are you thinking?' she asked, her fingertips against his cheek.

He shook his head. The shutters down.

*What had he seen in his mirror*, she wondered?

There was so much she didn't know about him. She thought of the first time she'd seen him at the airport, crossing the boarding lounge, backpack on, his knuckles raw.

She wanted to know everything about him, understand each marking on his skin: the raised scars, the ink of his tattoos, the deep lines at his brow. She wanted to know the story that brought him to Fiji, that had bloodied his knuckles, that had made him cast his phone in an airport bin. She wanted to know what he thought about in the long hours he spent beneath the skin of the sea. All of it. Every detail.

Yet she sensed that knowing . . . that asking . . . held the threat of unbalancing something fragile between them.

'Felix,' she said, propping herself up on an elbow. His face was deeply tanned, dark lashes sun-kissed at their tips.

His gaze met hers.

Those eyes. She felt the swift and delicious burn of desire at the centre of her. She wanted to press her lips against his shoulder, lick the salt from his skin.

But she also needed more from him. Needed to understand something of him to anchor herself to.

Her voice was low as she said, 'When you arrived at the airport, I saw you in the boarding lounge. It looked like you read a message and then . . . destroyed your phone.'

He held her gaze, but even while he was looking right at her, she could feel something in him retracting, closing her out.

'Felix?'

His lips pulled back over his teeth, a darkness settling in his expression as if he were battling something.

'It's okay, you don't have to—'

There was a painful bleakness in his eyes. She regretted asking – and yet she held herself still, needing to hear.

Then behind them there was a crackle of leaves underfoot.

Her gaze shot to Sonny: sleeping, safe.

The noise came again from the edge of the trees. An animal, she told herself. There were birds on the island, rodents too, although she'd not seen them – but she'd heard their scuttling, seen the discarded mango skins around camp that had been gnawed. She waited, looking into the green wall of jungle.

She felt it then: eyes on her still-naked body.

There it was again, the snap of a twig underfoot.

'Someone is there,' she whispered to Felix.

She thought of Daniel. Mike. Their ravaged faces, hollow-eyed stares.

Felix was on his feet. 'Who is it?' he called.

Only the chirrup of insects and the occasional drift of birdsong answered.

She looked in the other direction, her gaze on the trees – that's when she saw it. The silhouette of someone disappearing into the woods.

'Anything?' Felix called.

There was such darkness in his face, an anger that had uncoiled so swiftly, that she found herself saying, 'No. Nothing.'

They chose to return to camp separately. Whatever was happening between them was only for them.

Picking her way over the dark, rooted earth, the eerie sensation of being watched lingered. It was possible she'd made a mistake. Perhaps it was just a trick of light, a shadow rather than a person. Yet she couldn't shake the feeling that they hadn't been alone.

She glanced around. Wispy lichen hung from the branches, like years of gathered cobwebs. In the woods beyond, she heard someone clearing their throat. She paused, listening. She could hear a voice, low, mumbling.

With a hand curved around Sonny, she stepped forward, peering around a thick tree trunk, vines clambering up its length.

Mike was standing in the jungle, his face in shadow. He was saying something to himself as he kicked at the earth with his feet, head shaking. He was meant to be on the ridge top, watching for boats. *Him? Had he seen her and Felix at the stream?*

'Mike.'

His head snapped up, startled. 'Jesus, you gave me a scare.'

'I thought you'd be at the lookout.' The comment came out sharply.

'Dunny visit,' he said, with an apologetic shrug of his shoulders.

She flushed.

'Going to the stream?' he asked.

'Just been.'

He nodded. 'Found a new mango tree on my way to the ridge top this morning. Got a good haul. I'll bring them back to camp tonight.'

'That's great.'

'Little one all right?'

She looked down at Sonny. She ran her palm lightly over the soft fuzz of his hair, smoothing the base of his head. She'd come to learn the map of his body, the tender skin at the soles of his feet, the bow of his top lip, the delicious creases at his thighs and wrists. 'He's great.'

'Suits you, a baby,' Mike smiled. 'Made for it, I'd say.'

She pressed her lips together. Didn't know how to respond.

'Better get back to my duties. Catch ya later.'

She stood there for a moment, watching Mike shamble off through the woods.

*Made for it.*

That's what she'd once thought. But over the years of trying and failing to get pregnant, she'd begun to tell herself a new story. *You're not made for it.*

And now? Now, she stared at Sonny, feeling an intense rush of love and protection for this tiny little boy, who slept curled into the warmth of her body. Maybe her womb wasn't made for it – but her heart was. Her heart was made exactly for this.

She walked on, no longer thinking about the shadows lurking in the trees. When she finally arrived back at camp, Daniel's space by the fire was empty.

She was hanging her towel across a low branch, when he emerged from the trees, arms straining beneath a pile of firewood. His polo shirt was filthy and torn, and there was a sheen of sweat across his sunburnt forehead.

'You've been collecting wood.'

'Need to keep the signal fires going,' he said, throwing down the pile.

She remembered the shiver of someone's gaze trailing her. 'Did you collect it from near the stream?'

'No. Why?'

'I've just been there. Filled your water bottle,' she said, taking it from her bag.

As Daniel reached for it, his fingers enclosed hers. He leaned forwards, so close she thought he was about to whisper in her ear. Instead he inhaled.

'Vanilla,' he said. 'Vanilla and cinnamon.' He smiled without showing his teeth.

## 36

# NOW | ERIN

After the call with Felix's stepmother, a spark of energy returns. New threads seem to be opening – things I hadn't seen. There's something whispering at the back of my thoughts that I can't quite reach.

I push my fingers into the roots of my hair, pressing against scalp and bone. I rake my fingers down to the base of my skull.

Everything feels fragmented, shards of information that don't quite connect.

There's got to be another way into this, I think, pacing the hotel room.

The pilot, I know, is the key. The front door. But sometimes when you're locked out, your only option is to go around the side, search for a gap, an ajar window, a ledge that you can climb, until you can finally break your way inside.

I return to the folder on the plane disappearance, thumbing

through it, unsure where to go next. All this research – the long hours digging for information about the other passengers, the months of rallying members of CAAF and the British Embassy, the ongoing collation of news coverage scoured in search of a shard of information that might illuminate something – all of it building to what?

I lower myself into a chair, an elbow on the desk, as I leaf through more pages.

I pause on Daniel Eldridge's photo. *Passenger Five*, they called him. He's sitting in an office, hands clasped, wearing an open-necked white shirt beneath a well-cut suit jacket. His smile doesn't reach his eyes. Alongside his photograph, there's an article I unearthed some time ago about a property deal in Chicago gone sour. A former councillor is quoted claiming that Daniel Eldridge was both ruthless and untrustworthy. 'Eldridge reneged on his promise to create a community space in the perimeter of his city centre hotel, leaving locals up in arms.'

*Is the whisper about Daniel? Is there something I'm missing about him?*

Silence in return.

*Or is it Felix? Was he violent? Dangerous?*

I can't feel her. I can't hear her. But what I do know, deep in my gut, is that if Lori had made it off the island alive, she'd have found her way back to me.

*What happened to you?*

I slide my mobile across the desk and scroll through the day's news, hoping for something to spark. The pilot's death is still the headline in the *Fiji Herald*, but by tomorrow it'll already be kicked to the mid-section of the paper, until eventually it'll be no more than a footnote in readers' minds.

As I scroll, I come across an article in the *Guardian* about pseudocide – people who fake their own deaths – which cites

Captain Mike Brass's case. Decorating it is a picture of Nathan Brass and his mother. They're standing together in front of a weatherboard house, by the peeling bark of a eucalyptus tree. The photo must be old, as Nathan's hair is in a ponytail and he wears wraparound sunglasses and baggy shorts that come to his knee. My gaze stays with him for a few beats.

Nathan had no idea that his father was alive. My cheeks flush with shame thinking of the call he overheard to my editor, revealing I was a journalist.

There was anger there but, beneath it, something else.

Vulnerability.

What was it he'd said? Something about how his father had spent two years 'living in the fucking hills . . . fixing up bure huts for some German bloke. He chose that rather than coming back to his family.'

I study Nathan's image, pausing on that strand of conversation. I replay it again.

There!

I'd missed it before.

Nathan has given me a clue.

# 37

# THEN | LORI

There was a different energy on the island at night. Hope dissolved with the fading daylight, leaving a gloomy acknowledgement that they would be spending another night sleeping on the damp ground. On evenings like tonight when there was no fish, the mood was worse. The ceremony of a meal at least provided an architecture to the evening and, without it, the hours dragged.

Lori sat on the shoreline, the heels of her hands dug into the sand, head tipped back to the stars. Their twenty-ninth day on the island. The days passed in a shapeless blur, told by the growing pile of coconut shells at the edge of camp, the darkening shade of her skin, the extra notch she'd had to make on the belt of her shorts.

She tried to focus on the stars. If she could turn off the fear, the overwhelming desire to leave – if she could just be in this moment, then it was a strangely beautiful one, the

223

inky sea sighing onto shore, the stars bursting through the warm night, behind her the silhouette of trees and the scent of wood-smoke drifting on the breeze. A shooting star fizzed across the night – and with it a burst of memory shone.

She slipped Erin's mobile from her pocket and switched it on. Fifteen per cent battery. Leaving recordings for her sister had become a lifeline, a gossamer thread of connection.

'Know what I just remembered? That night you persuaded me to sleep out on the lawn with you to stargaze. You were what, thirteen, fourteen? Dad thought we were crazy, said we'd never last. But you were adamant.' She grinned. 'You were in your *Man, the universe is so vast* phase. I was just going along for the ride. We lay in our sleeping bags listening to Red Hot Chili Peppers on your Walkman, an earphone each. You kept rewinding "Under the Bridge" because it made you *FEEL*.' Lori began to sing the chorus, putting on the earnest American voice Erin always adopted.

'I swear I know every lyric from *Blood Sugar Sex Magik*.' She laughed. 'The neighbours' floodlight kept tripping on and ruining your stargazing vibes. You got in a mood and were about to go in, but then Dad came out with mugs of hot chocolate. Told us we should go inside, camp in the lounge if we wanted. So then we *had* to go through with it. D'you remember I was wearing your beanie because I was worried about getting bugs in my hair?' She paused, looking over her shoulder. 'You should see where I'm sleeping now. On the dirt every single night. Bugs in places you don't even want to think about bugs. No Walkman. No you. No hot chocolate delivery. It sucks,' she said, adopting Erin's teenage catchphrase. 'And I miss you. I may have mentioned that once or twice. Wherever you are right now, go sing some Chili Peppers for me, will you? I love you.'

She heard the light sound of footsteps through the sand.

She didn't turn, but closed her eyes, listening, trying to make out the rhythm of the steps. She could hear the light rub of fabric, the soft depression of heels through sand.

Felix, she decided.

The sky seemed to press away, her skin electrifying at the thought of him. Since the day at the stream there had been more – stolen moments when Sonny was sleeping, or Mike and Daniel weren't around. Without discussion, they were keeping things quiet – a glance cast her way, a portion of fruit left by her bed when she woke, her water bottle refilled at the stream without needing to ask – small little gifts.

She heard him getting closer, felt the butterfly flutter of anticipation in her stomach.

'Thought I'd join you.'

Lori jumped. Not Felix, but Daniel.

A blush heated her cheeks. 'Is Sonny okay?'

He shrugged. 'Probably.'

'Who's in camp?'

'Felix and Mike. The baby will be fine.' He lowered himself onto the sand, sitting too close, his elbow brushing hers. He had on a fresh shirt, which looked incongruous against the rucked-up hair, the patchy shadows of his stubble, the bite-riddled ankles. The 'before and after' Daniel, right here in one place.

'Christ, I'm hungry,' he said. 'No fish. Again.'

'Felix is doing his best.'

He turned, raised an eyebrow. In the darkness, his gaze remained on her.

She didn't want to sit here with Daniel. She started getting to her feet when he lightly gripped her elbow. 'Hey, I've got a surprise for you.' He reached into his pocket, pulled out a bar of something, and handed it to her.

She felt the paper wrapping, the dense weight of food in

her hands. She lifted it to her nose, inhaled. 'My God,' she breathed. 'Chocolate.'

'Yup. One Snickers bar.'

Her mouth watered as she inhaled it again. 'Where did you get this?'

'My hand luggage. Didn't realise it was in there. Found it hidden in a side pocket earlier. Thought it was a fucking mirage – but here it is. So,' he said, glancing at her. 'Shall we?'

'Eat it?'

'No, do a celebratory dance around it. Course eat it!'

'Shouldn't you share it out?'

'I am. With you.'

'I mean, with everyone.'

'Sharing this four ways? What's the point? It'll barely be a mouthful each. Anyway, Mike can go fuck himself if he thinks he's having any of my food after he necked all the alcohol.'

'And Felix?'

'You don't think he's skimming off fish just for himself? Course he is. Come on, Lori. I'm eating this now. If you want half, it's yours. Otherwise I'll manage it on my own.'

'I can't,' she said, passing it back to Daniel. 'We share everything.'

'In that case . . .' She heard the tear of the wrapper, could smell the chocolate as he raised the bar to his mouth and took a bite.

'What are you doing?'

'Oh . . . wow . . .' he mumbled. She could smell the sweet creaminess, the burnt sugar of the caramel. The peanuts crunched between his teeth. All that flavour, those calories.

As he lifted it to his mouth for another bite, she found herself gripping his arm. 'Wait.'

Before she knew what she was doing, she was guiding his

hand towards her mouth. She put her lips around the bar, took a bite. Her mouth exploded with the sweet richness of chocolate, the salty bite of peanuts. 'Mmmm . . .'

Daniel laughed.

Then she did, too, chocolate smearing her lips, her taste buds dancing in delight.

He took another bite, then held it out to her again. It was the most delicious thing she had ever eaten. She wanted to savour every molecule, but she also just wanted to tear through it, teeth and tongue and lips.

She guided in the last bite, her lips meeting Daniel's fingertips. She could feel the low hum of appreciation from her own throat. Then suddenly he leaned close, his mouth on hers, the taste of chocolate pressed firm against her lips, something sour and forceful beneath it. She pulled back, shocked, but his fingers gripped the base of her skull, pulling her into him.

She shoved her hand hard against his chest. 'What are you doing?' She was on her feet, sand spilling from her shorts.

He was up on his feet too, palms opened. 'What?'

'You kissed me!'

'And?'

'You're married!'

'We're on a fucking desert island, Lori. Normal rules don't apply.'

*Normal rules don't apply.* The words echoed darkly in her thoughts. She was acutely aware of the distance between her and the camp fire; her and safety; her and Sonny.

'Don't touch me again,' she said, teeth gritted. Then she jogged up the dark beach, the taste of chocolate souring in her throat.

\* \* \*

That night, curled into the dirt, Lori slept fitfully. The memory of Daniel's mouth forced against hers slid, belly-first, into her dream. The sour taste of him filled her mouth, the glimmer of threat in his eyes. His voice, hot in her ear, *Normal rules don't apply*.

Then the dream loosened, crawled across the earthy dark forest floor, towards four dead bodies lying shoulder to shoulder. One by one, each body was dragged from the shade of the trees, pulled towards the waiting ocean, heads lolling back, hair trailing through sand.

Ruth. Jack. Kaali. Holly.

Like driftwood, bobbing endlessly with the currents.

After a beat, there came a fifth body. Shrouded by a blanket, it was being dragged by the wrists through the hot sand. The blanket peeled back, exposing a pair of lifeless feet: slim ankles, a glossy pink pedicure beginning to chip, exposing dirt-cased toenails.

Her feet. Her body.

Lori was being dragged to the shore, body limp, meaty fingers around her wrists. She couldn't see the face of the person dragging her, but she wanted to tell whoever it was to stop! – that she was still alive! But when she tried to speak, she had no voice.

She felt the liquid cool of the water meeting her, separating each strand of hair, slicking her clothes to her body, gaping open her top.

Salt water filled her nostrils, the back of her throat, pressed down on the sockets of her eyes. As she sank beneath the surface, at first begging, then screaming silently, she heard the words distorted through the water.

*We had no choice.*

Whose voice was it?

Mike's?

Daniel's?

Felix's?

She woke coughing into the night, skin slick with sweat. She heaved herself upright, wiping a hand across her mouth. Looking around the dying fire, her gaze mapped the shapes of the three men lying in the dark, her thoughts still burning with the question: *Who?*

## 38

# NOW | ERIN

I drive with the windows down, feeling the rush of warm wind against my skin. The sky is heavy with clouds as I head inland. Another downpour looks imminent, and the heat is building, holding the moisture in a heavy, humid blast.

I'm headed for the Hibiscus Crest Resort, where Mike Brass spent the last two years of his life working under a false identity. It's Nathan I've got to thank for the lead. He told me that his father had been living in the hills, working as a handyman at a resort run by a German owner. The police must have given him the information, not wanting it released publicly. All I had to do was search for resorts in the hilly, more remote interior of Fiji, and then call each one, asking for the name of the manager, waiting until I heard a German name.

The island changes the further out of Nadi I drive, high-rise resorts giving way to plantations of pineapple and sugar

230

cane. Villages dot the roadside and traditional thatched bures squat in clusters. The air smells earthy, verdant.

I'm reminded how much I love driving. There's a freedom about it – pedal to the floor, the world rushing by, just out of reach. I remember the feeling of passing my driving test and roaring away from the test centre, no instructor in the car – just me – marvelling, *I can go anywhere.*

Where I went? To pick up Lori, of course.

I pulled up outside our house, honking the horn until she ran out in her short summer dress, hair loose at her shoulders. She drummed her palms against the car bonnet, squealing, '*You passed!*'

'Sure did!' I said, dancing behind the wheel, a grin splitting my face.

She climbed into the passenger seat, the car filling with her perfume. She leaned over the gear stick, hugging me hard. 'You're fucking brilliant!' She didn't care that she'd failed her test first time. Her value was never based on mine – and I loved her for it.

She turned up the music, loud, and I pulled away in a squeal of tyres as Lori grappled with her belt, laughing. In the rear-view mirror I saw my father at the window mouthing, '*SLOWLY . . .*'

We drove and drove with no idea where we were going, just taking roads on instinct, Lori flinging out an arm, saying, 'That way!' both of us knowing that it would unfold exactly as it was meant to. It wasn't about where we ended up – it was about blasting out music, tossing our hair, feeling forwards motion – but mostly it was about freedom, possibility. We drove until the petrol gauge hit empty and we realised we only had a tenner between us to refill it.

On the way home, we pulled in at a viewpoint overlooking the river, and sat on the bonnet of the car, like American teens we'd seen in a show, and talked about everything that the summer ahead held in store – parties and boys and trips to the coast with me behind the wheel. We didn't know that, three weeks later, our dad would die of a ruptured brain aneurysm and, instead of enjoying a summer of partying, we'd be spending it talking to funeral directors, solicitors and bank managers. We didn't know that, while our friends were dancing in nightclubs and sleeping till noon, we'd be grappling to understand probate and inheritance tax.

Now, as I slow into a bend, I wonder whether sitting on the bonnet of that car was one of the happiest moments of my life: me and my sister together, hearts full of the future.

Following a narrow track that climbs up a hillside, I finally see the sign for the Hibiscus Crest, a secluded eco-resort which, from the tired-looking exterior, is long past its heyday.

I park the car and climb out, the engine ticking. The sky feels heavy, threatening rain. It's close, as though it contains the weight and boom of thunder. The heat is oppressive inland; there's no breeze washing in from the sea.

As I stretch, rocking my hips from side to side, I feel a prickling sensation at the back of my neck. I turn, half expecting to find someone watching me from the shadows. I stare at the other cars and the treeline beyond, but there's no one there.

Shaking off the feeling, I take the path towards reception. The air in the hillside seems thicker, humming with insects. At the reception desk, I ask if I could speak with the manager. After a long wait, a friendly older man arrives wearing a greying T-shirt and a pair of red plastic-framed glasses. He smiles as he greets me, introducing himself as Wilhelm Becker.

'I'm a friend of Anne Brass's, the wife of Captain Mike Brass, who I believe worked here.'

'Oh,' he says, brows lifting. 'Is Anne not coming now?'

I hesitate. 'Coming here?'

'Yes, she wanted to collect Charlie's things.'

I've no idea what he's talking about.

'Sorry – Mike called himself Charlie while he was working here.'

'That's right,' I say. 'I said I'd do it for Anne.' It's a bare-faced lie and I can feel my face reddening.

'Good of you.' After a moment, he says, 'I feel such a fool for not recognising him . . . for *liking* him.'

'You had no idea who he was?'

He almost flinches at the question. 'Of course not! I took over the resort a month after the plane disappearance. I'd been in Germany – hadn't followed the press frenzy. No pilot's uniform, a shaved head, glasses: it's enough. None of us here recognised him. You see what you see.'

'Yes, you're right.'

He nods. 'I'd better show you his things.'

He walks away from the main reception and around the side of the hotel.

Assuming I'm meant to follow, I keep pace. While the building feels a little dilapidated, the gardens thrive. Tall ferns reach skyward, between bursts of red and yellow flowers. Perfume-scented bushes flank the pathways, and the grass is springy underfoot as we walk.

'I didn't like to move anything, so his belongings are still in his room. Course, the police visited briefly, but there was little to see. They were only here a moment.'

Sounds about right.

We pass through a gateway, and the ground becomes uneven and sloping, where half a dozen small wooden outbuildings are raised on stilts. At the edge of them, one stands alone. He points to it, telling me, 'That's where Charlie – sorry, Mike –

233

lived during his time here. He told us he had been widowed and needed a little extra income, but that it would affect his pension, so we paid him off the books. Truth be told, I felt sorry for him. He seemed down on his luck, you know?'

'Did he ever have visitors?'

'Not that I know of. Kept himself to himself. Took his meals in the staff kitchen. Never one to socialise. Preferred to spend his time in the company of books. He worked hard, always got the job done. If a man comes to you offering to work, wanting cash, not talking about their past, you don't ask questions.'

'What about his days off? What did he do on those?' Then I add, 'Anne was wondering how he spent his time.'

'Went for walks through the hillside. That was about it. Never went down into the town like most of the workers. Like I say, he kept himself to himself.'

'Did you ever have any suspicions about him?'

'Honestly? None at all. Shocked us all to hear who he really was.' The manager checks his watch. 'I'm afraid I've got to get on. You've caught me on payroll morning. Are you okay on your own?'

'Of course.'

We walk to the cabin, which he unlocks.

'All right then. I'll leave you to it. If you need any help, one of the reception staff can come and find me.'

I thank him then, as he leaves, I step into the room where Mike Brass started a new life.

At first, I think there's been a mistake, that the room has already been cleared. It is sparsely furnished with a simple bed, teak desk, and low chest of drawers. There are no personal belongings, just a fan perched on the desk, alongside a book titled, *Plants of the Pacific*.

Closing the door behind me, I move to the chest of drawers. I slide out the top drawer and find a well-thumbed historical novel, along with a biro and spiral-bound notepad, which is empty of writing. The drawer below houses a meagre set of folded clothes: three tired T-shirts, a loose shirt torn at the cuff, underwear, socks. To the side of the chest of drawers, a pair of work boots wait.

I move to the bedside table and open the small cupboard beneath it: mosquito repellent, paracetamol, sunglasses, tissues.

I glance around the room, amazed by the sparsity. There's no radio, television, or mobile phone. No alcohol. Not a single photo or personal item. Two years in this room?

I crouch to look beneath the bed. There's a rucksack, which I pull out by the straps. At first, the rucksack seems empty, but as I push my hand right into it, I feel something hard, metallic. I grasp it, pulling it out.

I'm holding an old-fashioned tea tin, a rusted picture of a plant on the front. I shake it once, hear the light rustle of paper inside, and something heavier that rattles. I tussle with the lid, yanking hard to free it.

The first thing I see is a smart gold pin badge reading: *Captain Mike Brass*. It would have once been pinned to a uniform or pilot's cap. He has kept this – a symbol or totem of a past that's disappeared. There's a wallet-sized photo too, worn at the edges, the colours faded. It's a family snapshot showing a much younger Mike standing with his wife and two children. They're in a garden somewhere, standing by a fence, all four of them smiling. It's a simple moment, and I'm learning that when the world pulls away, cracks open, it's a moment like this one – captured in the photo – that you would give anything to come home to. The centre point of it all. Family.

Beyond the room, I catch the sound of voices, and my ears prick up. I raise myself from the floor and look through the window.

The manager is striding across the lawns, arms swinging at his sides. Someone follows just behind his shoulder, who I cannot fully see. The manager raises a hand, pointing in the direction of this cabin. His face looks altered, brow furrowed, something determined in the set of his mouth.

Then, as the second person emerges, I suddenly see why the manager is hurrying in my direction.

It's Nathan Brass.

I've got moments until they're upon me.

I return the photo and badge to the tin – discovering that there is one more item inside. It's a creased tourist leaflet advertising feast nights, hula dancing, and Fiji's biggest water-park. I'm about to push it back into the tin, too, when I notice a faint mark in the corner. In smudged biro, there's a single question mark hand-drawn on the page.

I unfold the leaflet and, in the middle, discover a printed map of the Fijian archipelago. Nadi airport and the resort Lori was due to fly to on the island of Limanji are both ringed. A dotted line runs between the two. The planned flight path?

I can feel the vibration of footsteps hitting the wooden steps that lead to the cabin.

There's a second line diverting from the path – one that never reaches Limanji, but instead ends in a remote section of the map. There, a tiny fleck has been circled three times. And within it, is the question mark, which seems to be asking, *Here?*

The footsteps have reached the door and I look up to see the handle turning.

I stuff the map into the back pocket of my shorts. Then

return the tin to the backpack and slide it with a foot beneath the bed.

The manager fills the doorway, face puce. He holds the flat of his hand towards me. 'Whatever you're touching – stop!'

I raise my hands slowly into the air.

'I'm so sorry,' he says to Nathan Brass. 'This woman claimed to be a family friend. I had no idea you hadn't given your permission.'

I face Nathan, his eyes stony as they bore into me.

But even as he stares me down, adrenalin is gunning through my body as I realise what I've stuffed into my back pocket . . .

A map – marking the island.

# 39

# THEN | LORI

Mike gripped the knife handle in a closed fist. He kneeled at the foot of the tree, his pilot's cap lopsided and a tangle of white, greasy hair sprouting from beneath it. His arm trembled as he dragged the knife tip down the trunk, scoring it with another slash.

Across the camp, Lori counted the tally.

Day thirty.

A month they'd been here.

An entire month.

She turned away, crossed the leafy earth towards Sonny. He was napping in the bassinet, and she crouched down, watching him through the gauze of the mosquito net. He liked to sleep with his arms thrown back, fingers curled into fists. A mosquito was poised on the outside of the netting, waiting, and she pinched it between her fingertips, blood smearing from its crushed body. She flicked it to the ground, wiping the blood against her already-stained shorts.

She was seized by a head rush as she stood, the trees spinning and tilting as she tried to focus. She was suffering with dizziness more often as her hunger soared. Like everyone else, weight had dropped off her, leaving her hip bones sharp, her stomach no longer pleasantly doughy, but taut. It seemed ludicrous to have wasted so much of her life on wanting to be skinny, on thinking it was a goal, a mark of glory. Now the prominent sight of her collarbones and the lean stretch of her arms scared her.

'Anyone want coconut?' Felix asked, who was squatted low to the ground, shredding the husk and tossing the fibres into the embers of last night's fire. His dark T-shirt strained across his back, revealing each ridge of his spine, the sharp blades of his shoulders. He was managing to bring back fish every day or two, but she suspected the hours he spent in the water were expending more calories than he was able to replace.

'Please,' Lori said. Her stomach felt permanently hollow, a sensation she was growing used to, but what she found harder was the way her energy and focus dissipated within moments of beginning a task. 'Can you pour the milk into Sonny's bottle for later?'

'Course.'

The tin of formula was almost empty. She'd been supplementing it for some time with coconut milk, and had begun introducing solids, too – mashed banana or mango, with flakes of fish on the days Felix had success.

'I need that,' Daniel said to Mike, indicating the knife.

Mike, who'd finished carving the trunk, turned and looked hard at Daniel. 'What do you say?'

Daniel placed his palms together. '*Please*, Captain Crash, may I have the knife?'

Lori watched as Mike stepped forward and held out the knife, blade first.

As Daniel reached out, Mike unlocked his grip from the handle, allowing Daniel to take it.

'Arsehole,' Daniel muttered beneath his breath. Then he slumped down onto a tree trunk, rounding forward to inspect the heel of his foot; Lori saw the balding patch at the crown of his head. He used the tip of the knife to try and cut out a thorn. It'd embedded there days ago, and now the red, inflamed skin had spread, the entire heel print teeming with infection.

Daniel's mouth twisted, teeth gritted, as he pushed the metal tip deeper into the wound. He snarled with pain, then tipped back his head, screaming, 'You fucker!' He stabbed the knife into the log and stood.

'Easy with the knife,' Felix said. 'We don't want to blunt it.'

'Not going to blunt it from gutting too many fish,' Daniel shot back.

A knot of tension moved in Felix's jaw as he said, '*You* wanna get out there?'

Felix was the only one of them who regularly went into the sea. They'd discussed whether anyone else wanted to try spearfishing, but none of them was a strong enough swimmer. To reach the big fish – the eaters – Felix had to swim half a kilometre each day, out beyond the shallow atoll to where the ledge dropped off and there was a deep channel. Lori knew that reef sharks prowled there, cruising through the dark channels. They didn't pose a real threat, Felix had assured her, but she'd overheard him and Mike discussing a sighting of a tiger shark spotted through the binoculars on lookout.

'I'll give it a miss,' Daniel smirked. 'The Bear Grylls role suits you better.'

Felix stared hard at Daniel, his shoulders pulled back.

She could feel Mike watching the interaction with interest.

The tension between all three men was right there, every moment, simmering just beneath the surface. One wrong move, or comment, or look, and it would boil over.

'Anyone found more banana trees? We're almost out,' she said, in an attempt to defuse the tension. 'Sonny needs to eat more.'

*Sonny.* He was the reminder to all of them to keep their heads together.

Felix lowered his gaze from Daniel and stepped away. He moved to the fire, continuing to rip fistfuls of fibres from the coconut shell, tossing them into the embers. His brow creased as he reached for something at the edges of the ashes. 'Where did this come from?'

'What is it?' Mike asked, who was pushing a bottle of water into his bag, ready for the walk to the ridge.

Felix peered at it. 'A Snickers wrapper.' His head snapped up. 'Who the hell has been eating Snickers?'

Lori's face flushed with an instant, fierce heat.

'Daniel?' Felix asked, on his feet now. 'This yours?'

A bark of laughter. 'Why are you asking me?'

'You didn't say anything.'

'Neither did Lori.'

She could feel the heat burning in her cheeks now. She studied her hands, which were filthy, the pink nail polish long since chipped away, and when she looked up, she found all three men staring at her. 'I'm really sorry . . . I had some of it last night.'

'We shared it, okay?' Daniel weighed in. 'I found the bar in my luggage and halved it with Lori. We were going to give it to everyone, but you were asleep by then, so . . .'

Last night it felt like a small thing – a few illicit bites of a chocolate bar – but now in the harsh morning glare, with

Felix studying her, it felt like a betrayal. Particularly after all the energy he committed to spearfishing, diligently sharing everything he caught.

'We ration all our food,' Felix said, looking at her. 'We split everything four ways. That was the agreement right from the beginning.'

'I'm sorry,' she said.

'One less mango for us tonight, Lori,' Daniel said, his tone insouciant.

She saw Felix's lip curling, fingers clenching into fists.

*Keep it together*, she silently pleaded.

He was just about to drop the wrapper, when his gaze narrowed, reading something. Then he looked up, directly at Daniel. His voice was lethal: '*Multipack. Do not sell separately*,' he read. 'You sure it was just the one bar you found?'

She saw the flicker of amusement pass over Daniel's face. Of course he hadn't chosen to share his only bar with her!

'Ate the others on the first leg of the flight,' he said, not even bothering to sound convincing.

Felix scrunched up the wrapper, letting it drop at Daniel's feet. 'Next time you might want to do a better job of getting rid of the evidence.'

It would have been so easy to destroy the wrapper, to throw it right into the flames. To have put it at the edge of the camp fire so that the flames didn't even lick it seemed careless.

More than careless.

Daniel had *wanted* Felix or Mike to find it, she realised. She could sense he was poking at something, wanting something to come unstuck, watching it unravel. She remembered the feeling of being watched at the stream when she was with Felix, eyes trailing her body. Daniel? She sensed that sharing the Snickers bar was some sort of private game, about forging an alliance, or weakening one with Felix.

'I should never have accepted it,' she said, furious with herself.

'Don't be like that, Lori. You were happily eating out of my hand last night, licking the chocolate clean off my fingers.'

'That is not true!'

Daniel grinned, something fibrous stuck between his top teeth. 'Relax. We ate a bar of chocolate. It's not the end of the fucking world.'

'It's the principle,' Felix hissed. 'We share everything.'

Daniel turned then. 'Everything?'

'Everything,' Felix repeated.

'I don't know, it seems like you're getting more than your fair share of some things,' he said, eyes sliding towards Lori.

She felt something cold move through her stomach.

She saw the knife just beyond Daniel, its silver blade stabbed into the log. She imagined the cool touch of the blade, the firm grip of her fingers curling around the handle. With just a single movement, she could snatch that knife and push it deep into someone's throat. A pulse of energy fizzed beneath her skin.

Felix took a step closer. 'We've heard Lori apologise. I'd like to hear it from you.'

Daniel stood. 'You want me to apologise for eating two mouthfuls of chocolate?' The two of them were nose to nose, the heat of the jungle pressing close.

'That's what I want.'

She was still acutely aware of the position of the knife. It was in reaching distance of any of them.

'First a *please and thank you* lesson from the captain, and now you, too? Didn't realise I was at finishing school.' There was something untethered about Daniel, the rapid blink of his eyes, the twitchy jump of his fingers. 'If I don't apologise, what then? Do I get detention?' He laughed, spittle flying from his lips.

Lori glanced to Mike, imploring him to do something – but he was standing back, eyes bright.

'Know what?' Daniel continued. 'Out here on this island, you might think you're something special with your spear gun. But back home, back in our real lives, you know who you are, don't you? You're the bloke who serves me my meal in a restaurant, or the one behind the till in a petrol station when I fill up my BMW, or the guy who cleans my suits. You are that guy.'

Felix's gaze narrowed. Lori watched the muscles in his arms tightening beneath his skin. He'd become strong and lithe – an animal poised to fight.

When Felix spoke, his voice was slow, lethal. 'You have no idea what guy I am.' His eyes flicked briefly but deliberately towards the knife. 'I don't think you want to find out.'

The shrill caw of a bird sounded in the canopy above.

Daniel took a step towards the knife. Lori thought he was reaching for it – but instead, he raised both hands in surrender. '*Sorry*,' he said in an odd, singsong voice. He dropped his hands. 'There. That's my apology. Toss me a few fish heads now, eh?'

A vein at Felix's temple pulsed. In a flash of movement, he seized the dive knife, grabbed his spear gun and mask, then disappeared from camp. They all listened to the crash of branches as he made for the beach.

After a few moments, she turned to find Mike pulling on his backpack, then hooking the binoculars around his neck. 'You're going, too?'

Mike nodded. 'Lookout.'

She wanted to say, *Don't leave me with Daniel*, but that would put a voice to something she wasn't ready to admit.

Daniel limped through camp, muttering to himself. He kicked over a stack of coconut shells, cursing at a fresh shock of pain in his foot. 'Fuck!'

She rolled her eyes.

Catching her, Daniel rounded on Lori. 'What's your problem?'

'Don't make us your enemies, Daniel.'

'You'd rather be friends?' he leered, insinuation dripping from his tone.

She thought of everything she could say – that he disgusted her; that she'd rather be on the island with anyone but him; that he was weak and self-serving – but she was too exhausted for a battle with someone who courted them. Instead, she chose a question: 'Could you watch Sonny for me for half an hour?'

The magic bullet.

He responded exactly as she'd guessed. His eyes lowered as he said, 'I've got to get the wood.' Then she watched as he limped away into the jungle.

It was only when all three men had gone that Lori felt the tension unlocking in her shoulders. She moved to the bassinet, carefully lifting out Sonny. His body was warm and supple as she held him to her, burying her nose in the soft pelt of his hair. Tears stung the corners of her eyes as she rocked him in her arms. 'You and me,' she whispered.

40

# NOW | ERIN

My heart pounds hard in my chest as I face Nathan. I'm acutely aware of the press of the map in my pocket.

'I'm calling security,' the resort manager says, taking out his phone.

Nathan turns towards him. 'Thank you, but that won't be necessary. We do know each other.'

'But you said you hadn't arranged for anyone to clear out your father's things?'

'A miscommunication,' Nathan says, causing the manager's eyebrows to rise. 'Thank you for your help, but if it's all right, we'd like to clear out his stuff alone.'

The manager looks between us, then pushes his glasses up the bridge of his nose. 'Very well, then.'

As soon as the manager leaves, Nathan moves into the room, shutting the door behind him.

He says nothing, just stares at me.

I feel something in the air shift. An electric charge, as if all the air is being squeezed out, something bigger filling the space. I'm not sure if I'm scared – or something else.

He steps forward and my muscles involuntarily tighten, but he only passes me, as he looks around the room.

I hear the slow trudge of his boots across the wooden floor, then a deep sigh. 'I needed to see it,' he says, 'this life he's been leading. And here it is. A cabin on a hilltop. He chose this.'

'I'm sorry,' I say. And I am. For all of this. For coming here. For what Nathan and his mother have suffered. For what I've suffered. For what the passengers, the other relatives, all of us, have suffered.

'Why are you here, Erin? You've talked your way into this room and are rooting through my father's things. What is it you're looking for?'

'What I've always been looking for,' I say simply. 'Answers.'

'For your story?'

I raise my chin, look him straight in the eye. 'For me.' I hold his gaze as I say, 'I quit my job yesterday.'

'Why?'

'It didn't feel right. My heart wasn't in it.'

He surprises me by saying, 'I could see that.' Then further still by adding, 'I'm sorry about the way I spoke to you at the hospice.'

'Don't be. You'd just lost your dad, Nathan. I just stormed into the hospice. And . . . God . . . I'm sorry for what you overheard on the phone. Honestly, I was never going to write that story. I was never going to write about you.'

He shrugs.

We both fall into silence for some time. Then, eyes lightly skirting the room, he says, 'Find anything useful?'

I feel the crinkle of the map as I shift my weight, thinking of the question mark poised on that tiny island. I understand why Mike has kept this map, just like he kept the photo and captain badge: they are mementoes to remind him it was real. His family, his job, the island. Pieces of the man he used to be, carefully kept, hidden away.

Nathan is watching me, waiting for my answer. I've come too far on my own to share it with someone else now. 'Nothing,' I say.

He looks at me intently, as if he's waiting for something more.

I lower my gaze, telling him, 'I should go.'

I pass him and, as I reach the doorway, Nathan says, 'I don't know if this will help . . . if it will mean anything, but my dad said something before he . . . died.' He looks up, face uncertain. 'He was mostly drifting in and out of consciousness . . . he was confused, saying odd things. But he mentioned that there was a ridge top on the island. Said something about binoculars.'

My ears are pricked, senses alert.

Nathan goes on. 'He said your sister's name – and that he was sorry.' Nathan shifts. Glances at me, then away again. 'He said, "*It wasn't an accident*."'

The hairs on the back of my neck stand on end. 'What wasn't an accident?'

'I don't know. Sorry. I couldn't make sense of it. He just kept saying, *It wasn't an accident*. It may be nothing. It is probably nothing.'

'Do you think it's nothing?'

Nathan looks at me, as if deciding something. Eventually he shakes his head. 'His face, Erin, he looked . . . I don't know how to describe it.' He thinks for a moment and then says, 'He looked haunted.'

A shiver ripples down my spine, the spidery run of it leaving me with goosebumps.

My fingers slide involuntarily to the map in my pocket, testing the crackle of paper through denim. I glance at Nathan, wondering if I should tell him. Our eyes lock, and I feel it again – that pulse of a connection, the air charged.

Do I trust him enough to share what I've found?

His brow dips, a question in it.

I feel myself hesitating. My fingers slide away from my pocket, falling free at my side.

I've come this far alone, I decide, breaking eye contact. It's the only way I know how to be.

# 41

# THEN | LORI

Lori dusted an arc through the warm sand with her fingertips. Even in the shade, the midday heat was fierce. Beside her, Sonny lay on a blanket, kicking happily as he gazed up at the changing shadows spliced with light from the palm fronds above. Contented gurgles merged with the clicks and chirrups of the jungle.

'You're a wonderful little being,' she said, and his eyes brightened at the sound of her voice, seeking her out. She dipped her face closer, rubbing her nose against his.

He gurgled in response. That sound. It was golden. In all of this, it was the one thing.

She dipped her face again, nose to nose, his light breath against her face.

Behind them, she heard footsteps, and glanced over her shoulder to see Felix coming through the clearing.

He went first to Sonny, squatting low to tickle his tummy

in a way that always made Sonny chuckle, bunching up his knees in delight. 'How are you doing, buddy?'

Sonny cooed in response.

'Two little gnashers now,' Felix said, spotting Sonny's two bottom teeth.

'He seems older with them,' Lori said. 'Less like a newborn, somehow.'

Felix sat beside Lori and they both watched as Sonny tried reaching for a shell at the edge of the blanket. 'He's doing okay, isn't he?' Lori said.

'He's doing great.'

A surge of gratitude filled her chest: for Sonny, for Felix, for this simple moment when they were safe, together.

She turned to Felix to try and communicate something of it, but his gaze was set on the horizon, clouded, preoccupied. His arms, deeply tanned now, were hooked over his knees, back rounded. With his thumb, he absently traced the black tattoo of the mountains inked on the inside of his wrist. Feeling her gaze on him, he turned, eyes meeting hers.

Heat spread through her. The strength of her desire was a surprise out here – but she welcomed it. She wanted to press herself to him, feel the contours of his body. She reached out, taking his hand, squeezing it. He looked down at their fingers, his expression remaining serious, distant.

'What is it, Felix?'

With his eyes still on the horizon, he said, 'I don't like how things are going.'

'Between us?' she said, straightening. 'If it's because of that Snickers thing, I'm so sorry—'

'No, it's not that. It's not you, Lori,' he said, turning back to her, his expression softening. 'Jesus, you and Sonny are everything. Everything good on this island.' There was a long pause.

She was already coming to learn that Felix needed time. He wasn't like Pete, who chatted freely and easily. Words came harder – and when they did, she listened closely.

'I don't like the atmosphere in camp, with Mike, with Daniel. Everything feels . . . I don't know . . . loose.' He shook his head. 'That sounds an odd word . . .'

'No, it's right.' She understood. The thin veneer of civilisation was already peeling back, exposing parts of themselves that scared her. She remembered the sour taste of Daniel's mouth pushed against hers. *Normal rules don't apply.* She'd not told Felix that Daniel had tried to kiss her – and knew she wouldn't.

'I know I'm in the water for a big part of each day, but Lori,' he said, his focus square on her, 'keep your distance from them, if you can.'

'You don't trust them?'

He looked at her. After a moment, she saw the shake of his head.

There'd been a sense of agitation shimmering from him all day, something unsettled that she couldn't place. 'The people we are out here . . . we're different. All of us.'

She blinked. 'What does that mean?'

He looked past her, back towards the horizon.

She waited at his side, the heat of the jungle enclosing them together.

'Lori, you don't know me. Not really. Not who I was before this.'

'I know you're someone who strings shells to wood to make a baby happy.'

His gaze flicked to Sonny, his expression softening again for a beat. When he returned his focus to her, there was an intensity in his eyes. 'Have you ever done anything – acted a certain way – where you don't even recognise yourself? It's like you're watching some other person, and . . . and it's not you, because you didn't think it possible that *you* would behave that way?'

Slowly, Lori nodded. *Yes, yes, I know.*

There was a painful bleakness in his expression.

'Before I left for Fiji, I . . .' He hesitated, gaze lowering to his lap. 'I went to my dad's house. I wanted to collect this book that belonged to my mother. It was a volume of poetry that she loved – it had her annotations on most of the pages. That's all I wanted. One thing, to bring with me to Fiji. But Dad wasn't in. My stepmother answered the door.' A tendon in his neck tightened. 'She told me she'd got rid of all my stuff. Everything. She'd warned me she'd do it – it'd been clogging up the spare room for months, or something. But I never thought . . . never thought she'd actually go through with it. Or that my dad would let her.'

Felix drew his knees closer to his chest as he said, 'It's hard to explain . . . the history.' His face was wracked with hurt. 'I told you my mum died when I was a teenager.'

She nodded. A car crash, he'd said.

'Mum had been following my dad – seen him driving to another woman's house. He'd been having an affair for months. Mum – she must've been gutted, not concentrating. She drove straight through a lane of traffic.'

'Oh, Felix.'

He continued, gaze set ahead. 'My dad, he didn't end the affair with the woman. He married her. Eleven months after my mum's death. Kiera Tyler. She even took our name. How fucked is that?'

She could feel the pain.

'That's who told me that all my stuff – my mother's stuff – had been dumped at a charity shop.' His eyes stretched wide as he said, 'I lost it. I fucking lost it.' Felix described how he'd crashed through the house, upturning everything. 'Kiera asked if my mother would be proud of the man I'd become.' He turned to her, his eyes filmed with pain. 'She wouldn't have been.'

She wanted to reach for him, but sensed it wasn't the right move.

'The next thing, my hand's around her throat. I'm not even thinking. I'm just pinning her there so she won't say another word.' His gaze held hers, like he wanted her to see – to know what he was capable of. 'I would've killed her. I think I would've killed her.' His voice was shaking. Tears welled over his lower lids. 'My dad arrived home, pulled me off. If he hadn't . . .' His gaze broke away.

His voice was lower when he spoke again. 'Dad called the police. Rang them right there. But I left – went straight to the airport. I kept thinking security would stop me, pull me up, say I couldn't travel any further. Except they didn't. No one stopped me. I just got on that flight to Fiji.'

'Felix . . .' she began, but he was shaking his head.

'You asked me a while back about the message in the boarding lounge. It was from my father. It said, *After what you did, I've got to make a choice. It's her, Felix. It's her. It's always been her.*'

His face crumpled, eyes screwing up, lips pulling back.

Now Lori reached for him, arms holding tight, bodies pressed together. She felt the shudder of his chest as he sucked in air.

When she and Felix returned to camp with Sonny, Daniel was perched on a tree trunk, sucking a fish bone clean. 'Been anywhere nice?' he asked.

'Leave it, Daniel,' she said, not in the mood for his jibes. Sonny had fallen asleep in her arms and she concentrated on settling him into the bassinet, tucking the mosquito net around him.

She watched as Felix gathered his mask, fins and weight belt. The water was where he needed to be right now.

'Anyone seen the dive knife?' Felix asked.

He strapped it to his ankle before every spearfish, using it to kill and gut the fish. As soon as he returned to camp, he placed it on the log where they prepared food so it could be used by everyone.

Daniel wiped the back of his hand across his mouth. 'Used it earlier to skin a mango. Should be in the normal place.'

'It's not.'

'Check the ground.'

'I have,' Felix said. 'It's not here. You definitely returned it?'

'Course.' He shrugged. 'Rinsed it, then put it back.' Daniel flung the fish bones into the embers, then limped across the camp to look. He still hadn't managed to get the thorn out of his heel, and now a throbbing red welt was oozing something yellow. As he glanced half-heartedly around camp, he said, 'Lori used the knife, didn't you?'

'Yes, earlier. Then I put it back on the log table.' Was that correct? Had she put it back? She'd been so tired recently, her concentration broken easily, hunger keeping her in a permanently fogged state.

'I can't spearfish without a dive knife.'

Daniel arched a brow. 'Isn't that what the spear gun is for?'

Felix's mouth tightened. 'The spear doesn't always kill the fish. Just pierces it. Can't swim back to shore with a fish thrashing on the end of the spear. Even if I did get it back, how do we gut it? A sharp shell? A stone? A piece of fucking plane wreckage?' He was glaring at Daniel, fingers tightening into fists.

'I'll help you search,' Lori said, her voice sounding faux-bright. She began checking the area where they prepared the food, scouring the earth beneath it, moving aside the empty coconut shells they used as bowls. Felix paced through camp, a line of tension furrowing his brow as he lifted blankets, cursing each time the knife failed to be revealed. Daniel took a branch from the woodpile and began sieving through the ashes of the fire.

After several minutes, the whole camp had been thoroughly searched – but there was no sign of the knife.

'Where the hell is it?' Felix muttered, gaze dark.

No one had an answer.

After a few moments he snatched up his spear gun and strode out of camp. She watched through the treeline, glimpsing him wading into the shallows, then disappearing beneath the surface.

'Bit uptight this morning, isn't he?' Daniel said. He was standing right at her shoulder, close enough that she could feel the heat of his body radiating against hers, could smell the stale stink of his breath.

When she didn't rise to the bait, he picked up a stick, tucked it under arm, and announced jovially, 'Off to the gents.'

When Daniel had hobbled from view, she gave a final glance around, checking the camp was still empty. Mike was on the ridge top, Felix in the water, Daniel in the woods. She had a few minutes at most.

She went straight to the hold of the plane, removing Daniel's case and setting it on the ground. She crouched to unzip the expensive leather, catching the smell of aftershave cut through with something damp and unwashed. Pushing her hand inside, she found his wallet, thick with notes and two gold credit cards.

The heat was stifling, the trees crowding in close as she searched. From somewhere above came the shrill, urgent chatter of a bird. Her heart kicked against her ribs as she made herself continue the search, pushing aside mud-flecked polo shirts and a pair of shiny leather brogues she hadn't seen him wear. At the bottom she found his mobile, battery dead, and plush headphones in a circular case. Then she pulled out something delicate, wrapped in tissue paper. Peeling back the edge of the paper, she saw the lacy slip of a thong, the delicate strap of a bra.

'Don't think it's your size.'

She jumped, head snapping up.

Daniel was ahead of her, watching. His right hand was hanging loose at his side, his left was concealed behind his back.

If he had taken the dive knife, she realised with a bolt of alarm, he wouldn't have stashed it in his bag. He would have hidden it somewhere beyond camp.

'You're welcome to try it on. But . . .' he said, eyes trailing to her chest, 'I think you have bigger breasts than my wife.'

She dropped the underwear into the bag and stood.

'Looking for the knife, weren't you?'

Lori was so used to trying to please people. To be sunny and likeable, pretty and polite. But where had that got her? What she needed was grit. Determination. Fire. She raised her chin. 'Where the fuck is it?'

He looked faintly amused. 'What would I want with the knife? Have you thought about that?'

Whoever had the knife held an advantage over the others. It gave them power.

When she said nothing, Daniel said, 'If I had taken it, d'you think I'd just leave it idly around camp? I'd have it on me, surely.' He wiggled his eyebrows unnervingly. 'Right now.'

He stepped closer, and she felt the spread of ice through her veins.

He was still holding one arm behind his back – and suddenly he pulled it in front of him, raising both arms, making her jump. 'Go on then,' he grinned. 'Give me the pat-down.'

An anger flared deep at her core. It felt muscular and strong, so much better than fear. 'I'm the only woman on this island and perhaps you think that makes me vulnerable. An easy target for your careless sexism, or whatever the fuck it is you think you're doing,' she spat. 'But you've got no idea who I am, Daniel.' She drew herself up, eyes fixed on his. 'I suggest you don't push me.'

The smile was gone, replaced by a sneer. 'And I suggest,' he said, coming closer, baring his teeth, 'that you don't go through my fucking bag again.'

They glared at one another for a moment, the trees crowded tight around them, the air thick with heat. Then he turned and limped away.

Just as she released the breath she'd been holding, Daniel swung back to face her. 'You know who you haven't accused, don't you? The person who flew that plane,' he said pointing to the wreckage. 'The person who's already got the blood of four dead passengers on his hands. The person you were quick to help ditch the bodies for. So, before you cast your vicious little aspersions at *me*, how about you ask *him* about this missing knife? I sure as hell plan to.'

# 42

# NOW | ERIN

The sun's not yet up, but I'm standing in a fishing port, watching a man slopping fuel from a jerry can into an idling boat engine. A younger man in a vest lifts a spanner and bashes it against some hidden, misbehaving metal part. The clunk rings out across the morning.

Any moment now, I'm meant to be climbing into that wooden boat and heading out to an island that Mike Brass ringed on a tourist map. While I wait, I comfort-eat two muffins pilfered from yesterday's hotel buffet, which taste stale and over-sugared. I wash them down with a bottle of sun-warmed water.

I arrived here yesterday – an island called Rannatua – and found my way to this fishing port. This is true South Pacific island life, where the main port is little more than a bay with a handful of wooden boats pulled up on the shore. I spent an hour trying to convince a local named Rega, and his younger brother, to charter their fishing boat to an unnamed island I was pointing to on a map. It took much discussion with various locals, and most of the American dollars I'd brought with me, before we made an agreement. I told them – and anyone in earshot – that I'm a location scout for an educational programme.

Apparently it was too late in the day to set out, so I spent the night in Rega's sister's guesthouse, sleeping in a room with no fan and no mosquito net – and no sign of other guests.

I slip my mobile from my pocket. The battery is already low, so I dig out my power bank and let it charge, while I open Google Earth. The island is already there, waiting on my screen from my last search. I stare at this fleck of land on the most southeasterly edge of the Fijian archipelago. It is little more than a green thumbprint stranded amidst a wide expanse of seething blue ocean.

I zoom in closer until the island begins to reveal a dense canopy of trees and rock. A hem of white sand gives way to shallow turquoise waters. Beyond that, the island is surrounded by a ring of dark reef, fringed with white water cast from breaking waves. The island is unnamed, unmarked – and lies miles and miles from anything but ocean.

'Ready!' Rega shouts from the water, where he's standing waist deep, holding the nose of the boat steady, and beckoning me over.

I kick off my flip-flops and wade into the warm water. Rega takes my backpack from me as if it weighs nothing, and deposits it in the boat. I haul myself over the side with an absence of grace or dignity, and settle myself at the stern on a green wooden bench where the paint peels like scales. I'm trying to ignore the racing beat of my heart. This is fine. It's all good.

## The Castaways

The engine smokes as we turn from the shore and head out across the sheltered bay. I steal a look at the disappearing buildings, wishing I were inside one of them. Don't get me wrong, I love the sea – but I love it a whole lot more when I'm looking at it from the beach.

Once we round a headland, the wind picks up and the rise and crest of waves makes the boat lurch and drop.

I'm already regretting the muffins.

*Concentrate on the horizon.* Lori's voice is a small, welcome surprise, and I follow the instruction, focusing on the wavering line of the horizon. A warm, salt breeze washes against my face, easing the sickly churn in my stomach.

*You should be wearing a life jacket,* she adds.

She's always been bossy. But also, mostly right.

When I'm confident I can speak without vomiting, I put in my request for a life jacket. Both men laugh at me kindly and shake their heads.

I peer over the side at the broiling water, and tighten my grip on the bench seat.

As we motor, they trawl a fishing line from the back of the boat, reeling it in a couple of times to pull up huge clumps of weed and, later, an iridescent blue fish that Rega guts on deck, tossing the glistening entrails overboard. I watch the bloodied fibres drift away and my mind trips to prowling sharks, the depth of the ocean beneath us.

*Is this a mistake, Lori?* I silently ask. *Should I have gone straight to the police with Mike Brass's map?*

*Why didn't you?*

*I need to see it for myself. You know that feeling when you read a good book, and you're totally transported to the world within those pages? Your imagination has travelled there – and yet your body is not fooled: it knows you haven't left the sofa. Well, that's how these past two years have felt – like I'm researching all this stuff, but haven't actually left the sofa. It doesn't matter what anyone else tells me, Lori. I never saw you board that plane. I never saw the plane wreck. I never saw your . . . your body. I need those things. I need an ending.*

Several hours later, and still at sea, I am gripping the side of the boat, knuckles white, while the engine idles and waves smash into us, lifting me off the bench and slamming me back down.

Rega and his brother are looking closely at a map on one of their phones. They nod vigorously at one another, then turn to me and ask, 'This is the island?'

They point ahead towards a speck of land to our east. Clouds cluster above it; it looks impossibly isolated. The white beaches are startlingly bright, backed by a dense wash of trees.

I've no idea if Rega and his brother are right – whether this does match the island on Mike Brass's map, or even if he had circled the correct location – but this is my best chance. So I say, 'Looks like the one.'

The island, at first glance, appears flat, but then I see a gap in the trees at the eastern edge and the rise of land. Mike Brass – in his drug-addled, final hours – talked to Nathan about the island, about Lori. He mentioned a ridge top, binoculars, an accident. *I'm sorry*, he'd said.

From out here on the water, it's hard to gain a true sense of perspective, but looking at the island, I can make out a stretch of slate-grey rock climbing above the tree canopy. Could this be the ridge top Nathan mentioned?

I study it for a few more moments, my stomach pitching and falling with the waves. I imagine Mike Brass standing there, binoculars around his neck. Something happened up there and I need to find out what.

## 43

# THEN | LORI

Lori stood at the foot of the ridge, catching her breath. It stretched like a muscular arm of rock rising through the tree canopy, a giant fist of stony knuckles pumped into the air. She'd only made the ascent once before, the going too challenging to make regularly with Sonny strapped to her chest.

Ahead, Daniel was still just in her sights. He limped and scrambled his way through thick ferns strung with spider webs, using a branch as a walking stick. Sweat glistened on the back of his neck. She could hear the ragged draw of his breath, the scrape of feet through earth and tree roots.

She glanced down at Sonny, his cheek pressed against her chest, mouth slack in complete rest. She breathed him in, the almond-shaped eyelids, the wing of lashes, the perfect arch of his nostrils. Then she made herself push forward, following Daniel.

The shadows of the canopy thinned as they climbed higher than the treeline, following the narrow, barely worn path towards the ridge top. 'Daniel,' she said, catching up with him and reaching his elbow.

He swung around, mouth open, breathing hard. His face looked white and pinched.

'Mike might not have taken the dive knife. You know that, don't you? Don't just barrel up there and accuse him.' She'd seen the edge between the two men, growing sharper and more lethal with each day.

He glared at her. 'But it's okay to accuse me?' He held her stare for a long moment, then turned and shouldered his way through the fingering branches of a low-hanging tree. The branches parted briefly, before swinging back to close her out.

She wanted to turn back. She was light-headed with hunger and, more than anything, she wanted to sit in the shade with Sonny, and watch his face light up as she handed him the sweet, juicy flesh of a mango. But she couldn't. She'd seen the look in Daniel's eye – something loose, dangerous – and couldn't leave Mike alone on the ridge top with him. If one of them did have the knife . . .

Lori propelled herself upwards, calves burning, shoulders knotted with tension.

Reaching the top, she felt the welcome breeze against her face. It was a relief to escape the suffocating humidity of the jungle. There was something about being in the belly of it, the insects, the trees, the hiss and hum of it all.

The ridge top was the highest point on the island, offering a panoramic view of the ocean surrounding them. She glanced around, searching for Mike. The boulder where he usually sat was vacant. Then Daniel began moving towards the north of the ridge, gaze on the ground. He stopped.

Mike was lying on his back, hands resting on his chest, one ankle crossed over the other. His greying captain's hat was shielding his face from the sun.

Daniel's shadow fell over Mike. He lifted one foot, toe to the peak of Mike's hat, and flicked it clean off, so it skittered between two rocks, lodging there.

Mike scrabbled to his knees, hands protecting his face, shoulders hunched. He looked from Daniel to Lori, his brow furrowed with confusion, as if he couldn't place them.

'Great lookout you are,' Daniel spat.

She felt a flash of disappointment, too. He had a responsibility to them all to take his role seriously.

'What are you doing up here?' Mike asked, as he staggered to his feet, hands touching the crown of his head, as if searching for the cap. He had aged in the last weeks, a white beard now covering his jaw, deep pouches beneath his eyes.

'The dive knife is missing from camp,' Daniel said.

'I don't have it, if that's why you're here.'

'Answered that quickly,' Daniel said, one eyebrow cocked.

'We just wanted to ask if you'd seen it,' Lori intervened. 'Whether you'd used it this morning?'

He looked straight at her. 'I don't have it.'

'Want to look in Mike's bag?' Daniel asked Lori.

'If he says he hasn't got it, he hasn't got it,' she said firmly. She trusted Mike.

'And if I say I haven't got it?'

Lori moved apart from them both, setting herself near the edge of the ridge, but keeping a safe distance from the drop. She planted her feet wide, one arm cupped around Sonny, and peered out. With the extra height, the coral reef was open to her, and she studied the undulating shades of blue. Out on the ledge, where the shallow water dropped away into a darkened, deep channel, she could see Felix's silhouette.

Daniel limped to her side, a pair of binoculars around his neck. The breeze carried the sour tang of his sweat. He scanned the bay, remarking, 'Long way out, isn't he? Just drifting around like a piece of flotsam.'

Lori said nothing.

'Be nice to see him actually swimming, trying to at least catch something.'

'You don't swim after the fish. You find a position. You watch. You wait.'

'Spearfishing expert now, are you?'

She didn't bother replying, so Daniel turned his attention to Mike. 'What do you do all day up here, Captain?'

'You know what. Keep a lookout.'

'Didn't seem like it when we arrived.'

'I took a break,' he said, no apology in his tone.

Still with the binoculars raised, Daniel asked, 'How many boats have you seen go by?'

'None.'

'How about planes?'

'None.'

'Helicopters?'

'None.'

He lowered the binoculars and turned to face Mike. 'Strikes me as odd. We've been here, what, a month now? Not a single boat passing anywhere in the distance?'

'We're in the middle of the ocean. This could be one of the last islands in the archipelago. There are no shipping lanes. No, it doesn't surprise me—'

'Unless you're just not telling us. Letting them cruise by. Keeping those flares safely in the backpack over there so that there's no chance of us leaving. Maybe you're not content with killing half the passengers.'

There was a beat of silence. A bird erupted from the canopy below, its wings caught in the sunlight. It soared into view – then dipped again below the edge of the ridge. Mike seized that moment to grab the strap of the binoculars with a single fist, pulling it tight around Daniel's neck, like a choke chain, forcing him back a step, towards Lori, towards the edge.

Lori let out a cry of surprise, shocked by the flash of anger in Mike's expression. Daniel's heels were right on the edge of the ridge, eyes swivelling. His hands flailed to his throat, trying to prise the binocular strap free, but Mike's clasp was fierce, locked down.

Mike's lips barely moved as he said, 'Four people are dead because of my actions, my decisions. Four people who I reckon are far more deserving to be here than you, Daniel. Yet here you are. Here I am. Still standing.'

Daniel's fingertips reached towards his neck, trying to claw at the strap, but there was no purchase.

'Why you, eh? Why do you deserve to survive?'

Lori didn't move. She was aware she wanted to step away from the ridge edge, from these men, but she was frozen, as if any single movement or word could upset a balance that was finite enough to tip.

'Tell me . . .' Mike sounded genuinely curious. 'Why do *you* deserve to live?'

Daniel made a small choking sound, his face livid red. 'Wife.'

'Wife?' Mike repeated. 'You've got a wife. So that's why you should live? I've got a wife, but you know what? We don't talk any more. We don't sleep in the same room. We are strangers who live in the same house. That's what I've got. Does your wife love you?'

Daniel made the smallest of nods.

'Then she's an idiot.' Through his teeth, he whispered, 'What were you really doing heading out to Limaji, eh?'

Daniel gave a small shake of his head.

'Answer me.'

'Business trip,' he gasped.

'A development opportunity, you said.' He paused. 'That the truth?'

Daniel made a small squeak that sound like a 'yes.'

Mike shook his head, disappointed. 'Shame I know the owners. Their resort is the only one allowed on the island. They battled for six years before they got permission to build a dozen holiday bures. There's no way they can expand it.' He inched his face closer to Daniel's. 'So, I'll ask you again. Why were you going out to the island?'

Daniel's face was turning a deepening red.

She'd never seen Mike like this – eyes bright with anger. 'Mike, please—' she began, stepping towards him.

Suddenly Daniel's hand flew out, catching her by the wrist and yanking her to his side.

She screamed at the burst of pain in her wrist.

Startled from sleep, Sonny began to cry.

'It's okay,' she whispered, but her voice was thin with fear.

Mike's gaze flicked from Daniel to Lori, unsure. Beads of sweat clung to his brow.

A breeze twisted over the ridge, whispering of the drop below as it snaked around her bare ankles. One false move. That's all it would take.

'Let go,' she begged of either man.

Nobody moved.

*Not like this. This is not how it ends. Not with Sonny. Please, not Sonny . . .*

A roar of vertigo crashed into Lori. Her knees buckled, head spinning. The ground seemed to sway and tilt, looming away from her. Daniel yanked her harder to him, his breath ragged. As her vision swung, she felt the edge of the ridge only inches away, and beyond, nothing but a graveyard of jagged rocks.

# 44

# NOW | ERIN

*Is this the island, Lori? Have I come to the right place?*

Rega is leaning over the side of the boat, T-shirt darkened with sweat, as he points out shallow patches of coral. At the wheel, his brother navigates with caution, a deep band of concentration creasing his brow. I remain silent, understanding that coming aground somewhere as remote as this would be disastrous.

I glance at my phone again. No reception.

Rega cuts the engine and he and his brother haul two wooden oars from the floor of the boat and use them to pole their way through the shallowest sections. It is slow going and the heat is fierce, but eventually the boat makes it to shore.

I ask the men whether they've ever seen this island before, but they both shake their heads and Rega tells me, 'So many islands.'

He jumps out into the shallows, guiding the nose of the boat into shore. Then he holds out a hand, indicating I should come.

A cold dread keeps me gripped to the seat. I don't want to get out. I don't want to set foot on the island. What if it's the wrong one? What if I've come all this way and it's the wrong fucking island? Or, what if it's not? What if I find something that I don't want to see?

'Come!' Rega barks, impatient, as the boat rocks in the shallows.

My legs feel weak and uncertain as I clamber towards the side of the boat. I pass him my backpack, then I jump into the shallows, sea water splashing up my legs, soaking my shorts. I stagger onto the beach and Rega returns my backpack. He and his brother exchange glances.

Heart pounding, I turn and face the island.

The jungle hunches tight, almost impenetrable. The shore is tide-marked with browning palm fronds, the husks of coconut shells and island debris. There are no footprints, no sign of a plane wreck, no indication that anyone has ever set foot on this island.

Rega looks at his watch. 'Four hours, yes? We must make it back to Rannatua before dark.'

I agree, because there is no alternative. If the journey was challenging by daylight, it would be impossible at night.

The brothers move into the treeline, settling themselves in the shade, pulling a bottle of something cloudy from a bag, most likely kava. I'm thinking: *Don't drink too much – I need you to get me out of here safely.*

Then another thought lands, swift and sharp: *Can I trust them?* The men are muscled, fit. They say something to one another, then glance in my direction, laugh. I'm not sure if it's my imagination, but it feels like they sense my uncertainty, that there's a subtle shift of power.

Not a single person knows where I am, I realise.

*Is this how you felt, trapped on an island with strangers?*

With a final glance at the men, I begin walking up the beach, heart drumming against my ribcage.

The heat is relentless, the soles of my feet scorched by the hot grit of sand and sharp edges of shells. I pause, shoving my flip-flops back on, feet cased with sand. I move on, headed toward the ridge. It doesn't take long to reach its base where boulders stagger out into the water. Shading the sun from my eyes, I peer towards the top. The climb appears to be through dense jungle, rocks and undergrowth.

Nathan's words return to me again. *It wasn't an accident.*

I begin the ascent, hauling myself over a snarl of rocks. I grab at ferns sprouting in the cracks of boulders to anchor myself. I'm no Duke of Edinburgh medal holder, and it shows. I'm breathless and panting as I move through a thick crowd of trees, wary of unknown insects that could be lingering here in the dimness. The air feels heavier, thick with the scents of plants. I push my way forwards, hands grappling against branches.

The climb is hard and, by the time I reach the top, I'm sweating and breathless.

Up here, there's a clearing, as if earth has settled on a pinnacle of rock from some ancient uprising. I shrug off the backpack and stand with my hands on my hips, taking in the views of the island. To the west, a mangrove forest stretches out into the shallows, making the beach impassable, but the rest of the island looks as if it could be ringed on foot.

I turn another circle, more slowly this time, but there's no sign of a plane wreck. No sign of anything except trees, sand, ocean, sky.

A tension headache is beginning to pulse behind my eyes and I pull down my sunglasses, running a hand over the back of my neck. I look around the ridge, desperate for a sign that I'm on the right island. A sun-scorched leaf wheels in the breeze; a fly hums in the shade of a rock. But there is nothing else. The wind and weather will have long since washed away any trace of a footprint.

Looking out across the canopy of the jungle, richly dense leaves could be concealing anything. A plane wreck? Bodies? I shudder.

Maybe this was a wild mistake. There are hundreds of uninhabited islands and islets in Fiji. How do I know this is the right one? I've spent the last of my savings getting out here – and I could be wrong. What if Mike's map was a red herring? What if these guys in the boat have got the wrong island?

There's a movement in the corner of my eye. Down on shore, Rega is walking towards the shoreline. He bends, pulling at the rope anchoring the boat. I watch for a moment, the cool breath of unease winding through me. *What if he left? What if he and his brother climbed in that boat, right now, and just motored off?*

I'd be stranded here.

Lost.

Despite the heat, I shiver.

I feel the sway and lilt of the earth beneath me, my body adjusting to being on land after hours spent on the water. I'm too close, I think, turning from the edge, pacing back to the middle of the ridge.

That's when I see it, something gold glinting beneath the nub of a rock.

I step closer, crouching low.

A gold band of rope threaded around material. My fingers reach for it and I manage to tug it free.

In my hand, I'm holding a once-white cap with a navy

peak. Insects scuttle out from beneath it. There's a gold embroidered logo of wings on one side of it. It's filthy and dirt-stained, torn at the back, but I recognise it immediately: a pilot's cap.

A kick of adrenalin hits between my ribs: it's the right island.

They were here.

Lori was here.

## 45

# THEN | LORI

Blood crashed in Lori's ears as she stood with her back to the edge of the ridge. Daniel still gripped her wrist: bone and flesh and blood compressed. Her free arm braced Sonny, who continued to scream.

Behind her, the edge of the ridge loomed. Nothing beyond except sheer space – air spilling downwards to rock and earth and oblivion.

*Not Sonny. Not Sonny. Not Sonny.* She repeated the words in her head, over and over. A mantra. A prayer. *Not him. He's just a baby.*

Mike gripped the binocular strap tight to Daniel's throat.

She could see it in Mike's eyes. He knew. If Daniel went over, Lori and Sonny went, too.

Sweat soaked her top, slid down the backs of her knees. Tears bit into the corners of her eyes. Fear was sheer-white, blinding.

She began to hum. Lips together, a lullaby moved through her throat as air, weak at first, stalled. She continued. The vibrations filled the roof of her mouth, building, strengthening into sound.

Into comfort.

Sonny paused from his crying, shining eyes looking up at her. The humming tingled across her lips, filling the ridge edge, cloaking them all in something human and hopeful. Music.

Mike blinked rapidly, as if remembering where he was, who he was.

Lori continued the lilting tune, humming the swifts and curves of the lullaby.

Slowly, Mike loosened his grip on the binocular strap. Let go.

Daniel's body sagged and he fell forward onto his knees, hands clutching at his throat, peeling the binoculars from his neck, rubbing at the red mark.

Freed, Lori stumbled away from the edge, a surge of relief weakening her legs. Both hands circled Sonny, head bowing to plant kisses on him. 'We're okay,' she whispered into his hair. 'It's all okay.'

Daniel on his knees, teeth bared, screamed at Mike, 'You're fucking mad!' Then he staggered to his feet and limped across the ridge top. He crashed through the jungle, mumbling and cursing.

'You okay?' Mike asked. 'I'm sorry, I'm really sorry . . . I don't know what happened . . .' He trailed off. Colour was high in his cheeks, and broken capillaries mapped his nose. The pilot's cap was gone, white hair matted to his scalp.

'Nothing about this is okay.' Her clothes stuck to her, sweat cooling on her back.

'Really, Lori. I'm sorry, I never meant to put you and Sonny at risk. I shouldn't have let Daniel get to me like that.' He hung his head, ashamed. She'd glimpsed something in the dynamic between both men over the passing days, an edge of something she hadn't been able to put a word to.

She pictured the snarl of Daniel's lips, the rage ticking behind Mike's eyes. Then the word she'd missed came to her, swift and cold as a bullet.

Savage.

Lori was climbing down from the ridge, pushing through the undergrowth, when she heard her name being shouted.

Mike was calling to her.

She didn't pause. She needed to get back to the beach. Wait for Felix on the shoreline. Maybe the two of them could disappear to the stream with Sonny – perhaps even camp out there tonight. They could take their blankets, Sonny's bassinet. If it didn't rain, they'd be fine.

She ducked beneath a low-hanging tree, swiping away leathery leaves.

'Lori!' Mike's voice came again, louder this time. An urgency in his tone made her hesitate.

When he shouted again, the words chilled her.

'It's Felix!'

She took the binoculars from Mike, feeling the press of them against the bridge of her nose. Her hands were trembling.

She began to scan the bay, searching out his shape.

Endless, endless blue.

The salt breeze twisted indifferently over the ridge top. Sonny was quiet now, as if the earlier tension had left him subdued.

Felix's dark form appeared in the lens of the binoculars. He was far out on the reef line, near the ledge. Exactly where he'd been when she'd arrived at the ridge top earlier.

'He's not moving,' Mike said.

Fear squeezed at her throat. She blinked. Focused.

Through the binoculars, she could see his shape clearly. He was floating face down, limbs in a starfish position.

He looked so small – all that ocean, and only him.

Her pulse roared in her ears, but she told herself that he could just be looking at something beneath the surface, watching a fish below, stalking it ready for the kill.

'The spear gun has gone,' Mike said.

Eyes stinging with focus, she scoured the water. Her stomach folded in on itself. Mike was right.

Felix always swam with it at his side, kicking his fins to propel him through the water, so that the spear gun was ready and loaded the moment he needed it.

Trembling overtook her body. She fought to keep the binoculars steady. Something dark and inky surrounded his middle.

'Oh my God,' she whispered, ice spiking her veins.

There was a cloud of blood in the water.

# 46

# NOW | ERIN

The pilot's cap still in my hand, I turn from the ridge top. There's nothing else, except windblown dust and sun-scorched rock. I'm not going to find my answers here.

I scramble down from the ridge, sliding awkwardly in flip-flops. Earth and decomposing leaves snag between the rubber and my feet, each footstep gritty, my toes gripping for purchase. The jungle is thick and dense, and something about the humidity makes the air feel harder to draw. I don't remember the route I took up, but the sound of waves in the distance leads me in the right direction.

As soon as the terrain begins to level, I pick up my pace. I duck in and out of trees, eager to hunt out the plane wreck. I pass a stream in the centre of the island, where the water runs clear and deep, and later trees that are fruiting mangos and bananas. I'm alert for any trappings of life – rubbish, the ashes of a fire, a lost shoe – but the island refuses to give up its secrets.

After an hour or more of searching, I'm sweating hard, and the rubber Y of my flip-flops is working a blister between my toes. I wish I'd left my backpack on the boat; the bounce of it on my back ricochets up my spine.

'Come on . . .' I mutter into the empty jungle. 'The plane's got to be here somewhere.'

Sweat climbs the waist of my shorts, clinging to my lower back. I keep checking my watch, knowing that time is running out. The jungle is dense, stippled with shafts of light. There's something about the way the trees crowd out the daylight, and the earthy, mulchy scent trapped within it. Too many places to hide, too many shadows changing shape. An occasional slice of sunlight cuts through the canopy, blinding me.

It's beginning to feel hopeless. I traverse the same stretch of beach already marked by my footprints, and then duck through the hem of a mangrove forest, eyes peeled. Eventually I stop, out of breath. I take the water bottle from my backpack and drain half of it. I wipe the sweat from my face with the hem of my T-shirt, then check my watch. An hour until the boat leaves.

It's moored on the other side of the island and, to make it in time, I need to start moving – now. I can follow the ring of the beach and it'll take me right there. The pilot's cap is safely tucked into my backpack. It's evidence. Back on the mainland, I can hand it over to the authorities – let them take over.

But I need to see it. I need to see the plane wreck. I need to know . . .

I veer inland, pushing into the interior of the jungle. I'm not sure whether I've already circled this section of the island. The air feels heavier, thick with the scents of plants. I shove my way forwards, hands swiping away branches and thick ferns. Suddenly my toes are connecting with something hard and I'm tripping, falling forwards. The weight of my backpack pushes me down hard, and I land on my knees in the dirt.

Just a tree root, I realise, looking around at the dark knot of wood that tripped me. It felt iron-clad, like a hand hooking a foot. It's nothing, I tell myself, staggering a little as I rise, the violence of the fall knocking the wind out of me. I dust the dirt from my knees, watching a thin trickle of blood weaving down my shin where I hit the ground.

When I look up, I think at first that there's a gap in the trees. Light pouring through. Then I realise – it is not light, but something pale in amongst all the green.

I stumble forwards, gaze travelling across leaf-littered earth, beastly trunks, thin saplings. I push through branches bearded with moss, and suddenly I am sliding to a halt.

There, up ahead, I can see it clearly: the white body of a plane.

My hands clamp against my mouth. Shallow, ragged breaths.

I've looked at photos of this plane hundreds of times, with the single red line dissecting its fresh white middle – yet now that solid cylinder of metal is grounded in a jungle. Thick vines are knotted around the plane, reaching over the wings, veining it with stalks and branches. The entrance gapes open and the jungle has battered its way in, tangled vines seething into the plane's interior.

The horror of the crash hits me in the gut. I hinge forward, arms hugged to my middle.

*You were on this plane!*

I concentrate on drawing in air. Slowly, slowly. Breathe.

Near the wreckage, now I notice four tree trunks have been positioned around a ring of stones, wispy new growth rising at their edges. Blackened, waterlogged wood is piled beside it. Dangling from one of the trees is a long tube of rubber, knotted to a flap of something yellow. A shelter of some sort?

Slowly, I approach the plane, pushing past a shoulder-high bush with leaves like blades. The jungle is thick with unseen insects, the chirrups and clicks competing against the roar of blood in my ears.

At the entrance to the plane, I freeze. The floor is thick with dirt and decaying leaves, the belly of it darkened and crawling with insects. Hairs rise on the back of my neck. I can already smell it, fetid and repugnant: the stench of death.

## 47

# THEN | LORI

Lori ran. The flick of hot sand. The rasp of her breath. Sonny pressed close to her chest.

Ahead of her, Mike made for the water, elbows pumping, shirt tails flying behind him.

'What's happening?' Daniel called, who'd been tending a signal fire on the beach. 'A boat? Is there a boat?'

Mike threw the binoculars onto the shore, but didn't pause to strip off his clothes, just ploughed into the water and began to swim.

Lori halted on the shoreline, arms cradling a stunned Sonny, bouncing him too vigorously, heart exploding in her chest. She grabbed the binoculars, blowing sand from the lenses, then pinning them to her face.

'What the fuck's going on?' Daniel said, reaching her.

'It's Felix. He's not moved. He's just floating out there . . . There's blood!'

'What? Let me see.' He took the binoculars, pressed them to his sunburned skin. 'Could be fish blood. Could be. Yeah. Fish blood. He wears that stringer, doesn't he? Threads the fish onto it when he's speared them. It could be that.'

Lori wanted to believe it – *A cloud of fish blood, yes!*

Long minutes passed and Mike's pace began to slow. His stroke was becoming laboured, thick arms slapping at the water, head wrenching up for gasps of air. Everything felt painfully visceral – the sun burning hard against the backs of her shoulders, pulse crashing in her ears, and Sonny awake and murmuring, his cheek pillowed against her hammering heart.

She took the binoculars back as Mike reached Felix. Still, he didn't move, didn't lift his head from the water. She fought against the trembling that was overtaking her body, trying to keep the binoculars steady. Briefly she lost focus, searching the blank stretch of water until the tableau emerged again. All she saw now was Mike swimming back towards the beach, towing Felix face-down.

'Turn him over! He can't breathe!'

'What's happening?' Daniel asked.

'Mike's swimming him in. Felix isn't moving, he's face-down.' Mike was struggling, she could tell, the going painfully slow. His mouth was open wide as he slapped at the water with one arm, trying to tow Felix with the other.

She paced on the spot, unable to keep still, sweat building beneath her arms. Time dragged, just the wash of waves against shore and Daniel's voice at her shoulder. After a few minutes, she watched as Mike let go – just let go of Felix. His body turned slowly on the current, and then she saw it: a deep red gash through his middle, where blood swirled and muddied the water.

She unhooked the binoculars, tossing them onto the sand. 'Here,' she said, unbuckling the sling, and holding out Sonny.

Daniel reared back, hands lifted. 'I can't . . .'

'Take him,' she said, voice steely.

Watching Daniel's filthy hands accept Sonny went against every instinct in her body. She plunged into the shallows, crashing forward into front crawl. She was a weak swimmer, her strokes inefficient and uneven, clothes weighing her down. She pushed on, gasping for air, desperate to reach them.

Mike had resumed towing Felix, bringing him into the shallows now. Felix's face was still in the water.

'Lift his head up!' she shouted, saltwater stinging her eyes. 'Lift his fucking head! He can't breathe!'

But she knew.

She knew.

'Felix!' she was yelling. 'Felix!'

She trod water as they reached her. Mike was struggling to catch his breath. Through his gasps, he said, 'It's too late, Lori.'

'No . . . no . . .' She swam around to Felix's face, took his head in her hands, saw his eyes open but unfocused beneath the dive mask. She needed to get his mask off – he couldn't breathe properly, she needed to help him, she . . .

'Let's get him in,' Mike said, towing Felix the final few metres towards the shore. A swirl of blood inked the water.

Mike hauled Felix onto the beach, laying him on his back.

Lori stumbled through the shallows, falling on her knees at Felix's side.

'Felix . . .'

Her gaze travelled down his body, stopping at the tear that came right through the middle of him. Secret inner parts of him exposed. The stringer still intact around his waist, one fish head remaining, the body of it pulled free.

She knew what had happened. They all knew.

Behind her she could hear Mike. Caught the words *tiger*

*shark. After the fish, not him. Smell the blood miles away.* And beyond the words, Sonny fretting in Daniel's arms, his hiccuping cries building in earnest.

Blood from Felix's torso leached into the wet sand. His legs were splayed in his fins. Tenderly, she removed his dive mask, red indentations left against his skin. She pressed her face to his. Kissed his cold lips, his cheeks, his forehead. Tasted salt and the sea.

'Wake up,' she whispered. 'Please . . .'

*My life hasn't felt like a gift in a long time*, Felix had told her.

No . . . no . . . no.

She cupped his face in her hands, the dark weave of his beard in her palms. Her thumbs smoothed the soft, damp skin at his temples. 'Felix, please. Sonny and I need you.'

She felt a burning, bottomless pain deep in her chest, beginning to howl.

The sun beat down relentlessly, and the sea folded indifferently against the shore.

A wet hand on her shoulder.

'He's gone, Lori,' Mike was saying.

She shrugged him off. Hauled herself to her feet. She wanted to run to the ridge top – hurl herself right off the fucking edge! Or . . . or swim away from this fucking island, give herself up to the currents and the sharks.

She couldn't stay. Not without Felix. She lurched through the sand . . . tripping and righting herself . . . wet clothes caked with sand.

Behind her a cry pierced through the blaze in her mind.

*Go back. Sonny needs you.*

She slowed, hesitating.

*You can do this, Lori. You're strong.*

Her whole body was overcome by a deep trembling. Erin's voice?

*Not much longer now. I'm coming. I'll find you.*

She spun around, disorientated. Destroyed.

No Erin.

Felix's bloodied body on the shore.

And then Sonny . . . red-faced, screaming in Daniel's arms.

Daniel was holding him stiffly, his face turned away as if he couldn't bear the sound.

Everything was wrong.

Sonny needed her.

She ran back to him, taking him from Daniel, gathering him in her arms. She pressed kisses against Sonny's head, telling him, 'I've got you.'

Then she knelt beside Felix's body.

Over her shoulder, she hissed at the others: 'Go!'

She heard their retreating footsteps, the sand shifting beneath them as they left her on the shoreline.

She began to rock Sonny in her arms, letting the tears fall silently. She pressed her mouth to the crown of his sweet, warm head. 'Just you and me now. You and me.'

## 48

# NOW | ERIN

A damp, metallic smell inhabits the air inside the wrecked plane. It scuttles with insects and filth. Creeping vines map the seats and cling to the overhead compartments. Mike Brass claimed all the bodies were put out to sea, yet my gaze flits nervously, as if I'm going to find corpses strapped to seats.

I begin to search, sliding my hands into seat pockets, waiting to feel the hard shells of hidden insects. I crouch, looking low, head angled, then stretch onto tiptoe to peer all the way into the back of the luggage compartments. The plane has been stripped bare of possessions.

I clamber out, thighs gleaming with sweat, swatting at a mosquito that lands on my forearm. I pick my way over fallen branches, moving towards the plane's hold. Twisted vines are knotted around the handle, and it takes me several minutes to rip and snap them free. Eventually the handle is accessible and, with a bit of a grunt, I manage to release it.

A pile of weather-stained luggage, filthy blankets and empty plastic water bottles fills the hold. There, at the edge, is Lori's case, the wheels thick with dirt. I scramble forward on my hands and knees to reach it. I haul it free and set it down on the jungle floor, then stand for a moment catching my breath.

If I hesitate too long, I'll lose my nerve.

Wiping the sweat from my face, I crouch down and unzip it swiftly.

A sour, pungent smell, like stagnant water, hits me. Lori's once neatly packed clothes are now heaped together in a filthy bundle. Everything has been used, worn.

By her?

I pull out a camisole top with a frayed strap, smeared with charcoal and dirt. A dead spider drops from a crease in the fabric, tumbling into my lap. It seems impossible, horrifying, that these are her things. I remember this case living at the foot of her bed for the fortnight before our trip, clothes neatly folded and stacked inside. She added new items each day – a bikini, a tube of sun lotion, Grecian sandals, a pair of tan shorts. Now I hold up these same shorts, watching an earwig writhing free of the pocket, its body glossy and barbed. I drop them to the earth.

I want to run. Leave. But I make myself keep going.

I reach for her washbag next. Unzipping it, tiny mould spores explode in my nostrils. I rummage through empty tubes of moisturiser, shampoo, expensive eye cream – everything squeezed dry and smeared with dirt.

I slide my hands into each zipped pocket of Lori's case, pulling out her passport, a dog-eared novel, her purse, a mobile phone. I go to toss it aside but something gives me pause: I stare at it, confounded.

It's not Lori's phone – it's mine.

I left this phone in the bar where I'd met Mike Brass, two years earlier. I sit back on my heels thinking as I turn the phone over in my hands. Mike must have picked it up, is that right? And somehow Lori got hold of the phone. My thoughts spin with the whir of questions, trying to weave together the few thin facts into an explanation.

I try to turn it on, but the battery is dead.

An idea lands. From my backpack, I pull out my power bank. I find the lead and plug in this old mobile and watch the battery sign flash to show it's working.

I leave it to charge while I look around the abandoned camp. A circle of stones, overgrown by creeping vines, edge the long-blackened remains of a fire. Using my own mobile, I photograph what I see as evidence to take back to the authorities. I try to imagine Lori sitting here, waiting for rescue – but the image won't form. At the edge of the stone circle, something pearly catches my eye.

I reach for it, picking up a piece of fabric that's beaded at the top. It's a cream dress, the fabric bunched and stiff with dirt. Part of the skirt has been burned, a blackened hem fringing it. I remember it. I remember this dress – the day it was delivered to my flat in London. Lori came sashaying barefoot into the lounge, her skin winter-pale.

'What d'you think? Does this say cocktails at sunset?'

I'd glanced up from an article I was writing. 'It says, you need to shave your legs.'

'Single privileges,' Lori had grinned. 'Anyway, I've booked in for a wax. I've booked you one, too. Maybe they'll do your tash at the same time.'

I gave her the middle finger.

Lori twirled, the scalloped hem lifting around her knees.

'It's beautiful,' I'd told her honestly. 'Perfect for cocktails at sunset.'

Now the delicate fabric is torn and stiff with filth. When I attempt to shake it loose, the material remains stuck together. I tug at the hem and the dress peels apart. A red-brown mark spreads from the centre of it. My breath stalls as I recognise the dark stain.

Blood.

# 49

# THEN | LORI

In camp that night, Lori sat away from the fire. Sonny slept in the bassinet, quiet and undemanding, as if he sensed she had nothing left to give.

She'd taken one of Felix's T-shirts from his backpack and pressed it to her face. It smelt like wood-smoke and earth, and something deeper, muskier. She kept her eyes closed, breathing him in.

'Want some water?' someone asked.

She didn't respond.

'Lori? Water?'

She breathed harder into the fabric, rocking herself. *If Felix had had the dive knife*, she kept thinking, *he would've been able to protect himself better. Maybe he could have fended off the shark, or cut the fish free from his stringer. Maybe he would have stood a chance . . .*

She heard Daniel and Mike whispering somewhere

beyond her, caught snatches of words. 'Spear gun's lost . . .
nothing to fish with . . . Trees stripped of fruit . . . No one's
coming . . .'

She'd watched them drag Felix's body back into the sea,
just like the others. She'd not picked a frangipani to release,
or whispered words of prayer. She'd just stood on the shoreline, only half there – legs in the shallows, mind watching
from some distant place.

Now she heard a scraping noise. What was it? She tried
to flesh out the shape of it in the darkness. A faint sawing
beyond the low trilling of toads.

Suddenly, she placed it. Her eyes snapped open. In the
firelight, she could see Daniel was using a sharp shell to score
something into the bark of the tree.

The curve of his back blocked the notation, but she knew.

'No!' she said, lurching to her feet. 'Stop!'

She rushed across the camp, launching herself at Daniel,
yanking him away from the tree.

'What the—'

'Don't!' she cried. 'It's too soon . . .'

Her eyes found the marking. She was too late. There was
the list of the dead, Felix's name freshly gouged.

Morning rolled around, hot and still. Lori hadn't slept. She
lay with her eyes closed, listening. Mike's breathing was
rasped as he woke, a deep sigh, followed by the clicking of
joints as he stood, stretched. Then the zip of a bag, rummaging.
Next, the uneven gait of Daniel limping through camp,
mumbling and cursing to himself. One of them stoked the
fire, blowing hard at the embers, ashy smoke reaching her.
She heard jaws working around fruit, the flesh of a mango
torn and sucked and gnawed.

Neither man exchanged a word.

And then finally, finally, they left.

She wanted to keep her eyes closed. Sleep. Not face this day without Felix.

But there was Sonny. Soon he'd wake and need feeding, need changing, need carrying and caring for – and all of those things were hers.

When Pete left and she was at her lowest, Erin had given her one piece of advice. 'Make your bed and get dressed. That's all you need to do each day. Just that, okay?'

It had sounded stupid, simple – but Erin had been right. If Lori did those two things, she was up and out of her bedroom. And once those two tasks were done, the rest felt possible – never easy, but possible.

Her head spun as she pushed herself upright, light-headed with hunger. Her shoulders were knotted and stiff from a restless night in the dirt.

She shook out her blanket and folded it into a neat square ready for the evening. Then she peeled off her filthy top and shorts and dropped them in a heap on the earth. She dug through her case in search of something dry and vaguely clean. At the bottom, her fingers met a cream dress still folded neatly. She drew it out, realising it was the only thing left unworn. The fabric smelt fresh, and she fingered the smooth cardboard price tag pinned to the neckline.

She'd ordered it for the holiday, remembering the buzz of excitement when it was delivered. She'd slipped it over her head and waltzed into the lounge where Erin was sitting cross-legged on the floor, head craned over her laptop. 'What d'you think?' she'd asked.

Lori had been saving this dress. Cocktails at sunset, that's what it was for. That was what she and Erin had agreed. She'd thought if she left it in the case, if she didn't wear it on this island, then the dress would become a talisman, the promise of a time when she'd be safe again. Home. With Erin. She touched her bangle. *Together.*

She'd allowed herself to fantasise about introducing Felix to Erin. Erin would've arched an eyebrow that would have said everything: *Not what I was expecting, sis, but yes!* They would have liked each other, she knew.

She held the delicate fabric in her filthy hands, the moons of her uncut nails packed with dirt. She needed to remember who she was before. Everything felt too base. She needed to show the others. Remind them. They weren't animals.

She ripped off the price tag and pulled the dress over her head. The fabric was delicate and light, the scalloped hem brushing her mid-calves. If she ignored the bruising on her legs, and the way the dress gaped at her waist and breasts, she could almost feel the beauty of it.

She wished she'd worn it sooner. Wished Felix had seen her in this dress. She could picture that slow, hard-to-win smile that caused her stomach to flip. They'd had so little time . . . only a beginning. She squeezed her eyes shut against tears.

Behind her there was the snap of a twig breaking underfoot. She turned.

Daniel was standing at the edge of the clearing, his gaze on her, mouth slightly ajar. His arms hung loose at his sides, streaked with dried blood from a cluster of insect bites he'd scratched. A fly buzzed near his face, but he didn't move – just continued to stare.

*He watched me change*, she realised, her skin cooling. She tried to rearrange the dress, pulling the neckline higher, while Daniel's gaze slid like liquid over her body.

Standing in the shadows, his shirt torn, feet bare and filthy except for a bandage fashioned from a strip of fabric, he looked like something wild, forgotten. Patches of lengthy stubble clung to his narrow jaw and, above, dirt painted his face. Weight had dropped off him, skin clinging to the skeletal bones of his face.

At his side, his fingers fluttered towards his pocket.

*The knife*, she remembered. *Still missing.*

Her mouth turned dry and her pulse beat in her throat, like the wings of a trapped bird.

Daniel's expression was unnervingly blank, as if he were somewhere far, far away from himself. Instinctively she sensed that to move would be to incite something. She stared back, trying to communicate a warning. *Don't.*

His gaze travelled slowly from her face, sliding down her neck, and settling at her breasts.

That's when she moved. She turned, ducking low to the earth beside Sonny's bassinet. Hands trembling, she gathered his warm sleeping body, holding him to her.

*A shield*, she thought. *I'm using him as a shield.*

Still aware of the hot stare of Daniel's eyes on her back, she turned now to face him. He looked at her, then at the baby in her arms. His lips curled faintly – and then he was stepping back, head lowering, limping steps crashing through the jungle.

Lori shivered, hugging her arms around Sonny, the fresh cotton of her dress clinging to her goose-fleshed skin.

## 50

# NOW | ERIN

A slick of bile rises from the base of my throat as I hold up Lori's bloodstained dress.

*What happened to you? Why is your dress covered in blood?*

I wait for an answer, something whispered at the very centre of me, but all I catch is the breath of wind moving through the tree canopy, leathery leaves clattering.

Staring at the soiled fabric, I can't make sense of why it'd been put on the fire. Was someone wanting to get rid of it? The word *evidence* hisses in my thoughts.

I look up, right at that hulking wreck of the plane. Since Lori disappeared, my thoughts have swum through dark channels of possibility, but could always claw to the surface, breathing in the space of not knowing – where none of those fears could be confirmed. Yet now, it's all here, right in front of me: the brutality of the plane crash; the disturbing sight of her filthy belongings; and now this, her bloodstained dress.

The stench of death presses close: terrible things happened here.

I feel something in the wide pocket at the front of her dress, and pull out a clump of photos, glued together with print, blood, damp. The top image is lost – a blur of ink and blood. Carefully, I attempt to peel it free to reveal the photo beneath, but it takes the image with it. I try again with the next photo, but the same thing happens, the moisture sealing them into one mass. It is only the final photo that I manage to prise away with any success, half of the picture surviving. I hold it up and find I'm looking at the face of a young woman, amber hair sweat-slicked at her temples, her expression entranced. She isn't looking at the camera, but her gaze is turned towards the tiny baby in her arms, wrapped in a blanket.

I recognise this woman: it is Holly Senton, the young mother from flight FJ209. And this must be her baby, Sonny.

Why has Lori got a photo of the two of them in the pocket of her bloodstained dress? I study it closely, knowing I'm holding a piece of a puzzle that I can't quite fit together.

*What happened on this island, Lori?*

There's more. I know there's more. But time is running out.

I check my watch. Shit! I'm meant to be back at the boat in thirty minutes. I can't miss it. But I just need a little more time . . .

I return to my backpack and see my old mobile on the earth, still charging. The glass screen is scratched and cloudy, the case watermarked and lined with grit. I'm about to toss it in my bag, but find myself pressing the Power button, watching as the home screen lights up.

The screensaver is a photo of Lori. It was taken on a spring day in Lori's back garden, the two of us sun-drunk, bellies full of barbecue food. I love the smile lines fanning from her eyes, the easy upturn of her mouth. Every time I glimpse this picture, it says to me, *Home*. Not the red-brick house in the background, where Lori and Pete once lived, but my sister. Lori. She is home.

*I miss you, I miss you, I miss you.*

I scroll to the picture gallery. I want her here, crystal-bright in my mind. As I click on the gallery, Lori's face fills the screen. My heart flares: it is not an old photo I've taken. Here Lori looks deeply tanned, her hair wild and unbrushed. The dense treeline behind her is familiar and I recognise it instantly: this island.

Except now I realise it's not a photo at all. At its centre is the white arrow of a *Play* button.

It is a video.

## 51

# LORI | THEN

Lori hugged Sonny to her, listening to Daniel's retreating footsteps.

Then she moved to her case and slid out Erin's mobile, switching it on. Four per cent battery remaining.

Right now, all she wanted was to speak to Erin. To feel a connection. To remind herself there was hope. She tapped the *Record* button.

'Erin,' she whispered, her voice wavering on that single word.

How many times had they spoken each other's names? It felt so familiar, the dance of her lips, her tongue, the two syllables creating sounds that felt part of her.

She glanced down at Sonny in her arms, his cheek pressed to the neckline of her dress, eyes open, staring at her. Then she returned her gaze to the screen.

'Felix is dead.' The sentence choked her, stole the breath

from her lungs. She pressed her lips together, struggling to focus.

She swallowed, eyeing herself in the screen. Her skin was tanned, eyebrows unplucked and wild. Her eyes looked sunken, deep shadows lingering beneath them. Her hair was tangled and darkened with grease, hanging lankly to her shoulders. She looked a decade older, like someone she only half recognised.

'I'm scared,' she whispered. 'Yesterday, Felix was here, on this island, right here with me, with Sonny . . . and now he's gone.' She swallowed. 'He was spearfishing. Out in the water all alone. We think a tiger shark . . .' She broke off, head shaking. 'I loved him, Erin. I loved him – and he's gone.' She paused, waited till she had control of her voice again. 'The dive knife is still missing. I'm sure Daniel has it . . .' She looked around her. 'I don't trust him. The way he looks at me . . .' She swallowed, shook her head. Then she began to move, crossing camp. Mouth close to the phone she said, 'Erin, are you still looking? Are people still searching? God, I hope they are. I need you to find me.' She paused, angling the camera to the tally of slashes cut into the bark of a tree trunk. 'There. Thirty-one days. That's how long we've been here. Please, Erin. Please find me.' Then she lowered the camera to show the names below. 'I don't want my name to be on this list . . .'

She looked down at Sonny. 'Or his.' She kissed his forehead, heard the coo as he tried to communicate something to her. She dipped her nose against his, smelt his sweet milky scent. He gurgled, eyes brightening. She did it again. Found tears springing into her eyes.

She took a breath, then raised the phone to her face again and said, 'You know what I want? I want to record you a message at the end of all this. I want to be on a boat. I want to be safe. I want to be sailing back to the mainland. To you, Erin. I want to leave you a message on this phone, and tell you, *Erin, I'm safe. I'm coming home.* I've got to believe that, haven't I?' She glanced towards the tree. 'Not this tree, Erin. I don't want my name on this tree.'

Her head snapped up.

She listened.

Goosebumps rose across her skin as she made out the noise bellowing through the jungle: her name being screamed.

## 52

# ERIN | NOW

My finger hovers above the screen. When I press play, my sister begins to move. Her hair is lighter than I remember, and there's a scratch across her cheek that unnerves me, the skin raised and angry.

I'm gripping the phone close to my face, wanting to reach through the screen, touch her.

Then she speaks and her voice explodes in my head. 'Erin.' Her head shakes. Her lips part and she smiles, but it is a sad, unreachable smile, a quiver in her lips.

Eyes hot, breath held, I watch.

'I can't believe I'm recording this,' she says directly to me, 'that I'm even saying these words. My plane crashed. We're on an island somewhere.' I watch as she glances around, looking over her shoulder, the camera moving with her. I glimpse treeline, beach, blue sky. She was here! Right here!

After a moment, the video pans back to her. She describes

the crash, how the plane was off course when it went down. She tells me about Sonny, his mother dying in the crash. I absorb every word, watching as she shakes her head, pressing her lips together. I know that look – she does it when she is on the verge of tears and is trying to hold it together. I want to put my arms around her. I want to lean in, hold her.

Then suddenly her face is close to the screen. She looks right into the camera as if we are holding each other's eye. 'I'm scared, Erin. I'm so scared. And I miss you. More than anything – I miss you.'

*I know, I know. I miss you, too . . .*

I watch as she looks up, out towards the sea, as if her gaze is instinctively pulled to the horizon. 'Erin,' she says, finally, her voice breaking. 'I don't think I can survive this.'

The video ends.

My throat is choked. I cling to the phone, desperate for her to stay – to hear anything she has to tell me.

Flicking through the gallery, my heart flares to see there are a dozen more videos.

I know I should leave, return to the boat – but I need to know what happened.

I watch greedily, drinking in every detail of my sister. There's a subtle shift as her face changes, growing gaunt as the days pass, her cheeks hollowing. In some recordings, she seems upbeat, hopeful as she talks about childhood, sharing stories and recollections that hit me hard in the chest. In other videos, she talks about the island and her voice is flat and there's a worrying dullness in her eyes.

The next video I click, makes me freeze. Goosebumps rise on my skin as I realise Lori is wearing a cream dress – the same bloodstained dress bunched at my feet, with the cluster of ruined photos stuffed in its pocket. Yet here, in this video, the dress looks fresh, clean. Lori's face though – she looks exhausted, defeated. I bring the phone closer, trying to see the detail. It appears to be morning from the low light streaming through the canopy of trees. Her expression is taut, something distracted in her gaze. With Sonny pressed in her arms, she whispers, 'I'm scared. Yesterday, Felix was here, on this island, right here with me, with Sonny . . . and now he's gone.'

There's more and I listen closely, wanting to catch every single word.

'Erin, are you still looking?' she says in a rush. 'Are people still searching? God, I hope they are. I need you to find me.'

A shot of guilt punches right through me.

*I am, Lori. I am!*

Then she is moving across camp – this camp where I'm now crouched – and she is headed towards a large tree, its trunk gnarled and wide. The camera lands on a series of marks, as she tells me they've been on the island for thirty-one days now, and I see the slashes in the bark. Then there's a hitch in her voice. The camera angle lowers and I can see words gouged into the bark. A series of names.

*Holly Senton, R.I.P.*
*Ruth Bantock, R.I.P.*
*Jack Bantock, R.I.P.*
*Kaali Halle, R.I.P.*
*Felix Tyler, R.I.P.*

I hear the hitch in Lori's voice as she says, 'I don't want my name to be on the list . . . or his.'

I shiver.

On screen, Lori's head suddenly snaps up. There's a muffled, distant sound of someone shouting.

The camera peels away from her face and she is turning on the spot, moving through the jungle, away from camp.

Then she must reach the treeline because I can see the beach ahead of her. Out of shot, someone yells, 'Lori!'

Lori is running then, sand flicking up, her calves muscular and fast through the sand. The screen wobbles and distorts. I can't see what's happening clearly.

I hear Lori's voice. 'A boat?'

The screen lifts for one brief moment – as if Lori has raised her hand to point towards the horizon – and then the video cuts out.

I go back and watch it again, pressing pause on that final frame. Despite the pixelated quality of the image, it is clear amid all that blue. There is a boat – and it is headed towards the island.

## 53

# THEN | LORI

Lori came to a halt on the shoreline beside Daniel.

'Boat!' he cried, pointing.

With Sonny gripped in one arm, she lifted her free hand to shade the sun from her eyes, squinting towards the horizon. She'd spent enough hours staring at it to know the mind could conjure up images – a boat, a whale, a shipping tanker. But this – this dark shape didn't waver or disappear. There was something there, right on the surface of the water. It looked too small to be a boat. A log? Lost cargo?

She followed the shape, watching as it moved nearer. The angle of it shifted, and suddenly the long shape became clear.

It was a narrow blue boat – almost like a canoe – with a small engine on the back. There was someone on board!

She began waving wildly. 'Hey! Over here! Help!'

The boat was near the edge of the reef where the waves broke, but seemed to be turning away.

'Haven't they seen us?' Lori cried.

Daniel spun on the spot. 'Where's Mike? Where's the fucking flare!'

Lori continued waving her free arm, hollering, jumping up and down. Sonny kicked his legs excitedly. 'Hey! Over here! Hello!'

'It's leaving!' Daniel hobbled past her, straight into the shallows, clothes darkening with water. 'Wait! Wait!' he yelled, as he began to swim, arms thrashing at the surface.

His infected heel flashed as he kicked. He looked uneasy in the water, a jerking rhythm to his movements.

A wave slapped him in the face. He gulped a mouthful of salt water and began coughing before slipping briefly beneath the surface. He came up clawing at the water, gasping. She caught the flash of panic on his face and watched as he lunged at the sea as if searching for something solid, neck straining with the fight to keep his head above the water. But his body wouldn't seem to float, legs weighted, dangling downwards. Again, he slipped under.

She waited.

He surfaced finally, and this time he managed to make a few strokes, heading back towards the shore. It would only be a few moments before the water would be shallow enough for him to touch the sea bed. He staggered out, collapsing onto his knees on the beach. 'I couldn't . . .'

'It's okay,' she said.

He wiped his mouth on the back of his hand. 'The boat . . .'

Lori turned then, looking for it.

And there it was. A blue wooden vessel, no larger than a canoe, with a fishing rod attached to the rear. This was no mirage. It had entered the shallow bay – not leaving, after all, but finding a safer entry point – and now it was motoring steadily towards them.

\*   \*   \*

The sun beat down. Squinting against the blinding glare, Lori realised the boat driver was just a boy. A teenager. He was staring back at them, brown eyes wary.

This was it. The very thing they'd been hoping for. Someone to find them. Take them back to their lives. She'd imagined a rescue helicopter, or an expedition boat, or a seaplane flying overhead. Not this: a teenager standing in the shallows, wide-eyed and white-knuckled as he held tight to the nose of his boat. It looked barely big enough for one person, let alone all of them. A fishing rod was lashed to the back, and she saw a sun-bleached cool box used as a seat.

Lori had seen the same few faces every day for a month, and now she drank in this boy in his faded T-shirt, the wiry strength of his arms, the soft brown irises looking at them in puzzlement.

She felt a dizzying sense that she was standing close to the edge of something. Her heart was hammering, the breath in her chest swelling and falling. Sonny had settled again, an occasional gurgle and bat of his arms.

Daniel was back on his feet, clothes sodden, skin white. 'Help us!'

The boy took a step back.

'Please! We need to get off this island! Take us? In your boat.' He was speaking too quickly, too loudly, frantically. He limped into the shallows, coming to the other side of the boat. 'I go on this boat with you? Yes?' He was pointing to the seat, then began hauling himself up, the boat rocking violently beneath him.

In a flash, the boy had reached into the boat, and came up holding a large knife, the curved blade glinting in the sun. 'Back!'

Daniel dropped into the shallows, raising his hands above his head. 'Okay, okay.'

The boy, still gripping the knife, was looking between Daniel and Lori, eyes wide. She thought, *Any minute he's going to get in his boat. Leave. We'll have lost our chance.*

Behind them, Mike emerged from the treeline. He came to a stop when he reached the group. He took in the scene, then nodded at the boy. 'Bula.' *Hello, welcome.*

The boy nodded, repeating the greeting. 'Bula.'

'We need help,' Mike said, his voice calm, level. 'Our plane crashed. We need to get to Viti Levu, main island. We need a boat.' He pointed at the boy's boat, then widened his hands saying, 'Bigger boat.'

The boy nodded again, 'Big boat. Yes.'

'Where are we?' Mike asked.

The boy opened his hands. 'No name.'

'What island are you from?'

'Rannatua.'

'How long did it take you to get here?' Mike asked.

'One day.'

'Can you bring help? A boat? Bigger boat?' He pointed to each of them, held up his fingers. 'Four of us. Bigger boat.'

The boy nodded. 'Lo. Lo.'

Then, still holding the knife, he clambered back on board.

'Wait!' Daniel called. Then to the others he whispered, 'If he leaves, how do we know he'll come back?'

'What choice do we have?' Lori said. 'We can't all fit on the canoe.'

'I'll go with him,' Daniel said.

Understanding, the boy shook his head.

'I've got an idea,' Daniel said, turning towards the treeline, and limping in the direction of camp.

Mike said to the boy, 'One minute, please. Wait one minute.' To fill the silence, he indicated the boy's fishing rod. 'Good fish?'

The boy nodded. He pointed to the cool box lashed to the back of the canoe. 'Fish, yes.' He opened the lid and pulled out a huge fish that shimmered iridescent. 'Spanish mackerel.'

A stab of hunger cut through Lori's middle. She wanted that fish. Would give him anything for that fish. She looked at the boy, wondering whether she were stronger than him. If she could simply take the fish—

The thought was cut short as Daniel returned with something clasped in his hands. He held out a fistful of money for the boy.

Tentatively, he reached for the money.

From Daniel's other pocket, he pulled out a further bunch of notes. 'The rest when you come back? Yes?'

The boy looked at the money, then pushed it into the pockets of his shorts. It must have been a couple of hundred dollars, more even. 'Yes.'

'Fish,' Lori said suddenly, stepping forward. 'Can we have it?'

The boy looked at her, then the baby gripped to her chest. He leaned over the canoe, taking the fish from the cool box and passing it to her. It was already gutted, the belly sliced open, and she felt the solid, wet weight of it in her grip. She could imagine it cooking over the fire, thought of flaking the white meat for Sonny. They needed this. 'Thank you,' she said, saliva filling her mouth.

Mike stepped forward, saying something lightly to the boy, which Lori couldn't catch. The boy's eyes widened a little, then he turned and glanced back to Lori and Daniel, the lightest nod lowering his chin.

Then the boy was pulling the cord on the outboard motor, a light vibration of the engine hitting the water, the smell of diesel in the clear ocean air.

The rest of them stood on the shore in silence, watching the disappearing shape of the canoe, following its course east. After a time, it slipped away over the crest of the horizon and once again the ocean was empty, blue and dazzling.

Lori could feel the dry lick of thirst scorching her throat. She gripped tight to the Spanish mackerel, its tail cool and slick in her fingers. Blood dripped from its gutted stomach onto the sand at her feet.

'What did you say to the boy?' Lori asked Mike.

He looked at her blankly.

'Right at the end, just before he left, you said something to him.'

He shrugged. 'I just told him to travel safe.'

She watched him for a beat, unsure.

Daniel, who'd been staring after the boat, turned. 'What if that kid doesn't find his way back? What if he forgets the location? It's not like he had GPS or even a map to mark it on. He could get lost. I don't like it. Fuck, I should've taken that boat myself!'

'You really think you'd have made it to land?' Mike said. 'With no clue where we are, or how to navigate?'

Daniel moved towards him. 'At least I was willing to give it a shot. What about you?' He closed the gap between them. 'Where was the fucking flare?'

'I didn't see the boat, not till it was right in the bay—'

'How many boats have gone past that you "haven't seen"?' Mike held his stare.

'You don't want anyone leaving this island, d'you?' he seethed. 'Well, you know what? Too bad. A boat came! We're getting out of here! And when we do, everyone is going to know about how you fucked up. Crashed our plane! Made us get rid of the bodies—'

'I didn't make—'

'A cell. That's what is waiting for you.'

Mike said something back, but Lori didn't stay to catch it. She was already turning from them, leaving.

Sonny. That's who she needed to focus on now. Her only job was to keep him safe for just a little longer. She would take this fish, stoke the fire, feed them. Then she would wait.

Wait for the boat to return.

That was all she needed to do.

Hour by hour.

Moment by moment.

Survive until the boat returned.

Crossing the white-hot sand, Lori didn't realise it then, but Daniel had been right about one thing. He should have climbed on that boat, gone with the boy. Because if he'd left the island, then everything – everything – would have turned out differently.

# 54

# NOW | ERIN

I sit back on my heels in the earthy shade of the jungle. My breath comes high and shallow in my chest. I stare at the phone. A boat! There was a boat.

I'm desperate to understand more.

I know Rega is waiting. My time's run out. But I can't leave, not yet.

There is only one video remaining.

I press *Play*.

The screen is dark and unfocused, as if the record button had been accidentally knocked within a pocket.

I lift the phone closer, listening hard. There is a loud whir of background noise that I'm struggling to place. Then I catch Lori's voice. It is hushed, just broken fragments of it, as if her lips are pressed close to the phone. 'I'm in the plane . . .'

I glance up, seeing the wreck shrouded in the green arms of the jungle.

'It's Daniel . . .' she whispers urgently. 'All this time,' she says, her words catching. 'I can't . . .'

My fingers grip the phone, breath held. I need to hear every word – but they're rushed, whispered, as if Lori fears someone nearby is listening.

I suddenly place the background noise: rain. It sounds like a downpour battering the metal shell of the plane. Through the buffeting noise, I catch another word.

'Sonny.'

After that, all I hear is my sister, sobbing.

## 55

# THEN | LORI

Lori stood barefoot on the shore, beneath a sky blanketed with cloud.

She stared towards the horizon.

Empty.

Today. That was when the boy had promised a boat would be coming for them. Would it be a fishing boat crewed by an uncle or village chief, or would the boy have contacted the Fijian police? Would the report of the plane crash have already reached the relevant authorities? A rescue crew could be on its way. She allowed herself a moment to imagine it. The sight of a helicopter cutting through the sky, descending in a halo of lifting sand.

The image dissolved as the scale of the empty horizon filled her with doubt. There was only an hour of light remaining, if that. Surely a boat should have been here by now? What if the boy hadn't made it back to land, or if he'd not known the location of their island – couldn't find them again?

She listened to the slow purr and draw of waves, feeling the gentle shifting of sand. She tipped back her head, squinted. Didn't like the look of the dark clouds building in the east. Rain was coming. She could taste it in the earthy fullness of the air.

Despite the heat, she shivered.

Sonny slept on in the sling, cheek against her chest, lips pursed. She pressed a kiss to his head. Breathed in. This boy. She needed to keep going, keep hoping. For him.

There was no wind, not a breath. Wood-smoke from the signal fires hung in the heat. Nothing stirred. The sun-struck trees seemed to pant. Everything waited, still, heavy. The heat amplified the stillness; the coral-bleached sand, the dark-earthed jungle, her sweat-slicked body – all pulsing with it.

There was a quality to the air that kept everything suspended – as if the island knew. It was the pause between heartbeats. The halted footstep. The held breath. Waiting.

The weather broke. First the white clouds compressed, gathering and huddling close. There was a growing weight in the air, a sense of pressure building.

Then the wind arrived, blowing in from the sea, bringing a storm of dark clouds. It ripped the crests from the waves, sending spray high into the air, the sea becoming something broiled and angry.

The sand began to lift, rushing along in a stinging haze. She retreated to the treeline, arms shielding Sonny, pressing him against her chest as a gust barrelled past them. Behind them branches and fronds whipped together, clattering and whistling, punctuated by the deadly thud of coconuts plummeting to the earth.

She hurried into camp. Daniel was trying to lash down the life raft they used as their shelter, but it was flapping wildly, the rope snapping and cracking out of reach. 'Fuck!' he cried, as the rope was flung upwards with a gust, whipping against his cheek, before tangling around a branch. He fell to his knees, clutching his face.

'You okay?' Lori shouted.

He swore, staggering back to his feet.

'We should shelter in the plane. It's not safe here,' she shouted, gesturing to the branches that had already been snapped clean from trees, their green-white insides exposed.

They never went in the plane. It was an unspoken agreement, as if the space was bad karma, the smell of death still clinging to it. Even when it rained, they stayed in camp, huddling beneath the life raft or the wing of the plane – but they'd never seen winds like this on the island.

'I need to keep the signal fires lit!' Daniel shouted back. He'd spent the day collecting wood, laying half a dozen piles along the shoreline. 'I need to be on the beach when the boat comes.'

'No one will be on their way in this weather,' Lori said. 'It's too dangerous.'

But Daniel didn't seem to hear, just stalked from camp out into the driving wind.

The rain arrived, lashing down from the sky.

Sonny looked up blinking from his sling. Heavy raindrops slid down his face, even as Lori hunched forward, trying to shelter him. Outraged by the sudden change in circumstance, his brow crumpled and he began to howl.

'It's okay, it's okay,' Lori soothed above the roar of the weather. She scooped up a bundle of their blankets and Sonny's bassinet, then picked her way to the plane, the ground beneath her feet turning to mud, sky so dark that it felt as though the storm had dragged night with it. The trees were bending and groaning, palm fronds clattering above their heads. Her feet slid through the mud, slipping on an exposed tree root. She was hinging forward, her centre of gravity spinning.

She managed to right herself just in time. She looked down at Sonny in the sling. If she'd landed on him . . .

In the low light, the white metal body of the plane looked like a gravestone, the gaping mouth of it open to the elements. She climbed inside, holding on to the seat backs as she moved. She tried not to think of the air stewardess's body that had once lain where her feet were now.

The light was bleeding from the day, the rain ceaseless beyond the plane windows. She lowered herself into a seat, wrapping a dry blanket around Sonny. There was no formula left, so she tried him with a little coconut milk while there was still just enough light to see.

The rain continued to drum against the shell of the plane. The air smelt of moisture and earth and her own skin, damply salty. As Sonny fussed in her arms, not impressed with his new milk, she began to hum. The rhythm or tone seemed to soothe him, or perhaps it was just the company of another voice, but she felt his stiff little body soften, relaxing into his feed. His navy eyes found hers, and they held each other's gaze in the lowering light, eyes pinned to one another as if making a promise.

He was asleep before he'd finished his milk and she carefully removed the bottle from his lips, adjusting him against the warmth of her chest.

With a jolt, she realised that she was sitting in Holly's plane seat. She pictured Sonny – only a month ago – resting in the crook of his mother's arm as she'd held a bottle to his lips.

*He's not yours*, she reminded herself firmly as the final strokes of light leached away.

The wind buffeted the shell of the plane, gusting through the open door. An oxygen mask, still dangling from the ceiling, made a frantic series of thwacks as it connected with a seat back. Beyond it, she could hear the clatter of palm fronds blowing in the wind, and – at sea – distant waves rising and bowling.

The darkness was earth-thick, no shade or shapes beyond it. She wanted Felix. Wanted him so badly the pain felt physical. Peering through the window she hoped to glimpse a flame on the beach, but there was nothing but more darkness.

Sonny was asleep in her arms, the gentle purr of his breath lost to the wind. 'One more night,' she whispered. 'The boat will come back for us. It will be over soon.'

Desperate for distraction, Lori foraged in the seat pocket in front. Her fingers met an empty packet. Crisps, she guessed, unfolding it in the dark and inhaling the delicious smell of bacon. She brought it close to her mouth and tentatively placed her tongue against the foil. She licked. A burst of salt and a sweet, meaty flavour coated her tongue, her teeth, the roof of her mouth. She licked and licked, hunger roaring awake, saliva glands pumping. She edged her tongue right into the folds of the packet, tasting every final grain of flavour.

When the packet was licked clean, she rooted in the next seat pocket hoping for a discovery as good as the first. Her fingertips met something slim, firm. It was too dark to see what she held, but she felt along the edges of it and reached a triangular flap, which opened with ease. She was expecting to feel the stub of flight tickets or printouts of insurance documentation, but inside were glossy slips of card. Photos, she guessed.

The wind rattled the plane, an eerie, bone-shaking sound.

She slipped Erin's mobile from her pocket and pressed the power button. Two per cent battery remaining. The screen lit up the envelope. She'd been right; inside were half a dozen photos.

The first was a picture of a newborn – instantly recognisable as Sonny – with a hospital tag around a tiny, pink ankle, hair matted to his head. He was cradled in Holly's arms, whose face was blotchy and red, her hair sweat-soaked at the temples, yet her expression was lit with wonder. Lori could see the sheer, heart-stopping, expansive love – a bloom of it – lighting every plane of her face. Once, the intimacy of the photo would have struck her hard in the chest, because she'd never know what it would feel like to give birth, to hold her own baby in her arms – yet now, she felt differently. She hoped that one day Sonny would be able to look at this photo, and feel his mother's love, right there from the beginning. She wanted that for him. She wanted everything for him.

The next photo was of Sonny's feet, bare and perfect, ten tiny bud toes, the pink soles petal-soft. She knew the pleasure of cupping those feet in a single palm, marvelling at the lightness, the smallness, the absolute perfection of them.

There were more photos and she drank them in with a full heart – Sonny in a Moses basket, swaddled in a cream blanket, looking like a doll, mouth puckered, eyes open and curious. Sonny in a bath-tub, Holly's hand cradling his still-soft head, his umbilical cord browned and taped. Sonny swamped in a snowsuit, lying in a buggy.

Strange that Holly would bring these photos on holiday with her. Was she planning on showing them to someone? Or did she just want to see how far they'd come in the four short months of Sonny's life?

As she slipped the photos back into the envelope, the light from the mobile caught something else tucked at the back. A notecard. She pulled it free, angling the phone to illuminate it.

*To Daniel,*
*This is what you missed. We don't want you to miss any more.*
    *Holly and Sonny xx*

*Daniel?*
    She blinked. Re-read the note. What Daniel?
    Another Daniel, surely? Someone Holly was meeting at the island, that's what she told herself. Firmly.
    Because if the note was written to the Daniel on this island, then what did that mean?
    She stared at the writing, certain she was missing something. Holly and Daniel didn't know each other. Holly had flown from America with a baby. Daniel had flown from the UK to discuss a potential property investment on the island – that's what he'd told them.
    Then a thought snagged, something Mike had said on the ridge top, questioning Daniel about the supposed property deal.
    There was something else, too. The lace underwear she'd found in Daniel's bag. For his wife, he'd said. But was it?
    She thought of his expression when Holly's body had been carried from the plane. He stepped right back, cupping his mouth, as if containing something. He hadn't been able to help them dispose of the bodies, disappearing when Holly's was taken to the water.
    She tried to put an alternative narrative to the words in front of her, but the implication from that note pointed in one direction: Daniel was Sonny's father.

Her head was shaking. Not him; God, not him!

Did he know? He would have said something, surely?

Yet . . . Daniel and Holly must have *arranged* to go on holiday together.

Her thoughts spun back to seeing Daniel at the airport, in his smart open-necked shirt, a leather carry-on bag at his side. Had he talked to Holly in the boarding lounge? Lori had been so preoccupied with whether Erin was going to arrive, she hadn't been paying attention.

He was married, Lori knew. So, an affair that ended in a baby? He'd mentioned a work project in Chicago. Wasn't that where Holly was from? Is that where they'd met? Perhaps he had no idea about Sonny until he met Holly at the airport.

But she'd heard Holly say to the air stewardess that there was no father. 'It's just me.' And then Daniel was there sitting at the front of the plane, face white, asking to leave.

Sonny murmured in her arms. In the darkness, she adjusted him slightly, making a low shushing noise that she knew soothed him. She'd learned this over time, just like she'd learned that if she ran two fingertips slowly down his fore-head, between the groove of his eyebrows, he went still, calmed by the touch. She knew these tiny details about him because she had taken the time to care for him, to fall in love with him, to look after him.

Daniel – what did he know about Sonny?

Nothing.

Did he think that the truth he was the father had died with Holly?

As she felt Sonny's tiny heart beating beneath her palm, she thought: *I love you*. Even before she loved him, before she'd picked him up, before she'd seen those navy eyes gazing up at her, she would have helped him – because he was a baby and that is what you do.

But not Daniel.

In the first moments after the plane crashed – when there was numb silence, smoke billowing from the engine, passengers still strapped to their seats, dazed and helpless – Daniel had already left the plane. He must have pushed his way through the debris, stepping over the air stewardess, barrelling towards the exit. He didn't pause to help anyone, not even glancing at Holly, or stopping to check on Sonny.

That was the sort of man he was.

She turned the phone to herself, pressed record. She could barely hear herself think beyond the drum of rain, but she needed to tell someone.

Into the phone she whispered, 'I'm in the plane . . .' Her gaze flicked towards the entrance, listening. 'It's Daniel,' she said, her voice rushed. 'I can't believe it . . .' She felt the warmth of Sonny in her arms, the tiny thump of his heart. *How could he not want you?*

Tears streamed down her face. 'Daniel is Sonny's father,' she began, as the light on the mobile faded, the battery symbol flashing once, and then it was gone.

The battery was dead.

She sat there in darkness as the truth bloomed hot and ugly in her mind.

## 56

# NOW | ERIN

I stare at the screen, waiting for more. All I can hear is the sound of my sister sobbing as the weather lashes down against the plane.

And then I catch another rush of broken words.

'*Daniel is Sonny's father.*'

The recording ends, my sister's voice gone.

I stare unblinking at the phone.

*Wait, Lori. What? What do you mean?*

I shake the phone, scrolling back. But there are no more videos. That was the last.

I sit very still, blood roaring in my ears. I've played every message, heard each word, seen Lori right here on this island, studied the boat in the distance.

It feels like all the clues are laid before me, like shattered fragments of glass that it's impossible to piece back together.

I press the heels of my hands hard against my brow bones, thinking, thinking.

After a moment, I flick back through her messages, re-playing them. I want to have missed something. I pause on one of the recordings, play it back twice.

*'You know what I want? I want to record you a message at the end of all this. I want to be on a boat. I want to be safe. I want to be sailing back to the mainland. To you, Erin. I want to hold this phone and leave you a message, and tell you, "Erin, I'm safe. I'm coming home." I've got to believe that, haven't I?'* I watch as she glances away from the phone, towards the tree. *'Not this tree, Erin. I don't want my name on this tree.'*

Then I'm pawing through the videos again. I want to have missed it – missed the final recording where she tells me she's on that boat, safe. 'Where is it? Where is it?'

But I know.

There is no 'I'm safe' message.

*Why, Lori? What happened?*

I'm thinking, thinking . . .

*There's the blood. The dark stain of it on your dress.*

The answer echoes back to me, straight from her last recording. *'It's Daniel,'* she'd said.

I keep swallowing, as if I can't get enough air.

I stagger to my feet. Earth presses beneath me as I move through the camp, my gaze swinging from tree to tree, searching. Slowly, I circle the log seats set around a ring of stones. I pass one tree, then another. There. A thick-trunked tree that looks familiar. Its branches reach high into the dense canopy, and the heft of its base is gnarled, like the hide of an elephant. I recognise it from Lori's video message.

I'm moving closer, breath caught in my throat. My hands reach for the whorled trunk, feeling the dense solidity, the ridges of its wrinkled bark. Wisps of moss cling like an aged beard, and a thin march of amber-coloured ants descend in single file.

I angle my head in search of markings in the shady gloom. Yes, there. Something's been carved. I peer more closely, recognising a tally of slashes scored into silver-grey bark. With my index finger, I trail each groove, counting the tally of days the survivors spent on this island.

*. . . thirty-one, thirty-two, thirty-three.*

Thirty-three days – and then?

My palm smooths the bark, circling the thick body of the tree. Then I feel another series of depressions in the wood, my fingertips exploring the indents and cuts.

As I move around the base of the trunk, my breath stalls. I'm face to face with the carving of names Lori showed me. Not freshly cut, but aged, the wood darkened.

I read.

*Holly Senton, R.I.P.*

*Ruth Bantock, R.I.P.*

*Jack Bantock, R.I.P.*

*Kaali Halle, R.I.P.*

The next names are carved in a blunter style, as if the tool – or the user of the tool – has changed.

*Felix Tyler, R.I.P.*

*Daniel Eldridge, R.I.P.*

And then there are two more lines.

Two names I can't bear to see.

# 57

# THEN | LORI

Lori drove the sharp edge of the rock into the bark, scoring another slash. Day thirty-three.

She dropped the stone onto the earth and surveyed the empty camp.

Snapped branches and leaves littered the ground from last night's storm. The log bench, where foraged food was usually stored, was empty except for the browning skin of a mango being explored by a team of ants. Her stomach felt hollow, her mouth sour.

She pressed her fingertips into the knot of muscles surrounding her shoulder blades. She'd barely slept, the rain a deafening percussion against the metal drum of the plane, her thoughts ablaze with her discovery about Daniel.

She looked down at Sonny in her arms: *Daniel is your father*.

She left camp with Sonny, stumbling through the dripping rainforest onto the beach.

Her gaze – as always – went first to the horizon.

No boat.

The half-dozen signal fires lay forlornly on the rain-pocked sand, a thin drift of smoke curling from just one.

Sonny was restless in her arms. He liked to kick about on his back first thing in the morning, so she walked to the edge of the bay, where rocks and boulders crawled out into the mouth of the ocean. She stretched out a blanket and then set him down. She browsed the gaps between the rocks, searching for something to entertain him, passing over mouth-sized shells or a tangle of rope, and instead settling on a smooth piece of driftwood.

She lay on her side next to him, watching the brightness of his eyes as he tried to grasp the wood in his tiny fists. Light-headed from hunger, she wanted only to sleep. She rolled onto her back, making a pillow of her arms. She could feel the skin stretching taut over her ribs, the hollow arc of her stomach. Sonny's light gurgles drifted over her as she closed her eyes.

She longed for Felix. To hear his voice. To see him walking up the beach towards them. For him to lie on the blanket, fingers interlaced with hers. She wanted to talk to him about Daniel, about the boat, about—

'Lori!'

Startled, she sat bolt upright, a head rush making her vision spark with dark, floating spots.

Daniel was standing in front of her, shirt torn, eyes blinking rapidly.

She stared back at him, the spiky shape of her anger rising hotly in her chest.

'You need to help me with the fires!' His voice was too loud, too fast. 'We need the dry wood brought down from the jungle. I can't light them all.' He didn't even glance at Sonny. Didn't check they were okay after the storm.

She got to her feet. Faced him. 'No.' It was all she said. One word. One syllable.

Daniel blinked. 'No?'

She glared at him, distaste bitter in her throat. Before she knew what she was doing, she was pulling the envelope of photos from her dress pocket. 'I found these.'

She passed it to him.

He pulled out the photos, glancing briefly at the first image, Holly cradling a newborn Sonny. His face remained impassive as he flicked to the next photo, and the next, his expression barely changing. 'Why are you showing me?'

'Because they're yours. There is a note with them – addressed to you.'

A flicker of something then – unease?

He turned through the final photos until he reached the note. She saw the slow swallow of his throat as he read it.

*To Daniel,*
*This is what you missed. We don't want you to miss any more.*
  *Holly and Sonny xx*

When he looked up, she met his gaze. 'You're Sonny's father.'

He shook his head, half smiling. 'You're crazy!'

'Don't you dare lie!' Lori stepped forward, right in front of him. She snatched the photos from his filthy hands, pushed them into the deep pocket of her dress. Her teeth were clenched and she could feel tendons straining in her neck. 'Tell me the truth!'

He watched her, eyes narrowed.

She glared back, waiting.

Then his lips turned up at the corners and he laughed. 'So I'm his father.'

And then he shrugged.

\* \* \*

The dismissiveness of it, the sheer flippancy.

'All this time—'

'Listen, I didn't have a fucking clue about the kid, okay? I turned up at the airport. Thought I was just meeting Holly – except, there she was with this baby.'

'Sonny. His name is Sonny!' She glanced over her shoulder, to where he lay on the blanket, legs pumping happily. Turning back to Daniel, she asked, 'How did you know Holly?'

'I had a project going on in Chicago. Spent eight months out there, on and off. Holly worked in the hotel where I was staying.'

'Did you know she was pregnant?'

'She told me the day I was leaving. Said she was going to sort it.' He looked defensive as he said, 'It was the sensible thing. She was only young – and I wasn't about to leave my wife and move to the States. It had just been a bit of fun, you know?'

*Oh, I know*, she thought, her mind throwing out an image of Pete in Zoe's arms.

'Turns out she changed her mind.' He looked to Sonny. 'First I heard from her was a few weeks back. She got in touch, asking if I wanted to meet her for a holiday.' That shrug again. 'I thought, *Yeah, why not?* So I booked us a place in Fiji.' He sniffed, head shaking from side to side. 'Except she turned up with a baby.'

'What an inconvenience.'

'You,' he said, a finger stabbing towards her, his nail black with dirt, 'don't need to look so fucking judgemental about it. She tricked me. Duped me into meeting her.'

'*Duped* you? Is that really what you think? Holly had your baby. She brought him up on her own for four months – with no family to help. She got in touch because she must have been desperate. I doubt she was in the market for an exotic holiday – she would have just wanted you to meet your son, have a whole week with him, fall in love with him the way she loved him.'

'She should've told me.'

'If she had, would you have met her?'

He didn't answer.

She looked over at Sonny, who was waving the driftwood in his tiny fist. 'Weren't you even a little bit intrigued?'

'Look, I tried, okay? I looked him right in the eye, gave his cheek a stroke, but hell, I don't know what's wrong with me. What's missing. I wanted to feel it. But there was nothing there.' His words were rapid, tension radiating from him in waves.

She remembered waking on that first morning on the island, Daniel reaching into the bassinet briefly. Then, moments later, he had shambled away, leaving Sonny crying.

'Is that what you call trying? One quick attempt, and you're done?'

He didn't answer, just turned to the sea, a hand rubbing at his scalp. 'I need to get out of here. Off this island. Where the fuck is the boat?'

'If we get out of here,' Lori said, 'what then? Sonny's got no one.'

He swung around, chin jutted forward, eyes narrowed. 'You're not going to say anything, are you?'

'What, so you can saunter back into your old life? Back to your wife?'

'Yeah,' he said, stepping closer, gaze steely. 'That.'

Her head shook as she saw the depth of his selfishness. The occasional flickers of charm she'd glimpsed in the earlier days on the island were turned on for gain. 'I'm not keeping your secrets.'

'Righteous bitch,' he spat, a vein pulsing in his temple.

She turned away, wanting to put space between her and Daniel. She was bending to reach for Sonny, when she felt a sharp pain in her wrist. Daniel yanked her around to face him.

'You don't walk away from me!' His expression had darkened. His grip was iron against bone.

She scanned the bay for Mike, but the white stretch of beach was empty. He would be high up on the ridge top at the far end of the island. A flare of unease spread through her chest: she was on her own.

'You're not going to say a fucking thing,' he seethed, so close that she could smell the foul tang of his breath. He touched his pocket with his other hand: the dive knife, she guessed. Only a hand distance away.

He'd had it all this time.

Behind her, Sonny must have sensed the change in atmosphere as he began to whimper, a strange hiccupping sound. 'You're scaring him. Let me go.'

'You need to promise you're not going to say anything.'

She wanted to tell him to go fuck himself, but he was gripping her wrist so hard the pain was making her eyes water. She needed to get to Sonny. 'I promise,' she said, finally.

'I don't want him. I mean it, Lori. You can have him. Keep him.'

'*Keep him?* My God, who are you?' She tried to push him away with her free hand, but he grabbed that arm too, pulling her close. She could feel the clash of his ribcage against her breasts, the thrust of his hips against hers. He held her still, panting.

She could sense it, something shifting dangerously in Daniel.

She was aware of the heat of his body against her. 'Get the fuck off me!'

'You sure that's what you want?' he said, lips close to her ear. 'Felix is gone now.'

'Don't,' she said, and she caught it, the fear in her voice. She had nothing: no weapon; no one to call for help.

Sonny continued to cry, but the noise was wrong, spluttering and broken. She wrenched her head around – caught a glimpse of his face, bright red, fists batting at his throat. The piece of driftwood he'd been playing with lay splintered on the blanket.

*He's choking!* she realised.

Then she was screaming at Daniel, 'Sonny's choking! Let go!'

'I've seen you up at the stream,' he said, as if she hadn't spoken. 'Little prick tease, aren't you?'

Sonny was struggling for air, his face turning puce as he writhed on his back, unable to hook the wood from his mouth.

She kicked out, her bare foot connecting with Daniel's knee. He gave a sharp, sudden cry. It wasn't enough – not nearly enough. His hand jabbed out, bullet-fast, and slapped her around the face. Then he was pushing her roughly by the shoulders. She staggered back, towards the rocks, heels connecting with stone. She could feel her legs buckling; could see the funeral-grey boulders from the corner of her vision; could feel the weight of Daniel against her.

Even as she was falling, she was aware that Sonny needed her, that she had to reach him, that somehow she needed to hold on. The field of her vision seemed to expand as she drank in the expanse of island – the wide, clouded sky from which their plane came spiralling to earth; the fringe of the ocean where Felix once swam, his gaze fixed on the sea bed, searching the currents for fish; the hunkering jungle where she and Sonny slept beneath the canopy, curled together through the long nights.

In a blink, it was gone. There was nothing but the force of Daniel's body against hers, pushing her down, and then finally – the moment she knew was coming – the sudden, violent connection of the back of her skull against rock, before the world fell dark.

## 58

# NOW | ERIN

Something within me collapses, my spine rounding, body curling in on itself. I stare at the name carved into the tree trunk.

*Lori Holme, R.I.P.*

My head shakes.

*No, Lori. No . . .*

Fingertips press against the scarred wood, wanting to change it, to rip the bark clean off, to shoulder down this tree.

*Oh God, oh no!*

And below it, another name.

The brutal, final blow.

*Sonny Senton, R.I.P.*

I slam my fist into the tree trunk, once, twice, my knuckles exploding with pain.

I tip my head back, wailing something wordless into the canopy. The insects silence. Birds stall. The sky bleeds.

I can't bear it.

Lori dead. The baby dead.

My head is spinning. A hot wash of nausea rises, fierce and sudden. I'm on my knees in the dirt, stomach pushing towards my throat. I retch. Bile splatters the earth and the backs of my hands. An acidic heat burns in my throat. Beneath my palms are dirt and twigs and leaves. All decomposing. Everything dying and decaying.

The jungle breathes around me. Heat throbs damply against my skin. These trees, breathing giants, have seen everything, spectators to whatever unfolded on this island. Crouched here, beneath the humming rainforest canopy, my hands and knees pressed into the dark earth, I want to feel it.

Behind me, I hear a creak, as if a branch has been depressed underfoot. My eyes snap open and I spin around, scrambling to my feet, scanning the camp. The question leaves my lips as a whisper. 'Lori?'

I wait, breath held, my gaze travelling to the shadows between the trees.

'Lori?' I say again, her name louder. My lips, my tongue, the vibration of my vocal chords, the familiar rhythm of that name spoken. It's like my body remembers, a warm echo of all the times I've called to her through the years. 'Lori,' I shout now, bellowing, roaring. 'Lori! Lori! Lori!'

I am turning, spinning, hands reaching blindly, searching for her . . .

And then I hear it. My name. Called to me within these hollowed depths of the jungle.

'Erin.'

I freeze, fingers outstretched.

Everything is distorted, confused. Shadows where light should be, leaves in place of sky, heat instead of air.

It is wrong. The wrong voice. Male.

'Erin? Time to go, yes?'

I exhale sharply, chest compressing. It is Rega, calling from somewhere beyond the treeline. He says something about the boat, the light. His voice is urgent, annoyed.

Somehow I manage to mumble that I'm coming, that I'll be there in a moment . . .

I wait, listening for the sound of his footsteps receding.

My hands grip the roots of my hair.

*I don't want this ending, Lori. I want you. I fucking want you! You begged me to help you, but I didn't do enough. I'm sorry . . .*

I sob into the empty jungle, grief submerging me. Through the blur of tears, I see the plane wreck and understand that I didn't come to this island looking for its crumpled remains. What I came here for was bigger than that, sculpted out of hope. In the deepest part of me, I believed – I wished and longed and prayed – that if Lori had survived the crash, that somehow she would still be here, alive, on this island. Waiting for me.

But she isn't.

I've reached the finish line.

I've found the island, the plane wreck, Lori's belongings, her recordings.

I understand as much about her death as anyone can.

I've got the answers I've been looking for.

But the one thing I don't have, will never have, is my sister.

## 59

# NOW | ERIN

A boat ride awash with silence in the lowering light, Rega and his brother exchanging glances.

A sleepless night in the dimly lit guesthouse, where I refuse the offer of food with a shake of my head.

A morning flight, temple to window, eyes glazed, as I'm returned to Fiji's main island.

When the wheels touch down, my body goes through the motions. I breathe. I walk. I show my passport and tickets when asked. I filter with the crowd, a shadow hanging back, silent and breaking.

I sleepwalk from the terminal and find a taxi.

As I slip into the air-conditioned cool, the driver turns, asking in a bright voice, 'Where would you like to go?'

Expression blank, I give him three words.

\* \* \*

Now I stare out of the taxi window as we hurtle down a busy street, shops and restaurants passing in a blur of colour. The rush of buildings, looming billboards, roaring buses feels overwhelming, an assault on my senses. I look down at my hands. Turn the silver circle of my thumb ring around and around.

'Here?' The taxi driver asks as he pulls onto the pavement. I see the wary glance of his eyes in the rear-view mirror as he watches me.

I nod. I lean forward to pay him my last twenty dollars. Then I grab my backpack, and step out into the thick, fuelled heat of the roadside.

It's done. I've come to the end.

Now it's time to hand it over.

The taxi disappears into the flow of traffic. I'm left standing on the pavement, looking up at the faded blue sign of the Central Police Station.

I push open the heavy glass door. Dressed in three-day-old clothes, my hair unwashed and stiff at the roots, I probably look like a backpacker who has stumbled out of the rear end of a three-day bender and has come to report their passport missing.

If only.

I tell a young man with a wispy black moustache who staffs the desk that, 'I'd like to speak to Officer Enrol regarding the disappearance of flight FJ209.'

He looks at me sceptically. 'I'll see what I can do.'

My palm slams down on the desk, making both of us jump. 'Now.'

And then it begins.

I tell two junior officers everything I know.

I describe the island, the plane wreck, the tally of days

scored on a trunk. I describe a bloodstained dress, a cluster of ruined photos in the pocket. I say the words *Daniel, knife, my sister*.

They need to understand: Lori survived the plane crash – but was killed on that island.

They look at me, dishevelled and filthy, hands trembling around a beaker of tepid water. They exchange sceptical glances. '*You* actually went to this island?'

They don't believe me.

'Wait!' I say, pulling two mobiles from my bag. On the first I show them the photos I took as evidence, and on the second I press *Play* on the videos of Lori. As we watch Lori's face come to life, with the plane wreck behind her, one officer rubs a hand back and forth across his mouth, while another fetches Officer Enrol.

An hour later, there are half a dozen people in the room. Someone has brought in coffee. There's iced water. They plug in a fan. They ask me question after question. They bring out a map. I point, explain. They write things down. Make phone calls.

When I leave the police station, stepping out into the dimming evening light, I know the rest of the puzzle is theirs to solve. I've done everything I can.

It's over.

I've no money for a taxi and don't even know if my legs will make the hour-long walk back to the hotel.

As I trudge down the street, the police station abuzz behind me, I whisper:

*I did the best I could, Lori. I'm sorry it wasn't enough.*

# 60

# NOW | ERIN

Somehow, I make it back to the hotel. I stand beneath the shower, hot water pouring over my scalp, the scent of soap rising in a lather. I dry myself, put on fresh clothes.

I check the minibar: freshly stocked. Crouched low, I stare at those tiny, glinting bottles. Close it again.

I leave my room, drifting along the corridor. I'm barely there . . . a ghost, a spectre. I pass the long wall mirror, but don't pause or look, nervous to find my reflection missing.

In the lobby, Nathan is waiting for me.

He fills the low seat, thumb tapping against the armrest. He has on a short-sleeved shirt. No work boots, this time.

When he sees me, he stands. 'Erin.'

I didn't tell him anything over the phone.

I walk towards him, not sure what to do with my hands. I reach him. Shove my hands in the front pocket of my denim dress.

We don't order drinks. We just sit opposite one another

as I begin to talk. I tell him about the map I found in his father's room, about the island, the plane wreck, the police.

He listens to it all, eyes widening, growing taller in his seat.

When I'm finished, he just stares at me.

I can't tell what he's thinking. Whether he's angry, upset, disbelieving.

He clears his throat. 'You found the map in my dad's room – when I was there?'

That's what he chooses to say first. 'I'm sorry.' And I am. I've hurt him.

He glances down at his lap, then back to me. I expect him to say more about the map, but instead, he says, 'It was brave of you – going to the island.'

'The brave and the desperate have always been teammates,' I say, managing a small smile.

He smiles, too.

'I've got something to show you,' I tell him, taking out my old phone and setting it on the table. As Lori's video messages play, he leans close and I can smell him: soap and something mint-fresh. I notice the tips of his eyebrows are sun-lightened, that there is a faint scar on his cheekbone. When the video pans out to the plane wreck, Nathan's eyes film with tears.

Sometimes it's easy to forget that there were other losses on that plane, too.

When the videos are finished, he looks up at me. 'You never gave up.'

I lift my shoulders. 'And what do I have to show for it?'

'Maybe the police will find something else? Maybe there'll be more answers.'

'Maybe.'

We're both quiet for a time.

'I fly back to Perth in the morning,' he tells me. 'The funeral is Wednesday.'

His family have a body to bury. An ending. I press my lips together. I envy him that more than I can say.

'What about you?'

'Flight booked for first thing.'

'And then?'

I look up at the domed ceiling. 'Then I'm supposed to get on with life.' I can feel his gaze on my face. I concentrate hard on following the carved pattern in the ceiling so that I don't cry. 'I can't see what the shape of my life looks like without her.'

He's quiet for a time and then says, 'You don't need to see the whole shape. You just need to trust it's there.' He says those words with such tenderness, with such conviction, that my eyes lower, finding his.

We stare at each other. In the silence, I'm aware of each beat of my heart.

He unfolds himself from the chair, his height always surprising me. 'I need to get back.'

I stand, too.

*So this is it*, I think.

Nathan says, 'I would have come with you, you know?'

For a moment, I'm at a loss. Then I realise, he means the island. He would have come if I'd told him about his father's map.

'You didn't trust me.'

*I don't know how to trust*, I could say, but instead I lower my eyes, ashamed.

'Goodbye then, Erin,' he says.

He crosses the lobby. His leaving feels abrupt, wrong – but I've no energy left to make it right.

I stand there, alone, guests and holidaymakers passing through the hotel, their laughter pealing around me.

\* \* \*

A waiter spots me and comes striding over, smiling. 'Evening, madam! Will you be joining us in the restaurant tonight?'

I can't go back to my room. Can't sit alone with the minibar for company. With the balcony waiting. 'Yes.'

'And are you dining alone tonight?'

I nod.

'Come this way and we'll get you seated.'

The air is scented with warmed spices and the sweet aroma of toasted coconut. We pass tables filled with families and friends; conversations flow and laughter bubbles into the night air.

I realise there's one more thing I need to do.

I touch the waiter's shoulder. 'I'd like to sit there, please.' I point to the edge of the open-walled space, to the corner table that overlooks the floodlit gardens. A table I've sat at only once before.

He nods and leads me to it.

I lower myself into a bamboo chair. A candle flickers in a glass jar at its centre, casting tiny, jittery shadows. I order a drink without opening the menu. I watch the waiter remove the second set of cutlery. Beneath the table, my fingers dig into my thighs.

When the waiter leaves, I try relaxing into the chair, tuning in to the pleasing trickle of the water fountain beyond, but my attention is rooted to one point: the empty seat opposite mine.

It's where Lori sat on the first night of our trip two years ago. Hair loose over her shoulders, nails glossy and pink. I don't know why I'm making myself do this. For closure? For a bit of light self-flagellation after an already rock-bottom day?

My Mai Tai arrives with a fresh sprig of mint and pineapple bursting from the top. I raise the glass, toasting the empty seat. 'To you, Lori.'

I can feel eyes on me and think, *So what? Get a good look everyone. This is just the start of the show.*

I sip the cocktail. It's too sweet, sickly in my mouth. My stomach contracts.

I set down the glass with a smack. I push the menu away. I've no appetite, anyway. I don't want to order a meal that will only end up scraped in a bin. I'd hoped there'd be a pleasing symmetry to being here – the hotel, this table, the Mai Tai – but there's nothing.

I scrape the final coins from my wallet, scatter them beside my drink, then leave.

I descend the steps at the far end of the restaurant leading out into the gardens. Motion over stillness. I pace through the stylishly lit grounds, then wind down a wooden path lit by solar bulbs, heading for the beach.

*This is where I ran after our argument. I left you, stormed across the sand, totally ablaze with myself. All that drama over nothing. As far as last conversations go, it was pretty fucking shitty, wasn't it? You know how sometimes you argue about something, but the thing you're arguing about isn't really the thing at all? There's another thing, a bigger thing beneath it, but either you can't see it, or you don't have the words for it? Well, I've been thinking about that bigger thing for a while.*

*What we were arguing about that night wasn't Pete's affair, or how I lived like a student; it was that we were both dissatisfied. Our lives weren't how we'd imagined them. We'd lost our parents; you were going through a divorce. I was caged by a city and career I wasn't in love with. We were looking at each other to see where it went wrong. We were looking for the person to blame.*

The pathway through the hotel grounds leads to the beach. I think I catch the faint press of footsteps behind me. I pause for a moment, listening.

There's no one there, of course, just the distant sound of diners, the clink of cutlery, the pulse of music.

I reach the beach where sun loungers have been arranged into neat rows, cushions stored for the night. The sand gives beneath my flip-flops, and I kick them off, then walk to the ocean's edge, plunging my feet in.

The sea at night is something warm and unknown and stirring. Its energy licks at my ankles.

I've not swum since arriving in Fiji. I know why: the sea means pleasure, it means holiday, it means relaxation – and I haven't deserved those things. For so long, I've believed that I should only feel pleasure when I no longer feel all the other things: the sadness, the loss, the fear. But emotions don't come parcelled neatly. They're shaken together and messy. Happiness laced with sadness. Hope tangled with fear. Love shadowed by loss. It isn't about waiting until I'm in a better place. Striving for a happy life. It's about having a *feeling* life.

I peel my dress over my head. Throw it onto the shoreline. And then I'm wading forward, feeling the rise of the sea inching over my flesh. The sea bed softens and gives beneath my feet. I lean forward, diving down beneath black silk.

Salt water fills my ears, a shushing sound of clicks and fizz. My muscles and limbs move fluidly as one. I slide beneath the water, weightless.

I can feel that strange tow – of wanting to keep swimming, right out there towards the dark horizon. To feel nothing but oblivion. The urge to do that is so strong it snakes around my chest, constricting something.

I want to be brave. To feel everything. But it hurts. SO. FUCKING. MUCH.

Lori's voice is raw in my heart. Those pleas for help trapped in a recording: *I hope you're still looking . . . I don't know if I can survive this . . . I'm scared.*

I was too late.

Too fucking late!

Into the water, I scream.

Cries bubble and gurgle, vibrating through the sea.

I surface, mouth wide, water pouring from my head, eyes wet and blinking.

I wade out of the sea, grab my dress from the shoreline, tug it on, panting. The material clings to my wet skin. Salt water drips down my neck.

I'm suddenly conscious that I'm not alone.

A prickling sensation breathes across the back of my neck, whispering down my spine. I'm aware of my ear lobes, my lips, the very tips of my fingers.

When I turn, I see the silhouette of someone further up the shoreline. Moving towards me, or away?

I pull my dress back on, which sticks to my damp skin.

*Nathan*, I'm thinking. A rush of feeling fills my chest. I want him to have come back. I want to tell him I'm sorry. That he deserved more from me . . .

I let my eyes adjust, taking in his shape.

Except, whoever is standing there is smaller than Nathan. A narrow set to their shoulders.

The person isn't moving. They are watching me.

The night draws close, a shiver travelling down my spine.

The person takes a step forwards and there is something about the way they move that feels so familiar.

I wait.

They are coming towards me and everything about the length of the steps, the poise of their carriage – all of it is known to me, like the way I know my own footsteps.

I blink.

*It can't be.*

Breath stalls in my throat.

There is no air.

My body flushes hot, then cold.

*It can't be*, I am repeating somewhere deep within me.

My hands are lifting to my mouth.

I've been to the island. I've seen the wreckage. I've found her blood-soaked dress. I've seen her name carved into the tree.

*No. It isn't you.*

'Erin,' she says.

# 61

# NOW | ERIN

My sister.

Standing on the dark beach.

My heart kicks against my ribs, blood roaring in my ears.

I grip the roots of my hair, squeezing. Dig my nails into my skull.

*No, this isn't real.*

I drop my hands. Turn. Start walking, but I'm stumbling, barely able to manage a straight line.

'Erin.'

My shoulders hunch to my ears. I don't want this. I don't want to be standing on this beach hearing my sister's voice. It's madness. I keep walking.

'It's me, Erin. It's me . . .'

I turn.

My head is shaking, saying, *No, it can't be* . . . But my

eyes are drinking in someone who looks so much like my sister that my skin feels as though it's being shocked by hundreds of tiny electrical currents.

'It's me,' she whispers again.

I begin nodding; small rapid movements that won't stop. *I don't understand.*

She looks different. Her hair – it's been cut to chin-length. *I've never seen you with short hair.* And it's darker – returned to its natural golden brown. She looks thinner, stands taller somehow.

Suddenly she is moving, crossing the space between us. Her arms are opening, hands reaching, and we are wrapping ourselves in one another, holding each other. The clash of cheekbones and hair and limbs locked tight, holding, hugging. We rock, swaying from side to side, a dance of sisters. I breathe her in, the particular warmth of her neck, the press of our collarbones. 'It's you . . .' I whisper, eyes screwed shut, gripping her.

I don't know if this is a dream, a hallucination. Whatever it is, I want it. All of it.

Our fingertips grip one another, as if feeling for the memory of each other's body, pulling it out of our DNA, our history, the memories printed in each cell of our being. Her shoulders shake in my arms; I feel the wetness on my cheek of her tears or mine. She kisses my face urgently, repeatedly, holds my shoulders, touches my hair, my cheek.

A low cry emerges from my throat, a choked sob from hers. Each other's names are whispered over and over.

We lean in. Our foreheads touch, tipping our gazes down to where our hands now link in the space between our bodies, still squeezing, communicating.

She looks at me, eyes liquid.

My legs have no mass to them.

I look around – sea, sky, night, the twinkling lights of the hotel – as if I'm going to find I'm in a dream.

I turn back – and Lori is still there, her hands wrapped around mine.

I stare at our entwined fingers. She wears the rose-gold bangle still, after all this time. *Together.*

'I don't understand,' I say, staring at her, blinking hard. My heart thunders. 'I thought you were *dead.*'

She presses her lips together, nods. Her eyes refill with tears.

'Dead,' I say again, as if it's the only word available. Then I let go of her hands and take a small step away. 'I thought you were fucking dead!'

'I know—'

'How could you?' My eyes are wide, head shaking, trying to grasp for logic through the crushing noise in my head. Each thought jolts me, causing flashes of pain. I want to go to her. I want to be away from her. I'm tearing in half . . .

'I'm sorry . . .' she mumbles into her hands, which are clamped to her mouth. She releases them as she tells me, 'I don't know how to . . . God, Erin . . . I . . .' She breaks off, emotion thick in her throat. She breathes out hard, emptying the air from her lungs. When she takes a breath, she raises her head and looks right at me. 'I've missed you so much, Erin.'

I shake my head so hard it feels like it's rattling. 'You survived?'

'Yes.'

'How? I . . . I don't understand.' Nothing fits together.

She hugs her arms around herself as if she is deeply cold.

In our silence, I hear frogs croaking somewhere in the distance and the lapping of waves at my heels. 'Where've you been? Why didn't you come home?'

Lori looks right at me, her gaze boring into mine as she tells me simply, 'I couldn't.'

I stare back at my sister. 'Why?'

There's silence. Into it, she says, 'I could never tell anyone what happened on that island.'

# 62

# THEN | LORI

Lori was lying on the ground. There was a deep, burning pain at the back of her skull. She could feel a crushing weight against her chest, holding her down.

She blinked her eyes open.

Daniel. On top of her. The peaty smell of his body filled her nostrils. His breathing was ragged and foul.

She tried to move, to twist out from beneath him, but she was pinned by his weight.

'Get off!' she gasped, her lips feeling thick and numb. She couldn't get enough air.

But Daniel was reaching a hand to his waist, a wild look skittering in his eyes.

*The knife! He must have the knife!*

She bucked, kicked, desperate to be freed.

Daniel grabbed her arms, pinning them at her sides, forcing her to be still. His face lowered, breath rank.

Heat and stench radiated from him. She knew what came next. All women knew. Daniel's expression was unreachable, like he'd disappeared, leaving only bones and flesh and muscle, pinning her down, dominating her.

She screwed her eyes shut, tried to retreat to a still place in her head.

Then she heard a small sound beyond her – and suddenly her eyes snapped open: Sonny! She remembered the driftwood, his red face, choking . . .

She began to twist, writhe. She clawed at the beach, breaking a hand free of Daniel's grasp. Her fingertips met something hard, jagged. A loose rock. They curled tight around it – then, in one hard, swift movement, she raised the rock and brought it slamming down against the side of Daniel's skull. She heard the crack – rock against bone.

She drew back, hit him a second time.

A third.

Daniel's grip loosened. She slid from beneath him, scrambling to her feet, head thundering with pain. She rushed to Sonny, her vison swinging.

His face was a deep, choked red, tiny fingers raking at his throat. She sat him upright, hooking a finger into his mouth, finding a piece of saliva-soaked wood at the back of his throat. She managed to free it, then applied a steady, firm thwack between his shoulder blades using the heel of her hand. Once. Twice.

There! He coughed, shooting a shard of wood from his mouth.

He let out a cry then; full-throated, wondrous. Air in his lungs.

'Oh baby!' She lifted him to her chest, smothering him with kisses. 'It's okay. You're okay now. I've got you.'

His fists gripped onto her cotton dress as he cried.

Dizzy with pain, she managed to hold him steady, circling a hand against his back, calming him. Soothing him.

She glanced over to Daniel. He was lying still on the beach. She saw a dark slick of blood spilling from the side of his head, seeping into his hairline. A chill spread through her chest.

'Daniel?' Her voice was high with fear.

Slowly she crawled towards him, Sonny clutched to her.

She stared at his chest, waiting for the rise and fall of air. Waiting, waiting.

Hearing the lapping of waves against the shore, like the ocean was breathing. The sky breathing. Everything breathing, moving, shifting. But Daniel – completely still.

She reached a hand to his throat, feeling for a pulse. Her heart was roaring, the rush of blood in her own ears, oceanic.

She already knew.

There was nothing.

He was dead.

Lori knelt beside Daniel. The side of his head was gluey with blood. A trail of it had seeped into his beard, pooled into the skirt of her dress.

*What have I done?*

Lori could feel it, the seismic shift of the moment. Like the sudden plunge of the plane as it went down, that knowing dread, right in the pit of her core, that everything was different now.

She'd killed Daniel.

If they got off this island, then what? Her mind was racing, speeding and sliding through the scenarios of what lay ahead – being pulled into an interview room, a trial, a prison sentence? What about Sonny? Where would he be? Separated from her – Lori in England, Sonny in the US?

None of it was right.

Blood raged in her ears. *Think, Lori.*

She looked up at the sea, right there in front of her.

That's where the other bodies were taken: Holly, Jack, Ruth, Kaali, Felix. All in the water.

That's what she needed to do.

She would say he died with the others in the plane crash. No evidence.

Lori resettled Sonny on the blanket, then went to Daniel. She took his ankles, trying not to look at the pus-filled wounds criss-crossing his heel. She began to pull – the splitting pain in her head slicing through her – but he was a solid, unmovable weight.

She wasn't strong enough. Her whole body was shaking. She wiped her mouth against her shoulder, thinking. There was no other choice: she had to get him in the water.

She took a deep breath, dug her heels into the sand and leaned back with all her weight. She felt the slow drag of his body through the sand. Pain tore down the back of her head as she inched towards the sea. Daniel's arms trailed behind him, blood seeping onto the sugar-white sand.

Sweat beaded across her skin as she heaved on. As soon as the water reached him, she felt his bulk lighten, the hem of her blood-soaked dress rising around her thighs.

She steered Daniel's body out beyond the shallows, taking him far enough so that the water was up to her ribs. There, she made herself look at him. Even in death, there was something about his expression that seemed sneering. If she hadn't lifted that rock, she knew what would've happened – how far he would have gone.

No, she wasn't sorry.

She turned from him but, as she did, she saw the ripple of water. Daniel twitched, eyes blinking open, fingers reaching.

The shock of it jolted through Lori.

No thought, only motion. Hands reaching out, iron fingers – hers this time – around his shoulders, pushing down, pushing him under.

Daniel's whole body flexed, legs thrashing. He fought against her, head lifting out of the water, an arm grabbing the neckline of her dress, tearing, pulling her down with him.

Bloodied salt water filled her nostrils, her mouth, as the rest of the world disappeared. The two of them, tussling beneath the surface, hands and nails and fear.

She managed to prise herself free, rising, gasping for air. She had the advantage of position, standing above him – so she pushed, and pushed, keeping him beneath the surface.

She held him there as he kicked and thrashed wildly.

Daniel's eyes were wide open beneath the surface, looking up at her through layers of water and salt, blood swilling from his head wound. Lori felt the shake in her muscles. Seconds passed. Silver bubbles of air rising to the surface. Jerking knees and elbows. The fierce grip of hands against skin. The ripple and splash of salt water. The burning witness of the sun.

And then finally, finally, stillness.

Daniel's eyes remained open, looking at the sky.

She let go, sucking in air.

Her chest heaved.

As he floated, arms spreading into wings, she remembered the knife.

They needed it to survive.

She reached into his wet pocket – but there was nothing there except empty fabric. She tried the other. Both empty.

The sea bed shifted beneath her.

\* \* \*

Lori's breath was rapid, adrenalin spiking in her veins. Her blood-soaked dress clung to her skin. *Off. I need this off!* She yanked at the wet fabric, tearing it from her skin.

The ruined dress slumped at her feet. She stood in her sodden underwear, breathing hard. *Now what?*

Everything felt surreal and distant, the jungle looming close. Watching her.

Hooking the dress over an arm, she gathered Sonny and stumbled back to camp. She could hear her own voice, breathless and over-bright as she tried to soothe Sonny – and all the while another part of her brain was screaming: *I've killed Daniel!*

Reaching camp, she threw her bloodstained dress onto the smouldering fire. The wet fabric smothered the embers, a twist of smoke choking from beneath the material.

Despite the heat, she was shivering hard. She began to hum. The sound was manic, distorted as it bubbled from her lips. She continued the tune as she lay Sonny in the bassinet, while she pawed through her suitcase, digging out a filthy pair of shorts and a vest. She dressed herself clumsily, her body overtaken by uncontrollable shaking. Her thoughts were scattered, sliding from one spiked edge of fear to another.

*I killed Daniel . . .*

Her breath felt high up in her chest, shallow and thin, like there wasn't enough air.

The humming faded to silence as she moved to the treeline, standing in the shadows of the canopy. She looked out over the water, searching for Daniel's body. *Was it even real?* Already the current had carried him further out of the bay, away from the island.

*His eyes*, she thought, remembering his wide, terrified expression beneath the surface as she held him down.

*Who the fuck am I?*

She looked down at her hands – saw blood beneath her fingernails. Her head swam.

Behind her came the crash of branches, the approach of footsteps.

Mike.

His pilot cap was missing and his thinning, grey hair was matted to his head. He faced her, a strange expression narrowing his eyes. Then he lifted a hand – his fingers filthy, nails long and dirt-filled – towards the binoculars that dangled around his neck. Tapped them once.

Dread, cool and leaden, washed over her. 'You saw.' Mike would've been up on the ridge on lookout, watching through his binoculars.

'Yes.'

'I didn't mean to . . . Sonny, he was choking. Daniel had me pinned down . . . I knew what he was going to do to me . . . I had to get him off. Get to Sonny . . .'

Mike's face was blank, devoid of emotion.

*Does he understand what I'm trying to tell him?* 'It was survival,' she said finally, her throat closing around the last word.

Still, Mike said nothing.

She pushed her hands into her pockets, hiding the blood in her nails. 'The sea . . . I put his body in the sea.'

He watched her closely. 'You drowned him.'

He'd seen it all! It sounded so brutal, so callous. 'I panicked.'

A beat of silence. 'Did you?'

Her eyes startled wide. She shook her head, confounded. What was Mike implying? That she'd planned it? That she *wanted* Daniel dead? That's not what happened.

*Was it?*

She pictured Daniel's face as she'd dragged him into the sea. She'd felt hatred boiling deep in her gut. She'd wanted him dead, hadn't she? She chose that. 'I . . . I . . . was protecting Sonny . . .'

Mike's voice was low. 'Or was it about *keeping* Sonny?'

She blinked, confused.

'Daniel was his father.'

Lori stared at Mike. His expression was cold, distant. 'You knew?'

He nodded, a small curling at the corner of his lip. 'I told you, there was no property deal. A man doesn't buy expensive lingerie for his wife on the way to a business trip. It was for someone else. For Holly.'

Her head shook as she said, 'Why didn't you say anything?'

He shrugged, and in that gesture she understood that he had been banking the information. Leverage. There for when he needed it.

Her skin studded with goosebumps. Had she misjudged him all this time? Had Daniel got the measure of him right from the start?

Mike turned away, his gaze returning to the water, searching out Daniel – the evidence of what she'd done. But then she saw what he was looking at – not Daniel's body, which had drifted to the far end of the bay – but something moving in the opposite direction.

'The boat,' Mike said eventually. 'It's here.'

They watched from the treeline as the boat navigated the breaking waves at the reef's edge. From a distance, it looked of modest size, with a faded sun canopy stretched across a small deck.

Mike raised the binoculars. 'Two people on board. The boy who came before, plus an older man.'

'What now?' she said, gaze switching between the boat and Mike.

Mike lowered the binoculars and faced her. 'What do you think will happen when the police find out about Daniel?'

Saliva pooled at the back of her throat. 'I . . . I . . .'

'You think you'll be going back to your old life? Taking Daniel's child with you?' His tone was blunt, deadly enough to strike.

'We . . . we could say Daniel died in the crash? Like the others?'

Mike's face stretched in surprise. 'Another life on my hands? Another dead body that I'm going to be held accountable for?' His head shook slowly from side to side. 'Don't think so, Lori.'

Lori felt her insides turn to ice.

'Then I'll tell them what happened . . . that it was self-defence.'

'Perhaps when you hit him with the rock. But after that? The second blow? The third? And then you dragged him into the sea. He was alive, Lori! You held him under. You looked into his eyes as you drowned him.' He paused deliberately. 'That is murder.'

She could barely breathe, think.

'But . . . I'll go to prison . . .' Her gaze swung to the bassinet. *Sonny. I'm going to lose Sonny!* 'Please,' she begged. 'Please, Mike! Lie for me.'

Mike looked at her for a long moment, his gaze cool. 'There is another way.'

Then from his pocket he pulled out the dive knife.

# 63

# THEN | LORI

Mike had the knife all along.

Not Daniel, Mike.

A chill shivered down her spine. She'd got everything so very, very wrong.

Mike had taken the dive knife at the expense of them all – to thrust himself on a ledge above the other islanders. A weapon meant power. It meant advantage. It meant Felix had gone out spearfishing without it – and been killed.

*Oh, Felix!*

Now she remembered how Mike had failed to set off a flare when the boat arrived. How many boats had he let pass while he'd been up there on the ridge top? Had he never wanted them to leave the island?

She stared at his sun-ravaged face, skin lined with dirt. He'd stepped so far away from himself – from the father and husband he'd once been – that there were no rules left. Just survival.

His fingers gripped the knife. If he took so much as a step towards her or Sonny, she would fight and scream and kick and tear. She would do whatever it took. She was ready, muscles primed, fuelled by instinct and pumped with adrenalin – she only needed to survive until the boat arrived. A few minutes away at most. He might have the weapon, but she was fierce, younger, faster.

But Mike didn't move towards her – he turned away.

She watched as he shambled through camp, headed for the area just beyond the fire.

He stopped at the foot of the tally tree. His hand reached out, touching the bark, trailing to the far side of the wide trunk where the list of the dead was inscribed.

*Holly Senton, R.I.P.*
*Ruth Bantock, R.I.P.*
*Jack Bantock, R.I.P.*
*Kaali Halle, R.I.P.*
*Felix Tyler, R.I.P.*

He raised the knife, the tip touching the bark, and began to carve. She watched as the tree was gouged by the metal point, bark flayed, as – letter by letter – Daniel's name appeared.

*Daniel Eldridge, R.I.P.*

Her heart flickered with a tiny light of hope. *Is he going to lie for me?*

Mike wiped the back of his hand across his mouth, then crouched lower.

Below Daniel's name, Mike began carving a fresh line. Lori watched each cut of the silver blade, felt the tree retract. She saw the letters emerge slowly, knew what was coming,

Her name.

*Lori Holme, R.I.P.*

'No,' she whispered, head shaking.

Then below it, Mike wrote a final name.

*Sonny Senton, R.I.P.*

They were dead.

'What is this?' she whispered.

Mike ran a finger along the flat edge of the blade, dusting away the curls of wood shavings. 'We let everyone think we're dead. We disappear. You and Sonny have your life; I have mine.'

'But . . .' She shook her head, hands rising to her mouth.

'We set foot on the main island, announce ourselves – then it all kicks off. The press. The investigation. You said the word yourself: *prison.*'

'But your family, your wife . . .'

He looked at her, eyes shining. 'It was pilot error, Lori.'

She blinked. 'What?'

'There was never any problem with the fuel line. I made a fucking mistake, okay?' His voice was cold, detached. There was no remorse in his expression. 'There was a gauge on the fuel tanks. I should've switched from main to auxiliary. I missed it—'

'Wait. What? You *missed* a switch. All this . . .' She broke off, thoughts spinning. He'd been lying to them from the very beginning. 'The night before the flight,' she said, realising, 'it wasn't just one drink in the bar with my sister, was it?'

His eyes glittered dangerously.

Then she remembered the air stewardess lying in the plane aisle, in a pool of her own blood. She had said something, words bubbling from her throat, an intensity in her eyes as she said, *I should've stopped him.* 'Kaali guessed you'd been drinking, didn't she?'

'Listen,' he said, stepping closer, teeth bared. 'None of that matters now. It's what happens next that counts. The minute they find the island, all the questions begin. You know what happens to me, don't you? Prison.' A vein pulsed urgently at his temple. 'And what about you? Murder. Disposal of the body. I'll book you the cell next to mine.'

The boat was motoring nearer. It had made it over the reef and was now gliding across the bay. They only had minutes.

'And then what happens to Sonny?' His voice softened. 'Lori, you are a good mother to him – I've seen that. He needs you. This way, you'll stay with Sonny. No one will take him from you.'

Her whole body was trembling.

She glanced at the tree, her gaze burning down the list of the dead.

'Where's your name?'

Mike looked at her. There was something different about his eyes, a glittering blaze of excitement, or madness. 'The list has to be one name short.' He added, 'Last man standing.'

She understood: that's how Mike saw this. A game. A tactical game.

And Lori had lost.

# 64

# THEN | LORI

Lori hauled herself onto the waiting boat, ribs scraping against the splintered wood. She slipped, landing hard on her knees on the deck. She scrabbled upright, arms outstretched, signalling for Sonny.

Mike passed him to her, and she folded her arms around him, whispering lightly as she carried him to the back of the boat. She lowered herself onto a wooden seat, the hem of her shorts soaked, and sat in the shade of a canvas canopy. The engine toiled, diesel fumes clouding into the midday heat, the smell speaking of industry, people, and the machinations of a life she'd been ejected from.

Propped on her knee, Sonny was almost able to sit up on his own now. His eyes were alert, drinking in the new setting, and she caught a glimpse of the little boy who was beginning to emerge.

At the bow, the older man held the nose of the boat steady

in the shallows, while Mike struggled to clamber on board. He grunted as he tried to heave himself over the side, the boy needing to reach out to help drag him up.

Mike collapsed onto the deck, shoulders slumped – and she watched his struggle to get back to his feet, grimacing with pain. He shuffled towards her, breathing hard. He slumped onto the wooden seat, the stench of him lifting from his sweat-cloaked skin.

'No bags?' the boy called.

Mike and Lori shook their heads. They'd left all their possessions on the island, bringing only a bottle of coconut milk for Sonny and some cash she'd taken from her purse. If the plane wreck were discovered, it would look as if no one had made it off the island.

The boy hauled up the anchor, the metal tooth of it dripping wet as he clanked it onto the bow, before vaulting on board, wiry muscles contracting.

'My son said there were four of you,' the older man said, pushing up the peak of his faded baseball cap to look at them.

'Three,' Mike said, pointing to each of them in turn: *Mike, Lori, Sonny.*

The boy shook his head. 'There was another man.'

Lori's arms tightened around Sonny. They would never get away with this.

'What other man?' Mike said calmly. 'This is all of us.'

The boy's brow creased, unsure. 'No. The man who had money.'

Mike pulled a wedge of money from his breast pocket, just like they'd agreed. 'Yes, I gave you half the money last time – and now here's the rest.'

The boy looked confused, but his father was reaching for the money, tucking it deep into his pocket, thanking them, his teeth flashing yellow as he smiled.

Mike stood, reaching into a back pocket, to reveal a second wad of cash. 'We want you to have this, too. But,' he said, looking between father and son, 'you tell no one that you found us here.'

The boy and father showed no surprise at the request, as if their silence had been prearranged.

'Do you understand?' Mike asked as the boat idled in the shallows.

They both nodded. As the father reached for the extra money, Mike held it tight. 'Do we have your word?'

Dark eyes on Mike's: 'Yes.'

When they turned back to the front, she hissed at Mike, 'You said something to the boy when he first came to the island, didn't you?'

Mike didn't even turn to look at her, just kept his gaze steady on the horizon, his voice cool. 'If he kept quiet, returned with help, I said I'd double the money.'

She felt the blow of the final betrayal: Mike had always planned to find a way out.

If Lori hadn't killed Daniel, would Mike have? And if she hadn't agreed to this plan, would she and Sonny be dead, too?

She felt the vibration of the engine against the backs of her legs as the boat turned, nose to the horizon.

She looked back towards the dense thatch of jungle concealing the plane wreck. Apart from the remains of the signal fires on shore, the island looked deserted. Everything had a surreal, dreamlike quality to it, as if she'd conjured the whole thing.

The water, struck by the high sun, shimmered with scales of light. Squinting, she watched wavering coral gardens passing beneath the hull as they glided across shallow reef.

They nosed towards the outer edge of the bay, where the

ocean turned a darker shade of blue and the thunder of waves strummed. Suddenly, she gasped. Ice creaked in her veins as she froze, gaze on the water.

There, floating near the port side of the boat, was Daniel's body. He drifted face up, arms splayed at his side, shorts ballooning. Salt water fanned through his hair, exposing the jagged mess of his skull, the skin broken and raised. His eyes were open, staring unseeing at the sky.

She clamped a hand over her mouth, tasting the metallic tinge of blood beneath her nails. Saliva slicked the back of her throat.

Mike followed her gaze. Surprise registered in the rise of his brows, a flicker of something at the edges of his mouth.

If the boy or his father glanced this way, they'd see Daniel's body. It would all be over.

*What now?*

Mike rose to his feet, approaching the front of the boat, where father and son stood, navigating a path.

'Thought I saw something – over there,' Mike said, pointing east, in the opposite direction of the body. 'What's that in the water?'

Father and son looked to the empty stretch of sea, searching.

'I saw a fin. A dolphin, perhaps? Or shark?'

'Many sharks around here. I don't see it . . .'

'A dark fin, about this size,' he said indicating with his arms. 'There it is again.'

Mike maintained a steady flow of talk and questions, the men's attention never breaking from him or the sea ahead. Gradually, Daniel's body slipped further from view, rocking in the boat's widening wake.

\*     \*     \*

In the thirty-three days Lori had spent on the island, she'd imagined leaving it over and over, picturing a rescue boat or a search helicopter, relief seeping through her chest like honey. But never like this.

The father turned towards her. 'Your baby is beautiful.'

She glanced down at Sonny, the soft pelt of his hair against her chest, his tiny pink fingers gripped around her thumbs. She went to speak, to say something – *he's not mine; his mother died* – but found the reply dissolved in her throat.

*Your baby.* Those two words. They were for her.

Watching the green kiss of the island recede, she felt the warm stir of Sonny on her lap. The weight of him no longer strained her back. Her body had adapted, her muscles strengthening to carry him, her heart expanding.

Apart from the people on this boat, the world thought all the passengers on flight FJ209 were dead. Circling her arms around Sonny, she decided: *Let them.*

# 65

# NOW | ERIN

I twist the ring in the cartilage of my ear, as I listen to my sister's explanation.

I can't take my eyes off her. I'm afraid that if I look away – even for a beat – she'll vanish again, a puff of smoke dispersing into the night. I listen intently as she explains how she eventually arrived here on the main island, disappearing into the remote interior with Sonny, Mike striking out alone. I try and keep up as she describes the difficulties of those first few weeks living off grid, without papers and only a little money. But they survived. She'd survived much worse, after all. Now, she and Sonny live in a simple one-room shack that she rents for next to nothing, selling paintings to a gallery in town to keep afloat.

Lori finally stops talking. She stands in front of me, the two of us silent.

I don't know what to say. What to feel.

The sea breathes steadily at our backs.

'Where is Sonny?'

She turns, pointing behind her. I hadn't noticed before – but now, on the dark beach, I see there's a buggy parked in the sand between two sun loungers, a small child asleep with a thumb slack in his mouth.

I stare at this little boy, as if he's been conjured by a magician. In the moonlight, I can see he has fair auburn hair and smooth white skin.

*They survived.*

As I look at Sonny, at ease in sleep, I realise that, for two years, I've been looking at every angle of the plane's disappearance. I considered the possibility that Lori survived, yet discarded it with the impulse of instinct, because I believed that if she'd survived, she would have returned to me. We are sisters. We would never abandon each other.

And then . . . in the wake of the pilot's reappearance, I'd imagined Lori trapped on the island, and began to suspect each of the strangers on that plane. Circling her. Stronger. Dangerous. I dug and pawed, examining and hypothesising. All the clues I unearthed – the bloodied dress, the missing knife, Lori's videos – arrowed to Lori's desperation to leave the island.

What I failed to see was the most obvious thing of all.

Yes, Mike threatened her; yes, she was terrified of being sent to prison – but ultimately, when I peel away these layers, the only way I can see it is that Lori made a choice.

As I stare at Sonny, head lolling peacefully to one side, dark wings of lashes closed, I realise that there was only one thing that meant more to Lori than being a sister.

Being a mother.

\* \* \*

Despite the humid warmth of the night, I shiver.

I think about the wall in the spare room of my flat, papered with articles and news clippings, photos and questions. I think about the lonely nights when I've sunk a bottle of wine just to anaesthetise something I couldn't look at, or all the other ways I did it – bringing men back, working late, keeping moving so I didn't have to stop, to feel. So that I didn't have to hear that voice in my head, over and over, telling me it was my fault. The inner critic, so fucking quick and vicious, reminding me at every turn that it was my doing, I deserved this. That I'd let Lori down.

But here she was, this whole time.

I stare at her, still getting used to this new version of my sister, with her dark hair and lean body. She holds herself differently; nothing marked, not that I can put my finger on, but there's something about the way she stands. There is a presence about her, a seriousness, the way her feet are firmly planted. As if there is something grounded at the centre of her. Even on the dark shoreline, I'm close enough to see new laughter lines bracketing her mouth and fanning from the corners of her eyes.

A burst of outrage slams into me. 'You've been here, living your life, happily. But me? I've been *devastated*.' I hate that word. So overused. In the media everyone's devastated about something – yet I can't think of an alternative because that's exactly how I feel. My normal state has been derailed. And all the while, Lori has been here with Sonny. 'You could've let me know, Lori! You could have called. Sent me a message. Written to me . . .'

'I did. I wrote to you dozens of times. Started letters, drafted emails. But I could never go through with it, because a letter isn't enough. Nothing is enough. I called you too . . . heard you pick up, heard your voice. But what could

I say? Even now – having you here, right in front of me – I don't have the words to explain.' She shakes her head. Asks me, 'If I'd written to you, would you have accepted it? Let me go?'

I look at my sister. 'No.'

She nods lightly, as if this confirms something for her.

'Why now? Why come here now?'

'I found out you were here, in Fiji, still looking for me after all this time.'

'I never stopped.'

'I follow you on social media, have done ever since I . . . I disappeared. I use a fake account. I needed to know how you were. To be able to see you. I needed you to be okay.'

'But here? How did you know I was at the hotel?'

'You came back to Fiji. Where else would you go?'

She knows me – has always known me better than anyone. Tears are brimming over my eyelids. Lori was nearby the whole time.

'After Mike died, I came to the hotel to find you – but you'd already left. I . . . . I thought you'd returned to London, that I'd missed you.' There's a pause. 'You found the island, didn't you?'

Slowly, I nod.

Lori is watching me. Her gaze trails my face, my hair, my clothes, then travels back to my eyes. She's trying to read something in what she sees.

'I saw it all. The plane wreck. Your camp. The lookout. Lori, it was . . . brutal.'

Lori blinks, a fresh stream of tears spilling over her cheeks. 'Yes.'

'I've listened to the messages you recorded for me.'

The expression on her face – a half-frown of surprise – is an expression so much like our mother's that longing strikes me in the gut. Suddenly she is taking my hands in hers. Her gaze is so intent, I feel as though she is swallowing me, absorbing me. 'Recording those messages – feeling like we were speaking to one another – that got me through, Erin. I missed you so much.'

My big sister, right here, alive.

She squeezes my hands, her palms smooth and warm, secure against mine.

I want to lean into her, feel her arms around me again.

But I am rock, stone, earth.

I can feel a sob clawing from the deepest part of me.

My thoughts are flying, hot shards, spitting, thinking about the last time we saw each other. Jesus, the loss – so sudden, so unexplained, a finality without resolution. All the anger and hurt left between us, our final argument tangling everything. All I could see was the jagged knot at the end of us, where the threads were torn apart. I needed her to help me untangle it, work through the colourful, strong threads that once bound us.

All this time, I've been searching for the truth.

While she's been here. Living her life with Sonny. Her new family.

And I am alone.

I can feel the strange shape of my features, lips peeled back, brow collapsed, teeth bared. I'm breaking, tearing.

'Erin,' she whispers, her breath warm against my skin, 'I love you.'

*I can't do this.*

'I've missed you so much,' she tells me again.

My hands pull free, reaching up to my ears, blocking her out. There's no space. I'm bursting. I'm going to split open.

'Please, Erin . . .'

I can feel the heat of my arms wrapped around my head.

She's still talking. Words, words, bowling at me, like I am being stoned by them.

Then I'm tilting forward, rushing across the beach, sand stinging my calves. Legs pumping, arms dropping to my side. Running. Back towards the hotel, the bright lights.

When she calls after me, I run harder. I'm fast and put distance between us in moments.

Skin coated in sweat. Muscles burning. Just the roar of my pulse, the hard draw of breath. Feet against earth. Sweat trickling down the back of my knees.

I wanted her.

And it's too late.

She abandoned me.

Racing through the gardens, I pass uplit shrubs, ghostly shadows reaching across the stone path.

When I reach the hotel, I stop, looking up at the open-walled restaurant, the table where we once sat – now empty.

I've done this before: run from her, out through these gardens.

I can't keep running.

I can't.

## 66

# NOW | ERIN

Lori reaches me. She parks the buggy quietly to one side of the dark path. The hotel lawns are springy underfoot as we look towards the twinkling lights of the restaurant. 'The last place I saw you,' she says to me after a time.

I nod.

In the evening dark, sprinklers send soft jets of water towards the thirsty earth. 'Earlier, you said you didn't get in touch because a letter or email couldn't explain what happened.'

'That's right.'

I'm looking at her closely, thinking. 'Maybe it was more than that. Maybe you didn't write to me because of guilt. I'm not just talking about Daniel's death – I mean afterwards, your decision to disappear.'

She stares at me, the words settling.

'Mike didn't force you to lie. You had a choice, Lori. A hard one, I know, but still a choice. At any point in the last

378

two years you could have stepped from the shadows, handed yourself in to the police. Told the truth.'

She holds my gaze, looking me straight in the eye.

'But you *chose* not to. What about the relatives of the passengers? What about Daniel's wife? Jack and Ruth's children? Kaali's daughter? We didn't get to hear what happened. You could have given us that.'

I can hear the emotion in her voice as she says, 'I'm so sorry for it. For how much you've suffered, how I've hurt you.' Her hands reach for me, but I step back.

Another thought bursts into my mind. 'That last time we saw each other, right here – I've thought about it a lot. Replayed the things we both said. My mind has this habit of taking the worst bits, the hardest things, and then playing them on a loop when I'm alone, when I'm trying to sleep, when I'm working my damned hardest to be happy.'

She is listening, lips pressed together, eyes damp with tears.

'You know the bit I replay the most? The most painful thing to hear?'

She knows, of course she knows.

'You reminded me of the promise we'd made after we lost Dad. The promise to tell each other everything. To be there for one another. *Together.*'

She presses her palms together, brings the tips of her fingers to her mouth.

'You said to me, *You let us down.* Us. Because we've always been an us.' I shake my head. 'God, that hurt – because it was true. I let us down when I didn't tell you about Pete's affair.' I take a breath. 'And now . . . it's you, isn't it, who has let us down? You picked a new life. That was a choice made for *you*. Not for us. There was no *together.*'

\* \* \*

Lori says, 'You know what I thought about as our plane was going down?' Her eyes are shining, quick and livened. 'I thought about the life I *hadn't* lived.' She takes a breath. 'Up until then, I'd charted my course as a straight line – school, college, university, marriage, teaching. I wanted to build this perfect family life, my own little fortress. Inside there was going to be you, Pete, a gaggle of kids.' She stops. Her head shakes slowly from side to side. 'But it didn't work out. The children never came. Pete left. You were starting a new life in London. There was nothing inside that fortress, just empty, brittle walls.'

Lori's gaze flicks briefly past me, to the water. 'When I was strapped to that plane seat, the earth rushing right at us, that's when I felt it – all the possibilities that curved away from that straight line. It was like this space opened in my chest and I could feel everything, this energy, connecting me – like I wasn't separate from everything, but part of it all.'

I'm silent as I try and comprehend this.

'Those weeks on the island – God they were brutal, Erin. I was scared, and half-starved, and terrified for Sonny – but, but it was also strangely beautiful. Like being stuck in a nightmare that's shot through with your very best dreams. The island shattered those fortress walls. Stripped me back. And maybe . . . maybe I needed that.' She stops. She is staring at me, willing me to understand.

And I do. I see it – the new strength in my sister.

I can see Lori on that island more clearly now, the fishing boat approaching, Daniel's body floating in the water – and then Sonny, there in her arms. It's impossible to rationalise the tangled scale of her decision. It was so much harder, so much bigger, than anything I can imagine.

'What now?' I say. 'Are you going to tell the police?'

Her head shakes. 'Like you said, Erin, I made a decision.

Mike didn't force me. Not really. Once I left the island, at any point I could have held up my hand, told them what I did.'

'But you chose Sonny.'

She nods. 'I'm sorry.'

'You could go to the police now. You could say Daniel died in the plane crash. No one needs to know. Mike was the only witness.'

'But how could I explain my decision to disappear? I've kept Sonny. I've withheld information. It would never work.'

'The police know the location of the island now – I've given them the map, shown them your recordings. They'll go to the island, find the wreck.'

'Yes, and they'll see that some of us survived for a few weeks. They'll see the list of names carved on the tree, believe that we died on the island.' She pauses. 'The other relatives – they'll get their answers now.'

'What about me?' I ask, hating the weakness in my voice. I feel as though I am about to lose her all over again.

'I want you in my life, Erin. God, I want that more than anything.'

A punch of silence. Weighted, hard. 'Not more than anything.'

Behind us, an eruption of laughter bursts from the restaurant, causing our gazes to flick towards the warm, bustling space.

'I fly back to London in the morning,' I tell her eventually.

'I can't go back there, Erin. You understand that, don't you?'

I look at her in the darkness, pulse racing. 'So, what happens to us?'

# FOUR WEEKS LATER

# LORI

Sitting on the veranda, I watch Sonny push a red car along the deck, a soft *vroom* vibrating from his wet lips. Above us, the sky is sheer blue and cloudless. Sonny turns into the sun, squinting, seeking me out. Checking where I am like an anchor point.

I smile, reassure him.

The day after Erin returned to the UK, the police finally discovered the island where Captain Mike Brass crash-landed our plane. The wreckage was searched. They found the fuel tank three-quarters full, the fuel gauge unswitched. The investigation is still under way, but pilot error is the unofficial line.

News teams scrambled over the story, rehashing the details, speculating about our disappearance and deaths. The remains of the camp were investigated, our luggage bagged as evidence. No one but me and my sister knows the truth. What happened during the thirty-three days on that island is dark and clammy, and sometimes it twists so hotly around my heart that it keeps me awake in the night.

I think about what I did to Daniel. That I am capable of murder.

When that is too hard to bear, I remind myself of Felix, of Sonny, and that I'm also capable of love. Great love.

I slip my phone from my pocket and look at the blank screen.

Still no word from Erin.

She returned to London. I was in touch a week ago, asking if she'd think about coming back to Fiji when the media frenzy dies down. Whether she'd consider staying with us for a while. I want, so badly, to try and repair things.

She said she needed time to think about it.

Patience has never been my strong point. I type, *Have you decided? x*

Sonny climbs onto my lap, and my arms circle him. As I look out across our tiny dirt garden, towards the valley, I find myself wondering, *What if Erin and I had never come to Fiji? What if Mike Brass hadn't captained that plane? What if a rescue team had found us sooner?* Sometimes the *What ifs* overwhelm me with their limitless answers and outcomes. But of course, there is only one outcome. The now. This moment.

I glance down at my phone.

Nothing.

Instead of getting lost in the past, or fearing the uncertainty of the future, I try and hold tight to this moment.

For now, there is Sonny. And somewhere – on the other side of the world – there is my sister.

# FOUR WEEKS LATER

# ERIN

I haul the cardboard box into the lounge, setting it in the centre of the carpet. The sofa's gone – collected by the Sue Ryder charity van, me apologising for the red wine stain on the armrest and God knows what other stains on the cushions I turned over.

The rest of the flat has been dismantled, everything given away, except for two boxes which are stacked with photo albums and books I couldn't part with.

The only thing left on the wall is the painting Lori gave me when I first moved to London. I grip the edges of the canvas, removing it carefully. I turn it over, reading her inscription on the back. *So you can have a place to come home to in the city.*

I carry the painting towards the window, studying the river that once flowed through the garden of our childhood home. I think about its path, running towards the sea, speaking of a home that travels, not limited to one place, but that is always moving, shifting, changing.

I place it carefully in the box of things I'm keeping.

Next, I go to Lori's old room. The walls are bare, paint-work darkened where the articles and photos have been peeled free. There's no bed in here now, no bookshelf, no desk. Everything has been emptied, packed away. I stand in the doorway, arms folded, leaning my shoulder against the door jamb. All those nights I spent in here, sitting on Lori's bed, staring at the wall in search of answers. I used to think I could hear Lori's voice in my heart, speaking to me, guiding me.

Except, it was never Lori's voice.

It was my own. I had that strength inside me the whole time.

My mobile vibrates with a message. I slip it from my pocket and read:

*Have you decided? x*

I pull Lori's door shut for a final time. As I turn, I see my backpack by the door, passport tucked in the front pocket.

I think about this life in London that I'm leaving: skating past death on my bike, lungs clogged with pollution; prodding and poking and cajoling stories from people; rushing faster and faster to keep up with a notion of success that feels empty. Life is too short to get stuck in the wrong one, to be working hard to beat a path forwards. I don't want to shove to the front for the right quote, or work through the night to get my copy filed. I'm not lit by it. Quitting my job was the right decision.

Beyond the windows, I hear the drone of a plane flying overhead, sending the windowpanes humming in their frames. The sound no longer makes my stomach flip with dread. Instead, it makes me think of possibility.

I touch the screen with my thumb, Lori's message lighting up.

I take a breath, then type: *I'm not coming. Sorry.*

I can see the double tick as she reads my message and I imagine her eyes widening in surprise. I can picture the prick of hurt flickering across her features.

Her reply arrives almost immediately: *You're staying in London?*

I begin to type, *Not London, no.*

I think of the long flight ahead to Perth. Nathan has offered to pick me up from the airport, said I could crash at his for the first couple of nights – and from there, well, I'll see. I've got a working visa, and one month's pay in my bank account. I'm hoping the landlord of this place will return my full deposit to buy me a little extra time. Enough to tide me over while I work out the rest of the details.

As I consider how to word my reply, I think about Lori's explanation of how she felt as the plane came crashing down, the life she'd not yet lived.

I want to live mine fully, fearlessly. So I type a single line, one I know my sister will understand.

*I need to find my own island.*

# Acknowledgements

This book. What can I tell you? It's been the most challenging book I've ever written. The version in your hands comes in at 97,000 words – but I'd estimate that I've written closer to a million words. The fact that I made it over the finish line is down to the support and encouragement of several wonderful people.

Firstly, my editors, Kimberley Young and Charlotte Brabbin. They've read this book at every stage and provided feedback when I wasn't sure where to go next. I love working with the team at HarperFiction, who are every bit as passionate about stories as their authors.

The team at Greene & Heaton have been fantastic, as always. Judith Murray is the very best literary agent I could imagine working with, and her guidance and support have been invaluable in helping shape this novel.

A huge thank you to Emylia Hall, a brilliant writer and wonderful friend. She has read several drafts of this novel and been on hand to talk through everything from plot issues and character arcs, to book titles and jacket design. Our daily chats make working on a long, solo project infinitely more pleasurable. Emylia, thank you.

I'm also grateful to both Emma Stonex and Heidi Perks,

who generously gave excellent, thoughtful reads of this novel. Their feedback dramatically helped shape the finished copy. Thank you also to Faye Buchan, Lizzie Kerslake, and Becki Hunter for reading the final draft of this book, and giving just the right boost of encouragement, which helped me recognise that it was time to press *Send*.

Many thanks to Richard Powell for his help and advice regarding planes – and how to crash them! All mistakes are very much my own.

As ever, my ongoing thanks and love to my parents and parents-in-law, who are on hand to proof-read, help with the kids, and drop in with baked treats to keep up morale. I'm so grateful to have such a wonderful support team on my doorstep.

Then there's James, Tommy and Darcy. My family, my tribe. The three people I would happily be cast away with. I love you.